ST. MARTIN'S

MINOTAUR
MYSTERIES

"Atkins' research into blues history adds depth and context to the always entertaining story, which whizzes by like an old, familiar song heard on the car radio late at night." —*Chicago Tribune*

"Now, in this second novel, his maturity as a writer comes through strongly. He's comfortable with Travers, and we are too. Atkins also believes in meticulous research, and this illuminates the path of his story so well." —*The Tampa Tribune*

"The author builds the tension inexorably without surrendering control or resorting to pointless interludes of crowd-pleasing mayhem. When Travers arrives at the answer he has been seeking, the payoff is swift, sharp, and as unequivocal as a brick through a plate glass window." —*The St. Petersburg Times*

CROSSROAD BLUES

"*Crossroad Blues* sings. It proves that big guys can write, and that Ace Atkins can write better than most." —Robert B. Parker, author of *Sudden Mischief* and *Small Vices*

"*Crossroad Blues* is like a classic song. The right feeling, the right note, at the right time." —B. B. King, blues legend and author of *Blues All Around Me*

"Ace Atkins comes roaring out of the starting blocks with a fast, funny, suspenseful first novel that has it all." —James W. Hall, author of *Under Cover of Daylight*, *Red Sky at Night*, and *Body Language*

TURN THE PAGE FOR MORE PRAISE . . .

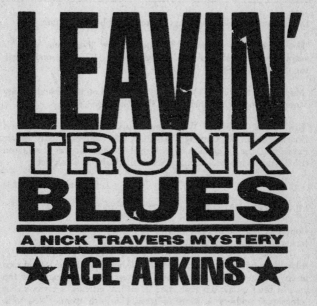

LEAVIN' TRUNK BLUES

A NICK TRAVERS MYSTERY

★ ACE ATKINS ★

St. Martin's Paperbacks

Lyrics from the following songs are reprinted by permission:

"Lonesome Blues Highway." Traditional from "Lonesome Valley" / adapted by Ruby Walker. © Copyright 1957, 1978 Diamond Music Inc. Copyright renewed (BMI).

"Merry Christmas Baby." Words and Music by Lou Baxter and Johnny Moore. © Copyright Unichappell Music Inc. (ASCAP).

"Key to the Highway." Words and Music by Willie Broonzy and Charles Segar. © Copyright 1941, 1968 Universal-MCA Music Publishing, Inc., a division of Universal Studios. Copyright renewed (BMI). International Copyright Secured. All Rights Reserved.

(*continued on p.* 323)

LEAVIN' TRUNK BLUES

Copyright © 2000 by Ace Atkins.
Jacket photograph by Jay E. Nolan.

Library of Congress Catalog Card Number: 00-029691

ISBN: 0-312-97718-2

Printed in the United States of America

St. Martin's Press hardcover edition / July 2000
St. Martin's Paperbacks edition / October 2001

St. Martin's Paperbacks are published by St. Martin's Press, 175 Fifth Avenue, New York, NY 10010.

10 9 8 7 6 5 4 3 2 1

for ian fleming and muddy waters

ACKNOWLEDGMENTS

This book started over a glass of whiskey and ended with a bottle. I appreciate everyone who believed I was still alive after the last two years. My editor, Pete Wolverton, supplied the guidance I needed and the time I had to have—your insight made all the difference. But remember, your wife still has all the taste in the family. Lindy, thanks for passing it along. And thanks to the coolest agent in NYC, Andrew Pope, for taking care of business while I write and providing great conversation when I need it.

Great thanks to: Eddie King, former Chess studio musician and veteran bluesman, for his stories on his long trip to Chicago and the world he found; my personal hero Chick "The Stoop Down Man" Willis for the great jokes and views on the current blues scene; Ed Komara, head of the Ole Miss Blues Archive, for his patient reading of the manuscript and sharing his immense knowledge of blues history.

To my colleagues at the *Tampa Tribune*: Leland Hawes for his file on the Great Migration, fine editing eye, and great friendship; Orval Jackson, the legend, for his files on the prison system and gritty taste of Tampa luncheon holes; Joe Brown for his great memories of the South Side; and Ladale Lloyd, Alabama man, writer/artist, for sampling Tampa's finest soul food cuisine and leading me through the trial process.

Special thanks to: all the folks at my X, Blind Willie's; Eric Bibb for spiritual inspiration when it was greatly needed; all my friends at the Suncoast Blues Society for their support; Larry Lisk for the great hours of blues radio every week on WMNF; Jay Nolan (aka Deuce) for being the best caffeine-addicted photog in the business; my sister Paige and her Hudgins' clan and my mother, Doris, for their friendship and love. A very special thanks to Shelli for traveling this lonesome blues highway with me (next time you've got to try the coffee at the White Palace Grill) and for listening to this story about a thousand times. As for Bud . . . Bud, man, for a dog, you're a great human being.

I traveled to Chicago not knowing a soul and ended up leaving with many new friends: Donna Metz with Chicago Neighborhood Tours, you were a wonderful guide; Tony Mangiullo, drummer, bar owner, poet—thank you for inviting me into your blues home at Rosa's Lounge (next game is mine); all my good buddies I met on a wonderful night at the Checkerboard Lounge; David Turim, *Chicago Tribune* researcher, for helping me find Eli Toscano and the truth behind his death; Jon Harris for his incredible hospitality on Dearborn; and thanks to my friend Gerri Oliver, owner of the Palm Tavern—all right, I'm done, now. Gerri, how 'bout that drink?

Nick Travers would like to thank the following writers and musicians for their great knowledge and continued inspiration: Francis Davis, *The History of the Blues*; Robert Palmer, *Deep Blues*; Willie Dixon, *I Am the Blues*; Robert Santelli, *Big Book of Blues*; Sandra Tooze, *Muddy Waters: The Mojo Man*; John Collis, *The Story of Chess Records*; Paul Trynka, *Portrait of the Blues*; Gayle Dean Wardlow, *Chasin' That Devil Music*; and Greil Marcus, *Mystery Train* for some deep thought on the man himself—Stagger Lee. Without a doubt, Mike Rowe's *Chicago Blues: The City and the Music*, Isabel Wilkerson's "A Great Escape, A Dwindling Legacy" from the *New York Times*, and Nicholas Lemann's *The Promised Land* (book and inspired documentary series) provided the greatest hunk of soul behind this work, with an incredible story of some courageous people: Muddy, Sonny Boy, Little Walter, Memphis Slim, Memphis Minnie, the list is endless.

Remember, Free Ruby and keep her alive.

Well, there's a road
that leads to glory,
through a valley
so far away.

Nobody else
can walk it for you,
all they can do
is point the way.

—Sweet Black Angel, "Lonesome Blues Highway,"
King Snake Records, 1957

To become aware of the possibility of the search is to be
onto something. Not to be onto something is to be in despair.
—Walker Percy, *The Moviegoer*

SO MANY ROADS. *So many trains.*

I stood on the station platform that July of '55 with my suitcase made of paper, and ambition burnin' in my soul. As I waited for the City of New Orleans to billow black smoke into the eggshell blue sky of a Mississippi summer, I thought back on my past life. About being born the ninth child of a sharecropper in a windowless, clapboard shack outside Clarksdale. About my daddy leavin' with a whore for Chicago when I was six and the disappointment in my mama's face.

She was a stout black woman with hands like anvils who kept us all workin'. I rubbed the tips of my fingers together and could still feel the thorns of the cotton piercin' my skin as the sun wrapped the Delta in a hellish halo. I could still hear the cicadas buzzin' and boilin' in the trees as the old fieldhands moaned and hollered to pass time. It was a steady hum of parched voices waitin' for mercy and peace. We would leave the fields drained and soaked with sweat. Our muscles knotted in our fingers.

Before I'd cook a supper of salted ham and biscuits, I brought my sacks of cotton to the scale. Mr. Williams, a white man who wore black glasses shaped like cat eyes, would peek at the weight then back at me. Never spoke. Just spit. Then he would tell me to move on.

Yeah, move on.

We were all movin' on at the time. There wasn't a soul in the

Delta that didn't know someone who was goin' to Chicago. I guess my daddy just got bit by the bug early. Never did see him when I got there.

In Mississippi, everyone was talkin' about jobs in the meat packin' factories and in the steel mills. Payin' four times what we made in the fields. 'Course, the ones not replaced by machines only made 'bout a dollar for every pound of cotton picked.

I knew I was leavin'. When I got old enough, I used to sneak out to juke houses on the weekends. Me and my girlfriends would stay out all night just hopin' one of them mens would let us sing at Red's juke. We used to have a time out there. I'd imagine I was Bessie Smith or Memphis Minnie.

I always knew I wanted to be known. Always knew I was born to be somethin' more. That's what Chicago was—a chance to become me. So the day after my nineteenth birthday, I stood on that platform, my thin yellow dress flappin' round my legs, and heard the train whistle blow like a dronin' harmonica.

It was the sweetest sound.

But Chicago wasn't my answer. City life engulfed me like fire upon brittle paper.

Five years later, I was given a room in an Illinois state prison. They say I killed Billy Lyons. Some say for love. Others for money. But that wasn't the truth. Truth is somethin' I've seldom known in the last forty years. I am imitated, duplicated, and faded out of history. My music today is barely recognizable.

I am the blues.

PROLOGUE

Christmas Eve
Chicago, Illinois

STAGGER LEE WAITED to kill Nick Travers where the old railroad tracks converge in a city of rust and rotting wood. The faded freight cars sat in coupled decay like still ramblers in a forgotten section of Chicago where brittle metal chains and warped springs littered the snowy ground below. In the moonlight, his breath crystallized before him as he gripped the handle of his blue steel .44.

There used to be a time when those old cars moved with hope and promise, he thought, filled with hungry people wanting to be part of it all. But that was before it fell apart, before their dreams drained into a world of shit.

In the distance, the blinking red lights above the skyscrapers pulsed like blood in his veins. Red hot and burning his mind. That hatred pumped through him like acid, making his muscles tight and jaw clench. Just like in the fifties when he was a pro wrestler in Memphis. Black Hercules, they called him. Six foot six, three hundred pounds. All man.

A cold wind ripped through the sliding door's gaping hole but Stagger Lee didn't try to stomp his feet or rub his hands together. The cold was nothing. A warning signal from the brain. Tonight, he wanted to keep quiet. He was on the hunt. Travers would tramp through the snow any minute and he'd take his ass out.

Stagger Lee felt the torn, bloody flesh at his side and smiled. He was about to give this man Travers a special present in return.

He wiped the red smears from his fingertips and adjusted his black leather trench coat.

Through the boxcar opening, Stagger Lee heard the zoom of cars over the Roosevelt Road bridge and the crunch of granite buried beneath someone's feet. The steps and slurred singing moved closer. Some kind of Christmas tune. This man Travers really was a fool. Stagger Lee clutched the .44 tighter. He liked the way the cold steel felt. Solid. Strong.

More singing echoed off the old metal cars as the hot blood dripped down his side. The man began to whistle "Silent Night." Stagger Lee knew Travers had no idea it was his time. He probably never thought this would be the last minute he would breathe or feel a cold night. Stagger Lee liked that power. The grim reaper of Chicago.

The sound of whistling and crunching feet moved down the aisle of cars. Stagger Lee's heart raced and he felt his nails dig into his palm around the gun. He waited and readied every muscle. His breathing came in low, ragged gasps. The blood boiled in his ears like a man trapped below the water's surface about to break through. His exhaling breath clouded his eyes.

He couldn't wait.

Stagger Lee lunged from the car. He grasped the man by his red coat and thrust him against the old railcar. He could see the fear in the black bum's eyes. The man's eyes bulged from under his Santa hat as his feet dangled below. Stagger Lee held him for a few moments before he set him down and smiled.

The bum smiled back.

Stagger Lee slid his gun in his overcoat pocket and grabbed the ice pick that hung from his belt.

The man's smile dropped as Stagger Lee thrust the pick into the man's ear and let him slump to the ground. He reached down with one hand and held the man's quivering body like he would a mechanical doll. The man moved in some kind of convulsions. Dead, but the body just catching on to the idea. He tossed the writhing body into the boxcar.

Shit.

Stagger Lee hopped back in and closed the sliding door. The rusted wheels screeched. He put another few holes in the man's head, blood misting his face, until the man stopped flopping around.

The last thing he needed to do was scare off Travers. Everything was a mess, everyone was dead, and this was the last chore left undone. Heard Travers was a real tough southern boy. But this wasn't the South Travers knew. *In Chicago, every corner was a crossroad.*

1

Five nights earlier,
New Orleans, Louisiana

JoJo's Blues Bar was a warm shot of whiskey, a cold Dixie on the side, and blues that could exorcise demons like a voodoo priestess. The bar stood in a narrow brick-and-stucco building off Conti Street where a blue neon sign spilled light onto beer-stained asphalt. As Nick Travers walked through its beaten Creole doors, he could feel the music under his buckskin boots and deep into his bones. The last of the New Orleans blues joints put a good hum in his heart.

Gold tinsel and plastic holly hung across the bar and jukebox. Fat red pepper lights winked on stage as Loretta Jackson growled her deep holiday blues like a lioness on the prowl:

> *"Merry Christmas, baby,*
> *you sho' did treat me right.*
> *Bought me a diamond ring for Christmas,*
> *now I'm livin' in paradise."*

JoJo's wife had the whole smoky bar flowing with the music. Whistling. A few yells. She had just started her first set and already had the crowd working, her red sequin dress wrapping her large brown body.

Nick wandered through a mass of dancers by the jukebox as Felix flitted behind the deeply scarred mahogany bar to fill orders. His bald head and the multicolored liquor bottles glowed in the blinking blue lights. At JoJo's, there was heat, there was whiskey, and there was music. Felix didn't even look Nick in the eyes as he popped the top from a Dixie and slid it down the bar.

Nick removed both gloves with his teeth and tucked them into the side pocket of his jacket. Some of the foam spilled on his hand. Cold, but warmed the soul.

He leaned forward, placing his elbows on the bar, and stared at the black-and-white photographs of the long-dead greats: Guitar Slim, Huey "Piano" Smith, Professor Longhair, Babe Stovall, and Little Walter. Nick glanced at the photo by the end of the bar and raised his beer. Underneath sat an empty bar stool. A seat once reserved for a man they called Henry.

"Nick, you would fuck up yore own funeral," JoJo said in a rich baritone voice from the darkness behind him. "Yore an hour late."

"It's all the fashion now," Nick said, as he lit a cigarette.

"Oh . . . yore late for fashion . . . well, goddamn, I feel much better."

JoJo had on a suit tonight. Black and creased to perfection. He was a sharp black man in his sixties with white hair and a trimmed mustache. His hands and fingers were thick from years of manual labor, and he wore scars on his knuckles from fighting in jukes all around Mississippi.

He was a great musician who never quite made it. He'd played backup on some of Loretta's recordings, but for the most part he was the man in the shadows. JoJo started the bar back in the early sixties, something for him to do while he waited for fame that would never come. But today there wasn't a blues musician alive who didn't know about the man's juke. *A little Delta on the Bayou*, JoJo always said.

"You been down at the peep show, haven't you?" JoJo asked as he frowned. "Down on Bourbon watchin' young girls havin' sex wit' goats."

"Donkeys," Nick said, sipping on the cold Dixie. A Blackened Voodoo with a nice beaded label. "That and finding a little religion."

"Oh shit." JoJo raised his eyebrows. "You kicked Jesus' ass, didn't you?"

"Let's just say he's been *saved*," he said.

"You can't do that. Beat up Jesus, man. Ain't that sacrilegious or somethin'? I mean, you kicked *Jesus'* ass."

Jesus was a street grifter who worked the park benches by St. Louis Cathedral at night, dragging a cross on his back and asking for tips. An old sax player Nick knew gave the jackass his rent money to pray for his dead mother. The old man was drunk and lonely and the grifter had used him.

"I got Fats's money back," Nick said, pulling the wad of cash from his pocket and placing it into JoJo's palm. "The only Christian thing to do."

"Guess that man deserve it then. Gettin' his ass kicked like that."

"Damn, that guy smelled bad, looked like he combed his hair with Crisco," Nick said, blowing smoke away from JoJo. "Make sure Fats keeps some of this until his gig New Year's Eve."

"You got it," JoJo said. "Thanks."

JoJo's eyes grew soft and he gave a pleasant wink. Nick patted his hunched back and flicked the cigarette into an ashtray by his elbow. That's why he liked JoJo's place, everything was real convenient. Cold beer to the left and an ashtray to the right. Hard drivin' blues on stage. *What more could a man want?*

"Loretta pissed?" Nick asked.

"Hell, I don't know. I ain't scared of my woman," JoJo said. "You think I'm one of those pussies who calls their wife 'the boss'?"

Nick laughed and pulled out a Hohner Chromatic harp. "She mind if I join her?"

"I don't know," JoJo said as he let out a long, deep chuckle. " 'Fraid to ask."

Nick had known the Jacksons for almost twenty years. Hard to believe it had been that long. When they met, he'd just come to Tulane and had fallen in love with the old city. Felt like he'd always belonged here, like his old spirit had wandered down those bleak alleys before. One Saturday night, while exploring the Quarter with some teammates, Nick had discovered JoJo's. They'd been stumbling around and looking for some refuge from the rain.

Months later, a scuffle in the bar's parking lot forged his life-long friendship with JoJo. After Nick had tossed two men around like they were blocking dummies, another man had poked a gun into Nick's ribs. At about the time Nick caught his breath, JoJo had rounded the corner with a couple of cops. Not only did JoJo save Nick from the guy with the gun, but also made sure the cops didn't haul his ass off to jail. After that night, Nick gave JoJo and Loretta passes to all the football home games. Hell, he didn't have any family to use them. His mother was dead and his father was too drunk to care.

When his father finally died from a broken heart and a rotted liver a few years later, JoJo and Loretta became his only family. They were the ones who waited for him all night in a rainy parking lot when he returned from his father's funeral. They were the ones who had him over for dinner twice a week and coaxed him to join their mostly black church.

The Jacksons were his only constants from his time at Tulane, to playing for the Saints, through his pursuit of a doctorate in Southern Studies at Ole Miss, and back to Tulane to teach blues history. *Constants*.

Nick drained the last drop of beer, snuffed out his cigarette, and smiled. He felt a tingling buzz in his feet as the blues swirled around the old brick room in a sweet blend of notes. Loretta waved him up to the old wooden stage where JoJo had already looped his Shaker microphone around a stand. The guitar player scooted over to give him a little room in the hot lights.

"Well, well, look what the cat dragged in," Loretta said, placing her hands on her big hips. "*Mmm, mmm*. Sho is fine for some white meat. Say Nicholas, a new woman got you tied up yet? No? Well, let's get you plugged into the Queen of New Orleans' blues and wrap yo' mouth around that ole 'Key to the Highway.'"

Nick started into Little Walter's mellow rhythm with Loretta breaking into song:

> *"I got the key*
> *to the highway,*
> *feel loud and bound to go.*
> *I got to leave here runnin',*
> *'cause walkin' much too slow."*

The hustled evening melted into slow blues burning in the pit of his stomach. Through the fog of a few beers and Loretta's relaxed vocals, he bonded with the rain tapping against the glass on Conti. The crowd of dock workers and tourists nodded to the music as the world became a warm mix of green, red, and blue in the dark shadows.

At the end of the second set, Nick gave Loretta and JoJo hugs and ambled toward the old twin doors to stumble home to Julia Street. For some reason, he drank in the whole scene. The Christmas lights, the way the juke blared in the corner, the chipped paint on the brick walls, and the way the bags crept over JoJo's wise, old eyes.

This was the place. Everybody has their X, that sacred spot where you feel most comfortable in the world. To Nick, JoJo's was that special spot. A darkened cave of happiness. Tonight was a moment. You can't create a moment. Moments are sporadic. Moments just happen.

2

AN UGLY WINTER rain fell the next morning as Nick studied the graystone buildings of Tulane University. Through the leaden glass of the Jazz and Blues Archives, he watched students under a rainbow of umbrellas bring color to the darkening day. Next to him, a portable cassette deck played Charley Patton singing "High Water Everywhere." His croaking voice told the story of the 1927 flood when the Mississippi River broke the levees around the Delta. The flood left farmers stranded on telephone poles and Indian mounds as everything they knew washed away. Must've seemed like the mean side of the Bible.

"Does anyone need the song played again or have any questions about the final?" Nick asked, his feet rocking like a pendulum below the desk. No one answered as the students shuffled paper and clicked their pens.

Today, Nick's knees and joints felt stiff with the rain. He'd taken a morning jog along the Riverwalk to sweat out the alcohol and did a few sets of weights in the bottom floor of his warehouse. Didn't help. The music he loved so much rattled like tin in his injured mind.

After Patton, Nick played one of his favorite Robert Johnson songs, "Love in Vain," for his Delta blues class. Johnson sang about a man with a suitcase in hand watching his woman leave the train station—the red and blue lights of the caboose trailing off into a Mississippi night. A great poetic moment.

"Remember, Johnson's role in the development of blues may have been a little overstated," Nick said as the cold rain sluiced down the windows. "Like any other great artist, he took a sampling of others from his era. Kind of like making a good jambalaya. Only add the best meat. . . . We've compared pieces of Lonnie Johnson to Johnson's 'Malted Milk.' He obviously borrowed some of the supernatural themes."

"What about Sonny Boy Williamson?" a student asked. "Was he there the night Johnson was poisoned?"

"No," Nick said, in a tired cigarette-damaged voice.

"How can you be sure?" the student asked. "I thought Sonny Boy said Johnson died in his arms."

Nick liked the kid. He always wanted more than the scraps Nick threw him.

"Rice Miller, Sonny Boy Williamson II, was a great harmonica player," Nick said, scratching the stubble on his chin. "Man spanned the prewar period to Chicago. Love his music. Even wrote my dissertation on his life. But Sonny Boy was a known liar. Hell, he stole the *real* Sonny Boy Williamson's name to make himself famous. He traveled with Johnson. But no, he wasn't there the night Johnson died. Trust me."

Through the window, Nick could see the dead grass in Tulane's mall area, leafless oaks, and more students ready to get their ass out of Dodge. The vibe of expectation was absolutely palpable. Or maybe it was just self-serving.

"You said maybe he wasn't murdered by a jealous husband?" the student asked again. "That's not what I read."

"You won't find it in any books . . . it's just a theory," Nick said as his students turned back to their tests.

Nick loved teaching but he longed to get back to his research. He tried to schedule the classes for fall and winter, so he could spend the spring and summer crisscrossing the Delta, knocking on doors and running down thousands of leads. Good field research was about patience. About hours and hours of interviews to find arcane details about blues singers' influences and personalities. He'd spend almost the entire summer running down relatives and old friends of Eddie Jones, aka Guitar Slim, in the Mississippi Delta. The research was for a book on Slim he'd been working on for the last five years.

He knew so many professors were content with obsessing over details of the original blues singers from before World War II that they didn't focus on the players of the fifties and sixties. If those lives weren't recorded while their contemporaries were still around, so much would be lost. That's why he roamed Chicago, the Delta, Memphis, and parts of Texas searching for their faded moments. Armed with little more than a good cassette recorder and a notebook, Nick wanted to make sure extraordinary lives were not forgotten.

It was a tradition started by the early blues trackers like Alan Lomax, Sam Charters, and Gayle Dean Wardlow. White men whose love of the music sent them knocking on the doors of blacks in a segregated South. The work often gained suspicion from both races. But trouble from Klan members or redneck sheriffs was now something out of tracker's lore. Today, the danger came from canvasing shithole neighborhoods. Sometimes a gun wasn't a bad addition to the notebooks and recorders. Gangs and guns sometimes interfered with getting a good oral history.

Someone tapped on the classroom's heavy oak door.

Out in the hall, Randy Sexton grinned at him like a fool. Real shit-eating smile like he'd heard some nasty joke about a weasel and a monkey. Short guy with a curly head of brown hair and the face of a cherub. He wore a frayed brown sweater and black jeans, the size of his eyes enhanced by thick glasses.

Randy was the head of the Tulane Jazz and Blues Archives and a genius writer on the history of jazz. The man could tell you anecdotes about Louis Armstrong and Rampart Street in such incredible detail you could smell the sweat on the dancers' bodies and taste the bootleg whiskey. A wonderful historian and storyteller.

"Fuck off," Nick whispered out in the hall. "My students are deep in thought."

"You have a package downstairs."

"Thanks."

"Don't you want to know who it's from?"

"My letter from Santa returned again?"

"No."

"Miss March Ninety-one? She got the tickets to Jamaica and the thongs?"

"Keep guessin', smart ass, I signed for it."

"Your wife?"

"Easy there, partner. How about your prison pen pal."

"How 'bout her?"

"Package is from Illinois. Maybe she agreed to the interview."

Nick was silent. He could hear his students moving in their creaking seats. Someone coughed. Another sighed. The rain drummed on the windows of the old building.

"Come down after you're finished," Randy said, raising his eyebrows. "I'll start drinking the Jack you keep in your bottom drawer. Maybe Christmas came early."

The rain stopped about the time the last student turned in his final. The cold water hung in beads off the oak trees like forming buds. Nick grabbed the tests and stopped in the hall to talk with a few students. He said he might make it over to The Boot for a few rounds to celebrate the quarter's end.

Then he headed downstairs to his office.

The archive building was built during World War II and still had that great architecture you seem to only find in a Frank Capra movie. Rounded hallways and big oak doors with frosted glass. Inside his office, Randy sat next to Nick's sagging metal bookshelves filled with almost every work ever published on the blues, along with unfiled photos and interviews that would eventually be cataloged into the collection.

"Drinking on campus?" Nick asked, hanging his brown corduroy jacket on an old oak hat rack and finding a seat in a brittle office chair.

"It's the last day of classes before Christmas . . . who gives a shit," Randy said, taking a big swig from a coffee mug stamped with the Dixie beer logo. "What happened to the days when a midday drink wasn't frowned upon? The martini lunch? A nice glass of wine with your meal?"

"When Americans began taking life too seriously," Nick said as he propped his boots up on his desk and poured himself a thick measure in another mug. He exhaled a long breath and picked up the legal size package and shook it.

"Would you open the fucking thing?" Randy asked.

Nick slid his thumb along the back of the letter and pulled out a couple sheets of paper, as thin as onion skin, along with two black-and-white photographs. The letter was filled with careful cursive lettering. Just like all the others.

"Well?"

Nick set aside the photographs and read the letter. He pulled out the bottle of whiskey in his desk and poured another shot into his mug. He read the letter again and leafed through the pages.

"She said she'll do it," Nick said.

"No shit. Ruby Walker? That's like DiMaggio and Salinger rolled into one."

Ruby was a blues songstress who'd spent the last forty years in an Illinois state prison for murder. Nick knew the story all too well. They called her the Sweet Black Angel when she performed in the late fifties. Made a few recordings for King Snake Records and had a big hit with a song called "Lonesome Blues Highway." Beautiful song with great lyrics about leaving the country for the city. About forgotten friends and family. About starting over and taking new chances and leaving behind what was familiar. But her career was cut short when she was convicted of murdering her lover, the owner and producer of King Snake. Guy named Billy Lyons. She stabbed him while drunk out of her mind and dumped the body in Lake Michigan.

"Take off, man. Do it. Not many of these stories roll around."

"University will pay my expenses?" Nick asked.

"Yeah, but no lap dances this time."

"Palmer House?"

"Motel Six."

"What if I make up the difference?"

"Fine with me," Randy said shrugging. "If you stay, you'll just get drunk and sing sappy Christmas songs to yourself. Or listen to those Alan Watts tapes."

"Still can't find Elmore King," Nick said. "He's the one who gave me the idea in the first place."

"He's avoiding you?"

"Making me feel like a leper at a singles bar."

"Maybe you can grab him in Chicago," Randy said. "Why do you think Ruby changed her mind?"

"Loneliness. Her letters seemed, I don't know . . . sad."

"No shit, she's in jail. What do you expect? Joy?"

Nick picked up the photos Ruby had sent. The pair of black-and-white images were of a young light-skinned black woman and a sharp-dressed black man.

The woman wore a flowered Japanese-style dress and a pillbox hat tipped at a jaunty angle. Behind her stood a false background of a forest surrounded by a stone fence made of paper. She stared straight into the camera as if she possessed some knowledge of the grimness of her future.

The man wore a snug overcoat with his hand stuck in a Napoleonic pose. He had a pencil-thin mustache and wide-set, serious eyes. Behind him was a backdrop of a tropical sunset. Crooked palm trees and a manhole-size paper sun. A water-stained rip spread at his feet in the photograph like an earthquake's fault.

For some reason, the song "Frankie and Johnny" came to mind: *"He was her man and he was doin' her wrong."* Nick refilled his mug to warm a cold, cold feeling.

3

ABANDONED CREOLE TOWNHOMES and empty red brick ware-houses sat stagnant on Julia Street like ships from a forgotten armada. The heart of the Warehouse District was stuck in a transition. A collection of restaurants, art galleries, and antique shops were mixed with the occasional wino flophouse and skid row bar. Coffee shops, crack houses, and a Zen monastery nestled side by side.

Years ago, Nick had restored a 1922 lumber storage into a loft apartment with a garage on the first level. A small blue door led to his second story, sealed with square, industrial windows blurred with time. Thick blankets hung from a tattered laundry line to keep away the winter chill.

He parked his 1970 gunmetal gray Bronco in the parking garage below and bounded up the metal steps. At the top of the landing, the sliding metal door was partially open. He heard his speckled coffee pot gurgling on the stove and saw JoJo seated at an old table by the windows reading the *Picayune*.

"Brought you a po'boy from Johnnie's," JoJo said. He wore a red cardigan over a white shirt with tiny blue and black checks. He tucked a pair of glasses in his shirt pocket and looked up from the paper. His wingtips were replaced by cheap, white sneakers.

"You ever hear of Billy Lyons?" Nick asked, pouring JoJo some coffee into a chipped mug. "Owned King Snake Records in Chicago."

"Heard of King Snake, but don't know nothin' 'bout Lyons," JoJo said. "Why?"

"Headin' up to Chi-town," Nick said, placing the mug in front of JoJo. "Woman convicted of killing him agreed to an interview. Remember the Sweet Black Angel?"

"Yeah, 'Lonesome Blues Highway' . . . that thing Elmore was talkin' 'bout."

"Yep."

"Lots of *real* nice things in Chicago," JoJo said, smiling a wicked grin. "When you leavin'?"

"A train leaves in two hours but I've got about thirty finals to grade," Nick said, pulling a tattered army duffel bag from under his bed. He threw in a few pairs of blue jeans, thick socks, thermal underwear, thread-bare flannel shirts, a heavy black wool overcoat, a watch cap, and his Tom Mix boot knife.

He could almost hear the pleading guitar, rattling maracas, and urgent drumbeat of Bo Diddley in his head. *The big city called.*

"I'll drive you to the station," JoJo said, blowing steam off his coffee. "Take them papers and send 'em back in the mail. Randy ain't gonna care. For a woman like Kate, I'd quit my job and walk buck naked in the street durin' Mardi Gras."

"Who said anything about Kate?" Nick asked, tossing a travel kit into the huge bag. "Did I say a damned thing about Kate?"

"Kid, don't twist my dick in a knot," JoJo said, removing the wax paper from his sandwich and taking a bite. "I've known you too long."

Nick opened and closed desk drawers searching for pens, notebooks, and his cassette recorder. He stuffed a pack of unopened tapes and a carton of Marlboros into the duffel bag and zipped it closed.

"What's the story about the Sweet Black Angel?" JoJo asked.

Nick told him the little he knew about Ruby Walker.

"I always thought Loretta would kill me too, *but you never let your right hand know what your left hand doin'.* What you gonna do when you get there?"

"Hook up with some old contacts on the blues scene. Get her history recorded."

"Chicago." JoJo sighed. "Man. Always felt I was missin' something by not moving up there. Damn, there was a time when it seemed like the whole state of Mississippi was hoppin' the Illinois Central."

"The Great Migration."

"Who could blame 'em?" JoJo said with a wad of sandwich in his cheek. "When you were from Mississippi and played the blues, it was like bein' black twice."

Nick sat down and unwrapped his po'boy and ripped open a pack of Zapp's crawtaters. JoJo leaned back in his chair and narrowed his eyes as he worked on his sandwich. He crossed his arms in front of him.

"So Elmore said she got a raw deal?"

"Yeah, but he might have been talking to the rabbit sittin' beside me," Nick said with his mouth full. Nothing better than a fried shrimp po'boy with plenty of sauce picante. The red sauce oozed through his fingers and onto the wooden table.

Last January, Elmore King was in town to play the Super Bowl halftime in one of those tributes to New Orleans music that doesn't make any sense. King, the master of the Chicago West Side guitar sound, was surrounded by the spinning umbrellas of an old jazz procession. It was like putting Yo Yo Ma in a conga line. But King didn't seem to care. He had his check and a room at the Hilton. Didn't even stay for the whole game; he surprised JoJo down at the bar by sitting in a set with Fats and the house band. King kept his turquoise-studded cowboy hat down over his eyes as he worked his Stratocaster like an evil woman. He played through a torrent of emotions bubbling from his guitar as if there was an electric hookup to his soul. He was really making that thing scream as he shook his oily locks.

When King walked off stage, Nick felt JoJo's Blues Bar was about to tip over onto Conti with the boiling energy. King just tipped his hat after a song where he licked the strings with his tongue. He joined Nick and JoJo in a back corner table and Nick asked him if he wanted a beer.

King said he wanted a Crown Royal. *A bottle of Crown Royal.*

Nick gladly paid and the men sat in the deep darkness of JoJo's trying to embalm their brains. The conversation shifted from women to the old circuit, to friends long gone, then back to women. But during Fats's last break, King started talking about the early days in Chicago. He said he was damned hungry when he stepped off a Greyhound bus but couldn't even afford a stick of gum. As the amber level fell in the Crown bottle and JoJo left to close up, King talked about being discovered by songwriter Moses Jordan and cutting records at King Snake.

It was the beginning of the West Side sound as the South Side/Mississippi masters like Muddy and Wolf were reaching their zenith.

You remember Ruby Walker? Nick had asked.

Then an ashen look swept across King's face like rain clouds across Pontchartrain. It was as if a deep sadness floated to the surface and tears rimmed his eyes. He shook his head, downed the last of the Royal, and said, *That woman got caught in a tornado of shit she never understood. She rottin' away while we drink. Ain't that a waste?*

King's whole being was seemingly wounded by the thought of the past. He stared into a deep corner as a midnight winter rain scattered outside the open doors. The rain released musty closet smells into the French Quarter as King tipped his sweat-ringed black cowboy hat again and politely excused himself. He never returned to JoJo's and Nick hadn't talked to him since.

JoJo wadded up the po'boy's wax paper, breaking Nick from his reverie.

"You think her story's worth you freezin' yore ass off," JoJo said, fingering away some shrimp from his back teeth.

"I need to hear it."

JoJo nodded. "Be careful. All right? Don't want you comin' back home in pieces."

JoJo stood and motioned for Nick to follow him to Julia Street where he parked his 1963 Cadillac El Dorado. He opened the long passenger door and pulled out Nick's Browning 9 mm. Nick slid the gun from the leather holster, checked the side release, and ran a thumb over the walnut handle. It felt good and thick as he ejected the clip and placed it inside his corduroy jacket.

"Thought you might want her back," JoJo said, crawling out from the old car and locking his doors. "Them shitheads ain't hangin' out on Royal anymore. Guys were nothin' but a bunch of gay bikers, man. Thought they was in a gang or somethin' 'cause of the way they dressed in all black and shit and givin' me a mean eye when I was parkin'. But shiiit, last night I seen one of 'em kissin' another fella like he was suckin' on an egg, and thought they don't want nothin' from this old man."

" 'Cept your ass."

"Yeah, yeah, yeah," JoJo said. " 'Cept my ass . . . fuck you."

A homeless man wheeled his shopping cart off St. Charles and began to search through a Dumpster. He wore a black-and-red hunting cap and Sun Records T-shirt. Nick had seen him before down at the St. Charles Laundromat. He started to yell to him but the man turned in another direction.

"Say hello to Kate," JoJo said. "Not many men get second chances."

"Come on."

"Remember what I tole ya," JoJo said.

"Is this the thing about shitting in one hand and wishing in the other?"

"No."

"Not criticizing a piano-playing dog?"

"Would you please shut the fuck up," JoJo said. "What I was about to say is just when you think everythin' ain't workin' out for you, when you think that ain't nothin' goin' right and the world or God's against you . . . you got to realize everythin' happenin' jes the way it's supposed to be."

4

THE TENEMENTS BUCKLED with new folks from Mississippi in late 1956. I wanted to complain about the dirty streets to my sister but she was so proud of her new home. She washed each dish as if it was a jewel and hung her ragged laundry as if it were spun from gold. I remember the late evenings when I sat on those old crooked steps to smoke my daily cigarette and find some peace from her complainin', her husband's yellin', and kids' cryin'. The sound of the neighborhood's laundry, hung from cords and stretched between buildings like a collection of flags, cooled my mind.

By the end of the month, I was on the street. The husband kept comin' on to me and my sister imagined it was my fault. So I took my paper suitcase, my ten dollars in my shoe, and left. I walked the rain-slicked streets at night and slept durin' the day in vacant buildings. I felt like some kind of dog trottin' around without direction.

When I found Dirty Jimmy on Maxwell Street, I hadn't eaten for three days. After the third song, he disappeared and bought me a plate of greens and corn bread. I almost choked tryin' to rush it into my body. Jimmy played harp like an angel, I'm tellin' you, and we became friends. Half the bucket of cash we made was mine.

But I continued to walk. I found work at a laundry where I got blisters on my fingers as long as snap peas. But it was work and it was more money than I had ever known.

I lived at a paper-walled rooming house till Billy Lyons walked over to me and Jimmy one day at the market. His suit was creased within an inch of his life and his shoes shined like a silver dollar.

He told me I sang like a man. I laughed at him, my eyes lookin' at the ground, but two weeks later I'm in his bed. He poured champagne over my brown body and blistered hands. He made love to me and left flowers by my mouth as I slept.

The music surrounded me as if I were swimmin' in blood-red wine. I was drunk with it.

I sang at Pepper's, The Purple Cat.

I was at parties at Muddy's house. I remember he was all twisted up in a fine suit. He told me I got somethin'. He told me he sees somethin' in me like Broonzy saw in him. Spann was there, playin' a piano in the corner. Drunk. A sombrero cocked on his head, as he pounded out his heart.

The whiskey flowed with the blues. I couldn't get enough. Blackness. Swimmin'. Blackness, back in the sea. Billy and I fightin'. He's out whorin'. I'm out workin'.

The world spun and I fell through it. The lipstick on my face was a jagged curve as I tripped off the stage in the middle of the first set. I blacked out. Felt myself swimmin' in Billy's blood. So thick I couldn't reach the surface.

Then I woke up.

A single bulb burned and rocked above my head and I knew I had been dreamin' again. My sister is dead. Billy is dead. And it's lockdown time. I heard the locks crack through the concrete walls as I turned my pillow. I closed my eyes, waitin' for sleep to come so that I could return to my dreams, Billy, and my promised land.

5

IN CHICAGO, THE snow fell in ashen flakes as large as Annie's hands. She watched the crystal patterns drop and burn as soon as they touched the black asphalt on Wabash Avenue. The snow almost didn't look real as the cars' headlights cut through the white curtain and into the hotel bar. Bet she could walk out and catch the frozen wetness in her mouth like when she was a kid.

The Cass Hotel was a real gangster-looking place. Sandstone blocks topped with a dozen stories of sturdy brick. She sat on the first floor in a bar called the Sea of Happiness with her partner Fannie. A model cutter ship hung over beer taps and about a dozen neon signs buzzed in the plate glass windows. A couple of video games pinged away along the back wall as a jukebox played bad eighties music.

She and Fannie watched the man slinking down at the end of the bar over some drink as thick as maple syrup. The little fat guy wasn't a social drinker. He was a professional on a mission. His beady black eyes were like slits as he downed the last drop, coughed, and moved his neck like a dodo bird. Made Annie sick to know she'd have to see him naked by the end of the night. Bet he had a dick like a little wet noodle.

Fannie yawned next to her. The long-legged black woman just wasn't in the mood, Annie guessed. Fannie just sat there all prim and proper with her legs crossed and her tongue running around a straw.

What a woman.

Fannie could've been one of those women who made money modeling underwear. She had a tight body filled with good curves and bumps and skin the color of the inside of a Milky Way bar. Wide-set almond-shaped eyes. But what Annie liked best about her partner and best friend was the scrolled tattoo above her pierced navel. Real sweet-girl-gone-bad look.

Fannie, the perfect black love machine.

Annie rubbed her hand over the little smiley face near her own breast and looked at the mirror in front of her. Maybe she wasn't that bad. Kind of cute with blonde hair cut as short as a boy's and wild blue eyes. Pert little nose too.

But she wasn't looking for a man. Already had one. *Willie, her butcher knife*. He'd never let her down. She remembered when she and Fannie were both growing up in the Robert Taylor projects, Willie became her best friend. Sometimes, she would stroke him under her pillow as she heard the screaming from the floors below.

She thought about the time when she was fourteen and that man, who smelled like garlic, grabbed her boob and tried to put her hand on his dick. They were stuck in a stairwell and the man was panting and making all kinds of dog noises. He gripped her small boob so tight she thought he was going to try and rip it off. But before he could get the second button undone on her shorts, she had the knife halfway in his belly.

Yeah, Willie was her man.

Butcher Knife-Totin' Annie and Fast-Fuckin' Fannie. Together they could do anything they wanted. Now that Fannie was out of jail for those B and E, possession, and prostitution charges, they'd take on the whole fucking world.

The Oriental bartender plunked down another orgasm for Fannie and a shot of Bacardi lemon rum for herself. There was a ratty captain's hat sitting on his head like he thought he was being cool as he flashed some rotten teeth. Pimple marks dotted his face and he had a sweaty white bandanna cocked on his neck.

"What you lookin' at, Chinaman?" Annie said. "You just gave us what we want, so go away dick brain."

The bartender frowned, then grinned and blew them a kiss.

Guess you really couldn't blame the guy for staring at all their leather-and-lace glory. Fannie had on the tightest black pants Annie had ever seen. Looked like she'd spray painted her legs. And her low-cut red sweater really brought out the tiger tattooed on her right breast. The old beast growling.

She watched Fannie sip out of the glass like she was the damn Queen of England, her legs crossed and locked in a vise. The short man at the end of the bar looked like he was about to start drooling.

"Maybe you should just cut the crotch out of your pants, woman," Annie said. "That'd make it easier for all your men."

"Girlfriend," Fannie said, taking another sip of the orgasm and licking the rim. "Please kiss my black coochie."

"Promise?" Annie asked, raising her eyebrows and smiling a rubbery grin.

"Girrrl . . . you are *too* sick."

"We got work to do," Annie said, patting her side where Willie lived. His cold steel firm.

"You got a plan?"

"One of two things," Annie said. "I can stick Willie up his ass and make him disappear or you can fuck him to death."

Fannie grinned and uncrossed her legs.

In a fake British accent, she said: "I'm quite glad us ladies still have options."

The two girls shielded their mouths with their hands as they snickered.

8

IN THE BLACKNESS of a Mississippi night, Nick watched the Delta landscape roll by from the Amtrak car window. The barren shotgun cottages, tired mobile homes, and brittle patterns of dead cotton fields shot out in strobelike flashes as he kicked off his old boots and took a sip from a stainless steel flask. The thumping metal on metal pounded a rhythm in his ears.

Kate Archer, JoJo had to bring her up. He just had to plant that seed in his mind to sprout and grow until he stepped off the train in Chicago. *What a friend.*

Nick heard she'd taken a job with the *Tribune* after a failed relationship with an Uptown restaurateur named Richard Brevard. A man she was supposed to marry. She must've met Richard shortly after she'd found Nick in bed with that lanky blonde two years ago. Nick remembered the vacant look on her face as she rolled back his warehouse door. She saw a strange woman sitting in her robe and drinking out of her favorite mug.

Kate had shot him a look that wasn't exactly hatred, just a drained expression of absolute disappointment. She said in an even, dead-sure tone, "You're such an ass."

But there were other memories. Better memories. Nick could still feel the heat of her dark skin when they made love in his warehouse. Aaron Neville on the stereo. Both of them loaded with Dixies, whiskey, and blues. The best time he'd ever had.

Maybe JoJo was right. Maybe this whole trip was about her.

Some kind of masochism to see if she would kick him in the nuts this time. But she was worth it. If only he could talk to her for a moment, he'd feel better. He was never much for closure. In fact, he thought the whole concept was bullshit. Endings are seldom neat. They're sometimes jagged and ugly. But he needed something . . . another *screw you*. Another chance.

Maybe he was just bringing hope with him, a dream of something that could never happen. Nick sipped the whiskey again and stared back at the blues highway and laughed at his situation. He felt New Orleans melt away in the flickering light, the history roll by, and the endless black night reconnect to a past that once showed hope to an entire generation. The train rolled, bumped, and vibrated his back. Thinking about the old travelers made him feel good.

Nick could imagine them now as he turned out his overhead light and pulled down his narrow bed. He could almost smell the migrants loaded with shoe boxes full of fried chicken and biscuits staring at the same Mississippi night. There were stories of women kissing the floor of the railcar as they crossed over the Mason Dixon line at Cairo, Illinois. *Trading what was familiar for what could be*.

The journey of the blues started somewhere outside, somewhere in a heated evening about a century ago. The blues was born in the rich, brown earth of the Delta, a region stretching two hundred miles from the Peabody Hotel in Memphis to the edge of Vicksburg, Mississippi. It was once a frontier of mean swamps with bears and water moccasins, a land broken in by blacks who worked from sundown in levee and prison camps. Sometimes at gunpoint.

From that soul-breaking work came the blues. Like their African forefathers, they used songs to make the work pass—sometimes alone, others in unison—as they picked cotton, unloaded steamship cargos, or beat their tools into the rich earth. Soon, they coupled the hollers with guitars and harmonicas.

The music worked its way into backwood shacks where couples danced, bathed in sweat, as the music brought back the spirit. The early players thumped drumbeats on the buckled, wooden floors making the guitar talk back to them. The instruments just an intimate extension of the players' voices.

Blues became a core of Delta life and of the southern black community.

And in the late thirties and forties, blues followed that community. About five million blacks left the south between World War II and 1970 for northern cities in a shift that changed the complexion of America. It used to cost about twelve bucks for a ticket from Clarksdale to Chicago on the Illinois Central—about a week's pay for most. Some families, like Old World immigrants, had to split up. They would send money home to bring everyone over to the other side.

In 1943, Muddy Waters caught a train to Chicago with nothing but a yearning soul, a single change of clothes, and his old Silvertone guitar. He knew fame was just a trip away.

Nick believed that's when the blues really left the Delta and started a new life in the Windy City. Muddy would help mold that country sound into a tightly backed band with piano, drums, bass, and harmonica. The future of the blues arrived with Muddy at the Twelfth Street Station.

When he was finishing his Great Migration project at Tulane a few years ago, Nick traced the routes of the Delta greats from Mississippi to Chicago. The change was bone-jarring. The Mississippi Delta was a fertile oasis. Everything green and alive. Chicago was industrial. Gray and cold. But for sharecroppers making inhuman wages, if anything at all, Chicago was about hope. They would've probably traveled to the depths of hell to escape the poverty and racial barriers.

Nick imagined folks like Muddy and Ruby Walker and the absolute loneliness they must've felt approaching the belching smokestacks of Chicago industry. Did Ruby wait for a train in Clarksdale with a suitcase made of paper filled with everything she owned as Nick had read? Big boasts to farmers in Mississippi about how she was going to make it in Chicago? About how she was going to come back driving a long, shiny car throwing money out her window at country relatives? But when the cold night cloaked around the train, it must have been like traveling to another planet. The boast becoming an internal fear.

Bright lights, big city, gone to my baby's head, Nick thought, closing his eyes.

Today, most of that hope was gone. The Twelfth Street Station was now a barren field at Twelfth and Michigan, and much of the South Side was nothing but rotting slums and burned-out shells. In Muddy's and Ruby's time, Chicago was a place where blacks could make it, where wealth was as obtainable as someone's work ethic. But today, many blacks were taking that same blues highway back to the Delta. Somewhere, the dream had become an economic nightmare.

The lights of the small towns and lonesome highways scattered across his face as the train rolled through the cold neverending night. As he fell asleep, he imagined Kate's face close to his. Brown eyes like sunlight hitting morning coffee. Perfect dimpled chin. Reminded him of a young Ali MacGraw about the time of *The Getaway*. He imagined her pulling the dark brown hair from her eyes and pursing a smile into the corner of her mouth.

I've been gone so long, I know things ain't what they used to be.

7

AN HOUR LATER, Annie and Fannie had their arms around the little man as they led him up to his apartment on Rush Street. Place was over a pizzeria and Annie could smell the crust, cheese, and sauce baking into a symphony. Made her mouth water as she watched the guy fumbling with his key for the hole and missing the entire knob.

"Baby, let me slip in it," Fannie said, guiding his key into the lock. "Mama will take care of you." The hallway was covered with muddy, red carpet with blue lights shining in a cavelike glow. Looked like they were inside a carnival ride. *Step right up, see what it's like to live in a shithole.*

Fannie smoothed her gloved hand over his greasy head with about four long hairs plastered over a bald spot. Over his shoulder, Fannie made a queer-looking face like she'd just stroked a dead chicken. Annie smiled back at her friend and could feel her heart pounding in her chest like a bass drum. She crushed her lip with her teeth.

The man stumbled into an apartment that smelled of pizza and cat piss. He had an unmade bed under a window heater with clothes strewn around the room like they'd flown out of a blender. Dirty grippie underwear littered the floor along with crushed cans of Hamm's beer. Real class act. Didn't even seem worth the effort. But this was the man, and they had a job to do.

The man fell onto his bed, turned on an AM clock radio,

unbuckled his pants, and pushed his loose polyester trousers to his ankles. The radio droned an old ABBA song as he put his hands behind his head and spread his legs. His legs were skinny, white, and covered in coarse black hair like some kind of fucked up Chia pet.

"I want you, Blackie, to get naked and put your muff in my face while Blondie over there kisses my lizard," he said with a thick tongue.

"How about a little smoke first?" Fannie asked.

"Shit, that's all you whores think about," he said.

The man rolled off the bed and reached into a flimsy night-stand for a pipe and a plastic Baggie. Next to the radio, he had one of those dumb-ass ceramic baseball statues with the bobbing head next to a picture of an old woman in a casket. Annie licked her lips as he popped a fat rock into the pipe and thumbed the lighter. The sweet orange flame licked the bottom of the glass.

The drunk man took a deep hit, coughed, and lay back into his bed like the caterpillar from *Alice in Wonderland*. He passed the pipe and a rock to Annie. She wrapped her lips around the glass, lit it, and sucked in deep. She felt the smoke burn through her lungs, into her limbs, and out her toes.

She passed it to Fannie, who burned the last rock in the Baggie. Her partner's eyes crossed as she inhaled the blue smoke.

Make it all go away. All go away.

Annie could see the amoebas crawl over her eyes and disappear. As she started to float, the man yanked the pipe away from them, pulling the brake on their wild ride. He set it on the bedside table.

Annie slid her hand inside her black leather jacket but Fannie shrugged her off and laughed. Fannie took a wide stance and dropped her vintage letterman's jacket to the nasty floor. She pulled the red sweater high over her chest, so the little man could see her bra. Then she started slow and deliberate, stroking her long fingers over her tight stomach and around her navel. Her gloved hands moved over her rib cage and up to her breasts.

Annie's heart felt like it was going to explode.

"Oh baby, that's the way I want it," the little turd said. "Keep on with that shit, get them pants off, down to your knees."

"How 'bout another hit?" Fannie asked.

"That was it," he said, slumping back into his yellowed pillows.

Fannie slipped off her boots and dropped her leather pants. She sat beside the man on the bed, his eyes flitting and darting over her body like some kind of crazed monkey at feeding time. Fannie let the man touch her leg. He was shaking now.

"You too, you too," he said, looking at Annie with his teeth chattering.

Annie gritted her teeth, pulling off her leather jacket and setting it on a broken kitchen chair. She turned her back to the man, her vision flickering, and tucked Willie into the side of her pants with the handle barely poking from the top. She could feel his sharp coldness on her hip as she walked across the room and closed the curtains above the space heater.

She sat beside Fannie on the bed and waited to get this shit over with.

The man shook like some old fucker as Annie put her arms around Fannie and kissed her neck. For some reason, men always went for that shit. They loved to see two women hot for each other or cat fighting. Showed how damned stupid they were. Too dumb to see they weren't needed.

"You wanna see it, baby?" Fannie asked.

"Mmm, we want to show you," Annie said, her vision blurring. "You are just *sooo* hot."

The man licked his fingers and ran his hand over his bald spot.

"Over there in the kitchen," the man said, slightly slurring his words. "I got another rock."

Annie moved away from the bed and into the kitchen. Under the sink was a box crammed full of more Baggies and two huge packs of pure coke. They felt like bricks in her shaking hands. One was covered in blue plastic wrap and the other in red. *All she needed to know.*

Back on the bed, Fannie moved her hands to the man's rod. The little man was rocking now as she moved her gloved hand up his leg. She grabbed hold of his wrists and pulled them over his head. Even at the foot of the bed, Annie could smell his dirty armpits. Fannie yanked the man's belt from his loose pants and bound him at the wrists.

"Now, now," he yelled. "Do it. Do it!"

Annie pulled Willie from her pants as Fannie moved to the other side of the bed. Annie jumped on him and traced the blade from his throat to his chest and smiled.

"Stagger Lee said hello."

"You fucked with the wrong man, mister," Fannie said, biting a cuticle and spitting it away. "That ain't your coke."

"Oh shit. Oh shit. Oh shit."

"Yeah, 'oh shit' is right, numb nuts," Annie said as she stabbed the knife in the center of his chest. His eyes crossed as he mewed and slumped into the pillows. A big O caught on his lips as a red bubble appeared, froze, and then popped.

8

THE COLD STUNG Nick's face and hands as he stepped onto the Union Station platform with his army duffel bag and great expectations. He buttoned the wool overcoat and pulled a black watch cap down on his head as he exhaled a long stream of smoky breath tainted with whiskey. It was early Thursday morning, December 21, and the booze and tight quarters hadn't been kind to his old body. He felt sore and stiff as he followed a trail of people into the terminal.

Union Station was like going back about a half dozen decades. The columns, statues, and wooden benches in the football field-size terminal made travel seem important: The ceiling was an arc of hundreds of glass panes shining bright on a world that still spoke of Al Capone, men in fedoras and red-lipped women smoking unfiltered Chesterfields.

Chicago. Capital of the blues. A man's voice reading schedules droned from speakers above.

Nick loved travel. Travel was about hope and the opportunity of adventure—about the only thing he missed from playing football. He remembered the dirty jokes on bumpy airplanes, the two-ton linemen with tiny earphones in their ears bopping to an unheard beat. He liked the camaraderie between the guys—some zealous Christians who recited prayers over the phone while others played with waterguns in the halls of four-star hotels.

He also enjoyed the simple pleasures—the way managers laid out uniforms as if they were armor. Socks perfectly cuffed, pants folded by your pads, and helmet buffed with a tight shine. The money was great too. He made more money in those few years than he would probably ever make playing or writing about the blues.

But he hated the preparations. The stress. The way the blue-collar fans pelted players with hot dogs and insults when you lost. His asshole coach who tore up a treasured copy of *Catcher in the Rye* because he was reading too close to kickoff.

The idiot never understood it calmed him.

There was a falseness about playing in the league, a feeling that you were disposable, that you were just sitting in a position being readied for someone else. Average players of the past were not revered. Most aging players, even great ones, were treated with pity, like greyhounds ready to take the needle. Most of the guys Nick knew were now broke. Guys who made a few hundred grand a year now had nothing to show for their time but cracking joints and ruined bodies.

For Nick, the giggling groupies with frosted hair and fake tits disappeared into the bottom of a Jack Daniel's bottle. *He was done anyway.* His shoulders couldn't make it without the cortisone and his head pounded with the monotony. Saints' fans were wearing paper sacks on their heads and professional football was starting to hold all the promise of a day's pass to an auto show.

In just a moment of rage, his whole career was gone.

His coach had benched him for most of his last season in favor of the laziest rookie Nick had ever met. When Nick got into a Monday Night Football game and racked up several sacks, the coach took him out again. The rookie had cleaned the dirt from his eye and was ready to go back in. The coach was making decisions not on how to win games but how to please the front office. Something snapped.

But it was worth it, just to see the wide-eyed shock on his coach's face as he threw him to the Astroturf and dumped the

Gatorade on his head. An hour later, he was drunk at JoJo's and had been there ever since.

Nick looked around the limestone cavern of the station as if he were lost.

Seemed silly now, but he half expected Kate to be there. JoJo trying to push fate and maybe giving her a call. But she wasn't. He was unknown wandering through a crowd that didn't give him a glance. Absolutely anonymous. Maybe it was better that way. Conduct a few interviews with Ruby and get out of town. Leave their past alone. He walked through the marble and gold to Jackson Street. The wind outside felt like ice water flowing into his lungs as he tossed the duffel bag over his shoulder and grabbed a cab to the Palmer House.

■

An hour and a half later, Nick headed south on Interstate 55, a Styrofoam cup of coffee between his legs and a McDonald's ham biscuit mashed between his hand and the steering wheel. He had his radio tuned to a public station as he thought about the ways to ask a woman about killing her lover. He thought about the Great Migration, Ruby's chilling voice, and the little he knew about King Snake Records. Through a haze of clouds the sun burned, white, distant, and alone.

9

SEVENTY-ONE MILES outside Chicago, the Dwight Correctional Center stood like a medieval fortress. Didn't look like a prison. Looked like a mental institution during the Depression or an old college campus. Buildings made of stone with pointed towers. Nick drove his rental car—which resembled a white Tic Tac—into the visitors' lot and shut off the engine. He finished a cigarette, flicked it into the weeds, and walked inside, passing through various gates and checkpoints.

The halls echoed with bolts popping and buzzers sounding until he was ushered into a sterile room to wait for Ruby Walker. Basic white cinderblock decorated with crooked law enforcement posters. The floor was concrete and the door was metal. No windows. Just the annoying burn of the fluorescent lights above.

Prisons were a part of the blues, the same way railroads and bars emanated with the music. Bukka White was a well-known slide guitarist when he was convicted of shooting a man in 1937. He spent a year at Parchman Prison in Mississippi before meeting Nick's hero, Alan Lomax. Lomax, the first great blues tracker, recorded White for the Library of Congress.

Lomax also found Leadbelly, who was sentenced to Angola Prison in Louisiana. Leadbelly, the king of the twelve-string, was serving his second term in prison for murder. Impressed by Leadbelly's powerful voice and knowledge of folk songs, Lomax petitioned the Louisiana governor for a pardon. In 1934, the big man went to work as Lomax's personal chauffeur.

Nick was also no stranger to the Farm. Over the years, he'd interviewed several prisoners at Angola. A prison meeting was nothing new. He drummed his hands on the table and adjusted the cassette recorder.

After a few minutes of staring at the ceiling, the door opened and a white female guard walked in with a tall black woman. The woman was lanky and rawboned with darting black eyes. She had an oval face with high cheekbones and weathered brown skin. Her gray hair was cut short and it frizzed loose above her ears. She kept her hands in the pockets of her denim jumpsuit as she took a seat.

Nick stood and smiled. He tried to imagine the Sweet Black Angel from the photographs, her hand delicately wrapped around a thick silver microphone, her eyes shut, and her mouth wide open in song. He thought of the slight space between her teeth and the sheen of her skin speaking of smoldering sexuality.

Now she just looked worn. Tired.

Nick sat back down, reached into his coat for a notebook, and fiddled with controls on the recorder. His watch cap and gloves lay on the table. The guard leaned against the wall smacking gum.

"Miss Walker," Nick said. "Glad to meet you, ma'am."

Ruby nodded, looked down at the tabletop, and crossed her arms over her chest. It was cold in the room. Felt like a cellar. But her arms over her chest and downturned head showed little excitement. He hoped she didn't regret the invitation.

"I appreciated your letters," Nick said, smiling. "Enjoyed every one."

Ruby wiped her nose with her right hand and stared at the buzzing lights over her head. She shifted in her seat, crossed her arms again, and turned back to Nick. The sound of her stiff denim was briefly interrupted by the guard's cracking gum.

"So, why'd you choose me?" Nick asked. "After forty years, you could have spoken to anybody."

Ruby shrugged.

"I'll make sure your story is cataloged into the archive at Tulane. Probably follow up with an article published in a blues history magazine. Several research papers . . . Ruby?"

She looked back up at the ceiling as if waiting for divine intervention. Seemed more talkative in the letters. Maybe she had trouble being around people.

"I'd like to start at the beginning," Nick said. "Maybe cover some old ground from what you wrote. . . . Heard you're a good cook."

Ruby slowly brought her head down to her chest and raised her eyebrows. She nodded as if seeing Nick for the first time. "Appreciate that," she said in a rough growl with only a trace of a Mississippi accent. "But with these ingredients, it's like turnin' dog shit into chocolate pie."

Nick laughed. Ruby and the guard didn't crack a smile.

"Remind me to skip lunch," Nick said. Still laughing alone.

No one spoke for a few uncomfortable seconds. Nick looked down at his notes. "Tell me more about 'Lonesome Blues Highway.' Big hit?"

"Went straight to the top," she said with dead black eyes. "You know that magazine *Cashbox*? They called it pure gold. Billy couldn't press 'em fast enough."

"You cut how many, ten others?"

" 'Bout a dozen."

"Which ones were your favorites?"

"Dude, you're askin' questions from way back." She sighed. "Let's see, 'Blues Highway.' I wrote that. Couple of Memphis Minnie numbers, 'Please Don't Stop Him' and 'Fashion Plate Daddy.' And 'Tie Yo' Monkey in a Knot.' "

Nick sang:

> *"When you see that woman*
> *dressed so fine,*
> *And you got lovin'*
> *on your mind,*

You better tie,
You better tie,
Yo' monkey in a knot."

Ruby listened to the words, her face intent. The guard laughed and turned away. Guess he never would make it as a singer. But maybe he'd loosen Ruby up.

"Moses Jordan wrote that one?" Nick asked.

"Yeah, Moses wrote most of my songs."

"You still see him?"

"He's come to see me a few times," she said. "He sent a few letters. But your friends have a way of forgettin' when you're inside. Used to have this big woman in here who told me that. Said forget your friends. Forget your family. Only person you can rely on is yourself."

"Last year, Elmore King told me you got a raw deal," Nick said. "You know why he would say that? You two close?"

"I thought you said you wanted to hear *my* story," Ruby said. "You said you wanted to know *all of it.*"

"I do."

"Aren't you gonna ask me why I pointed that gun at Billy?"

"All right—why'd you point the gun?"

"After forty years, those things start to rattle in your mind," she said slowly. She never looked Nick in the eye, reciting what she had to say like a bored minister working with an old sermon. "You fill your cell with books and your mind with the past. I still see it in my sleep. Wakes me up."

The cassette recorder whirred in the silence. Nick scratched his cheek and shifted in his chair. He smiled at her again. Her face was without expression.

Ruby leaned back into her seat and laced her hands in her lap. "Me and Billy was fightin' over money that day," she said. "They tried to make it seem like I was jealous but he owed me for my records. We'd been through for a long time."

"Seems like you loved him a lot."

"I did."

"But you didn't kill him over love?"

Ruby looked up from her seat. Her face drawn, her eyes hooded. "I didn't kill him at all. Don't you know that yet? Didn't you read my letters?"

He should have realized what this was about. An interview granted after you listened to some long, hard bullshit story of innocence. Most prisoners had spent so much time alone and in law libraries that they really believed they never committed the crime. Nick could play the game. He had before. When they got tired of repeating the stories, they finally tell you things you want to know about their music. Besides, Elmore King thought she was treated unfairly. Maybe that was a story in itself.

"Who would want to set you up?" Nick asked, trying to seem sincere. Maybe not looking too good doing it.

"If I knew, I wouldn't be here."

"Any ideas?"

She shook her head and looked at her hands. Short nails. Winter chapped.

"Billy owed a lot of folks money. I was just standin' in line. Could of been a lot of people. He used to run numbers, hookers, you name it. Made Al Capone look like a mama's boy."

"What about appeals?"

"Done 'em all. Hope can be mean, so I quit . . . Used to think I deserved what I got. I took my sentence but always thought I'd get out."

"What about parole? Seems like you're the model prisoner. You've cooked, served forty years."

"Yeah, well, there was some trouble 'bout fifteen years ago."

"What kind of trouble?"

"Guard. Man guard was messin' with me. Tryin' to touch me and things."

"Did you complain?"

"Yeah, I complained. I stuck a fork right up his ass in the kitchen. Had to have surgery to get it out and got me in solitary for a month. Had some cross-eyed psychologist tell me I had a problem with men and pointed things. Said I had issues with my daddy. Ain't that somethin'? I never knew my daddy."

"And that was the end of parole?"

She took another deep breath, staring at the floor and rocking in her chair. "The board told me I was still a threat on the outside. Hell, took me three years just to get back into the kitchen."

"Listen, we don't need to get into all that yet," Nick said. "I want to hear about when you were young, your recordings, leaving Clarksdale."

"What do you mean, you don't want to hear *all that* yet?"

"Your guilt or innocence isn't my business. I'm a historian. I want to know about your life."

"And bein' innocent ain't a part of my life?" Ruby asked.

"Not all of it."

She stared straight into his eyes. She wasn't mad. Just worn. She looked like a person suffering from severe sleep deprivation begging a doctor for a pill or some advice. Her eyes dropped somewhere into an open space and again nodded with an understanding only she knew.

"Ruby, I've been on a train from New Orleans all night. We'll get to your story . . . be cool."

"Don't be coolin' me, dude," Ruby said. "Uh-ah. Why do you think I gave you a chance? Spent my days tellin' you my story in those letters? That was my insides I wrote."

"You heard about how handsome I was?"

Ruby blew out her breath and leaned back into her chair. "Look like that face been in some fights to me."

The guard behind her laughed. Nick looked up at the guard and raised an eyebrow.

"Where'd you get that scar?" Ruby asked. "Fightin'?"

"Quarterback kicked me in the face."

"Reason I answered you is I checked you out. I keep up with blues. I know what's goin' on out there and the sad state of things. Reason they ain't deadened my mind yet."

"How did you check me out?"

Ruby had her shoulders pinched together and her head in her hands. She rubbed her rough brown hands over her face and said, "I read about you helpin' that man in Memphis."

Nick looked away and down at his notes.

"That old dude whose manager left with everything he owned. Said you found the man at a strip club in Jackson."

"Biloxi."

"Said you went to jail for a few days."

"Yeah."

"Man called you a saint."

"He said I once *played* for the Saints."

She skimmed her hand over her short gray hair. It was if she was searching for the glistening tresses she once owned. He had an hour for this interview and was losing time fast.

"Tell me about growing up in Mississippi," Nick said.

"Why?" she asked. "Nobody cares."

"Your music was and is important. People still listen to it."

"Who? No one knows me."

"I do."

"And you want to hear my story from the beginning. Everything?"

"Yes, ma'am."

Ruby looked down at her hands and inhaled a long breath. She blew it out and looked back at the masculine guard. The female guard rolled up on her toes and looked away.

"I'll make you a deal, dude," Ruby said. "I'm tired. Look at me. I'm a mess. That's another thing. Don't want no pictures. You hear me? I want to be remembered for what I was." She pulled the denim material from her chest. "Not this."

"What's the deal?" Nick asked.

"You find out what happened to Billy and you get my story."

Nick laughed. He could feel his face flush with embarrassment. "That was forty years ago."

"You tellin' me?"

Somehow this always happened. He had a weakness for

involving himself with his subjects. He knew he'd helped Will Roy get his cash back from his manager, done odd jobs for friends like tracking down Jesus for Fats. But what Ruby was asking was something altogether different. He should learn from his mistakes. *Willie Brown, Henry.*

"I'll see what I can do."

Ruby leaned her head to the table. He could see the top of her matted hair and the chaffed skin that had formed on her elbows. Ruby was eroded. Her body, her soul. Everything about her seemed to have been stripped away. It was a state Nick had seen before. So clear, it appeared like a photograph from his past.

"You still keep in contact with anyone from the old days?" he asked.

"Just one. But hadn't seen him for a couple years. Peetie Wheatstraw. He hasn't done nothin' but suck up every last cent I made on the outside. Said he was my agent. That he'd take care of me and all that kind of mess. We ain't talkin', but Peetie knew all them folks."

"Where can I find him?"

"Last time I heard, he was workin' at a men's shop on the South Side called the Soul Train," she said. "Been doin' that ever since he got out of the business. . . . Other than that, don't know what to tell ya."

Ruby cocked her head and watched Nick's face. "So, you gonna do it?"

"I'll ask around during my research," Nick said. "That's all I can promise."

She stretched out her hand. Nick shook it. She felt warm and small. He smiled at her again. She looked down at the concrete floor dabbed with cigarette butts.

"So your family were sharecroppers?" Nick asked.

"Slaves more like it. We worked on a plantation outside Clarksdale. Beautiful place. Still think about it. Can just see the way thunderstorms would roll over the Delta. Looked like big black islands that would beat the dirt for hours. . . ."

10

NICK DECIDED TO loop back through the South Side and search for Peetie Wheatstraw early that afternoon. Peetie was about the only lead he had on King Snake and shouldn't be too hard to find. You start with the easy ones and work backward. After a few minutes of searching though a soggy White Pages by a Burger King and consulting a folding map, he was on Forty-seventh Street, riding low in the stubby Tic Tac, heater cranked in the slushy gray cold, as the dilapidated brick buildings and crumbling Eastlake homes whizzed by in his peripheral vision.

He tried to imagine the neighborhood in the forties and fifties. He thought of the days when Forty-seventh cut through the heart of Bronzeville, a working-class neighborhood of hotels, shops, and theaters. He thought of the excitement of when Cab Calloway played the Regal and fresh faces from Mississippi cotton fields drank in an endless row of blues joints. Trading brogan shoes and overalls for creased suits and mack daddy hats. When Billy Lyons breathed and Ruby Walker was the hottest female blues act in town.

As he drove farther into the neighborhood, to the core of the South Side, the images of the past were shattered by liquor stores, check cashing joints, pawnshops, and storefront churches that hadn't had a service for twenty years. The neighborhood was a land of outdoor drinkers and men in black leather jackets and do-rags with cigarettes loose in their mouths. There were razorsharded parking gates, rusted stop signs, burned-out brown-stones with plywood windows, and crumbling buildings decomposing into trash-strewn lots.

It was a forgotten place. An apocalyptic world. Chained. Gated and covered for rediscovery.

Nick already knew Peetie Wheatstraw's name but not for any connection to King Snake Records or the blues scene of fifties Chicago. Peetie Wheatstraw was a brooding piano player with a potato-shaped head from St. Louis in the thirties. He was known for his songs about sex, death, and the supernatural and often bragged that he was the devil's son-in-law. But that Peetie Wheatstraw died more than fifty years ago in a car crash. His real name was William Bunch and used the name Peetie Wheatstraw for show. Wheatstraw was the trickster from black folklore. The evil spirit waiting at the crossroads.

Nick had never heard that name associated with King Snake. He would have remembered it. But so much about King Snake is unknown. It wasn't like Vee Jay or Diamond where oral histories were told so often they became redundant. Over forty years, names can become lost and people forgotten. Especially the money men.

Five minutes later, Nick walked through a narrow alley next to the store.

Soul Train Fashions sat inside a tri-corner, three-story building with a long row of plate glass windows wrapping the bottom floor filled with candy-colored suits, Stacey Adams shoes, and fedoras with feathers. A hand-painted sign in red and green said DON'T LET THE PREACHER CATCH YOU OUT OF STYLE.

When Nick pushed the door, a buzzer sounded and a lock released. Inside, the store had cheap wood-paneled walls and smelled of cellophane packaging and new shoes. Rows and rows of suits stretched to a back counter. Lime green, cherry red, sky blue. Hats sat behind a locked glass case like relics in a museum. A purple bowler hung in the middle as the crown jewel with a smallish yellow feather tucked into its band.

"Hello?"

"Hold up. Hold up. Be right with ya."

A black man in a purple suit with a pair of two-toned shoes in his hand walked out of a small cove. The man's hair was relaxed like a doo-wop singer and he wore a thin mustache below a large wide-spread nose. His skin was deep black and stretched tight against his skull like Little Richard after his fifth face-lift. Nick could have sworn he noticed a trace of lipstick.

"You Peetie?" Nick asked.

The man placed the shoes on a stand filled with a rainbow assortment of colors. He stopped and returned his eyes. "What's it to ya?"

"I'm looking for a man called Peetie Wheatstraw." Nick introduced himself and offered his hand.

The man's wide grin turned downward as he studied Nick's face, shaggy hair, and beaten work boots. His eyes rolled up to his arched eyebrows.

"I can tell you ain't lookin' for no suit."

Must be.

"Heard you were Ruby Walker's agent."

"If you lookin' for collectin', stand in line, boy, 'cause whole bunch of folks lookin' for a dime from the Peetster. You hear what I sayin'?"

"I'm not here for a shakedown," Nick said. "Hate to disappoint you, but I'm just a blues historian."

"No shit," Peetie said, his shoulders hunching with laughter. "You know you're gettin' old when you become *history*."

"I'm lookin' for anything you remember about the old scene and King Snake Records."

"Man, make my ole dick hard to hear you askin'. Goddamned, ain't thought about King Snake in quites the while."

"You got time to talk?" Nick said, never hearing a source aroused over his own history.

"Listen, man, I was about to close up. You can go with me if you want. Just down the street. Good greens and corn bread."

"I could eat," Nick said. The early-morning biscuit was long gone.

The winter sky had begun to turn black outside and hard wind rattled the front door. Peetie opened the glass case full of hats and pulled out the purple one. He slipped the bowler on his head and grabbed a trenchcoat off the rack.

"Gotten colder than a Minnesota well-digger's ass," he said with a giggle. "Where you from, Travers?"

"New Orleans."

"No shit. I grew up near Rampart Street. Left when I was sixteen . . . you come all this way to ask about King Snake?"

"Yep."

"*Ooh, well well,*" he said, tying the purple trenchcoat around him. "Lets go get down to business."

They followed the iced sidewalk down the block to another storefront, a place called Connie's. The sign said it was the Best Soul Food on the South Side. That was the interesting thing about Chicago, these pockets that could be right out of the Mississippi Delta. As soon as Nick walked through the door, the smell brought him home.

Peetie dropped his head and the hat fell into his hands. He found a seat by the window to the kitchen and sat down. There was a velvet painting of a black Jesus by the cash register and silver and red tinsel wrapped the serving window. A blackboard listed the specials: oxtail, chitlins, smothered chicken, pork chops, macaroni and cheese, collard greens, field peas, cabbage, corn, and corn bread.

The smell was better than the most expensive perfume. Give Nick a woman that smelled like soul food and he was hooked. Peetie yelled his order to an unseen cook and Nick did the same. He got chicken and greens with sweet tea. Only in the South and on the South Side.

"Love that smell," Nick said.

"Smell like a fat woman to me. You ever have a fat woman, man? I promise you never go back. I likes them with meat shakin' on their bones."

Nick kept on his wool coat. He could feel the cold sweeping in from cracks by the door as he took off his watch cap. "What made you leave New Orleans?"

"Did some things I wasn't real proud of," Peetie said. "Made some folks mad and didn't have much choice. Hard to keep straight down on Rampart in the day. Know what I'm sayin'? Lots of pool halls, women of the evenin' and the such. Man tried to cut my pecker off before I left. Ain't that some shit?"

"Man, I'd leave town too."

Peetie just started laughing.

"You were telling me about Lyons."

"Blues was nothing but a hobby to him. Man ran numbers, poker dens, hookers. You name it, it had Billy's finger in it. . . . But I don't want to give you the wrong idea 'bout him. Billy was kind of like that English dude, Robin Hood. I mean he'd give you the last bite of his chicken pie. I seen him down at the YMCA with a suitcase filled with silver dollars handin' them to folks so country they still had cow shit on their boots."

"Mind if I take a few notes?" Nick asked. This guy was too much. A little flaky but a real quote machine.

"Shit, man, I know what you're sayin'. I mean like right now. I'm thinkin' all about Ruby and Billy and shit, but havin' a hard time makin' it happen. It's like when you watch a movie and really love that bitch. Like I was watchin' this film with Cary Grant. That thang with the crop duster and all that shit? Anyway, man, I laughed my ass off seein' him when they poured that booze down his neck and made him drive that car. Aw shit, man, he was mouthin' off to his mama at jail. Ain't that some shit?"

"Oh, yeah. That's some shit, man."

Peetie's hands flew around as he talked with rapid-fire emotions. His face contorted with excitement as he jumped from topic to topic.

"Met Ruby today," Nick said. Two old women in pillbox hats waddled in and took a seat next to the front door. Peetie nodded and laced his hands before him.

"How is Miss Ruby?" Peetie asked, very cool. Smoother than a pig coated in STP.

"Not good."

"I'll have to go down and see her one of these days."

"She said you mishandled her money."

"Did she?" His eyes got big with phony surprise.

Peetie walked away for a moment and placed his purple hat on the rack. He brushed some imaginary dirt from his pants and stared straight ahead. Nick decided to drop the money issue until later.

Peetie wouldn't say shit if his mouth was full of it.

They talked a while about some big hits for King Snake and some of their main talent. Some Nick knew. Elmore King and Moses Jordan. And some he didn't. Peetie remembered some anecdotes about Lyons as a South Side kingpin and Ruby's first appearance on stage. He said she stood there shaking with fear in the hot stage lights before bursting into a raunchy song.

"What's this all about, man?" Peetie asked. "Nobody asked me a damned thing about King Snake for thirty years. And nobody sure has asked me 'bout Billy Lyons. So what's up with all this?"

"Like I said, I'm a music historian. I'd appreciate anything you know about King Snake and Lyons's death."

"Ooh, well, well," Peetie said. "You buyin'?"

"Yep."

"Connie? Connie, give me two pieces of corn bread," he yelled. "You want to know why she killed him, right? Let's slice through the bullshit. That's why you is here."

Nick smiled.

"Now who's gonna know that besides three folks? Billy, Ruby, and God. And two of them folks ain't talkin'. I didn't talk to Ruby a long time after all this shit went down. Maybe like ten years, but I went to see her at Dwight and ask her if she gettin' a cut. . . . Fucked up her money? No, sir. Maybe I made some bad investments, but no sir, I was lookin' out for that woman."

"What did you invest in?"

"You were just standin' in it . . . that store. It gonna turn a profit one of these days."

"Why would she kill Lyons?" Nick asked.

"Everybody say Billy was foolin' 'round, right?"

Nick nodded.

"Maybe that's true. Maybe it ain't. That man stone-cold loved that woman. I ain't lyin'. When he heard her sing his old face would start shakin' and you'd catch him kind of rubbin' his eyes. So, he loved her, right?"

"So why?"

"Ruby was down them last few months before she killed him," Peetie said. "Man, she went down fast. I used to couldn't book that woman enough. Shit. The whole town wanted her from the South Side up to Rush Street. But when she got hooked on that sweet, sweet cocaine, I couldn't get her a gig singin' for supper. Nobody likes an addict. Man, one night she fell off stage. I'm talkin' headfirst into a table. Blood on her head. That's sad. Just sad."

"She was fucked-up when she attacked Billy?"

"Yeah, probably. But it was about cash. She was sleepin' in alleys again." Peetie lowered his voice. "Put down that notebook. Let me tell you somethin'. Cool? Between us? I loved that woman. When she sang I could feel my soul smile. But she started whorin' for cash. One time, I had to beat a man with a baseball bat in some low-rent hotel to get him off her. Some greasy piece of shit was layin' on top of the Queen of the Blues. Man, made me want to puke . . ."

Peetie put his fingers to his mouth and shook his head.

"What?" Nick asked.

"Uh-uh," Peetie said. A void of expression hung on his face.

Nick stuck the notebook in his pocket and ran his hand over his stubbled jaw.

After a minute Peetie said, "She was robbin' Billy when she killed him."

All Nick could say was, "Jesus."

"She sucked you in, huh?" Peetie asked.

Nick nodded.

A black woman with her hair knotted into a gray bun walked out with two Styrofoam containers and two paper cups. She glared at Peetie. The food steamed up some wonderful smells when Nick opened the top. The woman turned on a soul Christmas tape while she cleaned up. Otis singing "Merry Christmas, Baby."

"C'mon, man," Peetie said, leaning close into the table and shaking his head. He ticked his tongue and rubbed his bottom lip over his mustache. He left his food untouched. "Don't let that old woman confuse you. She just OJin' on you, man. Prison will do that to a woman, get her mind convinced she didn't do it. But she got Billy's blood on her hands. That much I know. Police found Billy's blood all in her bed."

Nick dug into the greens. Crisp with small pieces of salty ham. The corn bread melted in his mouth. He listened to Otis sing and sighed. He thought he was on to something. Pretty stupid, he guessed. People were in prison for a reason. He just trusted too easily.

Peetie studied his face. "You all right, man?" he asked.

"Yeah."

"Listen, them days weren't all bad. Man, I remember goin' out drinkin' with Ruby after her shows down at the Palm Tavern. Guess that about the time when 'Blues Highway' came out. She'd have her driver pick us up and we couldn't pay for a drink all down Forty-seventh."

"Must've made a good chunk of change to have a driver."

"Not really. We had to. Ruby couldn't drive worth a shit. That country girl never learned."

"You know where I can find some other King Snake folks?"

"Most of 'em dead, man. Like I said, I been out that loop."

"No one?"

Peetie shook his head. "Sure don't, man. Wish I could help. I mean, like I seen Moses Jordan around and stuff but you got to have an engraved invitation to say hello to that fat fucker."

Nick nodded.

"Ruby really had the thing. Somethin' that made people just want to be around her. To this day I don't know what happened. But I guess I blame Billy. When that fell apart, something in Ruby died."

Nick played with his food, sorting the ham from the greens. He'd lost his appetite looking for something that wasn't there.

11

ANNIE KNEW HER knives. She didn't care for a bowie or a switchblade. They were all flash for cash. Just give her something that was made for carving a turkey or skinning a carrot and she was in heaven. So simple. The best knives were carbon steel with some nice wood wrapped around the tang. Most people didn't know what a tang was, but it was the extension of the blade you didn't see. You have a short tang and you were really screwed. Kind of like a guy with a short dick. She kept a seven-piece wooden block set on her nightstand beside her lava lamp and vibrator.

All her knives were forged, hammered out from a thick piece of steel. She liked the blade hand-ground by a master cutler. Make that edge so sharp it could cut through a tin can like it was butter. *She loved them all.* Willie was a butcher knife but he had friends like a carving knife, boning knife, cleaver, bread knife, and even her little shearpoint paring knife for those special occasions. One time she hid the paring knife in the crack of her ass to get by some club security. She jabbed a guy good as he sat on the toilet snorting coke.

Dead by the time she and Fannie hit the back door.

She leaned back into her waterbed, the waves making her a little seasick, and used a sharpener to turn the pages of her *Archie* comic. Fannie lay on the floor by the bed painting her toenails green.

"You want to get some coffee? A little latte? Hit the shops?"

"No," Annie said, bored and staring at Betty and Veronica playing catch at the beach in bikinis. Archie talking Veronica into playing in a Frisbee contest only to get beaten by a dog. Annie giggled. That Ronnie's so uptight.

When they made it big, she and Fannie could live like that. They'd find a little white bread town to settle down in. Maybe she'd buy an ice-cream truck. Fannie could find a rich man and be just like Veronica. They'd meet their Archie and Reggie. No Moose, please. Moose was such a fuckin' idiot. Who the hell walked around saying *duh* all the time? They needed to lock that retard in some kind of insane asylum.

"Sheesh," Annie said, popping her bubble gum and playing footsie with herself.

"What is it, baby?" Fannie said, dotting her pinky toenail with the polish, pulling her long feet to her mouth and blowing.

"Moose is just so damned stupid. Just kind of pisses me off."

"Yes, baby. You told me."

"You think we'll ever be like that? Livin' like Betty and Veronica or those rich women in *Cosmo*. All worried about the kind of shoes we wear or if our belts clash with our panties?"

"Don't be talkin' about *Cosmo*, girl. I just saw a cashmere turtleneck and a pair of silk taffeta pants that I'd kill my grandmama for. Hey, let me show you somethin', Miss Gemini. Almost forgot."

Fannie put her feet to the ground, extending her toes to the sky. She reached under the bed and pulled out the latest issue of the magazine. Its cover read: *Is his orgasm really important?*

Fannie licked her lips: " 'A creative door opens. Say yes to a new interesting project and don't be afraid to take risks.' "

"What the hell does that mean?" Annie asked.

"It means we in the same ole rut. Stagger Lee said last night he wanted us to go back to the South Side and work in some of his jerk shacks. I don't ever want to do that. Me and you sitting in them shitty old buildings waiting for some old man to come in and want to get his rocks off. I don't even like to blow my nose in Kleenex anymore."

"We'll run before we do that again."

"He'll find us," Fannie said. "So you best put that out of your mind."

Annie rolled over on her bed, the waves beating against her spine, and looked at her ceiling filled with miniposters of teen heartthrobs and pages from her favorite *Archie* books. Didn't matter if she was in her twenties, she'd never give up her friends. When she lay awake at night, some old man's scent still on her, she'd stare up there at all those smooth-chested guys and friends from Riverdale laughing away.

"You know, baby, clothes make you feel good," Fannie said, pulling off her sweatshirt and rubbing lotion down her chest and arms. "Sometimes I feel like I could take on the world when I got a sack of clothes with me. And I saw somethin' yesterday at the thrift shop that would make you shine like a bright penny in the sun. So beautiful. Sky blue leather skirt and top. Rabbit fur trim around the neck."

"Too girly," Annie said, blowing out her cheeks with air.

"Too girly?" Fannie rolled her eyes. "That ain't even the best part. Hey, throw me some Bubblicious."

Fannie caught the open pack and unwrapped a juicy piece. "Also found a pair of closed-toe platform shoes that felt *sooo* soft in my hands. Little wooden crisscrosses on the heel. They must've belonged to the same person."

Annie's cell phone rang beneath her pillow. Fannie brushed the dark hair from her eyes and started to massage her face with oil. She hated dry skin.

Annie picked up the phone and rocked her knees over her head.

"Hello?"

"I need to talk to Stagger Lee."

"Who's Stagger Lee?"

"Don't whisper bullshit in my ear, woman. It's Peetie."

Annie groaned and tossed the phone to Fannie. Fannie wiped the grease from her knuckles and daintily picked up the phone.

"*Yesss.*"

Annie tossed her legs back over her head and rolled to her side. She halfway listened to Fannie gab with the man until she switched off the phone. "Well?" she asked.

"Well what?"

"What was that about?"

"A creative door has just opened," Fannie said, laughing.

12

CHICAGO RAMMED INTO your soul like a fist. Made you feel tougher, bigger. The city was gray concrete, red brick, and silver-mirrored windows. A meeting of the decades in a mishmash of architecture that loomed over the avenues like walls of a canyon. Heat rose from sidewalk vents. White Christmas lights burned from bare trees and red bows wrapped green iron streetlamps. The smell of garbage drifted from back alleys.

The city noises bleated in Nick's ears after he parked just off the Magnificent Mile and fed the meter. He adjusted his watch cap over his ears and searched for Doyle Brennan's place among the monoliths looming overhead. If there were some old King Snake folks about town, Doyle would know where to find them.

Besides having probably the largest jazz and blues music store in the country, Doyle had his own indie label and was a tracker of sorts. He knew more about the golden age of blues than most professors Nick knew combined. Doyle was an old buddy of his instructor at Ole Miss and one of the first white guys to frequent black clubs in the late fifties and early sixties. A frustrated musician, like Nick, who turned to another profession so he could stay around the music.

Nick followed a back alley toward the river as a speckle of snow drifted across the asphalt.

The record store sat on the bottom level of a glass and concrete building and smelled of incense and plastic. Old blues promo posters lined the walls: hot pinks, sky blues, and electric greens spelling out such incredible shows as Little Walter Live or a Muddy Waters doubleheader with Sonny Boy Williamson. Days when the blues pounded the soul and shaped the identity of Chicago. The posters were curled at the edges, a few water-stained.

A teenage kid in a black Stones T-shirt with a diamond nose ring smoked an herbal cigarette behind the cash register. Nick asked if Doyle was around and the kid nodded to a back door where the man had kept his office for the past fifteen years. Nick turned the knob and walked into chaos.

Among the floor-to-ceiling bookshelves and file cabinets, papers were tacked on cabinets, taped on doors, and strewn across his desk. Styrofoam cups, several overturned coffee mugs, and piles of blues and jazz magazines lay on the floor.

Doyle sat with his head down, a cigarette burning in a black ashtray on his desk, and a fluorescent banker's lamp warming a book. A Memphis Slim record spun on a turntable behind him.

Doyle was a thick-bodied man with shoulder-length gray hair, a bushy beard, and the fleshy reddened cheeks of an Irish farmer. Nick knew he'd once possessed a heated desire to change the world. He'd walked with Martin Luther King Jr. in Chicago, helped register voters in Mississippi, and for years tried to help bluesmen recover their royalties.

Nick coughed. Doyle looked up and smiled. He awkwardly raised from his desk and offered his thick hand. He turned behind him and took the needle from the Memphis Slim record.

"Mr. Travers," he said, coughing into his hand. "A little late for the blues festival."

Doyle slumped back into his seat and kicked a wobbling office chair over to Nick. He pulled the chair back and took a seat. Shards of sunlight cut through the books, magazines, and records behind Doyle.

"Let me guess." Doyle studied his face. "You want something."

Nick lit a Marlboro and smiled. "I want to hang out with you.

Maybe go to the zoo. Buy a hotdog on the street. Skip through Lincoln Park."

"You smoking dope again?"

"I wish," Nick said. "No . . . actually I need to pick your nose. I mean brain."

Doyle opened a small refrigerator next to his desk and grabbed a couple of Harps. He popped the tops and slid one over to Nick.

"You got it," Doyle said, putting the beer to his mouth like it was a bottle. "Man, last time I saw you was in Holly Springs at Kimbrough's. Remember that woman who was all heated-up and drunk."

"My date?"

"Yeah, that woman you picked up. Ain't never seen a woman get all sexy with a door. She was gyrating and going crazy on that old thing. If I were a door knob . . ."

"All right, all right."

"So what's up?" Doyle asked.

"King Snake Records, Billy Lyons, and Ruby Walker," Nick said and took a sip. "Take your pick."

"New project?"

Nick nodded.

"Who've you talked to?"

"The Sweet Black Angel."

"Ruby talked to you?" Doyle asked before raising the bottle to his lips again.

"Yeah."

"I'm impressed," he said. "I once asked her to cut a record in prison and she told me to go fuck myself."

"You'd throw your back out."

"That woman could sing, man," Doyle said, ignoring him. "There weren't many women like her. I'd put her in the same class as Memphis Minnie or Bessie Smith. But her career proba- bly wouldn't have lasted much longer than it did. She sang old- style blues like Minnie. Probably would have hit the revival circuit in the sixties. But I don't think she could've adapted to the times like Koko or Etta. . . . Wonder if she still sings?"

Nick shrugged.

"Who else you looking for?"

"Just met a man named Peetie Wheatstraw. I guess this would be Peetie number two. He was new to me."

"I know Peetie Wheatstraw," Doyle said, sneering. "Only his name's not Wheatstraw. It's Jerome Tompkins. He didn't have a fucking thing to do with King Snake and don't let him tell you any different. He's a bottom feeder."

"Owns a place called the Soul Train."

"Only seen him on Maxwell Street." Doyle pointed his finger at Nick's chest. "But I wouldn't write down a word that idiot tells you. He's sucked a half-dozen players dry. Got no talent, although he says he plays piano. Shit, he plays a fucking Casio down at the new Maxwell Street Market. He has about as much business sense as my fat, hairy ass."

"Your ass is pretty smart, Doyle."

"Yeah, why don't you kiss it?"

"Don't want to get a razor burn," Nick said. "Hey, man, I could use some direction."

"Shoot."

"You and Moses Jordan still tight?"

"Yeah, yeah. Good thinkin', man . . . Moses Jordan and Billy Lyons were buddies from way back. Let's see," Doyle said fiddling with the cigarette in his hand. "Jordan had switched over to King Snake from Diamond. He was pissed off about not getting his fair share and I'm sure he was right. Anyway, I think he was pissed when Diamond wouldn't sign Elmore King. He thought King was damned near the second coming but the brothers at Diamond weren't impressed. King became one of Jordan's first projects with Lyons."

"King won't return my calls." Nick took a huge sip. He could feel the travel nerves wash away.

"He can be a moody asshole," Doyle said. "King's been babied too much. When you get your ass kissed everyday, you think you don't have to act human anymore. He's been wiping his ass with friends for the last ten years. You hear that last album? What a pile a shit. He gets a bunch of coke-sniffing Hollywood producers to give him a pile of cash and a hand job and he turns out something that sounds like twelve-bar hip-hop."

Nick laughed.

"But Jordan is still real tight with King so don't make any jokes," Doyle said. "He treats King like he was his son. And believe me, King treats Jordan like he was the shit. I don't know this but I've heard Jordan still gets a fifty-fifty cut on everything. One of those Elvis-Colonel arrangements."

"You know where King lives?"

"Bought a big-ass farm out in Woodstock. Man, it looks like the Delta out there. Has a big red barn, cattle, all kinds of shit. But he's in Europe . . . I can find out when he's supposed to be back."

Nick dumped his cigarette and started a fresh one. Somehow Doyle's office made him feel like he needed to constantly keep a cigarette burning. Smelled like the inside of a Vienna cafe.

"You remember that shitty VW van you used to have?"

"Yeah," Doyle said, giving Nick the finger. "It's parked outside."

Doyle lowered his eyes and blew smoke to the ceiling. Never knew he was so damned in love with his van. Maybe because he used to live in the thing in the early seventies.

"If you're looking for session players, good luck," Doyle said, finishing the beer in a gulp and dumping the bottle in the trash. "You remember Franky Dawkins?"

"Bass player?"

"Dead for years. I think he was robbed or something. . . . And what about Leroy Williams?"

"Don't know him."

"Barrelhouse piano man. Man couldn't read music but man, could he bang them keys. Listen to that old King Snake stuff— Ruby's songs—and I promise you'll hear his genius."

"Dead?"

"With a capital D. Heard he was manic depressive. So, when the music scene started to bottom out in the early sixties, he took a swim in the Chicago River." Doyle made a diving motion with his free hand. "Shit, you're the historian, look it up. Be nice to get Leroy's name back out there. He was a beautiful player. . . . so what else can I do for you? Want to hit the titty bars? Know this place where this woman makes her puppies into a hat."

"I want to talk to Jordan," Nick said. "Figured you'd be my best intro."

"Sure, I've got every phone number for that, man. You want to talk to him in the toilet?"

"Office would be fine."

Doyle picked up his phone and punched a number with his thick fingers. He stubbed his cigarette into the ashtray and stared at the ceiling. The kid from the cash register knocked and opened the door and Doyle waved him away.

"Moses? You got a second, man?" Doyle smiled at Nick and nodded. "Can you do me a favor? No." Doyle laughed. "No. No. You going down to the studio today? Great. Listen, I'm sending a good friend of mine over to talk to you. His name is Nick Travers, blues historian. You'll like him. All right. All right. What time? Thanks."

Doyle hung up. "I just got the touch," he said. "What can I say? How long you in town for?"

"Till Christmas, then Tulane cuts me off."

"Jordan will be at the old Diamond studio in an hour."

Nick looked at his watch; it was almost 3:30.

"What'd Ruby say?" Doyle asked.

"Said she didn't do it."

"You believe her?"

"I'd like to," Nick said. "But faith is a funny thing."

"No, faith is blind." Doyle chuckled and put the needle back on the Memphis Slim record. The dead piano player sang on.

13

NICK HEADED SOUTH again on Michigan Avenue to the old Diamond Record studio where Jordan kept an office. Diamond was a recording powerhouse in the fifties and early sixties after a pair of Greek brothers started the company in June 1952. Somehow, two guys that spoke English as their second language had a knack for recognizing talent. Almost every great bluesman and gospel singer of that period cut a single for the brothers. Unable to read music, the pair would sometimes hum out a rhythm for the hardened musicians. Nick remembered a recent documentary when Elmore King made fun of them: "How the hell am I supposed to know what blues sound like to two old white guys?"

Nick laughed at the thought as he passed boarded-up storefronts and warehouses in an area once known as Record Row. All the bruised buildings with shattered windows reminded him a bit of Julia Street on a weekend—a stillness. The recording companies were long gone and industry had found cheap labor somewhere else. This was the borderline, the industrial belt that once separated downtown from the South Side.

Nick imagined Little Walter, Jimmy Reed, and Muddy walking down these same streets, a new song in their heads. But before those guys hit the scene, Chicago was already home to some established artists. A white record producer named Lester Melrose was recording Tampa Red, Memphis Minnie, Washboard

Sam and Big Bill Broonzy for Columbia and RCA Victor in the thirties and forties.

Some might think that Muddy's blues were too hip, too electric cool for the old set. But really it was a reversal. Melrose's Bluebird beat relied on a light touch, a jazzy optimism. A mix of vaudeville and twenties novelty blues.

The bleak, desperate sounds of the 1930s Delta artists had evaporated.

When Muddy arrived in '43, his own sister told him: "They don't listen to that kind of old blues you're doin' now, don't nobody listen to that, not in Chicago."

After a failed effort with Melrose, Muddy would get a second chance with a style he'd learned from Son House and Robert Johnson. New independent labels were flourishing thanks to new, cheaper technology. Producers, like the Diamond brothers, also knew how to sell directly to their market—barber shops, salons, and stores in black neighborhoods.

In the late forties and early fifties, independent record labels exploded like umbrella salesmen in a New Orleans rainstorm.

All you needed was one big hit and you were off. Hell, Muddy was still driving a truck for a living when he recorded "I Can't Be Satisfied" and "Feel Like Going Home Again" back in '48, giving blues a kick in the ass. At first, producers weren't sure if Muddy's bottleneck style and almost field-hand moan would sell in the city. But the record sold out twenty-four hours later. Down on Maxwell Street, even Muddy had to pay almost double for his own song.

> *"Late in the evenin'*
> *I feel like a goin' home.*
> *When I woke up this mornin'*
> *all I had was gone."*

A little slice of the Delta seemed to hit the spot for black immigrants, just like Ruby's "Lonesome Blues Highway" reminded folks of the long journey. That kind of success, that kind of gamble, is why outfits like Diamond and King Snake started. The boom ended about the time Ruby went to prison. Rock 'n' roll and R&B were on the rise. Young blacks had turned their ear to new sounds and a white blues audience didn't exist.

Nick parked on a dead street where snowplows had stacked sludge like the banks of a dirty river. The iced wind blasted through his ears as he kept his hand on the car hood to keep from slipping.

The front door to Diamond, a two-story building with a wide aluminum canopy, was unlocked and Nick followed a hallway lined with pictures of old recording stars. A who's who of Chicago greats. At the end in a large room, a group of children in matching blue T-shirts painted walls while listening to rap music on a battered boom box.

"Mr. Jordan?" Nick asked.

A kid with a lazy eye and plugs of hair missing pointed upstairs.

Nick followed some rickety wooden steps to the old recording room. He heard someone whistling at the top of a rambling wooden staircase. Nick followed the slow tune into the old studio where he saw Moses Jordan in an undertaker black suit painting a door. Six black teens watched him demonstrate a painting motion. Jordan moved the paintbrush like he used to handle the drumsticks. Like it was born in his hand.

He gave the brush back to a kid with a pick in his hair and said, "That's how it's done."

Jordan looked like an old-time weight lifter with a bulging stomach and short legs. His brown face was wide and flat with eyes burning with a permanent irony. A little perspiration shined on his forehead with silver hair ringing his bald head in an almost metallic glow. Somewhere in his mid-seventies, Nick guessed.

"Travers?" Jordan asked.

Nick shook his hand. Great to meet the guy. Jordan was in a class with Willie Dixon, Wolf, Muddy, and all the golden-era guys. He'd seen him talk in about a half dozen documentaries and read endless interviews, but they'd never spoken. Still, he felt like he'd known Jordan his whole life.

"Gonna look like it did in the day," Jordan said. "Got the old equipment and asked the families of those who've passed on to donate instruments. . . . Sometimes I feel like they're still here."

"If they're remembered, they are."

Jordan held onto Nick's hand and looked him hard in the eye. "Doyle said I'd like you, Travers. And I'm beginnin' to believe him."

Most people thought of bluesmen as old guys wearing overalls and spitting off front porches. Incoherent. Illiterate. Jordan, like most, was the antithesis of the stereotype. Probably never worked a day in his life without shining his shoes, pressing his suit, and carrying a union card.

"So you want to talk about them dirty, lowdown blues?" Jordan said, laughing at his words and letting go of Nick's hand. "You know we're coming up on the anniversary. Place might not look like much yet, but you bring back the history and you get the tourists. You get the tourists, you get the redevelopment."

Nick pulled off his gloves and stuck them in the warm pockets of his wool coat. The layers of clothes were starting to make him feel like the Michelin Man.

"You'll have to excuse me," Jordan said, pointing to the loose groups of children working on the walls. "I've been trying hard to bring back some hope around here . . . they took away our jobs, gave us drugs, and turned us against ourselves. But I'm starting to see flashes of pride like when I first stepped off the Illinois Central from Greenwood."

"Spent some time in Greenwood last year," Nick said, watching a young girl painting fine touches on the mural. Windows on a crooked high-rise.

Jordan wiped his hands on a tattered rag. He checked his pants for paint. "Oh, yeah? I ain't been back in fifty years. And don't plan to."

"Understand," Nick said.

"But you know, we didn't come all this way to wear more

shackles," Jordan continued, his face full of heat and determination. "What's this around us but chains? At least sharecroppers had a damn thing to do instead of living off welfare. *Buying crack.* Do you know kids think it's always been like this? When I tell them about old Bronzeville they think I'm full of shit."

A young girl dipping her brush rolled her eyes. Guess she was waiting on another lecture.

"Man, I know you didn't come down to hear me preach," Jordan said with a grin. He grasped Nick's shoulder. "But you still gonna hear a bit anyway mixed with a few stories about Diamond."

"Actually, I wanted to talk to you about King Snake and Ruby Walker," Nick said, his voice reverberating off the hall's perfect acoustics. A holy temple of the blues. He peered through a Plexiglas window at a collection of old recording equipment coated in a layer of rust.

"King Snake?" Jordan asked, removing his hand. The old man sat down on an unopened paint bucket and sighed. There were fine flecks of paint in his silver hair. He laced his pudgy fingers in front of him and looked into Nick's eyes.

Jordan was cuing him up, wanting to gauge his intelligence, use his long-honed perceptions to see about this white man. A man who wanted to ask him questions about a failure.

"I'd love to hear more about Billy Lyons," Nick said, plowing though the mental prodding. He took out a notebook. "Sounds like a character."

"Billy?" Jordan asked.

"Yeah, Billy Lyons, Ruby Walker, King Snake. All of it."

"Can I ask you a question, Mr. Travers?" Jordan asked, licking his finger and wiping away a speck of paint from his shoe. "Why you like the blues so much?"

"The blues are about truth."

Jordan nodded. "What do you want to know?"

14

ANNIE FROZE HER ass off under East Wacker Drive waiting for Peetie Wheatstraw an hour later. The little shit said it was urgent and maybe worth a little money for his 411. Annie had joked with him, and told him sitting on a new sack of hemorrhoids wasn't news. But he kept pushing the shit so here they were, in between shopping, waiting for the old man to rat somebody out. About the only thing he was good for.

Wacker was a split-level road with a lower track snaking a little above the surface of the Chicago River. A long tunnel shining with yellow lights. A little world of its own with hidden doors and tunnels under the city. The smell of carbon dioxide gave Annie a little buzz as she and Fannie walked out toward the Michigan Avenue bridge.

She took a seat on the cold concrete wall and watched the brown river swirling by in frozen chunks. The river cut into a Y west of where they waited, separating the wealthy Uptown from the old Loop and the ugly West Side. It kept everyone from smelling each other's shit.

Across the river, she could see the Wrigley Building shining like a bright wedding cake.

Annie took a breath and rubbed her hands together as the cars zoomed behind them. Fannie readjusted some fluffy red earmuffs on her head and took a long drag off her cigarette. She wore a tan sweater with lace overlay and a mink collar, brown crushed velvet pants, and a mustard-colored jacket that felt like an old sofa. One of her favorites.

"Bitch," Annie said. "Let's go. My buzz is wearing off and my ass is about to turn to ice."

"Give him another minute, just to say we saw him."

"Why didn't he just tell you on the fuckin' telephone?" Annie asked. "I'm tired of all this *I Spy* shit. In fact, I'm tired of this whole damned thing. I say we take the cash we have, get on a bus, and head to New York. Shit, we'd become the queens of the city. You'd have all of Manhattan crushed under your platform shoes. All those dweeby guys would follow you around just like Veronica Lodge. They'd have little popping hearts exploding around their brains."

"Girlfriend. I'm sorry, but the world ain't a comic book."

"It can be. It can be, Fannie. I've seen pictures of places just like Riverdale. C'mon, let's head out."

"I don't want to wake up dead for Christmas."

"Stagger Lee can replace us with a phone call. He doesn't need us."

"He doesn't see it that way, Annie," Fannie said with a look like she was someone's mama. "Don't you see that? He sees he gave us something and now we owe him for it. You remember when we were turnin' tricks at Robert Taylor for five dollars. How old were you?"

"Fourteen."

"And what did he do?"

"Sold us out. Had us mule."

"It was better, wasn't it? Gave us clothes. Some crack. Place to sleep."

"Yeah, Stagger Lee's kind of like Santa Claus. Only he never laughs, he likes to cut people into little pieces, and he ain't fat and white."

Fannie leaned over the concrete rail down where the river-boats dock when it gets warm. "We'll always owe him."

"All right. C'mon, let's go. Fuck Peetie."

"Where?" she asked.

"Head over to Rush," Annie said. "There's an Irish pub down there. Lot of money. Lot of tourists. Let's try to get a big one tonight. That Italian shit wasn't really worth it. Except for the cocaine we gave Stagger Lee. Let's break five hundred at least."

"Five hundred?" Fannie asked.

"C'mon, we can do it."

"How much we have now?"

"Bout seventy-five," Annie said.

"How 'bout the Hyatt? Good rooms. Maybe we can find a convention."

"Got to be quick."

"We always quick," Fannie said.

Annie smiled and brushed her fingers over Fannie's hardened face. The city lights glowed all around them in the darkening twilight. Point zero. The center of the city.

Behind them, Annie heard a cough and turned to see a dark shape coming down the concrete steps from Michigan Avenue. It was Peetie in some jive-ass purple suit and hat. He smoked a long, thin cigar that smelled like burnt cherries.

"Peetie, we was about to leave," Fannie said.

"Yeah, Peetie. See ya."

"Hold on. Hold on," he said, walking down the last few steps and keeping his hand on the wall. The tires against the metal grate on the bridge made roaring sounds.

"We ain't got time for this shit," Annie said. "And we ain't payin' you no money for some lousy fool who owes Stagger Lee again. He finds who he wants to find."

"Would you shut up, woman," Peetie said, spewing the smoke from the side of his mouth. "This ain't nothin' 'bout that. Face to face."

Annie snorted. " 'Bye."

Some bum had built a fire down by the river and the smoke had just begun to rise. Barely alive but not quite dead.

"This ain't for public consumption," he said. "This for Stagger Lee only."

"You tell us and we'll see about that," Annie said.

"No, no, no," he said. "You two bitches ain't part of this."

Annie sprung from her concrete perch and kicked Peetie to the slushy ground. The blood roared in her head as she pulled Willie from her back pocket and stood over the quivering old man. Her foot was stuck on his chest and she could hear her own ragged gasps of air.

Peetie had curled into a little ball and covered his head with his hands. His hat rolled and spun on the ground like a quarter.

Fannie grabbed Annie's arm and soothed around her neck. "Annie? Annie? C'mon. You okay. You okay. C'mon, let him just tell us what he have to say. Let him just tell us what he have to say. Everythin' gonna be just fine. *All right*. C'mon Annie. Be my sweet little girl. C'mon."

Annie made a primal grunt and removed her foot from his brittle chest.

"What is it? What is it?" Annie screamed. "We're not going to give you a fucking cent. But *we will* tell Stagger Lee you were jerking our dicks around."

Peetie rolled onto his knees, his suit covered in black slush. He shook the slush from his hat, smoothed the feather, and put the hat back on at a crazy angle.

"You tell Stagger Lee," Peetie said, brushing his knees. "You tell him there's a man named Travers askin' all 'bout Billy Lyons. You tell him that, cain't you? Ya'll need to be cool about this. This ain't some street crack deal. This is serious. Real serious. Stagger Lee gonna want to—"

"Who's Billy Lyons?" Fannie asked, wiping the frozen crap from Peetie's shoulders.

"Old friend of Stagger Lee's," Peetie said. He was getting cocky now, trying to act like his pride was filled back up. "Just tell him. He knows where to find me. Cain't believe you ruined my suit. Man, this thing gonna cost me plenty. Now I cain't even put it back on the rack. I cain't believe it."

Peetie began to walk back up the staircase to Michigan Avenue and away from the deep tunnels and sludge below. His eyes looked red and he limped on each step. Fannie followed and slipped something in his pocket. She helped him get to the top and gave him a hug. Annie lit a cigarette and shook her head. That woman needed to toughen her heart. Peetie was a real piece of shit.

When Fannie skipped down the stairs, Annie asked her: "Why in the fuck did you do that?" She tucked Willie back into her coat. "Don't even think I didn't see you."

"Just some cab fare. That man so broke he can't even spend the night."

"That's funny," Annie said, snorting smoke from her nose. "Real funny. You think we need to see Stagger Lee?"

Fannie raised her eyebrows.

"Peetie's nothing but an ole fool with a broken dick," Annie said.

"What if he got somethin'?" Fannie asked. "One thing I will not do is mess with Stagger Lee. You know what he'll do. Beat us till we bleed on the inside. Our pride ain't worth it. Nothin' worth Stagger Lee shittin' a brick."

"We see him tonight?"

"Tonight."

15

JORDAN'S DOWNSTAIRS OFFICE was littered with black memorabilia. For some reason, the man chose to surround himself with reminders of the segregated South. Advertisements featuring coal-black Sambos eating watermelons and big fat mammies with huge grins. He had a complete shelf full of figurines of black boys playing and even a black iron lawn jockey holding a lantern at the foot of his desk. Jordan took a seat and leaned back in his creaking chair.

He watched Nick's eyes trail around the room and simply said: "It's a good way not to forget."

Nick nodded.

Jordan slid his Ben Franklin-style glasses onto his wide face and used his thick, bulging stomach as an armrest. Nick sat in a folding chair that Jordan had grabbed from the hallway. The room smelled of stale cigars and floral air fresheners.

"Billy Lyons, Billy Lyons. You know I did all the damn work? Wrote all the songs and ran all the equipment?"

Nick nodded. "Ruby told me a little."

"You talked to Ruby?" Jordan asked. His face filled with disbelief and questions.

"Yeah, met her this morning."

"You must be something," Jordan said. "After the killin' she shut us all out. Didn't want to talk to *no*body. What'd she say?"

"Said she's innocent."

Jordan grunted. His stomach shook with internal laughter. "I think Ruby's more full of shit than a Christmas turkey."

"She kill him?" Nick asked.

"Without a doubt."

"You see anything?"

"I just know it," Jordan said, pounding his fist on the desk. "Maybe she really doesn't remember stabbing him and dropping him in the lake. She used to have blackouts. You'd have a conversation with her at a bar. Like one night me and her sat down and had a real heart to heart. Talked about music and the Lord. The next day, I mentioned something about it and she said she wasn't even there."

Jordan took a deep breath and looked at the wall clock. Beautiful old thing. Dark black surrounded by green neon. Looked like it had hung on the wall for decades.

"Were you and Billy friends?"

"We were," Jordan said. "In spite of his huge ego, he was a good friend."

"I'm going to start recording now," Nick said, punching the button. "Go ahead. *Billy Lyons.*"

"I met Billy back in the fifties," Jordan said, obviously used to being interviewed. "Of course I didn't know who he was. He was an older man, I guess about forty. He came to a club where I was setting up with a little jazz combo. I had a big bass drum with me and he asked me about it. Wanted to know about my music and I told him everything I did for the brothers at Diamond."

"You didn't like them?"

"Not then. Not with what they were paying me. Back then, producer meant money man, song writer, arranger, and talent scout."

Jordan counted the list on his fingers. "I traveled all around the South looking for Chicago-size talent. New Or-leens. Memphis. Man, I even went deep in Alabama to try folks out. You ever seen a bunch of crackers stare at a black man driving a car worth more than their homes?"

Nick laughed.

"Well, anyway, I met Billy one spring night. I think about fifty-five. I remember women in flowered dresses smelling of roses. Billy was there dressed up in some fine clothes. White suit. White Stetson hat. So you knew the brother had money. He lit my cigar with this silver cigarette lighter with a snake on it. Rings on every finger. He bought drinks for me and the band and talked about this label he wanted to start."

Jordan looked over the end of his glasses at Nick. "Are you following me?"

"Yes, sir."

"I talked to him like he was just any guy off the street," Jordan said. "When he left, the bartender leaned over and told me. I knew the name Lyons but I never put the two together. You see, Lyons ran the South Side."

"So I've heard."

"He was 'the boss.' But he treated me like a man and I treated him the same. Later on, we met for a few more drinks. He owned a restaurant and paid for my dinner. Even took me to some of his *establishments*." Jordan leaned close and whispered, "*Cathouses*. Well, we became friends. He loved blues. Loved just being in the same room with blues singers. To Billy, they were the tops."

"Was he a badass?"

"Billy? Not to his friends. But to folks who crossed him he was a leg breaker. I just remember him taking publicity shots for the label with his little daughter. He dedicated songs to her and treated that girl like a princess. He wasn't married, I think his wife died back in Mississippi, but he loved that little girl."

"You know what happened to her?"

Jordan shook his head.

"Her name?"

"Oh, man . . . if you hadn't asked. Oh . . . I think it was Nat."

"What about money problems?" Nick asked. "I heard Billy had run out of cash before he died."

"He had. He'd win it, then lose it. But I think Chicago was

starting to change. Billy didn't deal drugs. Had to respect him for that. You dealed on Billy's turf and man, he'd hurt you. But some, in the end, were already picking off his territory."

"He'd rather go broke than deal?"

"Yeah, like I said, Billy was an unusual cat."

"When did you guys start King Snake," Nick asked, stretching out his legs and crossing his boots at the ankles. The snow had melted a wet ring around the bottom of his jeans.

"Well," Jordan began, "I was with Billy one night and started talking again about having to chase the brothers down for money they owed me. I was having a rough day. My match wouldn't even light my cigar. Well, Billy just reached out with that cigarette lighter and told me, 'How you like to help a brother out?'"

Nick smiled and pulled out a pack of cigarettes. He showed him the pack and Jordan nodded his approval.

"Just like that . . . help a brother out," Jordan said. "He said we were nothing but slaves playin' blues for white men to sell back to blacks. And I started thinkin' about that and the way I was treated and what I was paid. And then he said that golden word: *partner*. Two weeks later, I told the brothers to kiss my hole and we started King Snake."

Jordan shook his head.

"What about Ruby?" Nick asked.

He shook his head again.

"Ruby and Billy fought like you ain't never seen," Jordan said, picking up a porcelain mammie from his desk and twirling it in his hands. "They were always throwin' things and she was callin' him an ole so-and-so, this and that. But you know, we didn't think nothin' of it. That's just the way it was."

"Any one night stick out?"

"I remember one time Billy brought this skinny, young white girl to a session. I'm talkin' about a real hillbilly. She was crawlin' all over Billy and calling him baby doll and such. Well, here comes Ruby. She wasn't supposed to be there. It was one of Elmore's first sessions when he come up from Alabama . . . Well, Ruby bust in drunk and stoned with a gun. Man."

Jordan started chuckling as he put down the figure. "We ducked like we were soldiers. She was drunk and waved the gun around all crazy. Well, let's just say that stringy-haired hillbilly never ran so fast in her life."

"Maybe she had brothers."

Jordan laughed hard at that one. He chuckled for about thirty seconds, his eyes watering, and leaned back into his seat.

"Was that the day Lyons was killed?" Nick asked.

"Oh no, this was about a year before that."

"You remember her hanging out at the Palm Tavern?"

"No more than any other bar. Why?"

"I heard it was her place."

Jordan shrugged and looked at the wall clock.

"Did you see their last fight?"

"No, no. I'd left King Snake by that time."

"Why?"

"Creative differences."

"Like what?"

"Let's leave it at creative differences." Jordan's face folded in disappointment at Nick's lack of etiquette. *Fuck Emily Post.*

"You know anyone who was at King Snake to the end? Still living?"

Jordan shook his head and tucked his hands under his biceps. His black tie looked uncomfortably tight.

"Nobody?"

Jordan shook his head again.

"Elmore King?" Nick asked. "How long did he stay?"

He squeezed his eyes tight and shrugged. "Really not sure, man."

"I saw King down in New Orleans last year," Nick said, uncrossing his legs and standing.

He walked over to the trash can and ashed the smoldering end of his cigarette. "He told me Ruby got a raw deal with her conviction. You know why he would say that?"

"It's his right," Jordan said.

Nick sat back down and checked the red light on the recorder.

"What about Lyons's other interests? Someone else must've wanted him dead?"

"They did," Jordan said. "He was shot at twice that I know of. Once he took a round in his leg and had to use a cane for a month. Some gangsters shot at his car but his bodyguard slipped it into reverse, hightailed it out, and saved Billy's life. . . . But this was different. Ruby Walker killed that man. I'm just surprised she didn't do it sooner."

"But who else would've wanted him dead?" Nick asked.

"Why you so interested in that nasty part of Chicago blues? Man, there was so much more to King Snake than a killin'."

Jordan sighed, his face the complete picture of aggravation. Knitted brow. Squinted eyes.

"I know that woman threatened Billy's life about every day," he said. "I know that woman was mean. No, I didn't see anything. No, I didn't hear anything. But when I found out Billy was dead, I didn't even have to ask."

"You know anyone else who may have seen Lyons on his last day?" Nick asked.

"No, I don't. Billy had lost interest in King Snake. He had other pressures, you know."

"Yeah," Nick said slowly, the cigarette smoke rushing from his mouth. "Like what?"

"Just troubles . . . listen, I don't want anything negative to be written about Ruby or any of this. I've tried too hard to bring back the South Side without some bad shit from the past bein' smacked all over the place."

"I apologize," Nick said, watching the man's face harden. "I'm just a historian trying to put the jigsaw together. I've learned more about King Snake in the last five minutes than has been written in the last forty years."

Jordan relaxed and smiled. He offered Nick a cup of coffee and for the next thirty minutes, he served up some nice anecdotes about King Snake and the sequence of their first recordings. Old guy even got a little misty remembering all the musicians who were now dead. As Nick was about to stop the recorder and put in a fresh tape, the kid with the splotched Afro walked in and said someone had knocked over a paint bucket. Jordan growled and stood. Nick shut off the recorder and thanked him for his time.

"I'd like to talk again," Nick said.

"Let me take you to breakfast Saturday at my spot," he said. "Lou Mitchell's on Jackson. How 'bout ten?"

Jordan grasped Nick's shoulder again as they walked to the front door and talked of a drug march he'd planned for the week-end and his lost battle to save a section of Maxwell Street from demolition.

"Travers, you ever seen the monument?" Jordan asked with the door cracked. A brittle wind biting his back.

"Which monument?"

"*The* monument. At King Drive and Twenty-sixth Place. Tall bronze statue surrounded by concrete trunks."

"No."

"You should drive by there," Jordan said. "Call it *Monument to the Great Northern Migration* or something like that. Man waving to the north carrying his ratty old suitcase. Reminds me of the South Side story. We all came here with nothin' but dreams. Broke, filled with heartache for home. Guess everybody got that some time or another. Them leavin' trunk blues."

16

ANNIE TURNED UP the volume on the Prince tape as they rounded the corner toward the Robert Taylor Homes. She could see the high-rises get closer as Prince squealed off one of her faves. When she was a kid, she never understood what he meant when he sang that line about "used Trojans." But now she could just see those nasty things sitting inside that little red Corvette's glove box. Prince must've really felt bad knowing that girl was a ho. *Sing it, little man. Sing it.*

Prince always made her feel a little better about going back to the projects. Seemed like every time she got close, her gut did backflips. All the old smokestacks, lots filled with broken-down cars and shit, and all those empty meat packing factories made her want to scream. Kind of pissed her off too. She'd worked too hard to get pulled back into this world of crap. She wanted to run their piece of shit Suburu over the teenage crack dealers on BMX bikes and through the windows of the all-night liquor stores. The neon and fluorescent lights shined deep into her eyes. A vision in a desert of shit.

Annie turned onto State Street nearing a group of housing projects towering above the decay like upturned ocean liners. The Robert Taylor Homes looked abandoned beyond the chain-link fences with only a few lights in thousands of windows. Whoever thought they could put poor people in high-rises? That had to be one of the worst dumb-fuck ideas she'd ever heard. Like they wouldn't start robbing and stealing from the git-go. It was like locking up the criminals in the jail without any guards to keep order, like that movie *Escape from New York* when they put all those prisoners in the city and let them fend for themselves. Big fucking mistake.

Ghettos in the sky.

She parked the Suburu, duct tape on the windshield, up on a curb, and made a vibrating sound with her lips. A wino sat in the middle of an empty playground drinking some cheap liquor to keep himself warm.

"Goddamn, I hate going in there," Fannie said. "I hate this shit. I hate it."

"It won't take long," Annie said. "C'mon, I hate it too."

"You know it will. You know we'll be here all night long and what he'll make us do. You know he won't let us leave without showing he's in control. It's what he does. It's what he is. Like a big dog humpin' a little one."

"If Peetie finds him before we do," Annie said, "he's gonna be pissed. He'll hump us all at the same time."

"God, I feel nasty already," Fannie said. "We've come so far, Annie. I feel like I've just put on my best clothes and someone wants me to jump in a big pool of pig shit."

"I told you we can run," Annie said. "All we need is a plan. We could change our names legally to Betty Cooper and Veronica Lodge."

"Yeah, I always wanted to be a spoiled white girl," Fannie said. "What's the name of that butler she got? Fat dude? Cadbury."

"No, that's Richie Rich. Hers is Smithers."

"I wonder if he'd paint my toenails. Even wax my bikini area."

"You know he would. And he'd love it."

"Keep talkin', girlfriend, and you might have somethin'."

Annie giggled, opened her car door, and walked through a weeded lot to the high-rise. Fannie followed, cautiously stepping around the dirty Colt 45 bottles and the pieces of clothing littering the grass-splotched mud. The ground was like someone had emptied their suitcase from a high window. Annie looked up into the middle building, at a lone apartment shining in the cold night. *Stagger Lee.*

The early days in the projects with Fannie were nightmarish visions of the worst in human nature. Real crazy animal shit. People pissing in the hallways. Rapes. Murders. They had to rely on their street smarts. Shit, it was beyond street smarts. We're talking about the fuckin' law of the jungle shit. She couldn't even remember all the guys she'd poked with Willie.

A rusted metal door at the base of the building was propped open with a sawhorse. No lights inside. Annie tugged at a fallen chain-link fence until it fell to the ground. They walked inside a place they called The Hole.

"I hate it. I hate it. I hate it," Fannie said, walking blind through the blackness to the third floor. "Tell me about River-dale."

"Again?"

"Yes, again."

"They got that old malt shop. A beach. A high school. Bunch of white dudes with pointed noses."

Fannie made a little howling noise. "*Girrl*, I think I just stepped on something dead and it smells *so* bad in here. Smells like a man's bathroom."

Annie could see the top of the stairs and the light leaking from a door.

"Why doesn't he just move?" Fannie asked. "His brains in the blender?"

"Man won't let the past go. Still thinks he's the king of the black mafia. Doesn't know he's just a broke-dick dog."

Annie stopped cold at the top of the steps and waited for Fannie to bump into her. She reached back and squeezed her butt. The leather felt warm in her hands. Fannie giggled.

They'd always been good friends. Annie's mother had been a drugged-out whore and Fannie's father had been the plumber who'd found her mother in a gutter like a stray cat. He brought her mother home, cleaned her up, and even helped her get custody of her child—a young Annie. It was only the two little girls, like some kind of low-budget Brady Bunch.

Annie kicked open the door and followed the graffiti-sprayed halls to a door no different than every dozen they passed. Someone had crudely painted a sloppy heart encircling a thick peephole. Fannie slunked against the wall by the door and sucked on her lower lip. Annie tucked Willie in her coat pocket and removed the grime from her teeth with her tongue. She knocked and heard six different locks sliding away.

A young pudgy black dude wearing sunglasses and smoking a short cigar opened the door. He had on a black parka with fake fur around a loose hood and held a shotgun. Single action with a thick handle for a pump.

He pointed at them real serious. Then he smiled like fucking Buckwheat.

"Get up on my nuts if you wanna come on in," he said.

"Only the one?" Fannie asked.

"Yeah, only the one, Twondell?" Annie repeated. "We heard the other was a rubber one you paid twenty-five cents for in a gumball machine."

He grabbed his crotch and motioned them in. "Y'all can have a protein shake for dinner."

The room inside smelled dead. The walls were a collection of chipped paint from the last twenty years—splotches of greens and blues—with nothing in the room but a few dozen boxes, a stained bare mattress in the corner, and a buzzing refrigerator. Somehow the big man had figured how to rig some juice into his broken-down lair. A yellow bulb swung in the middle of the ceiling, scattering light on the empty floor.

Stagger Lee walked into the room naked wearing a spiked dog collar. He pulled open a huge refrigerator by the door and pulled out a small bottle of Coke. He nodded inside the refrigerator to all the other little green bottles.

Annie wrapped her arms around her stomach.

Fannie looked at the bottom of her clunky brown shoe.

"Twon, get me a towel," Stagger Lee said, before dropping to the floor and cranking out about thirty push-ups. His breath came out like a bark with his big, fat dong never leaving the floor. When he was done, Twon pulled open a pink towel for his boss and walked away into the next room. Stagger Lee gulped down the rest of the Coke and wiped his mouth with a forearm. He opened another bottle, popping off the top with his bare hands, and finishing most in one swallow.

Annie wasn't sure what the dog collar was all about. She never knew what was going through his sick mind. The man had to be past sixty years old with an obsession for staying young. Always working out and shaving away his gray hairs. Looked good for an old man though. Thick black muscles wrapped his body like bulging balloons of sand. His head a perfectly round cannonball. He crossed his massive arms and stared at the women.

"We saw Peetie tonight," Annie said.

Stagger Lee untucked his arms and finished the last of the Coke. The pink towel on his waist looked kind of like a tutu. Six foot six, three hundred pounds, in a pink tutu.

"He wanted us to tell you about a man named Lyons," Fannie said.

Stagger Lee rolled the little bottle in between his huge hands like it was clay.

"Well, he said you would know," Annie said. "Said, 'Tell Stagger Lee someone is looking for Billy Lyons.' Figured he was looking for some more money or somethin'."

Stagger Lee stood motionless.

"Said somebody was looking for who *killed* Lyons," Fannie said. "Yeah, said a man was looking for who killed him."

"Tell him, I don't give a fuck." Stagger Lee grunted and threw the green bottle against the wall. "Tell him he say the name Lyons again and I'll knock his fucking head off."

The girls turned to leave.

"Wait," he said, grabbing them both by their upper arms.

"He say who lookin'? Cops?"

"A man called Traveler or Travers."

"Peetie know where to find him?"

"I guess," Annie said and shrugged her shoulders as Stagger Lee leaned over and whispered his hot, angry breath into her ear. He said, "Bring me Peetie."

17

A DEEP URBAN night cloaked the street as if morning was not a possibility.

Nick's heart sank as he checked the address again and referenced his map. Right street. Wrong decade. The entire row of brick and rotting wood buildings where Ruby had lived had been destroyed long ago. Now, it was just a vacant lot at the cross street off Drexel Boulevard. Dead grass. A couple of old tires. A brittle wind rattled down the old boulevard as Nick rested his chin on the car's door and stared into the past like an idiot.

A block away, a single streetlamp scattered light onto a Dumpster filled with an old mattress as snow trickled down onto the dirty streets. Nick lit a cigarette and scanned the lot, trying to imagine Ruby's view. A view sharply different from the flat cotton fields outside Clarksdale. Brownstones, with castle-like turrets, sat empty by bare poplar trees. Chicago rose in a bright hub of buildings to the north. He could imagine the black Cadillacs, Buicks, and Hudsons parked nearby and the upper-class blacks who lived on the South Side. The women in stiff white clothing, maybe with gloves and hats, chatting down the busy street.

Somewhere a car alarm scattered the sounds of the late twentieth century. Where did all the people go? What happened to the black working class? What happened to Chicago, the promised land?

There would be no retracing Ruby's last steps tonight. No way of knowing how far she would have had to carry the body or the steps she would have to navigate drunk. Those answers had been wiped away by urban renewal, fate, and time.

All he knew was that Ruby lived in a second-floor apartment on this corner. She'd given him the address before he left Dwight. If she killed Lyons in her bed, it would have been a mighty long walk down those steps. Ruby had always been a thin woman. Maybe Big Mama Thornton could have hoisted Billy Lyons like a sack of potatoes, but not Ruby. If she couldn't drive she sure as shit would have needed help.

Nick still had a hard time imagining her stabbing Lyons. She told a story involving a gun but everything Nick had read stated Lyons was stabbed seventy-seven times. The number never changed.

The exhaust chugged like an electronic drumbeat. Nick got back into the car, his feet aching in his boots, his eyes heavy, and looped back south. If he couldn't find Ruby's home, he could still find her bar. Some things never changed and the Palm Tavern was one of those constants.

■

The Palm was wedged in a low brick building on East Forty-seventh Street down from the Met and the old Regal Theater. The bar was the place for entertainers like Cab Calloway and Duke Ellington back in the day. A place once filled with the who's who of 1950s black society. Businessmen to blues singers. The same owner had run the bar since the late fifties. Gerri Oliver. Nick stomped his boots outside and walked into the past.

The room was sad. Empty.

It was as if Gerri was waiting for all the ghosts to return. As if she never ventured outside her small business to see the Regal was gone, all the businesses closed, and the music that once poured from the taverns on Forty-seventh silent.

But the bar was impeccable. Padded leather booths lit with soft orange lights. A rose kept in a vase on each table. A gentleness and warmness about the place like a well-kept pair of wing tips.

Gerri stood behind the wooden bar, serving an elderly man in a fedora some whiskey in a smooth, rounded glass. Nick found a bar stool a few seats down and took off his jacket. Ella Fitzgerald gave a vocal workout from some hidden speaker. Across from him, silver tinsel snaked through bottles of booze.

Nick noticed a pay phone in the corner. He thought about what JoJo had said about Kate before he left. He had her number in his wallet. All he had to do was call her and ask for forgiveness. See if they could heal the tear he had created. But she'd moved on. You don't get second chances on major fuckups even though he'd loved her even before they'd met.

When he was taking graduate classes at Tulane, he'd noticed her running along the neutral ground and into Audubon Park. Kate was hard to miss. Dark brown hair in a ponytail swatting her sweaty back. Long tan legs dodging streetcars. He could almost set his watch by her 8:00 A.M. turn into the park.

He remembered one day, he was running late and parked his Jeep by the stone fence at Audubon. She almost ran into him as she gave the most brilliant smile he'd ever known. He felt like someone had plugged him into an amplifier when she said "excuse me" and trotted past. Thick, raspy voice like a jazz singer. Deep brown eyes.

But you don't follow a girl while she's jogging. He knew he'd come off like a pervert. Some kind of sex-crazed fool. *Excuse me, miss? I get really excited when you sweat. Can I smell your socks?*

So he'd waited. She continued to trot down St. Charles, turning on a dime into Audubon Park every morning, while he drew the last breath from his cigarette and smashed it under his foot. *The runner.*

The chase went on for months.

Then she stopped jogging. It was late fall and he began to wonder if she'd moved. Another lost opportunity. She was perfect, he thought. It was never meant to be. But one night he was flashing a ten-dollar bill for a bartender at the Columns Hotel when she wriggled beside him fighting for a space. She looked great in a black T-shirt, faded jeans, and Keds. His grin must've shown because she grinned back. The muffled roar of conversation in the dark Edwardian bar was deafening. A yell was a whisper.

He paid for her drink and followed her outside to the antebellum porch. She introduced him to some other *Picayune* reporters and asked him to sit down. They all got into some crazy two-hour conversation about hidden meanings and metaphors in *Scooby Doo* while the constant New Orleans rain swept off St. Charles. The olive green streetcars clanged by, their interiors brightly lit in the darkness. After the hours passed, only he and Kate remained.

Their table was a mess of martini glasses and Dixie bottles. She bummed a cigarette from him and admitted she didn't smoke. Her legs hugged to her chest as she inhaled. He was beginning to feel cocky when she looked at her watch, shook his hand, and darted out into the rain.

But the next day, he called her at the paper and asked her to dinner. After a hard-won twenty-minute conversation, she agreed. They had a date down by Pontchartrain with crawfish boil and a *fais do do*. A great outside venue where the beer came from trash cans filled with ice and the mudbugs were so spicy, they singed your fingers.

"You want a drink?" Gerri asked, breaking him from the memory.

"Just thinkin' about that," Nick said, his voice cracking.

Gerri was a light-skinned black women who looked a great deal younger than her seventy-odd years. Her hair was kept neat, white, and natural. Golden disks adorned her ears and she wore a loose-fitting pink shirt. When she smiled, the dark room became brighter.

"Double Jack on the rocks," Nick said, staring at the multicolored bottles across from him. A couple of unopened boxes of Johnny Walker, and a smooth, wooden African statue. He shook loose a cigarette and listened to Fitzgerald croon. There was a good energy here. Even in the silence and emptiness, you waited to hear the roaring laugher and clinking drinks of years ago.

Nick looked over at the pay phone in the corner of the bar and thought against it. *Leave it alone.* He introduced himself as Gerri laid down the drink. She was a legend who had been in several documentaries on the South Side. Even featured in a *New York Times* article on the migration. He believed she'd migrated from Jackson, Mississippi, during the forties.

He told her about his project on Ruby and King Snake Records. She said she remembered Ruby well and shook her head at the mention of Lyons's murder.

"She was something," Gerri said. "I miss the days when Ruby was here."

"A regular?"

"Oh yes," Gerri said. "This place used to be so packed on a Saturday night that a sardine couldn't find a place to stand."

"You remember her agent?"

"Peetie? Oh yes, the man would walk in and say, 'Gerri, give the room a drink.' Then he'd slip out the back door."

The old man at the end of the bar looked at Nick as if the world was out of focus and turned back to his whiskey. The music had stopped, and he could hear the buzzing of the neon sign in the window. *The Palm Tavern.* Nick laughed and wondered how JoJo was doing. He wondered if Felix was working his acrobatics at the bar and what Loretta cooked up for tonight's special.

Nick smiled. "When was the last time you saw Ruby?"

"I went to the trial one day. Felt terrible for her. She just let that man drive her crazy. Billy could do that. He was so handsome, sharp as the devil's tail. . . . You know she was here the night he was killed?"

Nick almost choked on his drink.

"Hold on . . . ," Gerri said, walking down to the end of a bar and picking up a steaming mug. "Herbal tea. Oh yes, I'm sorry."

"Ruby was in here?"

She closed her eyes as she took a sip of the greenish tea. The old man at the end of the bar studied his reflection in the whiskey glass.

"She must've killed him a few hours after she left. She had a whole table that night, with some other folks in her band."

"You remember who?"

"I'm sorry. That's been quite a spell ago."

"Was she drunk?"

"That's like asking is a swimmer wet. *Ruby was always drunk.*"

"More than usual. Did she act strangely?"

Gerri shook her head. "No, just normal. Told me, 'Gerri, keep it comin'.' Poor, poor Ruby drinkin' that ole Lord Calvert."

"Did you know her very well?"

"No more than the other singers. We used to have 'em all in here. They'd tell me things. Talk to me about their problems and cry on my shoulder."

"She ever mention her problems with Billy?"

"Oh sure, with his cheatin' and that type thing. When I heard what she'd done, I remember just crying for them both. It was just so awful."

"Everybody knew her?"

"Ruby was the queen of the ball. Every man's head, and I mean every man's, would turn. She was so beautiful. And folks who just made the trip north really appreciated her songs. She had one. Oh, what was the name of it?"

" 'Lonesome Blues Highway?' "

Gerri nodded. "Yes, people really loved that one. People connected, I guess."

The Jack flushed a warm glow into Nick's face. He rubbed his boots together as he listened. He could go to sleep right there. Find one of those empty corner booths and take a nap. Gerri wouldn't mind.

He looked at his watch.

He'd done his best today.

"You met any of Ruby's friends?" Gerri asked.

"Peetie," Nick said and laughed. "Moses Jordan."

"No, her *friends*. She used to have this gal who was always by her side. Couldn't go to the bathroom without her following. What was her name? Always wore one of those floppy hats. Not as pretty as Ruby. A little large. Hold on. . . ."

Gerri placed her tea on the counter and walked away again.

She returned holding a brittle wood frame. The bottom left corner of the glass was broken and the black-and-white picture had yellowed. But Nick could still see Ruby sitting among a group of people, drinks hoisted high in their hands.

"That's Ruby and over there is Billy in the Stetson hat. Never did like to have his picture taken."

Lyons was the only one with his head twisted away from the camera.

Gerri pointed to an overweight black woman sitting next to Ruby.

"That's the one I was telling you about. Florida. She and Ruby were real close. Worked to keep the fans away. And handle things. I think they both came from the same county back in Mississippi. Haven't seen her for years."

Nick stared at Florida's face. He wondered why Ruby didn't tell him about her. Maybe she was dead. Maybe she had drifted into time like Ruby's apartment and King Snake Records.

"You remember her last name?"

Gerri said she didn't. She walked away as the old man stirred at the end of the bar. The man laid his cash on the table and Gerri helped him into his heavy coat. She walked with him to the door.

An icy breeze shot into the bar as Nick stood and fished into his pockets for some cash.

"You mind if I borrow this?" he asked, pointing to the picture. "I want to make a copy."

"No, go right ahead. You say you're trying to help Ruby?"

"Yes, ma'am."

"Well, good luck then," Gerri said. She looked confused. "We miss her around here. Been a void since she left that I can't explain."

"Anything else stick out in your mind?"

"Not really," she said. "I knew the men in her band a lot better."

"Who?"

"Oh, Franky Dawkins. Leroy Williams. They were some great people. Makes me sick to think how they died."

"Yeah," Nick said. "Heard about that. Guess Leroy has some problems."

"What do you mean?"

"Had to be depressed, taking his own life."

"Who told you that?" Gerri said, plunking down her tea. "Man was murdered."

"I'm sorry, it's late. I guess it was Dawkins who killed himself."

"You gettin' some bad information, son. Both of 'em were murdered just after Ruby was put away. People used to say Billy had put some bad mojo on that place. Can you believe two such fine men killed so close to each other?"

Nick toyed with the napkin around the glass of Jack and shook his head.

"Mr. Travers?"

"You're sure about this?" Nick asked.

"Yeah, I'm sure. Those men were like family."

"How'd they die?"

"Both robbed. Cut up awfully bad. They threw Leroy into the river after they finished with him."

"You mean they were stabbed several times?"

"So many times they looked like a side of meat. Or so I'm told."

18

AT THE COOK County Jail, I gave up the flowered dress, the black high heels, and the ruby necklace Billy had given me. I lived there for months until the trial started in the beginning of 1960. My lawyer wanted me to confess. Said it would be easier that way. Said I wouldn't have to fear being put to death. But I said the truth would give me freedom.

He was a timid, little man with a violent stutter. He became confused givin' facts I knew by heart. Twice, he called me by the wrong name.

I didn't cry durin' my trial even as the prosecuting attorney strutted before me and made me into a drunken whore. He painted a picture of a woman who laid with them all. He said I liked men and women. He said I liked dope and whiskey.

He embarrassed my friends on the witness stand while people I respected watched on. Musicians from all over stopped by the courthouse. One day, I even saw Mr. Sonny Boy give me a strong nod. I remember it 'cause he had this suit that was half-black and the other half-blue.

I wondered what happened to Dirty Jimmy until I saw him on the stand. He told the story about me threatenin' Billy's life in September. I thought I was guilty myself, the way that attorney pulled it from him.

Florida stayed by me though. She wrote me letters and sent me food. And although she never came to see me in jail, I never lost respect for our friendship. Her words were like manna fallin' from heaven as the locusts gnawed around me.

The jury was all white. Mostly men.

One of them smiled at me every time the bailiff sat me down by my lawyer. It wasn't a good smile; he looked like he could smell me. Little bald man with black hair in his ears.

I used to watch all their faces durin' the trial. I knew people. I felt I could sense their feelings and with concentration, make them feel mine.

But change swept through them like a heated lightning bolt when that detective man took the stand. My attorney sank into his seat and rubbed his temples through the whole thing. Had to poke him to make him sit straight.

That detective nailed it on me. They brought in pictures of my bloody mattress and of the bloody sheets they found in a trash can down the street.

My lawyer tried to argue but it couldn't be undone. "Blood doesn't lie," the prosecutor said as he grinned with pointed teeth.

I thought the trial lasted forever.

Two days later, I got life.

The hammer came down on the bench like thunder through my soul.

19

FRIDAY MORNING, THREE days before Christmas, and Nick was already beat. He'd hit the Palmer House gym at 9:00 A.M., bench-pressed two-fifty for three sets of ten, shoulder pressed seventy pounds for another three sets, and finished with a few sets of cable pressdowns at ninety pounds. His triceps screamed and the front of his gray T-shirt was soaked with sweat.

After his last set, he took the elevator to the lobby and grabbed a cup of joe and a couple donuts. He dropped into a plush red chair and stared at the golden candelabrums, marble arches, and oriental rugs that filled the grand room. Fat naked ladies loomed in a fresco above as he sipped on the scalding coffee.

The Palmer House was classic Chicago. The hotel opened back in 1871, thirteen days before the great Chicago fire. Rebuilt several times after that. He'd heard it was the first hotel in the city with elevators, electric lights, and telephones. From cowboys to gangsters. Now it was a little 1920s and a little 1980s. A world of tiny chocolates on your pillow and a minibar filled with shots of Jack for six bucks.

An old woman in a mink coat glared at his sweaty T-shirt littered with powdered sugar. He winked at her. Never got this kind of attention when he stayed at the Motel 6 by the airport.

As much as he'd like to sit on his ass and enjoy the atmosphere, somewhere in the back of his mind he could hear Ruby's voice call. Her pleadings of love and moans of happiness. That constant humming vibrating her silver, honeycomb microphone. *The drained expression on her face.*

He thought about what Peetie Wheatstraw said about her robbing Billy. But seventy-seven times implied a mind-set much more than a drunken robbery. And if she was so drunk or stoned, how did she have the power to kill him and move the body? A second-floor apartment. No car.

Nick thought of the promise he'd made and a curiosity he'd created. *Dawkins. Williams.* He could pull records and see if Gerri had the story right about how the men died. He'd planned to dig up the court file anyway.

Ruby trusted him. He could see her wide, black eyes staring into his soul. Trust was not something that woman gave easily.

Nick knew people. He'd worked years on sifting the good stuff from the bullshit. About every other blues player he interviewed lied. Everyone played with Robert Johnson or Muddy Waters. Hell, it was easy to lie about dead people or playing at clubs that had closed their doors decades ago. How do you check references?

You could see it their eyes. You could hear the conviction in their voices. Call it a hunch. Call it using The Force. But whatever it was, he knew Ruby wasn't reciting a a tired mantra. Ruby thought she was innocent and unless she was a complete nutcase, then she was to be believed.

He was sure no one ever really worked to prove her story.

The last of the great female blues singers.

He might as well quit tracking the blues if he didn't keep his word. He remembered a conference a few years ago in Helena, Arkansas, where white, southern, self-proclaimed intellectuals debated arcane facts about long-dead musicians. After this historian Nick had always admired finished his hour-and-a-half lecture on Lonnie Johnson, he joined some back-slapping colleagues at the hotel bar.

After the man's fourth scotch, the man started telling some really borderline racist stories about some musicians he had been talking about an hour earlier with awe. He probably meant to share the story-behind-the-story thing with some men he trusted. But to Nick, he came off like a jackass. He thought it was funny the way an elderly woman lay in her own waste in her rusted trailer. In his speech, he called her brilliant. He laughed at a guitarist from Betonia who signed an autograph with an X. Earlier, he compared that man to Mozart. This historian painted blues with a intellectual fence that only the trained could understand. But personally, he scoffed at the music's ignorance.

You don't feign respect. You don't find stories of lynchings, back-breaking labor, and soul-tearing depression quaint. This was an opportunity to show you stand behind your sermons. What JoJo would call a "proving day." Ruby was also a second chance to help a woman who thought the world had left her.

Nick pulled the drapes open in his hotel room and stared across the gothic city. Steam and smoke worked from chimneys and vents. Battered fire escapes wrapped brick buildings like skeletons. Snow as fine as powdered sugar fell from the gray skies. *Time to hit the records trail.*

20

CHRISTMAS IN CHICAGO. New Orleans had its own traditions but somehow the deep cold put the season in perspective. Chicago was like a big family you desperately wanted to join, Nick thought, a big aunt with her meaty arms spread wide in welcome. Down on State Street, he lit a Marlboro and watched little mechanical figures dance, make pies, and turn pirouettes in the Carson Pirie Scott window display. He passed the tarnished copper clock of Marshall Field's and saw the white bulbs of the Chicago Theater burn in the distance. When he smiled, the wind hurt his teeth.

Nick walked north past an outdoor skating rink, to Randolph, and then over to the Cook County Building to pull death certificates on Lyons, Williams, and Dawkins. He hoped the bits of information he'd gathered from his tattered *Blues Who's Who* would be enough.

He waited in the basement of the building for about thirty minutes after giving an attendant death dates on the men. He knew their fates lived somewhere in the system.

In a hard plastic seat, Nick glanced through a ragged spiral notebook and watched people to pass the time. He thought about the brutal deaths of other Chicago bluesmen. Little Walter and Sonny Boy Williamson. Sonny Boy was the man who took a novelty instrument and turned it into a blues staple. "Good

Morning Little School Girl." "Early in the Morning." Beaten to death in '48 over a wallet, a watch, and three harps.

Little Walter Jacobs . . . Walter was the greatest. For years Nick had tried to draw that complex sound from such a simple instrument. His licks were perfection. A member of the original Muddy Waters's band and the man most credited with first amplifying the harp. Nick could still hear his teasing laugh on the alternate version of "Worried Life."

Some hustler killed Walter with a lead pipe over a back alley dice game. He was 37. Nick shook his head at the thought and scanned the room.

Dozens of people slowly moved over the linoleum floor in five lines for the official word on death and marriage. Hard to tell which from their faces. Soon, he became particularly interested in a young woman in a ragged fur coat at the desk. She reminded him of a young Madonna—mole above her lip, eyes painted like an Egyptian, and hair in dirty blonde ringlets. She gave him a few glances and Nick shot her a weathered smile.

She finally motioned him over to the desk with the crook of her finger. Nick jumped ahead of the crowd and met her at a corner window slot.

"Franky Dawkins, nineteen-sixty?" she asked, chomping some gum. She showed him Dawkins's full name, date of death, and a file number. "And here. This is William J. Lyons."

"Williams?"

"No record of Leroy S. Williams," she said.

"Could be a few years earlier or later," he said.

"I could try again," she said.

"I like your eyes," Nick said.

She stopped chomping and grinned. Her lips were the color of a fire engine.

"I could also check the surrounding counties," she said.

"Anyone ever say you look like Madonna?"

"You can stop now," she said, blushing. "You got it. *You got it.*"

Nick watched the line snake out the hall. The dirty water from slush-covered boots had wiped the floor in a muddy smear. The crowd looked like a Russian food line, with their bundled jackets and scarves covering their heads, moving with grim faces in the basement of the old rock of a building.

Madonna whistled for him about fifteen minutes later.

"You meant sixty-five," she said, looking over at a supervisor.

"Yes, ma'am."

"Sorry you had to wait so long."

"No problem, caught up with my sitting."

She slid across three death certificates on bonded paper crushed with an official stamp of Illinois. The room buzzed around him as he searched for cause of death on Dawkins. Multiple stab wounds. Homicide. *Williams?* Stabbed. Drowned in the Chicago River.

"Sir?" Madonna asked.

"Oh, I'm sorry," Nick said, paying for the certificates. He ordered three copies each. One for his files, one for the archive, and another for his friend Ed Komara at Ole Miss.

He thanked the woman and noticed a business card paper-clipped to Dawkins's death certificate as he walked away. Home number scrawled on the back. Nick turned back and waved. The woman shrugged and gave a weak smile.

■

The inside of the Cook County archives reminded Nick of an worn-out airplane hangar. A long-concave building made of stamped tin. Thick erector-set like beams, coated in rust, criss-crossed overhead. Metal warehouse lights shined down its corridors with metal shelves stacked ten feet high with employee personal records, court transcripts, and endless official documents. The place smelled like the inside of a worn paperback book.

A gray-headed woman with yellowed teeth slammed a sagging cardboard box onto a military desk at the far end of the archives. Gray light cut in laser sheaths above him from windows coated in dust and city grime.

"I appreciate it," Nick said.

She scowled.

"Thank you," Nick said.

"Your friend is a real jerk," she said.

"Thank you."

"Really, I mean it," she said. "Public record request doesn't mean 'thirty minutes or it's free.' We ain't fuckin' Domino's. You see all this shit? It took me all morning to find this file."

Even from his small insignificant pine desk at Tulane, Randy's presence was felt. He handed her the death certificates on Williams and Dawkins and politely asked for their files before turning back to the *State of Illinois vs. Ruby Walker*.

She gave a rotten sigh and trudged off.

Nick exhaled a long breath and scratched his bristly chin. He needed witnesses. Contacts. Right now, he was just rubbing a couple of sticks together to kick up a little fire. He needed to get into the scene of Chicago blues in the fifties. He had to imagine the rough texture and smoky fabric that held together the ramshackle blues joints, fledging record companies, and singers with faded souls.

Nick could feel the connection as he extracted Lyons's personal effect sheet.

The report read: one ring with ten stone sets, one ring with white stone set, one ring with two side stone sets, one money clip fashioned from a silver dollar with $3.96 attached, and a cigarette lighter marked with a snake.

Medical Examiner's report wasn't a surprise. Seventy-seven stab wounds. *Sometimes oral histories are right.* But Lyons was also shot once in the head with a .44-caliber gun, according to the report and the death certificate. Nothing of value had been taken. Nick rubbed his temples and took notes.

For the next two hours, he read through police reports, endless depositions, and the trial itself. Dawkins, Williams, and Elmore King were interviewed. They all said they saw Ruby fighting with Lyons the day he died. They all talked about the tension in Lyons's life and said he was about to lose the record company.

The trial lasted a couple of days. Ruby's public defender called a few witnesses that only seemed to help the prosecutors. Prosecutors said Ruby sometimes carried a gun on her right hip and had a violent temper. Ruby's defense attorney spoke vaguely of Lyons's enemies and known ties to criminal activities in the South Side. Both said Lyons was a gambler. A womanizer. Ruby was obsessed with her career. Prosecutors said that was her only interest in Lyons.

There was blood on Ruby's sheets and the detectives had found a murder weapon. A rusted ice pick coated in her fingerprints.

Nick flipped back to the deposition of a man who also saw an argument with Ruby and Lyons. The type was blotted and crooked from an old hard-banging typewriter.

Direct Examination

Q: Will you please state your name?
A: James E. Scott
Q: What is your address?
A: 645 Thirty-first Street.
Q: That is Chicago?
A: (mumbled affirmation)
Q: What is your occupation?
A: Musician.
Q: What was your relationship to Mr. Lyons?
A: Play harmonica on his records.

James E. Scott. *Dirty Jimmy Scott?* Dirty Jimmy was a pretty well-known session musician in the fifties and sixties, but Nick never placed him at those late King Snake recordings. Nick had seen an interview with him within the last few years. Maybe he was still around but surely not at a forty-year-old address.

Q: You saw them arguing?
A: Yes, sir.
Q: Was she upset?

A: Yes, sir. She called him all sorts of names. Things I can't repeat.

Q: Did she threaten him?

A: Yes, sir. She said she was going to kill him.

Q: Did she have a weapon?

A: Yes, sir, we all seen the gun.

Nick's heart sank. Everything fit too neatly.

Still, Nick wrote Dirty Jimmy next to the names of Elmore King, Moses Jordan, Peetie Wheatstraw, and Gerri from the Palm Tavern. Nick glanced back through the transcript. He listed the names for the prosecuting attorney, Ruby's defender, and a detective named Butler. He was the one who put her away with exact details about Ruby and the crime.

Nick found a battered Xerox machine and copied selected parts of the file.

"Williams and Dawkins?" he asked the clerk.

"I can't find anything with those names," she said. "Was anyone charged?"

"I don't believe so."

"You could put in a request for the homicide file but that could take weeks."

He made copies of their death certificates and scribbled his office number at Tulane on one of the pages.

The woman took the torn, musty box away to its hidden slot in the cavernous room. As Nick walked outside, he noticed random patterns of shoe prints in the thin layer of snow and ice.

21

STAGGER LEE STROLLED down the center of the Robert Taylor Homes with kids trailing behind him like he was the motherfuckin' pied piper. Not as many as there used be. A few years back, he'd sit in the playground surrounded by kids and hand out sacks full of presents. He'd give them bicycles, candy, and even twenty-dollar bills. Shit, money was nothing. Grew like a fungus around the projects. *Rock was working strong then*. Made a man forget about pussy, about his family, about everything but shoving cash into that pipe. Reason he never touched the shit. Hell, he just drank Coca-Cola and laughed at those fools.

He bent down to a little boy and gave him a couple of Tootsie Pops from his Santa sack.

"Merry Christmas," the little boy said in a small voice. Burrheaded child with wide eyes. Didn't understand how things worked yet. He thought the world was full of possibilities. Give him a week with Stagger Lee and he'd learn urban law.

Stagger Lee rubbed the boy's head. "You remember me. Okay?"

The boy ran off toward a row of boarded-up buildings with CONDEMNED signs shaking in the December wind. Kids were his future, always had been since he came to Robert Taylor. Babies cried in the apartments around him, choking and wailing into the world of crap they found. He gave them jobs.

The high-rise ghettos were about the closest thing to hell you could get on this earth. No one planned on the turf wars, the power out in the summer heat, or the open sewers that made your eyes water from the smell of decaying shit.

He stood and stared down the straight shot of State Street. The brick buildings made him feel like a forgotten king, all his people scattered to the wind. The snow was caked on windowsills and in door frames filled with rotted plywood.

A couple more kids walked over to him all bundled up in the cold. He handed them a couple of Walkmans. They'd been good this year, unloaded a whole bunch of shit. A couple of Twon's boys. Future gangs kids.

Stagger Lee was the one who brought the gangs all together. They all came to him for advice: Vice Lords. Disciples. Mickey's Cobras. In the beginning, he ran four lieutenants under him who controlled kids on the street corners. He liked them young. Teens could smell the cash.

Sure they died quick. If street punks didn't get them, the crack would. But the cops couldn't get to Stagger Lee. He never kept the drugs around him and never got close to the corners. To the Chicago police, he was just a shadow.

But his world was crumbling. Street corners were cleaning up and money was starting to flow back into the old neighborhoods. Damn if they weren't going to even tear old Robert Taylor down next year. The whole damn projects were going to be gone. Now, how was he supposed to run a business? Most of the buildings had already been closed, folks moving out. He made less money this month than he had in twenty years.

All he had to do was walk down the bare halls of The Hole and feel the low tide coming. He'd wait till the wrecking ball came and then he'd find something else.

Billy Lyons. His name was a forgotten friend. Reminded him of the days when whiskey poured into his hands like gold. He thought about those first days after he broke away from hustling in Memphis and the big hit that changed his life.

Stagger Lee adjusted his leather dog collar. *One last score to make.*

■

The Iranian man called his pawn shop the Gold Mine. The shop was only a few blocks away from the shells of Robert Taylor and used to be the place to trade in stolen TVs, car stereos, and jewelry. Man used to have so much hot shit moving through his shop, cops had to close him down about every other week. But now, the Gold Mine moved slow. The Iranian guy had a Christmas tree blinking behind barred windows and advertised a jewelry sale with one of those mobile plastic signs.

But Stagger Lee didn't give a shit about the man's gold. He just needed a tool. Yeah, if he took care of this Travers, like he did all the others, man would set him up. He could get enough cash to set up shop somewhere else, get the kids workin' for him again, and get out of the hole of shit where he'd lived for the last two years.

Stagger Lee pounded on the front door and saw the man scurry away from his seat—his brown face bright with fear—and disappear into a back room. Stagger Lee pounded some more and saw the lights go black inside.

So he'd be like this, he thought, as he walked down the row of concrete block stores. Nothing in them but For Rent signs. Stagger Lee saw a fat hunk of concrete on the broken asphalt ground and wiped the snow from its rocky edge.

He bounded back to the front of the Gold Mine and tossed it through the front door's glass. The door shattered and Stagger Lee cracked off the remaining pieces of ragged glass with the fat edge of his ice pick. Same old ice pick he'd used back in the stockyards all those years ago to chip off the ice from bloody sides of beef.

Stagger Lee bent at the waist and walked through the door frame and into the shop filled with outdated televisions, broken-down stereos, and six glass cases filled with jewelry. In the darkness, the cases of gold and silver glowed like something out of a fuckin' museum.

Stagger Lee searched the walls for what he needed as the old Iranian man walked into the room with his hands over his head. Shaking.

"Please," the man said.

"Where are they?"

"What?"

"I want a forty-four."

Man walked with his hands over to a side case and nodded his head down. Stagger Lee walked over, past a crate filled with discount porno movies, and looked down at dozens of Glocks and 9 mm's.

"I said a forty-four," Stagger Lee said, grabbing the man by his black hair and pounding his face into the black case. His face became a torn, bloody mess in the cracked glass.

"Please, please. I have family. Please."

"A forty-four."

The man slowly turned around and reached for a bunch of keys on his waist. His hands trembled so much the keys dropped to the floor. He looked down at the ground and back at Stagger Lee.

"You better get goin'."

The man reached down to the floor and reached for the keys. He turned back and unlocked a wooden case behind him. He kept his eyes on Stagger Lee as he pulled out a finely oiled, blue steel .44. *Just like he used to have back in the old days.*

He delicately dropped it into Stagger Lee's huge hands and raised his arms again. The Iranian man had a scruff on his face and a thick gold medallion around his neck.

"Good boy," Stagger Lee said. "I'll take it."

"Go in peace," the man said.

"I will," Stagger Lee said reaching into his black overcoat and pulling out a hollow-tipped bullet and inserting it into the spinning cylinder. "I will."

He aimed the gun between the shaking man's eyes and pulled the trigger.

22

NICK JUMPED ON a southbound El to Forty-seventh Street hoping Peetie could help him find Florida and Jimmy Scott. He rode the rambling elevated train and thought about the three men of King Snake and how their deaths could fit together. After the last jarring stop, he walked over to the Soul Train where an old woman told him Peetie was upstairs sleeping.

Nick took a back staircase to an apartment and knocked.

After a few minutes, the knob jiggled and Peetie opened the door wearing a tattered red kimono robe and a shower cap on his head. He rubbed his eyes and jumped back a few feet when he saw Nick. He tried to close the door, but Nick stuck a Tony Lama into the frame.

"Peetie, it's me. Nick Travers."

The man's tired eyes shot wide open. He backed up into his apartment, closed his robe around him like a prudish grandmother, and held his hands in front of his body. Nick thought he might piss down his leg.

"Peetie? You all right, man?"

"Yeah, yeah, yeah," he said. His head tilted and eyes turned to slits. He dropped his shoulders and gave a new look of understanding.

"You just kind of came up on me," Peetie said. "I was asleep, havin' some kind of wild dream about Halle Berry and a donut.

Man, I just wanted to keep that thang goin'. Hey, you just scared me is all. Not awake yet. It's cool. It's cool."

"You sure?" Nick asked, smiling. "I can come back. You look a little whacked out, man."

"No, come on. Sit down. How you know where I live at?"

"Lady downstairs told me."

"My auntie. She don't like me sleepin', say I'm a no-good drunk . . . and I don't even drink."

Peetie had a coffee table and a couple of wobbly director's chairs by a large bay window like you'd find in an old Victorian home. An unmade murphy bed leaned from closet doors and a twenty-year-old television sat on a crooked stand. Peetie walked into a small kitchen, yawned, and opened a lime green refrigerator collaged with naked Asian women.

"Hey, you want one of them Snapples?" he asked, scratching his ass. "Got me two cases of them down at the market for five bucks. Ain't that some shit? I'm gonna make me some coffee to wash ole Miss Berry out of my mind. My dick still wide awake."

Nick sat into the director's chair and looked out of the window down onto the street. A Yugo with tinted windows and curb feelers rambled past, blaring its stereo. A little boy walked a mangy dog down the slush-filled sidewalk. Steam belched from a crooked pipe at a restaurant across the street.

"Snapple?" Peetie asked again.

"Coffee's fine."

"Man, can't unload that shit. Some kind of iced tea. Nobody wants to drink tea out of a bottle. I just bent over on that thang. Hope you don't mind instant. Got me a deal on them Folgers crystals too. . . . You know they used to switch that coffee at one of them real nice restaurants downtown and nobody could tell the difference? All those rich folks thought they was drinkin' Colombian but they was really drinkin' this shit. *Wooh* . . ."

"Peetie, you remember a friend of Ruby's named Florida?" Nick asked, staring at one of the most complex collections of LPs he'd even seen. Floor to ceiling vinyl. Cassette tapes. Hundreds of boxed reel-to-reels.

Peetie bustled through a cupboard clanging around with some metal pots. He pulled out a tea kettle and tried to turn on his water. Under the sink, the pipes made a supernatural groan, and he scrambled to turn them off.

"Goddamn!" he yelled. "Sound like they hooked them thangs up to Cujo's ass. . . . How 'bout some hot tea?"

"That's fine, man."

He screwed the top from a couple bottles of Snapple and poured them into the kettle.

"Oh yes, I remember Miss Florida," Peetie said, lighting a match and catching the flame on his stove. "Oooh. Yes, she was . . . how does a gentlemen say . . . big-boned. Yeah, that woman was hauling some serious boo-tay. But she was always sweet to me . . . drove Ruby around." His voice got higher. "She was the driver you was askin' me about."

"What happened to her?"

"*Ooh, well, well,* I don't know. Man, I ain't seen that woman since Ruby was put in jail. Figured she left Chicago. Her cash cow gettin' milked in prison and all."

"You know her last name?"

"Mrs. Big Bottom?" Peetie laughed. "Awe, man, I can't remember. Hell, Billy was probably doin' her too. That's why he called his business King Snake. As in crawlin' all night long. You see what I'm sayin'?"

"Got it."

The tea kettle rattled over the flame. Peetie took off his shower cap and tucked it into a drawer. His relaxed hair was pulled in place by a series of silver barrettes. He didn't seem self-conscious as he plucked out each one, and then leaned into the director's chair with a small cigar.

"Nice collection of records," Nick said, looking over Peetie's shoulder.

"I figure I got to have more than three thousand in there. 'Course I got lots of the same thing. Dumb-ass musicians who thought they could pay me that way. Now, if they suckin' ass, why they think I want to hear their songs a hundred times?"

"Seventy-eights?"

"All speeds. All kinds. Blues, gospel, jazz, rap. All that shit."

Peetie stood and lit the end of his cigar and held it high in his hand. In his silk kimono and with slicked-back hair, he looked just like a woman. There was something androgynous and confused about him. His legs were stick thin and hairless.

"Were you around the day Billy died?" Nick asked.

"No, man. Like I said, I was financial. I let him deal with the talent. I just made sure they was treated with respect."

Yeah, and were never paid by Lyons.

"Why you lookin' 'round for her?" Peetie asked. "Thought I set you straight on Ruby. Thought you understood she lyin' out the ass."

"I need some more folks to tell me that."

"History?"

"Yeah."

"That's cool."

"Hey, man, you know where Dirty Jimmy's hangin' out these days?"

"The cemetery?" Peetie said.

"When did he die?"

"Oh, man, I cain't remember. But last time I seen him he looked like a skeleton in a suit. Drank himself into a world of shit."

"But you're not sure he's dead."

"I'd bet my ding dong on it."

"You should never do that," Nick said. "You know where he was living?"

Peetie shrugged. "Nah, used to just see him down at Maxwell Street playin' harp for some loose change. Didn't sound right blowin' without no teeth. Smelled real bad too. Raggedy ole clothes. Give a bluesman a bad name."

Nick felt an uncomfortable silence grow between them. He took a deep breath, waiting for Peetie to keep talking. "So who you been talkin' to?"

"You, Moses Jordan, and went down to the Palm Tavern last night."

"Yeah?"

"Yeah, I heard about what happened to Leroy Williams and Franky Dawkins. That must've been a rough time."

Peetie scrunched up his eyes and acted like he was going to cry. "Dawkins got robbed, shot down like a dawg," he said. "Man was like a goddamned brother."

"What about Leroy Williams?"

"Leroy didn't care for me too much," Peetie said, puffing on his cigar. "He was real strange. You'd see him all feelin' sorry for himself, slumped over his piano smokin'. You ask him somethin' and he just grunt. Real strange. Then you'd see him at a party and he'd be all smiles, gettin' you a drink. 'Course I heard, don't say nothin' bout this, he beat his wife a lot. He'd beat her then get mad at himself. I went to his funeral—you know he jumped off a bridge—and his wife had a broken nose."

"He was stabbed and dumped in the river."

"No shit?" Peetie's face contorted in surprise and wonder, his jaw hanging loose. "That ain't what I heard."

"So, no ideas where to find Jimmy or Florida?"

"Nah, man," Peetie said, walking back to the kitchen and pouring the tea. He moved toward the bay windows, balancing the steaming mugs. Frost and crystals coated the panes.

"You miss the old scene?" Nick asked, warming his hands on the tea and wondering where he would go next.

"You got no idea," Peetie said. "So, what you gettin' at with them men dyin'? You think that has somethin' to do with Ruby?"

"Could be."

"What you gonna do with all this?" Peetie asked and laughed. "Let's say you find out she didn't kill Billy. You goin' to the cops? 'Cause you got me real confused. You sayin' you historian but you comin' on like somethin' else."

"I've taken a personal interest."

"What that mean?"

"I'm still figuring it out."

"Well, man, if you learn somethin', let me know," Peetie said. "I sure like to know if Miss Ruby is innocent. Sure would feel bad about all those years she spent in jail. 'Course I ain't the one that's been stayin' away. All them people that loved her forgot about her like yesterday's garbage."

"What about old friends of Jimmy's?" Nick asked.

Peetie shook his head. "Don't know a one of that fool's, wish I could help. . . . Hey, you want to hit some clubs tonight? I can get you in free at the Checkerboard. They owe me a favor down there. Took care of some trouble with a band kept missing dates."

"I may take you up on that before I leave," Nick said. "But tonight I think I'm headed to Rosa's."

"I know the place," Peetie said.

Nick took another sip of the tea, not to seem rude, and stood. He shook Peetie's chilly hand and smiled. Peetie walked back to his shelves of records and carefully extracted a 45. He handed the record, embossed with the familiar coiled logo, to Nick and crossed his arms across his chest.

A copy of "Lonesome Blues Highway." Original. Perfect condition.

"I can't take this."

"It's yours," Peetie said. "You been nice enough to believe in Ruby."

"You're all right, man," Nick said, shaking Peetie's hand again.

"Sure I am," Peetie said, his face a broad smile of teeth and tight cheeks. "What you expect?"

23

MOST WINTER DAYS in New Orleans, the white sun would peak from the clouds and give a quick mental reprieve from the depression. Winter was a temporary inconvenience, not a way of life. Not Chicago. A flat roll of thick gray clouds blocked the sun. Endless rows of concrete and brick buildings stretched tall as if seeking to break the barrier.

On Forty-third Street, aka Muddy Waters Avenue, Nick watched a group of teenagers staring at their reflection in a cracked mirror propped against an abandoned warehouse. Next door, a wino sat on a bucket looking at his rotted shoes as a bunch of kids played hopscotch by a liquor store. The kids smiled and giggled, oblivious to the poverty around them.

When walking through a depressed neighborhood, it was best to act confident. Especially when you're white. Nick's light coloring made him look like a napkin waving in the wind. But he'd learned long ago to walk with purpose. Don't let others know you're watching. Look like you've got business. The heft of the Browning underneath his wool coat helped. A little.

He passed a peeling graffiti message telling all the world to EAT ME as two guys warmed their hands over a fire in a barrel. He heard the word *cracker* and someone call him a *crazy son of a bitch*.

He didn't stop to argue. Besides, they were both true. This was insane. He was starting to wonder if any of the pompous intellectuals at any blues conference would care if he risked his ass to get information. But like it or not, this is what he did. *He was a tracker*. And unless he wanted to become one of those men who talked about blues all day but were afraid to live the life, he had to keep plugging away.

A few years ago, Nick had become good friends with a man in this neighborhood named Theodis Meyer. Theodis ran a barber shop called the Upper Cut. He used to be a boxer and later kept dozens of faded photos and trophies around the shop in case anyone forgot. The Upper Cut was a hangout for original southern immigrants and bluesmen. They swapped stories and told tall tales about the old South Side and the blues and jazz joints, and the house parties that lasted all night and day.

Nick had a great time with the old guys on the last trip. They talked about the Great Migration and gave him a real feeling of the excitement of old Chicago. Theodis said there was so much neon, blues, and women, a man could get drunk without having a drop of alcohol. He said everyone was either starting a shift at the mill or coming off one. He said the South Side never slept.

Nick walked past a burned-out theater and another liquor store advertisement with the cartoon head of a bull. He knew he was getting close. Nick knew this would be the place to start if he wanted to find Dirty Jimmy. He'd already called all of the numbers in the phone book without luck.

Jimmy would be a real find. He was a Korean War vet who came to Chicago to make it as a gambler. But apparently, Jimmy played three-card monte better than poker and occasionally got in trouble with the losers. When he was down, he played harp at the old Maxwell Street Market for a few bucks. It was at the market Jimmy caught the attention of some record producers and made some decent harp instrumentals in the mid fifties. Nick had read where Jimmy took a job as a cabdriver in the seventies when the blues almost died.

After that, Jimmy disappeared.

Theodis would set him straight. Good to see the guy. He looked forward to sitting in the old spinning chairs and hearing the laughter of the old men. Maybe he'd get a shave, he thought, rubbing his jaw as a cold wind passed. The sky above was fat and gray with snow clouds.

As Nick looked back at the street, two teenagers in long NFL coats started to follow. They didn't talk and wore sunglasses with tasseled ski hats. Nick kept walking. Buffalo Bill and Jacksonville Jaguar.

"Hey, man," Buffalo Bill yelled.

Nick kept walking.

"You lost?" Jacksonville Jaguar asked.

So helpful. So kind.

There was a vacant lot filled with a jacked-up Oldsmobile and two men working on the engine. Nick felt someone push his back at his shoulder blades. Something snapped and he spun around and knocked the hand away.

"You better watch yo'self," Buffalo Bill said, laughing. He had a rounded face with plump cheeks. "Get your ass back on the El."

Nick stopped walking and sighed.

"Listen, kids, it's cold and I'm tired," Nick said. "If you want to get down, fight a little bit, that's fine. I could show you I have a gun and I'm sure you'd be impressed. Maybe you would even show me yours. But instead of flashing our dicks out on Forty-third Street, why don't you go home to your mamas? I bet they're at home baking you cookies right now."

"Fuck you, man," Buffalo Bill said. His eyes thin slits.

"Fuck me?" Nick asked and gave a palms-up gesture. "All right. Fuck me. Now what? We through?"

Buffalo Bill bit down on his lip and rubbed his fist into his hand. His shoulder dropped and he took a swing at Nick. Nick caught the kid's fist in his hand and twirled his arm behind his back. Jacksonville Jaguar elbowed Nick in the side, as Nick pushed the chubby kid down. Nick caught Jacksonville by the team jacket and tossed him yards away. Still as quick as when he shucked offensive tackles.

He breathed quickly and his knees felt weak. He waited for the kids to pull a blade or a gun from their jackets. This is how it happens. You're walking along one day, minding your own business, and someone wants to scramble your brains. Never comes when you're looking for trouble.

Nick swallowed, opened his coat, and showed his gun.

"Either of you kids have a piece?" he asked, trying to catch his breath. "No? Well, then I guess my dick's bigger. I win . . . now get the fuck out of here."

Nick walked away feeling like a target had been drawn on his back.

24

"**Did you know** the first man in Chicago was a black man?" Stagger Lee asked Peetie Wheatstraw in the far corner booth of the White Castle.

They were the only ones in the top of the L-shaped restaurant and Peetie felt buck naked. He shuffled in his seat and scanned the floor, before looking at the man. Stagger Lee had fourteen small hamburger boxes in front of him as he sucked on a Coke until it was dry. Then he began to crunch on the ice. "Du Sable," he said.

"No, I ain't so much for readin'," Peetie said, trying to keep cool, "Like my daddy said, 'I'll trade street smarts for school smarts any day. Books don't reflect no bullets.' My daddy was a trip, boy. Man sold hats down in New Orleans all from the top of his head. His whole store stacked *on top of his own body, man.* Can you believe that? On a windy day, business was just dead."

Stagger Lee just watched him as he picked up a stray pickle and flopped it on his huge tongue. His hands were folded before him and he wore a spiked black leather dog collar on his neck. There was a gold ring on his left hand that read NEVER.

"Ain't nobody want to see someone bring discomfort to you, man," Peetie said. "I just thought it would be in *both* our best interests to give you a little four-one-one on this man kickin' around. Billy Lyons's name really caught my attention. Hadn't heard that shit in years. Man, ain't that a trip?"

He could tell Stagger Lee was listening.

"He's been to see Jordan and Ruby. Heard he's trying to get her out of jail. Believes she didn't kill Billy. Ain't that some shit? Thought you like to know that." Peetie leaned in close and whispered. "He ask me this mornin' about Franky and Leroy. He knew the whole deal, man."

"You did right, coming to me."

"Me and you stayed in the South Side, brother. Some folks slippin' round the Jacuzzi sippin' champagne while we drinkin' Thunderbird and fartin' in the bathtub. You know what I'm sayin'? I know you don't care about no cops. Don't care about no jail. But I know you care about business. This seemed like business some folks might want to know."

Twon walked in from the side door with his parka over his head like he was an Eskimo. He looked over at Stagger Lee and the big man nodded. Twon walked back outside where it looked like it was going to snow. Real dark clouds. Heard the weather man say they were in for a world of shit tomorrow.

"Who is he?" Stagger Lee asked.

"Said he teaches blues history but don't make no sense . . . studyin' blues."

"Where can I find him?" Stagger Lee asked.

"Listen," Peetie said. "Things ain't been too great with my store, man. I ain't sold but two suits this week and some homeless fucker takin' my shoes. But he only take one of each 'cause he only got one leg. How the hell am I gonna sell one shoe?"

Stagger Lee stood and put on his black leather trench coat and kicked a hamburger box beneath the table with his silver-tipped cowboy boots. His belt buckle was even with Peetie's head.

"I ain't never asked you for nothin', man," Peetie said.

"Where can I find him?" Stagger Lee repeated.

"Man, I don't know."

Stagger Lee wrapped his thick hand around the back of Peetie's skinny neck and asked again. Peetie could barely speak through the pressure.

"I can find out," he gasped. "I can find out."

"You better, nigger," Stagger Lee said. "You try to con me and you'll find yourself full of holes just like your friend Billy Lyons."

Peetie wiggled out of the booth as Annie and Fannie slinked around the corner. The girls stood beside Stagger Lee.

Annie on the right, Fannie on the left.

Annie was all dolled-up today, had on some blue leather outfit with a fur collar.

"Y'all go with Peetie," Stagger Lee said. "You got that, Peetie? You show the girls this man and keep your mouth shut. Got that?"

Peetie looked at the two girls and shook his head. How was he supposed to follow the man with two dumb whores on his ass? White girl had her hair slicked down on her head like a man and the black one wore her hair in pigtails. Looked like some travelin' freak show. This was fucked up even for Stagger Lee.

"Listen, man," Peetie said. "I got this. Everythin' cool. All right? I'll get what you need, man. I don't need 'em going with me."

Stagger Lee played with the huge ring on his hand and his jaw muscles twitched.

"Ooh, well, well . . . ," Peetie said. "That's unless you feel real strong about the thang and we can work it out, man. We can work it out."

Fannie looped her arm in Peetie's and led him to the door. Annie walked behind him and pinched his ass.

"We gonna have a real fine time, Peetie," Annie said.

"A real wang dang doodle," Fannie said, leading him to his car.

25

ABOUT A QUARTER of a mile away from the scuffle, Nick reached another row of storefronts. It had been a couple of years, but he still remembered the corner with the beauty shop and decaying church across the street. On the other side of the barber shop's window, a group of old black men watched Nick's movements.

Place was a classic glass storefront with a fake snow MERRY X-MAS sprayed on the glass and tired, plastic holly lying on a dirty ledge. A broken electric barber pole hung by loose wires below a sign that read UPTOWN.

Theodis must've changed the name, he thought walking inside.

The men's heads turned back toward him. There were three old-time spinning chairs and mirrors illuminated with bright fluorescent lights. A poster of a black woman in a bikini holding a beer bottle was posted over the plywood where the men sat. No trophies or old pics of Theodis. Smelled of chemicals and burnt hair.

"Theodis around?" Nick asked.

One of the men gruffly said "no" and another spit some snuff into a bucket. Not exactly the fun crew he'd met who had shared their memories like Nick was a trusted friend. Nick smiled and walked over to the group. He felt like the party crasher who'd pissed on the wedding cake.

"You know when he's comin' back?" Nick asked.

"Never," said the spitter, as a long strand of brown drool dipped into the bucket. He wiped his chin and leaned back into his chair.

"What happened?"

"Moved," said the old man next to him. This guy had skin the color of ebony and steel-gray hair. He had scissors poking out of six pockets in his white shirt.

"Moved?" Nick asked.

"Mmm hmm," the barber said. "Sold me his business last year and drove back to Georgia."

Nick looked around at the loose group of five men. Didn't recognize a single one. Most of them looked to be in their fifties. Three of them wore checked flannel jackets and baseball hats, permanent looks of disappointment in their eyes.

Nick thanked the barber and walked back out into the cold. A police car flew by with its siren wailing. Icicles hung from a metal overhang. Rap music poured from a tenement building across the street.

He turned around and walked back into the shop. The same man spit. The barber read a paper. The others had cleaned off a moving box and were passing out cards. Nick could hear a loud ticking clock by the cash register.

"Can I get a shave?" Nick asked.

"Sure," the barber said. "My hands don't shake like Theodis." He neatly folded the paper, got out of his seat, and reached into the bottle of blue disinfectant for a long straight razor.

Nick rubbed the overnight growth on his face. Felt like the side of a matchbox. Maybe if he lit a match, they'd think he was tougher and open up a little more. More likely, they didn't give a shit. Nick took off his coat, folded the long part around the gun in the pocket, and laid it on the next chair.

"C'mon, c'mon," the barber said, rubbing the razor on a leather strop that made a popping sound.

"Just got off the train yesterday," Nick said, as the barber covered him with a sheet and snapped it around his neck. He pulled a lever on the side and Nick was thrown back and his feet propped up all at once. A La-Z-Boy with whiplash.

The other men in the barber shop remained silent as the barber covered Nick's face in hot foam. There was a *plink* of the poker chips and the sound of the man spitting. The clock continued to tick. Barber shop symphony. Maybe he could whistle, Nick thought.

"Yeah, I've come all the way from New Orleans looking for Theodis," Nick said.

"You must feel like a real ass right now," the barber said. "Phone call only costs a quarter."

Nick gave a short laugh and stopped.

"Actually, I wanted to find Theodis because I'm really looking for another friend and I thought he could help me. Knew a bunch of folks 'round here."

Nick kept one eye open to watch his reaction. The barber intently scraped his cheeks. The dull razor pulled his beard, making his eyes water.

"Any of y'all know Jimmy Scott?" Nick asked.

The barber continued to scrape.

"Nope," the barber said.

"Why'd Theodis leave?"

"Why do they all leave?" the barber asked. "It look like Disney World? He just got tired of the muggin' and the killin'."

"Thought he loved Chicago."

"We all did. *Once.*"

The barber had a sing-song quality to his voice as he worked. His voice almost hummed with resonance. If he started waving a watch in front of his eyes, Nick could go to sleep.

"You work for the government?" the barber asked.

"Do I look like I work for the government?"

"No, but ain't a lot of white people come around askin' questions."

The barber ran the blade under a faucet. He eyed Nick as he wiped the blade and started back to work. Nick could see the other men, all old and tired, studying his reflection.

"Folks call my friend Dirty Jimmy. You ever heard of anyone by that name? Used to be a musician. I think he drives a cab now."

The barber's face didn't show a thing as he moved to Nick's chin. The barber scraped away the stubbled gray hair that made Nick look like a stray dog. The hair on the sides of his head was almost completely gray now. Approaching forty real fast, felt like he was sixty.

"Y'all ever hear of him?" Nick asked again a little louder. He tried to be polite and keep his voice conversational.

"Nope," said the spitter.

Nick heard the squeak of a man pushing a chair away. It was one of the poker players. He had a baseball cap pulled low over his deep black face. The man coughed and walked into a back bathroom.

The barber lifted up Nick's nose and scraped away the hair above his lip. He cleaned the blade again and started on Nick's neck. The blade was hot from the steaming water as it scraped away around his throat. Maybe he should shut up until the man was finished.

"Men must really trust you around here," Nick said.

The barber pulled out a hot towel with tongs, held it over the sink.

"You like it hot?" the barber asked.

"Medium broil."

No one laughed and the barber slipped the towel on his face. It felt great. He could feel the travel sooth away. In the dark, with the towel over his face, Nick heard the shuffling and wheezing of the men around him. Somebody whispered, "Don't make no difference."

The barber removed the towel and jerked the chair straight. Nick stretched his jaw and ran his hand over his smooth face. The poker player had walked back into the room. He was standing, watching Nick's eyes in the mirror.

"Fine shave. How much I owe you?"

"Two-fifty," the barber said, sticking his thumbs under his belt.

Nick stood, paid him five bucks, and threaded his arms into

his coat. He looked at the row of old men. Not a single one looked him in the eye.

"I'll give fifty bucks to anyone who knows how to find Jimmy Scott," Nick said.

No one reacted.

Nick patted his coat pocket for his gloves and gun and walked back out of the shop. The late afternoon gray was beginning to fall into the night. Beaten cars rambled by on Forty-third Street. A prostitute wobbled down by the sidewalk and stuck her finger into her mouth. Nick looked down the endless urban row of crumbling storefronts and sighed. A crooked Christmas tree's lights blinked from a window.

Long walk back to the El. Maybe he shouldn't have turned the car back in at the hotel. He lit a cigarette and watched the tip burn as he walked toward the platform.

Someone tapped him on the shoulder as he felt for his gun.

"That money still good?" asked the poker player with the dark face. "Could use me some backup for the hand I just lost."

"Jimmy Scott?"

"I know where he's at."

"You fucking with me?"

Nick looked into the man's wind-burned eyes. He didn't blink or look away.

"Nah, man. I known Jimmy for thirty years."

"Heard he was dead."

"You heard wrong. Give me a hundred and I'll give you an address. Hell, he's sittin' there right now waitin' for you."

"Some friend."

"Last time I seen him, he clogged up my toilet. Ain't paid me yet."

"I'll give you fifty," Nick said flatly.

"Ninety."

"Fifty."

"Eighty."

"Fifty," Nick said, looking down the road and wondering if he should just toss his money to the wind. Instead, he counted the cash into the man's hand.

"You got yourself one broke-down old man, mister."

"You drive a hard bargain," Nick said.

The old man gave him the address before he walked back inside.

26

THE HOTEL SEEMED like a great place to check in after you'd lost your way in life. The lobby resonated with the same emotions as old folks homes, prisons, and insane asylums—complete abandonment of hope. Reminded Nick of the Riverside Hotel in Clarksdale where many great blues singers had spent their final hours. The place where Bessie Smith had died when it was a black hospital in the thirties. You could almost smell the death in its walls. In the lobby's dim light, a wrinkled black woman sat at a cracked rolltop desk. She had a bag of Chee·tos before her as she watched a tiny black-and-white TV with a comatose indifference. Her fingernails were dirty and her thumb was covered with a Band-Aid.

"Jimmy Scott?" Nick asked, placing his elbow on the Formica counter.

The woman looked over at him like a lizard and returned her eyes to the TV. She mumbled something that could have been Chinese, her eyes glued to the television.

"Does he live here?"

"Huh?"

"Is Jimmy in?"

"Three-oh-nine," she said in a breath laced with the smell of the Chee·tos and cigarettes.

He smiled. Maybe he'd spent that money on the right man after all.

Nick followed a dark hallway to a caged elevator littered with crushed beer cans and cigarette butts. He could hear someone playing an old hillbilly record and coughing in spasms as he pulled the cage closed and pressed the third floor. The old contraption shook upward with the floors rolling past. It was like an ascension into purgatory.

The elevator stopped with all the ease of a truck into a brick wall. Nick caught his balance and rolled back the gate.

Down the hall, he knocked on the wood door, thick with cracks that broke around the handle. The knob was glass and the lock was rusted. Nick smelled burning toast inside as he removed his watch cap.

He stomped the snow from his boots and the bottom of his jeans.

Finally, a gnomelike black man with jug ears opened the door and walked back into the room. He left the door ajar and Nick followed. The man hovered over a hotplate and turned over a piece of bread with a pen.

"Mr. Scott?" Nick asked.

"Jimmy's fine."

"Came a long way to find you, sir."

"You want some grilled cheese?" he asked, flipping his tongue around an upper row of dentures. His face bristled with white stubble. "Got that good government cheese."

"No thanks," Nick said. "Came here to talk to you about King Snake Records."

Jimmy continued to cook, his eyes intent on the work.

"Am I imposing?"

Jimmy looked over his room, bare except for a metal bed, a suitcase, and the hotplate. He shook his head and rolled his eyes. "Oh, I guess I'll have to postpone my dinner with Mayor Daley."

"Not going so good?"

"Been better," he said.

Nick introduced himself and shook the old man's hand. He told him what he did and what he wanted. Jimmy nodded as if it was something he was used to by now.

"Some English guys came over a few years ago asking me all kinds of questions too. Treated me like I was some kind of royalty. They took a couple of pictures and bought my record collection 'fore leaving me with a bottle a whiskey and one of them *Playboy* magazines."

Nick pulled out the bottle of Jack Daniel's he bought at the corner store and smiled.

"God bless your white ass," Jimmy said.

Nick offered him a cigarette and he accepted. Outside, the El train rattled by, shaking the wooden floor where they sat. But Jimmy was unaffected as he poured two generous measures of aged whiskey into plastic cups decorated with superheroes. The snow melted on the top of Nick's work boots.

"You saw the fight with Ruby?"

"Hold on," Jimmy said, turning up the cup and draining the whiskey. He put a hand to his head like he was having a migraine and then took a long drag of the cigarette. He smiled and rocked back into a ladder back chair with a view of a tenement building behind him.

The old building had two chimneys pumping long, thin lines of smoke. El train tracks twisted away before reaching the building's third floor.

Jimmy's eyes narrowed. "Yeah, I saw it. I was there as a favor to Elmore King. Playin' backup. We were recordin' that night but she was mighty drunk and mighty mad 'fore we even started."

"That was King's session?"

"Oh yeah, man. That was King. Let's see," Jimmy said, looking up at the ceiling and patting his knee with his hands. "Yeah, guess that'd be about fifty-nine, 'cause I know Billy weren't with us in sixty. Yeah, 'round then. Billy was broke as hell."

"I thought Lyons was rich."

"Sometimes. But that man gambled away every cent, a real crap-shootin' fool. Not just dice, man, but with bars that didn't draw no crowd. Or sinkin' a lot into the blues business. He lost some kind of money on King Snake. His time runnin' whores and numbers on the South Side 'bout gone."

"You think Ruby killed him?"

"Ain't for me to decide." He shrugged his shoulders. "That's between her and God."

"Could it have been the gambling? Someone he owed money?"

Jimmy leaned forward in his chair and reached for the bottle.

"Could be," Jimmy said. "That man owed everybody he knew and some he didn't. You don't pay yore debts to some folks and they gonna get yore ass. Yeah, I 'spect so. All I say in that court-room is I saw them fightin'."

"Who did he owe money to?"

"Man, I cain't remember. Here and there. You know . . . just some men. Let's see, there was this guy he hang with name Fat Tony. Man, he so fat they had to special make him these ugly pin-striped suits. He was some kind of criminal. I seen him and Billy in business."

"What happened to Fat Tony."

"Died in sixty I think. Got kilt while holdin' up a bank. Dumbass too fat and slow to run away."

"Anybody else?"

"Not that I recall. Nope."

"So, how'd you meet Billy?" Nick asked.

"Jewtown. I'd just moved from Biloxi and was doin' some record work. Had me a part-time job at a paper factory. But I worked cheap and I was good. That's what Billy wanted."

Nick hadn't heard Maxwell Street called Jewtown in a while. Years ago, it was a place where Jewish merchants set up shop. Now, it was mainly blacks and Hispanics selling everything from food to jewelry off Roosevelt.

"Ruby and I used to play there together."

"She didn't tell me that."

"Shit, I'm the one got her off the streets."

Jimmy stretched his legs before him. One tattered sock was red and the other bright green. The hair on his head looked like the soft dust on a bookshelf. He poured Nick another drink and what looked like a triple for himself.

"Why you care about Billy Lyons?" Jimmy asked.

"Some say Ruby Walker is innocent."

"Ruby? Man, I don't know if I'd trust that woman."

"But you said she *could be* innocent."

"Could be. I'm just sayin' I don't trust her."

"Why not?" Nick asked. He watched Jimmy squirm in his chair and try to evade eye contact. The man was holding back, but Nick knew pushing him would just make him more suspicious.

"Ruby changed after she got known, man," Jimmy said. "I took care of that woman for a long time. She lived on the street like some kind of animal. Didn't need to give her a place but I did. Shared my bucket with her but she never shared her bucket with me."

"Who else was around that night? Who was recording the night Billy died?"

"Same ole, same ole. King. Moses Jordan. All them dudes."

"Wait, I thought Jordan had left about a year before?"

"No, he was still around. He'd switch back from Diamond to King Snake all the time. Just like a bitch, cain't make up his mind. All the rest of 'em dead 'cept Moses Jordan and King and me. Dawkins dead. Leroy Williams dead."

"Dawkins and Williams were murdered," Nick said. "You know anything about that?"

Jimmy took another sip.

"Yeah, I heard those stories. Some folks say it was Billy come back from the dead to take their ass out. Ain't nothin' but ghost stories. Hey man, you got another one of them cigarettes?"

Nick handed him a Marlboro.

"Thanks. *Mmmm hmm.* Some folks even say Billy's soul still burns out on the lake. They say you can go out to Navy Pier and you'll see him ridin' them cold waves. That old green glow." Jimmy shook his head. "I don't believe it. Billy's dead and so are them other folks. Don't let no one fool you with stories about the King Snake curse and all that shit."

"You think their deaths are connected with Billy's?"

"Not unless Ruby escaped."

"What time you guys finish up that night?" Nick asked.

" 'Bout ten. Hot as shit. Man, I'd been blowin' so hard all day my mouth felt like cotton. My lips and tongue all fuzzy. But we cut some good blues, man. King just hittin' his stride with that rock sound. Real mean guitar. Billy kept turning me down, said harp didn't mix. Me and Elmore knew that was a bunch of shit. But I got paid the same, left, and went down to get some drinks at the Palm. . . . Ruby was there."

"How late?"

" 'Bout midnight I guess. I don't remember a lot. We was all drunk. Guess she went back and killed him that night."

"You remember her friend Florida?"

"Shit yeah, man. Good ole gal. Florida could cut up. Funny gal, drove Ruby around wearin' one of them . . . what do you call 'em?"

Nick shrugged.

"French name for a driver?"

"Chauffeur."

"Yeah, she'd just cut up wearin' one of them sho-*fer* hats. Good ole gal."

"You know what happened to her after Billy died."

"Naw, man, you know I was lookin' for her too. But I think she just got out of town. She was real tight with Billy and Ruby. Tore her up pretty good."

"You remember her last name."

"*Mmmm.* Tho-mas. I think. Yeah, that's it. Florida Thomas."

"You know what time Ruby left the Palm?"

Jimmy shook his head. "Damn, I was fucked up as a goat myself."

"Was she upset?"

"Oh yeah, she was cussin' all about Billy . . . but seemed just like man trouble to me. Not killin' trouble."

He looked over at a blank wall and took another drink. Nick handed him one more cigarette and they both waited for a while in silence.

"Man, I used to travel all 'round this country," Jimmy said. "When I was just out the service, I'd hop these big ole freight cars out of town and jump off when I got tired. I'd make a little money. Lose a little money. Sometimes hungry." He shrugged with his palms up. "Sometimes broke. Didn't matter, always had a ride. Man, I miss those old trains. Make me feel strong every time I hear one pass. That whistle blowin' in the night . . . *shiiit.*"

Nick stayed until he couldn't see the El tracks or the blackened tenement building. The old El rattled past every fifteen minutes in the darkness until Jimmy became incoherent. He'd told Nick about the ratty garage they'd converted into a recording studio and the way Lyons would deliver most of the records himself in an old mail truck he'd won from a butcher off Maxwell Street. He told a great story about Lyons tapping him on the shoulder for the rhythm he wanted and another gem about Lyons keeping a stray crow in his office that ate out of his hands.

Jimmy played a few licks on his harp and Nick repeated them back with the Hohner he always carried with him. The playing seemed to sooth the old man. His licks were still razor sharp.

"Goddamn that was a sad story about Billy," Jimmy said as a light snow began to coat the base of the thick windowpane.

"So what do you think happened to Dawkins and Williams?"

"Bad luck," Jimmy said. "I don't know *shit.* Why don't you ask Leroy's son . . . he runnin' some kind of junk store a few blocks from here. Remind me of that cat Fred Sanford livin' with all that shit 'round him."

"Where can I find him?"

Jimmy told him, speaking his final words for the night. He leaned far to the right and his eyelids half-closed. He rolled straight back in the chair. His eyes got big and he pointed his finger at Nick's chest like he was about to make a grand point. Then he started rolling with cackling laughter.

The old man rolled out of the chair and fell to the floor. Deep snores came from his nose.

Nick finished his drink and looked at the apartment. A bed with a dirty mattress, a piece of luggage in the corner filled with crumpled clothes next to a folding card table. No phone. No room service. Nothing to show for years of work and years of honing their art. The end for so many musicians. Musicians who once had made enough to eat from day to day, but when they got too old to perform, they were discarded like useless tools. Many get bitter. Most die in obscurity, too proud to ask for help.

Nick scooped Jimmy in his arms and helped him off the floor. He was light, just thin flesh and brittle bones. He placed him on the bed and pulled a musty blanket over his withered body. The El rattled by again as Nick turned off the light by the door.

He left Jimmy in the darkness on a forgotten shelf.

27

ANNIE WAITED OUTSIDE the old hotel in the passenger seat of
Peetie's candy apple red Volkswagen Beetle. The car had one of
those after-market hoods made to resemble a Rolls-Royce—like
anyone would be confused with this piece of shit—and shiny
gold hubcaps. She laughed as she lit up a joint and stared at the
winged ornament. Fannie was asleep in the small backseat and
Peetie was humming a song to himself like a moron.

That Travers guy had been in there more than an hour.

She took a long draw on the joint and stared down the empty
row of warehouses and burning streetlamps then back to the latest copy of *Betty and Veronica Digest*. It was kind of a collection
of their greatest adventures. This one had Mr. Lodge trying to
fake out Veronica, who was running up his credit card bills. He
told her to spend whatever she liked. The punch line in the last
box was that Veronica was so confused she had to go shopping.
Annie made a cough and gagging noise as Veronica, with her
blue-black hair, smiled, clutching a bunch of shopping bags.

"That him?" Fannie said in a groggy voice from the backseat.

"That's him," Peetie said. "Had him sit down with me yesterday over some greens and talk to me about the old days and
askin' all kind of questions about when I was makin' records and
Billy Lyons and New Orleans. I tell you—"

"How do I turn off this little turd?" Annie asked.

"Annie," Fannie said.

"I'm serious. I'm tired of this. It's like diarrhea of the mouth. Shit, man, shut up."

"Just tryin' to help you girls out. Me and Stagger Lee go back a long ways."

"Yeah. He said you were real tight. Said, 'If Peetie gets on your nerves, why don't you cut him up and throw him into the river.'"

Annie tongued the joint and scratched her nose as the big white man kept walking down the street. He was about six foot three and over two hundred pounds.

"Y'all like working for Stagger Lee?" Peetie asked. "Don't mean to imply nothin'. Just wonderin' if you like your work."

"Yeah," Annie said. "It's kind of like working at Disneyland. He loves us."

"Once again, don't mean to be sayin' nothin' improper 'bout my dear friend Mr. Stagger Lee. It's just you two ladies are just so fine. Beautiful women down to your toes. Just made me kind of curious. Like you can't find another line of work?"

"Fannie? You passed the bar exam lately?"

"Not lately, girlfriend. Still need to take my GED first then to med school."

"Oh, that's right. I forget. You're going to be a cootie doctor."

"Y'all afraid to leave him?"

Annie stared into the darkness and said: "You don't leave Stagger Lee."

"So what'd he tell you ladies to do? Kill the white man and that's it?"

"Duh—what else is there?"

Peetie grinned over at Annie and then looked back and tipped his hat to Fannie. "So much more, ladies. So much more. You got to think about your future."

"Sure, Peetie with you on our side, we can't lose," she said, rolling her eyes.

"*Shh, shh,*" Peetie said. "Don't look at him. Scoot down. Scoot down."

The man disappeared around the next street corner. Peetie cranked his ignition but the car wouldn't turn over. He cranked the key again. Ice clung to the still windshield wipers.

"You want us to get out and push?" Annie asked.

"Hold up. Hold up. She may be old but she got some fire down below."

The engine sputtered, caught, and Peetie turned into traffic following Travers. It was gonna be a long night. Annie straightened up in her seat and felt inside her old jacket—the one they'd bought today that looked like Daniel Boone with leather fringe— and ran her finger over Willie's blade.

"Knew he'd come here," Peetie said with a big shit-eating grin on his face.

"Think you can handle him?" Annie asked, stubbing the joint onto the heel of her platform shoe.

"Ain't a man alive could stay away from my trap," Fannie said. "All they got to do is smell me. They get a little whiff of this chocolate pie, how sweet it gonna taste, and *mmm-mmm*, they are gone."

28

NICK HATED TO do it. Been too long to pick up the phone and act like an old friend just blew into Chi-town. But there he was in the back of a South Side liquor store cradling a pay phone in his hand. He'd already paid for the six-pack of Colt 45 at his feet and another bottle of Jack Daniel's. Something had called him back here, made him stick the quarter into the slot, and dial the *Chicago Tribune*'s number. He even heard his own voice ask the news desk for Kate Archer. But she wasn't there. He got an answering machine and was damned glad of it. What came next was something out of Travers' jackass files.

"Kate?" Nick said, as if he could have gotten the wrong person. "I'm in Chicago. And could really use a little help. Need anything you guys have on a September fifty-nine murder of a man named Billy Lyons or the woman accused, named Ruby Walker . . . I'm staying at the Palmer House. Thanks."

Jesus. He sounded like an overanxious dork. He could have gone to the Washington Library and looked up the clips himself. He knew it. She knew it. Man, he came off like a freakin' idiot.

He grabbed his paper sack and walked back outside and down the block to the place Jimmy said Leroy Williams's son lived. The rundown house was surrounded by a chain-link fence with floodlights illuminating rusting metal chairs, floor lamps, patio sets, old metal beds, toppled dressers, and a stringless golden harp. Guess this is the place where old furniture came to die.

A pit bull with a mangy coat and yellow teeth gave a low growl as Nick shook the gate trying to attract whoever was in the house. He called out Williams's name a couple times as the dog acted like she was about to have a conniption or chomp through the metal.

"Hold on, Fluffy," Nick said to the dog.

A light switched on the porch and a man in pajama bottoms and no shirt popped out of the door. His gut hung over his waistband and a long cigarette lay low in his mouth. He had on a pair of gold round glasses, taped at the corners, and when he spoke his words came in clouds.

"What the fuck you doin', man?"

"Merry Christmas," Nick said.

"Fuck off."

"Happy New Year?"

The man glared at Nick as the dog tried some type of Olympic leap over the fence but fell onto her back. Snow covered the furniture in rounded shapes in the yellow light.

"You Mr. Williams?"

"Fuck off."

"Listen, man, I've come to talk to you about your father."

"My daddy's dead. You dumb-ass prick."

"Season's greetings," Nick yelled. "Listen, I know that . . . I want to talk to you about why."

Williams walked back into the house shaking his head. The lights fell across the junkyard, and Nick bent down to pick up his booze for an exciting night at the Palmer House. More drinking. Cable. Then the lights came back on. Twice as bright, in twice as many places.

Williams walked back to the front porch of the run-down two-story, this time in a ragged coat, and called the dog back inside.

"Lucifer! Get yo' butt back in here."

The dog yelped and turned back to the warm home. Williams ambled down the steps and weaved through the piles of garbage. He moved like there was a load in his pants. Back clenched, shoulders reared back.

Nick decided not to ask if it was true.

"What, you sellin', somethin' in the bag?" Williams asked.

"Just some booze for the night. You want a drink?"

"I don't drink." He looked through the diamonds in the fence. His face was round and weathered and wore an expression like he'd been shit on his whole life and never expected anything different.

"I know your father was murdered," Nick said, grasping his fingers through the fence. "I'm trying to make some sense of it."

"Ain't no sense to it," he said, spitting on the ground.

"Let me in and we'll talk about it."

"Fuck you," Williams said and turned to walk back inside his warm home.

"Give me five minutes," Nick said. "Your father was a great man. Heard he was one of the greatest blues piano men ever."

Williams turned back as his dog opened the loose door with her snout and trotted down to her master. She growled at the man's side until Williams grasped her by the spiked collar. He smiled.

"Was he that good?"

■

Nick sat in a ragged chair as Williams walked over and turned down the sound on a black-and-white television. The man sat back into a couch and reached into Nick's sack for a cold Colt and settled into his seat.

"Thought you didn't drink?" Nick asked.

"You want to leave, fuckhead?"

"No . . . I'm having too a good a time making friends."

Williams scowled and popped the top of the can. He drank a long sip then tilted the can for Lucifer. The dog licked the rim and then kissed her owner's face.

"Yes, yes, yes, baby. Yes, my little, little Lucy."

Nick raised his eyebrows. "Mr. Williams . . . What do you know about your father's death?"

"Nobody ever did nothin' about it."

"I think an innocent woman was set up by the same people who killed your father."

He scowled again and rubbed the wrinkles on the back of the dog's neck. The dog made a burping sound and dropped to her stomach, her head in Williams's lap. The man hit a button on an old coffee table and the sound came back on the television. Pro wrestling.

"Aw shit!" he shouted, watching two huge men collide with the mat.

Nick watched his face. It was as if no one was there, as if their conversation had never occurred. This was bullshit. Nick looked at his watch and groaned. He needed a hot shower, a hot meal, and some sleep.

"Goodnight," Nick said.

The man continued to stare at the television.

The room smelled like the inside of a military footlocker. Old-fashioned fat Christmas lights hung in the window by a metal walker and a box of dozens of canes.

As he hit the door, Nick glanced back. The man looked at him.

"Stagger Lee," Williams said softly.

"What?"

"Stagger Lee killed my father," he said, scratching the dog's stomach. "That's what my mama said before she passed on a few years back."

"Like the man in the song?"

"I guess . . . some folks say he ain't even real. But I heard about this man. They say he was the first to bring crack into Robert Taylor and Cabrini-Green. But shit, I don't know. I heard he was killed in some gang fightin' a few years back."

"You know why?"

"My daddy wasn't a good man. Never cared for us. Beat my mama. Let's just say, I wish I gave a shit."

29

FRIDAY NIGHT IN Chicago and Nick felt like pulling the hotel room's curtains shut, finding a western on TV, and washing down some warm Jack with the Colt 45. When you retrace the steps of the dead, you begin to learn life doesn't mean shit. You may work your ass off, be revered in your own time, but like Sam Chatmon sang, "We all go back to mother earth." These men weren't just footnotes in a history book. They laughed, drank, loved women, felt the blues, and all died in a horrific way. He could see their cold faces dried with blood and flashes of gaping wounds in his mind. *Forty years ago.*

He took a hot shower with the water slowly turning his blood back to a normal temperature. The water felt like small needles on his skin and his worn shoulders, lined with thick, diagonal scars. A little reminder of his football days, a probing scope, and a hundred dislocations. Maybe he was getting soft. Twelve years ago, he played the Bears in Soldier Field in a short-sleeve jersey. He could still feel the cold, brittle shock in his bones with each jarring tackle. But he wasn't thinking too much then: The pain in his shoulders was constant, his drinking was out of control, and he was engaged to a woman who had the depth of a pancake.

Her name was Lisa. Green eyes, blonde hair, and a simply perfect body. Woman never worked out, ate ice cream like it was air, but retained this tiny waist with perfect hips and breasts that would make Hugh Hefner's jaw drop. She couldn't walk in a room without every single man almost breaking his neck. She loved the attention and seemed to be plugged into every member of New Orleans' society.

Hell, the woman couldn't go take a dump somewhere without having to hug some person she'd met before. Nick felt like a damned trophy. The football player. The one who got her good seats to the home games and into all the closed parties.

But she seemed to have a good heart. Lisa was always there waiting at the New Orleans airport with players' wives and fans when he got off of the plane. She'd have on tight jeans tucked into cowboy boots with a low-cut T-shirt. Always with a brown paper sack holding a muffuletta and a six-pack of Dixie. He just didn't want to see the flaws.

They didn't start to crack wide open until he was kicked out of the league. Those were the days when his agent refused to answer calls, his investment broker dropped him as a client, and he had lost most of his savings.

Lisa had become a stranger to the townhome where they lived near Lake Pontchartrain. She said she needed space. She'd come in drunk or stoned and fall facefirst into bed. She would say she went out dancing or had dinner with friends. But New Orleans is a small town. Rumors start. Messages trickled back from third parties. And then one day, about three months after *the game*, she disappeared.

Most of his friends, his money, and his pride went with her. He sold off the townhome, paid his bills, and moved into the warehouse. It seemed for a while his whole world was swirling in a toilet. His drinking spiraled into a daily collection of Jack Daniel's on the side of Dixie. He lost about sixty pounds.

Mixed with the whiskey and self-pity came the blues. He absolutely enveloped himself in the culture. He drank with the players, practiced harp with JoJo until his lips bled, and even worked with some street players in the French Market.

The blues helped him put everything back together. He got his master's and went after his doctorate. The layers of age fell from his warehouse as he worked on her piece by piece. And during that time, he also met Kate. Together they made the finishing touches on the warehouse. Paint splattered in her hair and a smile plastered on her face.

It was as if he was rebuilding himself.

■

Downstairs was civility.

Couples huddled over low, round tables at a dimly lit U-shaped bar. Framed pictures of famous Chicago buildings hung on the walls. The whole room was made in dark woods and greens. Nick ordered a blessed Budweiser and eavesdropped. No shame in it. Just made waiting so much more fun.

A man had just neutered his cat. A woman had just bought a Victoria's Secret outfit to please her husband, and some guy was obsessed over his scratched Mercedes. Nick was starting to enjoy the unknown company and the gentle burn of the candles on the bar when someone sat in a chair beside him.

"I was saving that for somebody," he said, staring straight ahead. Little lights winked around the cash register.

"Someone I know?" the woman asked. He could feel his pulse quicken. Made him feel silly and sophomoric. His heart lodged somewhere in his throat.

"You used to know her," he said, still looking straight ahead.

Kate settled into the seat next to him and plunked down a manilla envelope onto the bar. She ordered a Plymouth gin on the rocks.

"So, how you been, Travers? Look about the same. A little more gray in your hair."

"Feel a little more gray," he said, smiling a crooked grin.

Kate pulled a comma of dark brown, almost black hair from her eyes and tucked it behind her ear. Lines of character had grown around her mouth and brown eyes. She pulled a smile to the corner of her mouth. Thick, full lips.

She had on a long gray sweater with a scooped V-neck and blue jeans frayed at the bottom. Somehow she made tan work boots look feminine. She had a thin athletic frame and delicate hands with short nails. Nick remembered her body underneath the clothes. Dark skin corded with muscle.

"Nick Travers. Haven't heard from the man in years and he calls me like a teenager looking for a date."

"I didn't know if you'd want to talk."

"No shit," she said, her face unconcerned. "Found some short clips on that Lyons guy. You can buy me dinner."

"Really?"

"You look surprised," she said, with a grin. Really enjoying watching him squirm.

"It's just . . ."

"It's just what, Travers?" she said as she raised an eyebrow. "You think I'm still pissed off about that bimbo you nailed in our warehouse? Screw it. I really don't give a shit anymore."

Kate took a long pull of the gin.

"You've gotten mean, woman," Nick said.

"Bet your ass," she said and nodded.

Nick drained the beer and watched her eyes. She closed her open-mouth smile and pulled the hair from her face again. It was as if time had fallen away. As if the spaces between their first meeting and today were only minutes apart.

Kate continued to stare, her arms folded over the bar, before she let out a long breath of air.

"Now, how about that dinner?" she asked. "I'm feeling Mexican."

30

WILLIAMS TURNED OFF the pro wrestling and walked back in his kitchen for a beer for him and Lucifer. His back ached from repainting those iron beds all day and he needed a little sweetness to take the pain away. Lucy trotted by his side as he found his last can of Eight Ball and cracked open the top. She whined by his side as he polished off the foam and turned up the can in the dog's slobbering black lips.

"Sweet baby," Williams said. "Sweet baby."

Man, he loved that dog. Ever since his wife had been eaten up by cancer two Christmases back, Lucy had been some kind of company. At first, he had made her sleep outside in a corral he'd made from old porch chairs and dressers. But one night, after the first frost, he'd walked outside and seen her fat nose all filled with snot and her sneezin' up a storm. He never knew a pit bull could catch a cold but his little baby was so sick. He brought her in and made her some hot milk and she'd slept in his bed ever since.

Williams hobbled back in the room as WGN rattled off the nightly news about some pawn shop owner being shot in the head down by Robert Taylor. Shit, what does a man expect. He wouldn't even roll down his car window in those parts. Live in the jungle, you better expect the lions to come after your ass. He took another sip and looked into his junk lot filled with mounds of snow. His floodlight rattled off the telephone pole as he took a sip, sighed, and scratched Lucy's ears.

Something crashed in his backyard.

He put the beer on the table as Lucy stood at attention, her ears perked, and sounded off some deep-down growls.

"Cool down, baby."

Williams walked over to the window and searched his junk lot. Fuckin' kids trying to steal some shit again. He trotted back to his kitchen and pulled out his shotgun, cracked it in half looking for shells, and popped it back together.

They'd get a dose of buckshot for disturbin' his night.

Lucy was wailing and scratching at the kitchen door. He opened the door and she ran into the lot. He followed with his shotgun aimed from his right eye.

He heard Lucy growling, metal clattering over in piles, and then some scuffling from a mountain of broken wooden chairs and tables. Man, she had someone good. He heard a man grunt real loud.

Williams laughed as he followed the scuffle to the other side of the mountain of junk. But when he looked down, he felt a brittle sadness through his body. He dropped to his knees and screamed. Never screamed before in his life, didn't even know a man was capable of it.

Little Lucy's head was twisted around facing her tail. Blood poured from her mouth with gaping holes all through her pink stomach. Her backside flopped around for a moment as he cradled her warm body in his hands and sobbed. She looked up into his face with her yellow eyes and made a puffing sound. He kissed her nose and rocked her as her body went limp.

He cried and cried until he heard another crash from a row of junk about ten feet away. With great care, he laid sweet Lucy on the cold, muddy ground and picked up his shotgun. This was it. He always knew he would kill somebody and tonight was it. Didn't care if they were ten years old, they were dead.

"Come out, you motherfuckers!"

He yelled again as something clacked again behind him.

He swung the gun toward the sound.

Nothing.

His breath rattled around in his head as he ground his teeth. The gun shook in his hand. He could feel the cold locking his fingers to the trigger of the gun.

"You motherfuckers!" he yelled again.

Then a mammoth hand covered his face as the shotgun was ripped from his hand. He felt his hand being held against a man's chest and heard the man's hot breath on the side of his face. He felt the cold end of his shotgun inside of his mouth as his legs gave out. A huge black man wrapped Williams's hand inside his own gun and as much as he tried he couldn't keep his own fingers off the trigger. And for a brief moment, Williams understood his life was over.

"Your old man didn't fight so much," the huge man said.

Williams tried to yell and bring an understanding to a moment that exploded into red and white and a shock of cold, black water he thought he could feel sweep over his body.

31

THE FRONTERA GRILL was a fancy Mexican restaurant on Clark Street that didn't take reservations and made tacos with catfish and enchiladas with free-range chicken. Not exactly Nick's kind of place. But Kate was glad to see him out of his element. Travers was always more comfortable in a Mississippi barbecue joint or a New Orleans greasy spoon than anywhere remotely gourmet. She watched him snake through the crowd to the bar and order her a margarita with plenty of salt. Red chili pepper lights blinked over the bar crowded with men in Brooks Brothers and women in Banana Republic.

Nick had on a decade-old blue flannel shirt and jeans with battered Tony Lamas. Kate laughed as she found a cove by the hostess and waited. Travers always stuck with the basics. Wore what felt good. Ate when he was hungry and drank when thirsty.

If only she could look at life so simply.

Tonight she was just about to hit deadline, trying to finish a story on a double homicide, when she remembered to check her messages. She was used to all kind of calls at the *Tribune*—irate sources, annoying flaks, and even holiday greetings from Jesus. But this was something way strange. *Nick Travers bustling by the Magnificent Mile for Christmas*. She still couldn't believe it. How long had it been?

After she filed her story, pulled and copied the clips on Lyons, she knew she had to go to the Palmer House. There was no question where she would find him. Of course, she knew it was a stupid mistake. But hey, it's Christmas. Or at least that's what she told herself.

She took a deep breath and watched him smile over at her. Damn guy stood out. Not 'cause he was the best-looking guy in the place—because he wasn't. It was more of his worn quality. Nick was like your favorite pair of pajamas. Warm green eyes and a husky voice. Always a little off balance and awkward. She bet by the end of the night he'd have something spilled on his shirt.

Nick handed her the margarita. No salt.

"A fifty-nine murder?" she asked, arching her eyebrow.

"There's a woman . . ."

"There's always a woman," Kate said, getting in a little jab. Felt good.

"There *is* a woman in jail," Nick said. "Brilliant singer. I've been hounding her for the last year to agree to do an interview. Finally, she agreed."

"Someone I know?"

"Ruby Walker. Sang under the name the Sweet Black Angel."

"*Ah-hah.* Woman charged with killing Lyons." Kate sipped her margarita.

Nick smiled. *Damn, why couldn't she stay mad at him? The woman was in her bed. He'd taken everything they built and torn it down just for one night.*

"She was convicted in sixty," Nick said, taking a swig of Dos Equis. "I pulled the court records and interviewed her yesterday. Met with some of her friends."

"Let me guess, she's innocent, right?"

"Something like that."

"I'm not making fun of you. You know, Illinois has a shit record with murder convictions? Eleven people in the last twelve years have been released from death row."

"She's not on death row," Nick said. "She's just forgotten."

A hostess led them over to a table by the window and Nick

ordered a couple more drinks and some chips. The margaritas were doing wonders for her stress. She remembered that time they were in Austin, she'd practically lived on them. Reminded her of Sixth Street and mariachi bands. The salsa was thick and chunky and filled with all kinds of wild colors.

"Clips were pretty thin," she said, passing over copies. She had handwritten dates on the two stories. "Pretty much briefs saying what had happened. Hate to say it, but we're talking the fifties. And she was black."

Nick nodded, studying the clips. Nothing.

"How far did the lawyer go with appeals?"

"Ruby had a little problem with a guard and she had a public defender who makes Bud look like Atticus Finch."

"Bud *is* Atticus Finch."

"How is the Bud man?"

"Lickin' his butt. Drinkin' out of toilet bowls. You know, all those tricks he learned by watching you."

"I was never that flexible."

"And if you were?"

"The world would be a better place." Nick leaned forward and tucked his arms in front of him. His shirt was rolled to the elbows.

"I have some really good sources. Enough to head home. You know, my job's not to be her detective, only to write about her life. . . ." Nick shook his head. "But I gave her my word I'd look into it. And the more I find out, the more I believe she was set up. Two men who were in her band were killed right after she was sent to jail."

"Her lawyer and the detective mentioned in the stories are dead too. Found their obits. Sorry."

Just like Nick to go on some half-cocked outing without a clue to help an old singer. She remembered one Sunday during Jazz Fest finding about a dozen musicians crashed in the warehouse waiting for Nick to make pancakes.

"What does she say?"

"She thinks Billy Lyons was killed in some kid of turf war. Apparently he used to run hookers and numbers."

"What about the court file?"

"They found bloody sheets in her bed and a murder weapon."

"What part do you doubt?"

"A lot of things don't make sense," Nick said. "Lyons was stabbed seventy-seven times and shot once. The detective said he was killed on the second floor of an apartment and the body was moved and dropped into Lake Michigan. How does a little— no offense—woman move a big man?"

"Maybe she just dragged his dead ass down the steps."

"And then what?" Salsa toppled from a chip into his lap. "Ruby didn't have a car and didn't drive."

Kate started to laugh. She put her hand over her mouth.

"I'm serious, I think she was set up."

"It's not that," she said, still laughing. "You could never eat without getting food on you."

Nick frowned and looked down at the salsa spot on his jeans and wiped it away with a napkin.

"So you just wanted these clips?" she asked.

"*Mmm-hmm.*" Nick smiled and leaned forward. His face grown serious.

"What is it? I knew you didn't take me to dinner for the company."

"You asked me."

"Oh."

"Could you run a driver's license check for me?"

"An AutoTrack?"

"Yep."

"On who?"

"Ruby's best friend," Nick said as he scooped some salsa with his tortilla chip. "Woman named Florida Thomas. Nothing in the phone book and she hasn't been seen in Chicago since the murder."

"I'll see what I can do," Kate said. "You have an old address or date of birth."

"She'd be around sixty."

"She could have gotten married."

"Or be dead."

"Who else have you interviewed?"

"I just found the son of one of the dead musicians. After insulting me several times, he finally told me who he thought killed his father."

"That's awesome."

"I'm not so sure. Told me a ghost story about a man named Stagger Lee."

"So?"

"Stagger Lee is a myth. Old South. And now maybe an urban legend."

"Could be a street name."

"That's true."

"I'll run it by some cops I know."

There was a pleasant hum of conversation around them as the Mexican guitar music played overhead. The Friday night crowd of gawking tourists and burned-out businessmen bustled by on Clark Street. The waitress laid down a plate of chicken enchiladas and catfish tacos. Another margarita, this time with salt. Another Dos Equis.

One drink at the Palmer House, she'd promised herself. One drink. Was it really her idea to have dinner?

"How are JoJo and Loretta?" she asked.

"JoJo just renovated the second floor of the bar into an office," Nick said. "Took us a few days to clean out all the crap he had up there. Weird shit like mannequins and saxophone parts. But they're doing fine. You know. Shows at night. Sleep all day. Church on Sunday. I miss 'em."

"Me too."

There was an awkward silence when she couldn't find the words to fill the dead space. He continued to watch her and she looked away.

"So you going to spill your guts?" Nick said, the taco in his hand.

"What do you want to know?"

Nick smiled and took a bite. "Why Chicago?"

"I don't want to talk about it."

Nick took another bite.

"We're still trying to work it out," Kate said. "What do you want me to say?"

"You finally realized he looked like a monkey and gave him the boot."

"He's a good guy," she said. "Don't get all cocky because I'm eating with you. I'd eat with the devil, if he took me out for Mexican."

"Even if the devil looked like a monkey?" Nick shoved the remainder of the taco into his mouth.

Kate frowned and took a bite of her enchiladas. Hot chipotle salsa and diced tomatoes. She finished her margarita as if it were water and licked the salty rim. They sat in silence for a moment.

"You ever think about fate?" she asked. "That if certain things wouldn't have happened, we would still be together?"

"You mean if I hadn't met the woman that night? That you wouldn't have met Richard?"

"Yeah."

"So what happened with him?"

"I left."

"Why?"

"He wanted me to be someone else."

"A gibbon?"

"See, you can't be serious for two seconds. The more important the topic the more you want to tear it down. Why is that, Travers?"

"I'm immature," he said, shrugging his shoulders. "I have a puppet in my coat right now. Want to see him?"

Kate studied Nick's face for a moment. All the light had drained from those green eyes. She looked at the deep scar sliced through his eyebrow. The waitress dropped off the check and Nick paid before they walked out onto Clark Street where their breath mixed in the cold air.

Neon lights illuminated rows of trendy restaurants and tourist bars. Irish music. Blues. Clark Street was like a supermarket for nightlife. A dirty taxi rolled by splattering the sidewalk with filthy snow from the black asphalt.

"What do you want?" Kate asked. No need to bullshit each other. Get it out into the open.

"You up for Rosa's? Blues? Drinking? A possibility of dancing?"

"No. What do you want from *me*, Travers?"

"Trouble." Nick looped his arm around her waist and tried to pull her close. She put a strong arm to his chest and backed up a good five feet. She just stood there for a moment looking into his eyes. A taxi rolled by scattering sludge across his boots.

"You are trouble," she said. Then she turned and walked away.

32

Rosa's blues lounge was a bar for black music run by an Italian in an Hispanic neighborhood. Nick had to give its owner, Tony Mangiullo, a lot of credit for his equality. Diversity at its finest, Nick thought as the cab rolled past storefronts selling hot peppers and Tejano music off Armitage on the West Side.

The West Side is where the second wave, the next generation of blues guitarists, got their start in the late fifties. The blues of Buddy Guy, Magic Sam, Otis Rush, and Elmore King all had roots in these neighborhoods. Billy Lyons was the first to give some of those guys their start.

Inside, Tony ran the pool balls around a green felt table with delicate ease. He was a skinny man with a long face, a thin beard, and mustache. He wore a Hawaiian shirt and a white Panama Jack hat. No matter how cold it was, Tony looked like he's just stepped off the cruise dock at Ocho Rios. Nick stopped the cue ball in midroll.

"Nick, my friend," Tony said in a lilting Italian accent, shaking Nick's hand. "How are you, man?"

"A woman I love just blew me off and I got splattered with slush on Clark Street."

"You want a beer?"

"It would help," Nick said, already studying the black-and-white photographs that lined the wall behind the pool table. Great images from old Theresa's Tavern. Old T's basement had closed back in the mid-eighties, but Tony had kept the institution's spirit alive in his place. Little Walter, Buddy Guy, James Cotton, and Sunnyland Slim all played the old venue. It was one of the first South Side clubs frequented by whites back when the audience was shifting in the sixties. Nick never got to journey into Theresa's smoky sin den to hear the blues but the stories were legendary.

Theresa's. Pepper's Lounge. The Purple Cat. All of them gone.

Still, Rosa's had that old blues lounge feel. Long wooden bar and scuffed wooden floors. Darkened room with a few neon beer signs. Thick jackets were piled high on the back of seats with everybody hunkered over beer and mixed drinks. Low red lights illuminated a high stage where instruments sat cold.

There was a different feel to a Chicago blues lounge compared to a Delta juke joint. The Delta was a quart of Colt 45 and a tin roof where the sound of a harmonica would rattle through your bones. Chicago was the red lipstick on a woman's cigarette, a double bourbon in a clean glass, saxophones, and driving guitars. So much the same but born from different needs.

Tony handed him a beer and a pool cue like he was giving Nick permission to joust before racking the multicolored balls.

He let Nick break. The balls scattered.

"You know Jimmy Scott?" Nick asked.

"I haven't seen Dirty Jimmy in years."

"He could use some work," Nick said as a solid blue ball went in a pocket. "Interviewed him a few hours ago. Wasn't doing too well."

"You tell me where he is and what I can do."

"He's just eating cheese and drinking whiskey," Nick said, taking another shot and missing.

"He likes cheese," Tony said, sizing up the next shot on a purple-striped ball. The cue ball kissed it on a far edge and pushed it in. "He used to make Kraft singles part of his contract."

"How's mama?"

"Very good."

Mama Rosa was Tony's partner. When Tony moved to Chicago

from Milan, Italy after an invite from the late Junior Wells, she was so worried about him that she soon followed him to America. She opened the bar to make sure her son had a safe place to hang out and hear the blues he loved so much. A great woman. A great bartender.

"How long are you going to be in Chicago?" Tony asked, nailing the yellow-striped ball.

"Till Christmas. Trying to get some information on some old players for King Snake Records. Want to find out about the death of the producer and owner. Guy named Billy Lyons."

Tony shrugged, missing the next shot.

"You remember the Sweet Black Angel?"

"I remember her records. People would get into fights over them in Italy. The Sweet Black Angel . . . she was so wonderful."

"Billy Lyons was the one she supposedly killed," Nick said, knocking a red ball in the pocket with the sound of a hammer.

"She still alive?"

Nick nodded before he tried to edge a green ball into the corner pocket but it stopped a hair short. "*Shit.* She's still in jail."

Tony knocked in the green striped and then the red striped. Looked like he had a run. Nick took another sip of beer.

"No money," Nick said. "Don't you think there should be a limit on punishment?"

"For murder or the way you're playing?"

"Like cheating on a woman. How long should you be punished for cheating on a woman?"

"Is the woman your wife?" Tony asked, missing a shot.

Nick shook his head and sized up another ball.

"Girlfriend?" Tony asked.

Nick nodded and missed.

"Ooh, tough shot," Tony said. "You sleep with someone's sister again?"

"That was a long time ago, man. Long time. And no, that wasn't it. How do you remember the shit I tell you? I barely remember it myself."

Tony made a thinking motion with his index finger to his head.

The show crowd started to gather at the door and Tony excused himself to take up the night's cover charge.

"Oh yeah, man, I see how it is," Nick said. "I got you on the run."

"I don't think so."

"Next is mama."

"Don't talk about my mama," Tony said, walking away, laughing.

Nick found a stool at the end of the bar, close to the stage, so he could watch Pinetop Perkins work his magic on the keyboard. It was the first time since he'd been in Chicago that he felt like he was home. He missed JoJo's groveling, Loretta's cooking, and the quiet rhythms of the Warehouse District. Nick lit a cigarette and watched Perkins take a seat at the piano.

The eighty six year old could find a depth of emotion from a piano like few others. Only Perkins could have taken over the void left by master Otis Spann in Muddy Waters's band. Perkins was Delta bred, a seasoned player who traveled up the lonesome blues highway when the music came to the Windy City. His résumé read like some mythic bluesman: traveled with Robert Nighthawk playing around juke joints, then backed up Sonny Boy II on the King Biscuit Time radio show before becoming a session player with Earl Hooker, Albert King, and Little Milton. It was a religious experience just being in the room, watching the man start into a boogie-woogie roll for an old Leroy Carr tune.

> *"I can hear that train whistle blowin'*
> *but I can't see no train.*
> *Deep down in my heart,*
> *it's like an achin' pain.*
> *How long, how long?*
> *Baby, how long?"*

Nick draped his jacket over his seat, finished his beer, and ordered a double Jack on the rocks. He could feel the warmness spreading in his chest as he felt the master's music roll through him. *The things he'd seen. The experiences he'd had.* Nick had never been a fan of the term *living legend*. Too often, it applied to a mediocre player grown old. But Perkins was Chicago blues. Great blues. The roll, the feeling, and the depth was like rereading your favorite Langston Hughes poem. An immediate connection with the simplicity. An awe of surprising depth.

More faces filled the narrow bar, shaking the snow from their coats and snuggling into the rich blues and a warm drink. Nick could imagine all those black faces, not far removed from places like Belzoni and Natchez, finding a little bit of home in that music. The Delta with an urban edge. Distant cries to Mississippi, to family, lost loves, and places that only existed in their minds.

Mama refilled Nick's double shot of Jack and gave him a warm pat on his hand. He walked around the bar and gave her a hug.

When he returned, there was a woman sitting on the bar stool. A black girl, looked to be in her twenties, with long black hair and green eyes. Looked like a Paris fashion model in platform heels, tight red leather pants, and a long rabbit coat over a halter top. She had a curvy Sanskrit-looking tattoo on her stomach and a tiger on her breast.

She drank tequila out of a shotglass like it was tea.

"Excuse me . . . my coat," he said.

"We can share," she said.

Nick smiled.

She put out her hand as if she were in a business interview.

"What's your name, baby?" she asked, raking her nails on the flesh of his hand.

Nick told her.

"You can call me Fannie."

33

NICK AND FANNIE stumbled out onto Armitage in the snow to catch a cab. He'd said good-bye to Tony and Mama and other friends he'd made in the cozy bar. Feeling good, warm, and friendly, he'd wished more Merry Christmases that night than he had in his whole life. Fannie had her arms clutched around his waist like she was holding a life preserver. Her breath rich with whiskey and smoke. His hand stayed on her hip as a couple of cabs sped past on the slush-covered roads.

Three Mexican teenagers in long checked flannel shirts walked in front of them, carrying a boom box.

"My apartment's just a hop and a skip," she said, giggling.

"No, no. Let me get you into a cab."

"Baby, see me home. *Please*."

A cab rolled before them, and Nick held open the door for her. She scooted across the duct-taped seat and rapidly fired off directions to the driver. Nick had no idea where they were going but let it ride. He remembered JoJo's advice about always being where you needed to be. But this was just a ride. He needed to make sure the woman was all right. He couldn't leave her just wandering around the cold streets. Drunk. Lost.

The passing lights in the windows made Nick feel dizzy as she snuggled her head into his neck and gave light pecking kisses. Nick smoothed her black hair and leaned back into his seat. The

Nigerian cabdriver gave a thumbs-up in the front seat as Fannie's kisses became more intense. She sucked on his neck and groped around his chest and arms in the shady light of an alcoholic fog. Hot breath in his ear as his hand brushed her warm stomach.

He delicately pushed her to the side as the cab soon slowed in front of a dimly lit brownstone. No particular neighborhood. A no-name street. Nick told the cabbie to wait as he walked her to the front door. The new-fallen snow cracked like wafers on the sidewalk.

"Wait," she said. "Wait just a damned minute." She walked back to the cab and leaned inside.

The cab took off.

"Hey, hey, hey, what are you doing?" Nick asked, leaning his back against the cold stone. The steps before him broke like ocean waves. His stomach rolled.

She patted the side of his face and tramped up some creaking green steps.

At an apartment door, she grabbed him close and pushed his back against the wall, forcing her tongue into his mouth. The door knocker was cheap and tarnished. Someone had wedged dried flowers under the metal.

He could feel her hand grip between his legs. She grabbed his hand and stuck it below her left breast.

Nick shook his head and pulled away.

They had had a good time at Rosa's. Good enough time to see her home. But this wasn't what he was looking for tonight. Too fast. Reminded him of a schoolteacher he'd picked up in the Quarter. The woman was so starved for the human touch, she quivered when his hand felt her cheek. But that was tender. Slow. This was all speed and strength, loose buttons, and ripped clothes.

She bit his ear and pushed open her door.

He did like the narrow shape of her eyes, the thin slits when she smiled gave her an oriental look. Inside, there was a long hallway covered in faux-wood paneling and a cheap reprint of

The Boulevard of Broken Dreams. Bogie, Marilyn, and James Dean all hanging out in some kind of immortal cafe. Moonlight bled into a window down the hall.

When Nick turned, she had slipped her halter top over her head. She wrapped her arms around him and he could see the full tiger on her cold breasts. The breathing was quick and heated as he moved his hands over her back and then gently pushed her away.

"You are really, really gorgeous, okay. And any other time, I'd be right with you but I can't do this. I'm . . ."

"Just stay a few minutes, I've been *soooo* lonely. Please, I'm just a little lamb. I'm not going to do anythin' to you you don't want done. How 'bout one last drink and we'll fade off together? I'll call you a cab and you can go back to your hotel. All right?"

"Sure," Nick said. "Sure."

She pulled him into a tiny room with pink walls. A cheap four-poster bed and dozens of teen heartthrob posters. A pack of stuffed animals on the bed.

"See, I'm just a sweet little thang. I'll get you another whiskey, just stay put."

Nick picked up one of the animals from the bed. It was a little dog. Ratty old thing with moth-eaten material and a missing eye.

He stood as she gave him the drink and pushed him back on the bed. She was still shirtless and he marveled at her large breasts with silver-dollar tips. Slats of light covered her body like prison bars.

He took the drink and smiled.

"Fannie, I really have to go. All right?"

"I just want a friend," she said, walking over to a tall closet door and disappearing for a minute. She returned in T-back pink panties and a see-through baby doll top. Her hair was pulled into pigtails. She flipped them behind her shoulders as she sauntered over to a flower-printed bureau and lit a candle.

Nick drank faster and started to rise again from the bed.

"Lean back and get loose," she said.

"If I get any looser, I'll melt."

"Then just drip away."

She pulled the drink from his hand, placed it on a nearby table, and grabbed both wrists. She held them in a tight grip with her clawlike nails biting him. In one quick motion, she jerked his hands above his head and pushed him deeper into the bed. She straddled him with her knees hugging his body and licked his face from his chin to his nose.

He felt rope being wrapped around his wrists and tried to wriggle his hands free. *Strong little thing.*

"Fannie . . ."

She ripped open his wool coat and pulled open his flannel shirt, running her tongue over his chest. She unbuttoned his pants and was about to pull them down when the closet door flew open.

A blonde girl clutching a knife rushed from inside.

Fannie rolled to the floor as the woman reached the knife high above her and leaped onto the bed. Nick pulled his arms forward hearing the wooden bedpost crack.

With his hands still bound, he pulled his knees into his chest and launched her off the bed. Her body rammed with a thud against the plywood walls. The candle knocked to the floor, scattering eerie shadows. Nick ripped the rope from his wrists with his teeth and jumped to his feet.

He faced the blonde woman who squatted before him.

She held the knife before her and slashed at his face.

The room spun and buzzed around him as he tried to evade the edge. He felt like he was going to puke. His stomach churned as the whiskey rose in his throat. She slashed again, and Nick made a wide punch to her stomach.

She grunted and fell to the ground.

The knife scattered on the floor. Nick scrambled to pick it up as he felt Fannie's heel on his hand.

Her boobs jiggled in the candlelight, a smile smeared on her full lips.

"Let it go," Fannie said, grinding her heel.

"Get the fuck off me," Nick said.

Nick pushed her down with his free hand and jumped to his feet. The blonde girl walked on her hands and knees for the knife as Nick kicked her hard. Square in the gut.

His actions seemed like some kind of awkward slow-motion dream.

The blonde girl tackled Nick to the ground and the air rushed from his lungs.

Fannie jumped on top, twisting Nick into a headlock and grunting with her effort. The blonde girl tried to squeeze and hold his legs but Nick kicked out of her like a pair of pants. He kicked her hard in the mouth and she gritted her bloody teeth, punching him hard in the stomach.

He tried to awkwardly stand like an Olympic weight lifter with the women's bodies clinging to him. He lowered his legs and stepped for the wall, smashing the women against the faux wood.

They let go.

He dropped to the floor for the knife. He held the blade in his hand as the women moaned and writhed on the floor. Fannie lay in a heap rubbing a swollen lip. The blonde girl was motionless, her face worked into a feral grin.

The breathing sounded like the last round of wind sprints. Grunted labored breaths working in the silence. Nick tucked the knife under his arm and pulled his coat shut. He loosely felt for his wallet and ran his hand over his face. The room twirled. He held the urge to vomit.

Stepping back, he heard the blonde girl plead for the knife.

"Please leave him, *please*," she sobbed. "Willie! Willie!"

Nick shook his head walking backward to the door.

He spun and ran down the steps to the no-name street in the unknown neighborhood. He chose a direction, jogging toward the brightest light. He stopped for a moment listening for any signs of the women following, bent at the waist, and threw up about thirty dollars' worth of good whiskey.

Nick wiped the foul foam from his lips and walked for miles

among the urban decay and unfamiliar surroundings. He felt like a lost dog. A clouded mind seeking something familiar. A touch of home. But the abandoned buildings in the deep midnight cold brought no comfort. *This mean ole city ain't nobody's friend.*

34

PRISON LIFE WASN'T hard to get used to. Not much different than Mississippi. Just live by the three rules: never look no one in the eye, work until they tell you to quit, and accept everything.

The guards first had me workin' in the laundry room. I must've washed enough clothes to fit Chicago. The heat from the presses sometimes would knock me out, but I was glad to keep my mind off Billy while I waited for my freedom. Soon, all my appeals were denied. My lawyer wouldn't return my letters and my sister stopped comin' to see me.

My best friend in the world became a three-hundred-and-fifty-pound woman with gold teeth named Queen. Queen was my prison teacher. She was a lifer who taught me how to get by. She once stuck a bull dyke's head in the laundry press after the woman threatened my life.

Queen knew my music and loved it.

She got me into the kitchen where she worked and taught me things about food I never imagined. The right way to salt greens and how to make crispy biscuits that strengthened your soul. She also taught me how to speak properly and about the Lord. Taught me how to trust in his actions and the path he had chosen for me. I became convinced the Lord wanted me here. Sunday services were all I looked forward to.

I cooked, read the Bible, and the years passed.

Queen died sometime around 1970. I don't know how that fat,

old woman did it. But somehow, she crawled on top of her sink, tied a sheet to a light and around her neck. No one claimed her body. We buried her in the ground so frozen it felt like rock.

I pretty much gave up too. My beauty had long since faded and my voice was broken and weak. Each day rolled into the next. Sometimes I didn't even know what year it was.

I thought about the cold earth where Queen was buried, and it somehow seemed to be a relief to me. Just like layin' down and goin' to sleep.

I had it all planned, until the letters from New Orleans started coming. This man, Travers, said he wanted to talk to me about my two years of being somebody. At first, I didn't believe it and left the letters in the back pages of my hand-tooled leather Bible.

I hadn't responded to anyone over the years. I wore my silence like a heavy coat. Gave me some kind of pride. But he kept tryin', and I decided to give one last act of faith. One last chance.

Memphis Minnie once told me every good kick in the butt moves you 'long. She'd twirl that six string and smile her bright grin, unaware of the shadows that had begun to fall.

35

STAGGER LEE WANTED Annie and Fannie to meet him at the Sears Tower early Saturday morning. Sometimes that big black man's ideas were just a little too crazy, Annie thought. Like he just acted on whatever kind of crazy shit popped in his mind. He wanted them to go on some kind of fucking elevator ride like they were tourists or something. You just didn't go to the fucking Sears Tower to hang out. That was when you were in school and had to hold hands with your teacher as you walked across the street. But that idiot Twon did whatever Stagger Lee wanted him to, and so there they were, riding on this super-rigged elevator that shot like a million fucking miles in the air like a jet pack or whatever.

Annie felt like she left her stomach somewhere on the bottom floor as Fannie stood across from her, laughing at her face turning green.

Annie didn't feel like laughing or smiling. She was pissed. That guy Travers had taken the one thing that meant more to her than her whole collection of *Archie* comics. How she longed to stroke Willie's clean blade and kiss his wooden handle. Bastard. Her stomach was bruised from where Travers had kicked her, and she had a loose tooth that she could rock with her tongue.

Fannie smoothed the nape of Annie's neck. "You okay, baby? You don't look so good."

"I'm fine. I'm fine. I just wish Willie was here."

"I know, baby. I know. We'll go to a pawn shop after this and get you one just like the one you had. We can call him Willie Two."

"Won't be Willie."

"Be better than Willie."

A teenage girl shot her a weird look.

"What are you looking at bee-itch?" Annie said.

The girl stared at the digital floor display, holding her breath.

Finally, the elevator slowed as they reached the moon or edge of the earth or wherever the fuck they were, and they all shot out of the elevator. On the top floor, a bunch of people gawked through tall glass windows and pointed at things. Annie had been here before but usually at night with her men. She would let them grope her as they looked down on the city like they were pissing on the world. What a time. *Shit.*

Fannie fluffed the rabbit fur on her coat and yawned. Fannie too cool for school. She wanted to get this over and go shopping. She had their whole route planned for Christmas Eve. Blow their whole damn load on the Magnificent Mile.

Annie looked down at thick clouds and fog and couldn't see shit. Through a thick, dark haze she could just make out the thousands of crisscrossed honeycombed caverns of the city. Down at Navy Pier and the lighthouse. Snow falling like bad reception on a television. So much going on. So much she wanted.

Maybe there was a way.

Last night, after they dropped Fannie at Rosa's, Peetie said they had options. He said he knew a way they could get out from under Stagger Lee and live. He said they had the talent and could take their show out of the projects. He said Stagger Lee was getting weak like an old dragon.

Then he sadly smiled inside the cold Volkswagen and said he knew a way to kill that dragon. He said, "Lay low and be cool and get ready to act when I say."

Of course she fucked with him about that. What was little Peetie gonna do to Stagger Lee, bore him to death with his bull-shit stories?

But it got her thinking. She walked over to a broad window and smushed her nose to the cold glass and thought about her future.

This is where she wanted to live someday. She would live all cooped up on the top floor and never have to leave. She'd have servants bring her Cocoa Puffs and *Archie* comics, and have Fannie as her gal pal to watch trash television and have pillow fights. Maybe she'd have a diving board that would reach outside where she could stand, squat, and piss on the city. Above it all. It would be like a heaven she'd created for herself. She'd piss on them all: on her whore mother, on their lazy-ass welfare daddy, and on Stagger Lee's slick bald head.

She felt a grip like a meat hook on her arm.

Black-as-night fingers wrapped her white flesh. She and Fannie turned.

He wore a black leather trench coat, black cowboy boots with silver tips, and that dumb-ass spiked collar on his neck. Surfer sunglasses wrapped his head. Stagger Lee looked down at them and then rested his hand on the glass to look at Annie's view. Twon wandered behind them to discourage anyone interrupting their privacy.

They had the whole northern view to themselves.

"What happened?" he asked. His deep voice seemed to rattle the glass.

"He got away," Fannie said, speaking up and tossing her hair toward Stagger Lee. Her black hair all loose and flowing like an Indian princess's.

"What did I say?" Stagger Lee asked.

"We tried," Fannie said.

"No. What did I say?"

"You wanted him dead," Annie said, speaking up.

"This isn't some kind of fucked-up game," Stagger Lee said. "The longer he's out there, the more it spreads. You rub shit around and it's just gonna stink more. I want him out. Wait . . . he see you two bitches?"

"Yeah," Fannie said.

"Both of you?"

"He seen me real good," Fannie said, making her eyes go soft. She licked her lips and fingers and rubbed her hand over the fluff of her coat. Her spit smoothed the fur.

"Girl, you can quit throwing your pussy around. I got socks I'd rather fuck."

Fannie snorted air out of her nose and tossed her hair over her shoulder.

"White girl. He see you?"

"Yeah, but not like Fannie. It was dark and I think he was drunk."

"Take his ass out. You hear me?"

"You kill Lyons?" Fannie asked, unpeeling a piece of Bubblicious and putting her hands into her coat.

Stagger Lee shot her a look like a cornered street dog. A vein in his temple throbbed.

"This isn't about killin'. Killin' is like breathin'. I wouldn't have you workin' just to cover up a killin'. This is about the sweet smell of money. You ever smell a fresh dead president's ass? Nothin' like it."

"A president's ass?" Annie said, wrinkling up her nose.

Stagger Lee glanced around the floor like an animal protecting a kill. No one was around. He stood still with his eyes turned toward her.

He reached out, and grabbed Annie by the throat.

Annie felt her air cut off and the blood rush behind her eyes. Her feet left the ground as her back thudded against the glass. She caught her feet on the guardrails gasping for a sip of air. She reached out, clawing at his hand, but it was like an iron vise around her neck. He shook her with his hand and rammed her against the glass again. She heard a cold crack behind her. Her legs tingled and her head swam, knowing she was an inch away from falling through the clouds.

The glass cracked again and she could hear Twon yelling at

someone to stay back. She saw Fannie grabbing Stagger Lee's arms and Peetie Wheatstraw smiling up at her. He tipped the edge of his hat as he chomped on a wet cigar.

"Killin' that man can wait," Peetie said, still grinning.

Stagger Lee grunted and dropped her to the ground. On her knees, she choked and gasped. *That motherfucker.*

Fannie helped her to her feet. Her left eye twitched as she stared up at Stagger Lee.

"Listen," Peetie said in a low voice. "Dog, I've been around a long time. I seen you with Elmore King. I seen you meet with him. Even seen him come down to Robert Taylor like y'all old friends. Somethin' to me just don't jive, right? So 'bout ten years ago I started thinkin'."

Stagger Lee's veins continued to throb in his head. Annie just knew any second he'd reach out and grab Peetie like a rag doll and toss him through the window. That cold December air would suck them out into the clouds.

Peetie slipped the cigar from his mouth and took off his bowler hat. He'd yet to take a breath. "I started thinkin' y'all got some kind of thang bindin' you together. And that thang got to be Billy Lyons. Do I lie?"

Stagger Lee folded his arms across his chest.

"Listen, dog, I know you ain't no Uncle Tom. I know you don't like cleanin' the shit off King's boots. So why do his work for him? I know business ain't happenin' down South. I see your world crackin' down under your feet. How you like to make one last big thang? I know you been thinkin' 'bout it. And I ain't talkin' about a little payoff. I'm talkin' about the whole thang. Let Billy, Leroy, and Franky make you what you deserve. You owe it to yourself, man. If the time ain't more right, I'll kiss my own ass."

Stagger Lee uncrossed his arms and put his hand down on Peetie's shoulder. Peetie finally exhaled. *Stagger Lee screws over this King guy. Then Peetie screws over Stagger Lee. Seemed like leapfrog to Annie.*

Stagger Lee said, "So what you got on your mind?"

36

EVEN ON LITTLE sleep and a nauseous stomach, Lou Mitchell's was a fine place to have breakfast in Chicago—the kind of diner JoJo would appreciate. Slouched old men in sweaters with hooded eyes. Cops with their checkerboard hats and thick jackets on booth posts. Lou's had been open about eighty years, the waitress said, but it resonated with the fifties. A green and white awning covered a stainless steel counter where waitresses in creased shirts, black ties, and aprons worked feverishly to fill cups. Hardcore coffee from filtered water and Colombian beans served with a prune and an orange on the side.

Nick thought maybe he'd have some dry toast. JoJo always said that burned bacon or a warm Dr Pepper did the trick. Nick swallowed two more chalky aspirin and warmed his hands over the coffee waiting for Moses Jordan. He wished he was in bed sleeping off his terrible headache. Drapes closed. Heater cranked. But he'd promised Saturday, 10:00 A.M.

Damn, Chicago was starting to make him feel like a whore at a Delta revival. Since he'd arrived on Thursday, he'd been in a fight with a couple of gang bangers and had wrestled for his life with two beautiful women.

This morning, he'd gotten back to the Palmer House about 3:00 A.M. and had a rough sleep for the next few hours. As he listened to the Hawk howl against his windows, he still saw the white girl's face worked into a feral grin. Blood on her teeth, a butcher knife in her hand.

Nick wasn't a true believer in bad luck and couldn't sleep. So he took a steaming shower, decided not to shave, and slipped back into his two layers of clothing. The thermal underwear had become another layer of skin under his faded jeans and flannel shirt.

Last night had been a series of stupid mistakes. First, he'd put the moves on Kate, probably severing any chance of a reconciliation. Then he'd gone home with a strange woman.

He could still smell her sickening sweet scent all over him. Almost like wet sugar.

Jordan walked in the front door shaking his coat and greeting a dark-headed woman at the cash register. A couple waitresses waved and Jordan stopped to shake hands with several people. They all seemed pleased just to touch his hand.

The old man laughed at a comment Nick couldn't hear and hung up his coat and houndstooth hat. He grunted as he slid into the vinyl booth and shook Nick's hand. He watched Nick's face and tightened his eyes.

"Man, you look like something bad."

"Feel like shit."

"You clubbin'?"

"Yeah."

"Man, that shit will kill you."

Jordan's broad face had small pockmarks across his forehead with small imperfections under his black eyes. He scanned the menu for about two seconds before snapping it shut. He had on a charcoal gray suit today with a tabbed collar and black knit tie. He grinned as he brushed the silver hair on the sides of his bald head with his hand and took in his surroundings.

"Best damned breakfast in Chicago," he said.

"Smells like it."

"So," Jordan said. "You get a chance to see our neighborhoods? I don't want you going back to New Orleans saying bad things about our world."

"Yes, sir, I did a little walking around."

"What'd you think?"

"Well . . ." He decided not to mention his run-in with the two thugs on Forty-third Street. "A lot of potential."

Outside it was so dark it looked like it was the middle of the night. Small flakes drifted down onto salt-corroded sedans already covered in snow. A waitress walked over and took their orders. Jordan ordered an omelette, a plate of bacon, Greek toast, orange juice, and more coffee. Nick ordered dry toast and more water.

"You know for us to succeed, strangers need to feel comfortable in our neighborhoods," Jordan said. "Man, there are parts I still don't want to drive through."

"No different from New Orleans. We have our good and bad. Yin and Yang."

"So, you're headed back tomorrow?"

"Christmas. Taking the train Christmas morning."

"You should be with your family," Jordan said.

Nick nodded. "My only family is back in New Orleans. I'll see them soon enough."

The waitress laid down Nick's toast and water and Jordan's omelette and bacon plate. He had to admit it looked pretty damned good. Maybe he should force himself to eat.

"*Mmmm,*" Jordan said taking a mouthful of omelette. "Sure you don't want anything else? It's on me."

"No, sir, I'm fine," Nick said. "But I would like to ask you a question."

Jordan looked up from his food.

"I talked to Jimmy Scott yesterday."

Jordan smiled, unconcerned. He took another bite of the omelette mixed with some Greek toast. His fat chin shook beneath his jaw.

"He said you were with Billy the day he died."

Jordan shook his head, averted his eyes, and brought the coffee mug to his lips. "No."

"He said he was playing harp, with Franky Dawkins on bass,

Leroy Williams on piano, Elmore King on guitar, and you on drums. He said you saw Lyons fight with Ruby that day."

"Dirty Jimmy Scott is a drunk, senile old man," Jordan said, raising his voice. His eyes hot. "He can't remember the last time he changed his underwear. He used to collect venereal diseases the way some do trading cards. Used to brag about his collection. Don't congratulate yourself on that find, son."

"So, you were *not* at the last session at King Snake?"

"No, sir."

"Who was? Did you keep the recording log? Who ran the equipment?"

Jordan laughed deep in his chest and added a wedge of omelette onto a slice of Greek toast. He had yet to look Nick in the eye.

"Billy Lyons ran the show. I was long gone."

"And Jimmy's a liar?"

"Jimmy's confused."

Nick added some orange marmalade to his toast and asked the waitress for a refill on his coffee. An elderly couple walked over to the table and introduced themselves to Jordan. He shook their hands, his face beaming with pleasure, as he talked about a youth group's art projects. The man said he'd love to see their work.

Jordan sat back down and finished the coffee. Nick was sure he'd probably pushed him too much. But he had more questions that had nagged at his mind since he'd woken up with the headache.

"Williams and Dawkins still around?"

"No, sir," Jordan said. "Died years ago. Both of 'em murdered. Fine men. Fine musicians who lost their lives because we couldn't control the streets."

"What do you think happened?"

"Who knows. I tried and tried to get the police interested. They just checked that robbery box on their reports and acted like we should fend for ourselves. That's what I'm talking about. Put that in your article. Those men were broken windows no one tried to fix."

Nick missed the connection but could appreciate Jordan's passion. He didn't mind listening, the coffee was great, he was inside, and he could feel the pounding in his brain stop to just an annoying hum. He took a deep breath and rubbed his temples. One more. One more. Asking these questions was like holding your breath and jumping into a cold pool. You just did it.

"You know the name Stagger Lee?"

Jordan looked like he had stopped breathing. Words caught in his throat. He straightened his knit tie and pushed away his plate.

"Yeah."

"I heard a man that went by the name Stagger Lee took out Williams."

Jordan slowly nodded.

"Dr. Travers, simple people have simple explanations," he said. "Who told you that? His son that's in the junk business? We got all kinds of stories on the street. If it makes him feel better to blame his father's death on a phantom then I'll let him. Lots of folks blame their lives on Stagger Lee. . . . Your car's stolen? Stagger Lee did it. Your home broken into? Stagger Lee did it. I'm afraid you just got told an urban folk tale."

"Maybe."

"No maybe about it. Stagger Lee's the man who haunts our dreams in the South Side. He runs gangs, right? He brought crack to the housing projects? And started turf wars? Hell, I even heard he organized Saturday night dog fights back in the sixties. They'd throw the loser onto the steps of a church. *Usually a church who was tryin' to clean up a neighborhood.* Those tales keep people from getting involved."

Jordan sipped his coffee and stared into the black day. His hands slightly trembled around the cup as he said, "Yeah, if Stagger Lee was one man, all our lives would be much easier."

37

NICK STUCK A quarter into a pay phone on Jackson and dialed Kate's number. He had a cigarette hanging loose in his mouth as he rubbed his hands together and stomped his feet. Shit, he'd dance the funky chicken if it'd keep him warm. His breath clouded in front of his eyes as the phone kept ringing, waiting for a machine to pick up. Kate was good and he wasn't too stubborn to admit he needed help.

A few years ago, she'd helped him search for a student of his that had disappeared in the Quarter. Maria, a Haitian exchange student who'd been abducted by some *ton-ton macoutes* and held in an old warehouse in Algiers. That spring, Kate helped knock on the right doors and eventually track down Maria. Brittle, alone, and scared shitless. He and Kate had spent a lot of time in hoodoo parlors, flophouses, and the projects.

He just remembered all that rain. Seemed like it would never stop.

Just as he was about to hang up, she answered.

"Hey," he said. His voice sounding gravelly and foreign.

"Apology accepted," Kate said. "Sometimes I just have to shake you from my leg."

"Listen, last night—"

"It's all right. I know you were drunk."

"Kate . . ."

"You smelled like Bourbon Street on a summer morning."

"Last night a couple of girls tried to kill me."

"What?"

"Can we meet? I'll tell you about the whole freak show."

"Two girls?" Kate asked, her voice sounding metallic and biting in his ear. "Was this a fantasy?"

"I'm headed back to Dwight to see Ruby right now. How about I'll meet you at the paper at two."

"You sound like hangover city, Travers."

"Maybe we should make it two-thirty?"

"You need to puke again?"

"I need to find Florida."

"Do what you need to do. I'll stop by the paper and bug our researchers. Thomas, right?"

"Yeah."

"There's a Starbucks right across from the *Tribune* on Michigan Avenue."

"Sounds good."

"Or maybe we could meet somewhere and get a big, bloody cheeseburger."

Nick could feel the bile rise in his throat. He made a gagging noise.

Kate laughed and hung up.

■

An hour and a half after leaving Chicago, Nick had the rare privilege of talking to Ruby in her cell. Her home of forty years. He sat on a bare blue-and-white striped mattress and marveled at the collage she'd formed on the concrete walls. It appeared she'd spent her days making a shrine to the blues. Magazine cutouts of everyone from Muddy Waters to Koko Taylor. Nick wished he'd brought a camera or would have thought to grab some video. This was incredible. In the center were three large cutouts: Memphis Minnie, Bessie Smith, and Ma Rainey like a holy trinity of female singers.

Ruby had a scented candle burning by a boom box that played some old Al Green Christmas music. She seemed skittish and agitated he was in her space as she folded and refolded clothes and organized dime-store knickknacks that filled a crooked shelf.

Nick offered her a cigarette and she peered out into a concrete corridor vibrating with prison conversation. The cell door was open and she accepted the cigarette, swiping it from his hand like a frightened animal. The bars on the door were painted light blue filled with countless rusted scratches. An old radiator boiled stale air down the hall.

"I found Peetie," Nick said. "At the Soul Train, just like you said."

She nodded as he flicked open his Zippo and lit her cigarette.

"Also talked to Moses Jordan and found Dirty Jimmy."

"Thought Jimmy was dead." Her cheeks hollow as she inhaled the smoke.

"He's still around," Nick said. He tried to relax but Ruby's pacing was making him nervous. He wanted her to feel comfortable because what he was going to ask wasn't going to be easy.

"Too bad," Ruby said. Maybe she meant it as a joke but she didn't smile. *Ruby never smiled.*

"You mean because he testified against you?"

"Man sold me out."

A plump black woman in an orange jumpsuit wandered by the room and stared into Ruby's cell. She rolled her eyes and asked Ruby, "What's up with this?"

"Conjugal visit," Nick said. "Please leave us."

Ruby ignored the woman and Nick and sat on the floor with his back to the concrete blocks. She puffed on the cigarette as if it provided every pleasure she would ever need.

"Did you hear what happened to Franky Dawkins and Leroy Williams after you got arrested?"

"I know they were killed." She ashed the cigarette in her hand. Her brown eyes lazy and distracted.

"Did you know they were stabbed like Billy?"

She shook her head, got off the floor, and sat beside Nick. She found the very edge of the bed and peered down at the floor worn from walking. A single tarnished drain stuck in the center.

"Odd coincidence. Don't you think?"

"I'd never hurt anyone like that."

"I know."

"I didn't hurt him."

"I know."

Nick looked up at the walls. "Looks like you've kept up with blues."

"If that's what you still call it."

"What do you mean?"

"It ain't blues. It's *faded* blues. All sounds the same to me now. People just repeat things they've heard. No one has their own sound anymore."

"Still a lot of good music out there."

"Some, but they're gettin' old like me," she said. "Kids want to play it loud. They don't understand it's about the guitar speaking for you, no soul left."

Ruby stubbed out her cigarette on the floor and left it there.

"Guards told me you could move out of this old cell. Find some better housing."

"To the new place?"

"Yeah."

"Why? This is mine."

Nick nodded. "Ruby, how come you didn't tell me about Florida. Sounds like she was your best friend."

"She was."

"That's pretty damned important."

"So what, dude?" She twisted up her face. "What do you want to know about Florida?"

"What happened to her?"

"I don't know . . ." She shook her head. "She left the next day. Ain't seen her since."

"Never?"

"No."

"You two mad at each other?"

"Lots of reasons. But I'd guess it had somethin' to do with Billy's daughter, Nat. She always wanted that baby for herself. And I guess when Billy died that was her chance."

"She took his child?"

"Wouldn't be the first time. Billy had to sometimes fight just to get his child back," Ruby said. "Say that for Florida. Sure did love that baby."

"Ruby, what happened that night with Billy?" Nick asked, playing with a loose thread on the watch cap. "I know you didn't kill him . . . but how do you explain the blood in your bed and the ice pick?"

"You sound like my lawyer," Ruby said. Her voice grew small as if falling into a deep well. Her shoulders hunched forward.

"What happened?" Nick asked.

He looked into her eyes and saw nothing. A look he'd seen out in the Quarter from derelicts and prostitutes. People who were so low, nothing surprised them. You could kick them and they wouldn't feel a thing. It was as if the pain had become so immense it had deadened her soul.

"Ruby," Nick said, taking her shaking hand. He took another deep breath. "Just hang in there. I'm so damned close. All right?"

Her future had closed. Pain did not exist and the world was becoming a place where she once lived. *She stood at the kitchen table, a light breeze rattling a curtain over dirty dishes, her eyes watching the clock. I asked her questions but she was already a ghost. To her, I wasn't even there.*

"Why not just tell the truth?" Nick said, reaching out for her hand. Establish a reality, a contact. "Let's get it all out."

Ruby pulled her hand away and wrapped her arms around herself.

"Let me tell you something," Nick said. "About ten years ago, I felt the same way. My story can't compare to yours. I can't even imagine what you've been through. But at the time it seemed like I didn't have a friend in the world. My mother died when I was ten and my dad died when I was in college. About the only thing I had back then was my career. When that ended, almost everybody I knew gave up on me."

Ruby turned to watch him. A single bare bulb burned in the small square cell.

"I found out my friends weren't true. My money had dried up. I started having pains in my chest because of worry. I would wake up in the middle of the night sweating."

Ruby clasped her small hands in her laps. Nick grabbed her hand again.

"Then, a great man I know told me to get off my ass. I sold off everything I had. My cars, my clothes, my house. About the only things I kept were my boots, a couple pairs of jeans, some good T-shirts . . . and an old harp."

He could feel her squeezing his hand. Her fingers were thick with callouses.

"What happened to your mama?" she asked in small voice.

"She gave up."

Ruby squeezed some more.

"You ever hear the name Stagger Lee?" Nick asked. He'd delved into that subject about as deep as he wanted to go. It was a place he'd kept locked away, hoping it never saw light.

Ruby shook her head, tears running down her dry cheeks, her gray hair poking from the sides of her head.

"Ruby, I need to know."

After minutes of stillness—as gates clanged shut and laughter reverberated off concrete walls with narrow windows filled with knives of light—she began to talk in a slow even tone. "Me and a friend. Me and Florida was drinking at the Palm Tavern."

Nick felt he could breathe again as he pulled out a cassette player from his old coat and pressed record. He tried to remain as still as he could. He tried not to show expression or excitement.

"I did a show at Theresa's and went to the Palm to calm down. You know? Elmore been recordin' with Billy. You know about all that mess? About me showin' Billy my gun and all that?"

"Who was at King's recording session that day?" Nick asked.

"I can't remember. I don't even remember being there."

"What about the bar? Who all was there?"

"I don't know. Like I said. Jimmy . . . Elmore."

"Why didn't King testify?"

"Said he didn't see me that night. Which was a lie."

"Why would he lie?"

Ruby shrugged.

King, his last piece. Why would he think she's not guilty? What had driven him to open up that night in New Orleans? Sit there as the rain drummed outside JoJo's and share his story? *He believed Ruby for some reason.*

"I need to find him," he said.

"If King don't testify for me, what makes you think he's gonna talk to you?"

"I know him," Nick said. "He owes me an explanation."

"Don't work that way."

"Was that the last time you two spoke?"

"Elmore came to see me about ten years ago," she said. "He brought me some things after the trouble with that guard. Said he was real sorry about not speakin' up for me. I told him to get out of my face, lessen he wanted to help. He just left. Didn't say nothin' except he was real sorry. Ain't that somethin'?"

"He say anything to you that night at the bar?" Nick asked.

"Dude, that was forty years ago," Ruby said, rubbing her hands together, "I can't remember every thing that man said. Let's just say we was both drunk and bitchin' bout Billy. He tole me not to feel bad 'bout breakin' in on the session like that. Said it didn't affect him none. I tole him I was sorry, just had somethin' I needed to get out 'bout that woman Billy was with."

"You said you were drunk. How did you get home? Florida?"

"No, she left . . ." Ruby shook her head: "Dirty Jimmy or Elmore, I guess."

"C'mon, Ruby."

"I don't know."

Ruby looked at the ceiling and rubbed her hands together as if she were lathering them with soap. "Damn. Damn. Damn," she muttered to herself.

"Just tell me what happened," Nick said.

"Been over this a million times," she said. "Been over this a million times."

"Let's hear it again," Nick said, moving the recorder closer to her. "Where did that blood come from?"

"I went to the Palm Tavern and got drunk. Had me a bottle of whiskey."

"You and Billy fought again?"

"No," Ruby said, so low he could barely hear. Something was drawing her eyes inward, pulling some musty file from a far corner of her brain. Something not easily accessible.

"I was drunk. I was drunk."

"But did you kill him?" Nick asked.

Ruby was shaking now. Not crying. Just rocking and hugging herself. The muscles in her jaws flexed.

"No," she said softly. "I felt him crawl in bed with me late that night."

"What time?"

"I don't know, I was so drunk," Ruby said. "He knocked over a pitcher I kept on a nightstand. And kicked a clock 'cross the room."

"Then what?"

"It was morning. I was in his arms and he was cold. Felt like a piece of steak on me and when I moved I was all wet and kind of stuck to the bed. The sun was up and it covered Billy's head and body . . . and that's when I seen it."

Nick waited. He wanted her to finish but couldn't speak. The cassette player churned and he felt his hands sweating.

"Billy was all cut up. Blood all around his shirt and head. His face look gray. I just remember screamin' and tryin' to just get out of the bed. But the sheets were all tangled around me. All those *goddamn* sheets tangled all around me. When I got out, that's when I heard that metal pick clang to the floor. Somebody put it there. Somebody want me to think I killed him.

"I was scared, I couldn't breathe, I was shaking all over and threw up. I called Florida . . ."

"She helped you."

Ruby nodded. "We threw away the sheets and that pick and . . ." Ruby's face ran with tears. "We put him in the back of Florida's Hudson and drove him out to the lake. I was just so scared. *I know it wasn't right. I know it wasn't right.*"

They sat there for what seemed like hours. Finally, she composed herself and spoke again.

"Go home, Dr. Travers. I always wanted to be known. Be remembered. You remember me, okay? But there's nothing else can be done."

"Last night, two women tried to kill me," Nick said. "I think someone wants me to stop asking questions about Billy. And I can't leave that unfinished."

Ruby didn't say a word.

Nick tried to give a reassuring smile. "I always remember what Muddy Waters once said. 'The only way to defeat trouble is to look it straight in the eye.' "

38

HALFWAY TO CHICAGO, Nick turned off the interstate and into a chrome and neon gas station that looked larger than a bus terminal. Place must've had fifteen pumps with two fast-food restaurants and a convenience store. He stretched his legs and hooked up the nozzle to the Tic-Tac as some Illinois redneck pulled up in a red truck blaring Elvis's "Santa Claus Is Back In Town." Maybe he could stomach some beef jerky and a Coke by now. His stomach started to grumble as he lit a Marlboro.

The redneck combed his hair in a pompadour, watching himself in the rearview mirror.

Nick knew he needed to find a way of turning up the heat on his sources. All of them were holding back. He just had to find what motivated them. What would cause them to turn out secrets buried for forty years? If he could just find Florida. She had to know more about the King Snake circle after Ruby was put away.

Nick thought about her downturned head and slumped shoulders. A blues legend being led down a concrete corridor to be left alone with her thoughts and atrophied experiences in a concrete cage. What did she think about? Was death the last thing that brought her hope? He thought about the confined spaces and not seeing the world since 1959.

As the pump cut off, he felt like he couldn't breathe. He flicked the cigarette onto the ground and smashed it with his foot. A patch of sky had broken free of the snow clouds showing a sliver of sunshine. The cold surrounded Nick like he was at the bottom of a frozen lake as Elvis sang on inside the redneck's truck.

After he walked inside and paid for some gas and some jerky, he found a pay phone close to the highway. First he called the Palmer House for any messages. Maybe Randy or Doyle had tracked down some more information. Nothing.

Nick hung up the phone and looked at his watch. Two o'clock. JoJo would be setting up for the Saturday night crowd. He'd be closed Christmas Eve and Christmas day. Probably a big show with Loretta, Fats, and the guys. She'd go all out decking the whole damn bar in that ugly silver tinsel and throwing home-made pralines to the crowd.

He could imagine the old wooden signs creaking in the winter wind under stucco buildings of dark red, green, and blue, the smell of incense leaking through the doors of voodoo shops. JoJo drunk on stage with a Santa's hat on his head playing harp. His old buddy Jay Medeaux down from the cop shop for his yearly brandy with Felix. Oz down from the midnight showing of *The Rocky Horror Picture Show* dressed in full Dr. Frank N. Furter gear, and Hippie Tom from his French Market bong stand with his latest teenage girlfriend. *Only in New Orleans.*

When Loretta picked up the phone like she didn't have time for bullshit, it gave him great comfort.

"Loretta?"

"Hey, boy . . . you home yet?"

"I'm stuck at a gas station 'bout thirty minutes from Chicago."

"Ain't that some shit."

"Listen, if I don't talk to you guys I just wanted to wish you a Merry Christmas. Okay?"

"Sure. Sure. You all right, Nicholas? You sound down."

"No, no. I'm fine."

"How's Kate?"

"How'd you know I found Kate?"

"I know you."

"JoJo tell you why I'm here?"

"One of those crazy things you do. Helpin' out some woman who killed her man."

"Yeah . . . the Sweet Black Angel."

"You're shittin' me? She's still in jail? Lord, that woman could sang. Used to sing a bunch of her songs when I was in Memphis. Had some real pipes. So when you gonna wrap this thing up and come on back home? Or you got other things on your mind?"

Nick laughed and pulled a pack of cigarettes from his coat. A semi rolled by on the highway blaring its horn.

"It's hard. Takes a while to put together all the pieces from forty years ago. Ruby's in jail. The old South Side doesn't exist and half her band is dead or isn't being straight. You get conflicting stories. Everyone remembers things their own way. Same old shit."

"Yeah, I know what you're sayin'. Couple of years ago me and the ole fart went back to Memphis for a party with some of the old school. Went back to the studio where I made my records, and Lord those memories shot out at me like ghosts from an attic. Things I ain't thought about for years."

"I've found a lot of ghosts but little truth."

"Hope you find what you're lookin' for."

"So do I. . . . Hey, I'll try to catch you guys on Christmas. Send the old fart my love."

Loretta cackled.

"And Loretta?"

"Yes?"

"I love you too. You know that, right?"

"Never figured it to be any other way."

39

ANNIE STARED OUT Peetie's car window at the most foreign landscape she'd ever known. Looked like another freakin' planet. Woodstock was so damned country that she expected any minute to see some guy in overalls picking a banjo. Kind of like that retard in that movie with Burt Reynolds who had no teeth and fucked-up eyes. Yeah, this wasn't the kind of place Peetie's Bug/Rolls needed to break down. They'd probably tar and feather them or string them up from one of those leafless trees they passed out on the two lane.

This was serious corn country with tiny white farmhouses and miles of dead cornstalks that looked like someone's stubbled haircut. Snow at their roots like a bad case of dandruff.

"Are we there yet, Daddy?" Fannie asked.

"Just about," Peetie said, driving with one hand. Man was wearing some stupid driving gloves. "King ain't had me out to the ranch in a few years. Guess I ain't sharp enough for him no more. Won't return my calls. Don't say hello at his club. That's what happens when you get famous, Miss Fannie. You think yore booty don't stink."

Peetie's little car rolled through a town of fast-food franchises, old-time diners, and shit-hole motels before he wheeled off onto another winding highway. After passing a bent, blue mailbox twice, he turned down the dirt road marked with a sign that read

CROSSROADS RANCH, with small guitars inlaid on the corners of the sign.

They passed a rotted barn and pulled in front of a big-ass white home with huge columns. Looked like something out of *Gone with the Wind*.

"Where's Miss Scarlett at?" Fannie asked.

Peetie laughed. "Yeah, King likes to believe he's still in Alabama. . . . Thinks he's some kind of cowboy. Always did. Even lectured me one night sayin' the movies had it all wrong. Said most of the cowboys back in the day were black. But I said I ain't never seen but one movie with a black cowboy and that was Sidney Poitier. And man, he had Apaches crawlin' over his ass like fleas."

Dozens of cars were parked on the lawn—BMWs, Mercedes, Cadillacs—as the lights burned bright in the huge home. Snow wandered down from the country skies as they stretched out of the car and drank in the whole scene. King had a huge run-down barn about fifty yards from where they parked—red and faded with its door wide open and bails of hay stacked nearby.

Huge stainless-steel troughs were full of beer and soda with rows of crisscrossed white lights hanging overhead. Thick barbecue smoke drifted in the dark air dotted by snowflakes.

Annie caught a flake in her mouth and imagined it was a sugar cookie as they walked past a bunch of idiots with smiles on their faces, wishing a lot of empty Merry Christmases. Peetie tipped his hat at a few ladies. He was having a grand old time in his ugly-ass yellow suit and yellow shoes.

"Man, you look like a banana," Annie said.

"Ooh well, well. Why don't you peel me then, baby."

"I'd rather not," Annie said, trudging ahead in the snow. "But me and Fannie been talking about your offer. . . . We just want to know the whole plan before we agree to anything. You been awfully cool with Stagger Lee too. You ain't lookin' to dick us over to get yourself in good? Are you?"

"Ain't nothin' like that. Okay?" Peetie said. "It's like you gonna rob a house. Right? Who am I talkin' to? I know you two is the B and E experts. So let's say you got a house you lookin' at and it look real good. Big ole thing with brick and trim and all that shit. But hey, the family ain't moved in. Well, Stagger Lee like that house. You know he's dry as a bone right now. Me? I'm just helpin' to fill up that house to let y'all do yore job."

"What job?" Annie said.

Peetie stopped walking and readjusted his bowler hat. He played with the snow with his yellow shoes. The dumb-ass grin disappeared. His ears slipped back and his eyes narrowed. He whispered, *"Kill that mean motherfucker. Can y'all do that?"*

She thought about Stagger Lee grabbing her by the neck as she rubbed the purple spots circling her throat like a necklace. If that man touched her again, she'd buy a new knife and carve his ass like a turkey. Get all that dark meat.

Annie watched Peetie's eyes. See if he was screwing with them. He didn't flinch. There was a dark light in there she'd never noticed before. It was as if another soul had been sucked in his body and his old shuck and jive had been flushed away.

"Can't believe you talked Stagger Lee into this," Annie said.

"We split the money?" Fannie asked.

"Yes."

"Even?" Annie asked.

"Like cuttin' up a pie." Peetie puffed on the sweet cigar and blew a smoke ring into the cold sky. More flakes fell from the blackness and about an inch of snow covered the ground. Their shoes made squeaking sounds in the fresh snow as they tramped along to the open barn.

She could see a bunch of backslapping crap going on inside and hear a small blues band playing in a far corner. Six-foot heaters sat in the center of the room with their big mushroom heads glowing red hot.

A black couple, decked out in some high-dollar holiday fashions, passed Annie, Fannie, and Peetie heading into the door. The woman gave a real sour-faced look to the girls as if they were nothing.

"She think we some skanky hos," Fannie said.

"Well, this is a ho-down," Annie said as the wind scattered tiny bits of ice into her face. She wrapped a scarf around her neck and gave a big, game-show grin. "Let's go inside."

"Man's having a Christmas party," Peetie said, smiling.

"What are they eating?" Annie said, looking at a long line forming inside. People passed a linen-covered table with men in chef's hats cutting off thick slabs of bloody meat. She saw more stacks of steaks and ribs.

"Roast beef?" Fannie asked.

"Yeah," Annie said. "Roast *beast*. What did we eat last year?"

"Shit on a shingle?" Fannie asked.

"Shit on a shingle," Annie said, slowly. "Now, what is up with that? This Elmore King guy getting to live it up eating the beast while we're on the outside. Don't seem fair."

"I guess you're right," Fannie said.

"I know I'm right."

Annie marched inside as a plump, black woman with about two tons of eye makeup met her at the door. She had on a long mink coat with a flute of champagne in her hand. Her plastered grin dropped when she saw the girls. Guess she wasn't a fan of leather and lace. The woman tilted her head in question. She looked like she was in her fifties with stiff black hair all woven into some kind of Aretha Franklin thing. Rings on her fingers and gold chains around her neck. *You're rich, we get the idea.*

"Hello, are you with the band?" the woman asked.

"No," Annie said. "Your husband invited us."

"Yesssss, Big Daddy be 'spectin' us," Fannie said, sliding into her street accent as Peetie wandered away.

"You girls know my husband?" the woman asked, looking them up and down. Her face shriveled like a dead flower.

"Oh, well kind of," Annie said. "He said he just couldn't get through Christmas without seeing his sweet thangs."

Fannie walked ahead into the room and over to a table filled with chips and dip and big pecan pies. Little cookies with red and green sprinkles. Annie shrugged her shoulders and followed.

The men seemed to brighten and part as the girls walked through the party. The women's eyes just narrowed and they began to whisper. Black, white, yellow. All kinds. All rich. She could smell their cologne, their new suits, and the alcohol on their breath. Poor people didn't smell like that. Poor people smelled like mothballs and cabbage soup.

Fannie stared over at a teenager, ran her tongue around her lips, and then poked it through a cookie. Made Annie feel butterflies just watching. Peetie grabbed a cold beer, sat down on some folding chairs, and finished his cigar. He tried to act important, like he didn't know them.

Guess they would just have to put on a show. Annie joined her partner near the treats. She cut a slab of pecan pie and topped it with M&M's.

The rich black woman looked like she'd faint when Annie picked up the pie with her hands and ate it like pizza. The woman and some white chick with a hard face walked over to them. The white woman wore one of those queer sweaters you make at home. Rudolph made of glitter and red balls. The thing looked like a fucking carpet.

"My husband will be with you shortly," the rich black woman said. She stood there, trying to make a big deal about being quiet. The white woman staggered behind her like she was about to spit out a little venom.

"That's just fine," Fannie said. "Don't take too long for Big Daddy to get his rocks off."

Annie could've kissed her as she watched the white woman begin to choke.

"That's right," Annie said. "Ever since he got a hold of that old-man dick pill, he been wantin' it all the time. We always used to hassle him on the street. We said, 'Daddy, how come you don't want no pussy?' But one day, he say, 'Okay, missy. Come give me a taste.'"

The black woman was hyperventilating. Someone get the woman a paper bag or slap her in her fat ass.

"He do like a little nasty," Fannie said, licking sprinkles off her fingers.

Peetie watched, looking down at the end of his cheap cigar. He pointed the moist end at some old fossil in a blue suit and laughed. The man had a wild Afro, almost like Don King's, and fat bags under his tired eyes. He placed his fists on his hips.

"The rabbit done died, sir," Annie said. "Please have kindness upon your child. I told you we should have used a rubber."

"I made my coat out of little Bunny," Fannie said. "You should come over to my closet and feel the little girl. Poor Bunny. She loved those carrots."

"You two get out of here," the man said. His black eyes looked like they were about to poke out of his head. "I said now!"

"C'mon, Big Daddy," Annie said.

"I've never seen either of you in my life," the man said. "Get out."

A small group formed around them. The blues band stopped playing as the harmonica player hit an off note. Everyone stopped talking as a slim black man wearing a long western coat, cowboy hat, and boots wandered into the room. He had a big plug of tobacco in his cheek and spit on the floor when he saw the women.

"Ladies, ladies," he said, wiping off his lips and smiling like he was in heat. "Do we know each other?"

The man in the suit just stood there staring. He adjusted his tie and took a step back. "Elmore, these your guests?"

Elmore kept smiling and spit again on the floor.

"What's your name, little mama?" King asked.

"Fannie."

"Lord, Lord, Lord."

The old woman snorted like a bull and walked away, leaving her husband standing in the dusty barn, a dozen onlookers watching him. Peetie strutted over to the group, switching the cigar around in his mouth, and stood a few feet from the cowboy man's face. He raised on his toes and blew smoke in his eyes.

"We'll talk later, Peetie," King said. "Now, get these people the hell out here."

"I think we need to talk now," Peetie said. "Stagger Lee wants you to make a little donation to the annual Billy Lyons Christmas fund."

King looked like he choked on his wad of tobacco.

40

Nick watched the Chicago River's cold water churn under the Michigan Avenue bridge in a slushy brown mess and thought about Ruby Walker, dying young, broken promises, and second chances. The gray Tribune Tower loomed over the bridge like a gothic castle. Spires. Flying buttresses. He half expected Batman to scale down the wall anytime as big chunks of ice fell from another bridge like melting glaciers. Nick studied the orange end of the Marlboro burning in his hand and took a warm breath of black smoke.

He flicked the grayed ash into the cold river and stomped his feet on the bridge. *Second chances.* He tucked his hands into his thread-bare wool coat as businessmen in fedoras and camel hair overcoats walked by, leaning into the wind as if someone held a strong hand to their chest. The Hawk had made its presence known. Out of the corner of his eye, he saw Kate walking across the metal grate, her brown hair whipping across her face in a white turtleneck, peacoat, and faded jeans. She held a manilla folder filled with loose papers in one hand and an extra-large cafe latte in the other.

"Sure you don't want one?"

"No, got a deal on this supersize cup at a gas station," he said. "They call it El Burro. Damn thing won't spill over. I could get you one for Christmas. Only ninety-nine cents. Free refills."

"You look like shit," she said, out of breath.

"Thanks."

"Was that a joke?" she asked, handing Nick the file and pulling her windblown hair from her brown eyes. "About the women?"

"I gave a ride to this woman last night from Rosa's."

"Is this X-rated?" she said with her hands around the cup and tapping her feet on the concrete. "Because if it is, I don't want to hear it."

"She was drunk," Nick said, raising an eyebrow. "And I didn't want her wandering around."

"Always the gentleman." Kate pursed her lips and made a sarcastic grin. She took a sip of coffee and started to walk back toward the Tribune Building. Nick followed, his coat flapping in the wind. His feet warm in two layers of wool socks and battered boots.

"Anyway," he said, almost bumping into a guy talking on a cell phone. *Asshole*. "When I got her home this other chick hops out of a closet with a knife and they both start beating the shit out of me."

"So, you were in her house?"

"Yeah, I tried to leave . . . but then she tied me up." He frowned. "Look, I know this sounds bad."

"Quit while you're ahead," Kate said. Her voice bourbon over cracked iced. "Poor kid, women just can't get enough of your ass."

"Tony said he'd never seen her before. I can't remember the cab company or where the hell the apartment was. I admit I had a few."

"A few?"

"Listen, someone wants me to stay away from Ruby."

"Now you're just being paranoid. Get a grip, Travers, no one wants to kill your broken-down ass over this. You almost got rolled by a couple of whores. Bad luck."

"I don't believe in luck."

"Did they ask you about her?" Kate said, stopping. She took another sip of coffee, steam seeping from the lid. In front of the doors to the Tribune Tower, a rush of people scattered around them in heavy clothes, walking with impatience. Nick readjusted his hat, completely content in the moment. Just standing there with a knocking beat in his chest with Kate so close. Just standing in the freezing cold, two feet from Kate Archer.

"No."

"Did they say anything about any of the people you interviewed? Or seem to know who you were?"

"No."

Kate smirked.

"Why would I make this up?"

"Who knows why you do half the things you do, Travers. Sympathy. Trying to get into my pants."

"Yeah, right." A perfect slash of lips. Dimpled chin. A diamond carat in each ear.

"Shit. Don't try to con me, Travers."

"Please. . . . Listen, these women were attractive. I mean beautiful women."

"Whores can't be beautiful?"

"You know what I mean."

"No, Nick, I don't know what you mean." She looked at the door to the *Tribune* and then back into Nick's eyes. "I think you got what you deserved. Going home with some woman you don't know and then surprised when she tried to rob you. C'mon. Don't try to play games like I'm one of your dumb-ass blondes. How drunk were you?"

"Like I said, I had a few," he said swallowing. His mouth filled with cotton.

"Looks like you made Tony plenty of money last night."

"She played me for a reason."

"Ruby Walker has been in jail for forty years," she said. "Why would a couple of young girls care if you were trying to talk to some of her friends? It doesn't make sense, Nick."

"You have the greatest eyes."

"Up yours," she said.

He put his hands in his pockets and shrugged. She pulled the folder from the crook of his arm.

"And you owe me big-time for this one . . . we found Florida.

My buddy in research, David, decided to check marriage licenses for a Florida Thomas. He found one from 1974. She married a man named Whitaker. After that it was easy as shit. He Auto-Tracked Florida Whitaker's car registered a couple of years ago. Address. Everything. All right here."

She shoved the papers into his chest. He read her notes rustling in the heavy wind, her handwriting so clean it looked like type. Nick let out a long breath. He thought about kissing her. Then thought better of it.

"A green Nova? Has to be one of the last ones still on the street."

"Why didn't Ruby know where she was?" Kate asked.

"She disappeared after Ruby was charged."

"Ruby know why?"

"She helped Ruby move the body."

They stood in front of the glass doors to the Tribune Tower for a few moments looking at each other. The world swirled by, the stoplights changed color from red to green in the never-ending grayness, and a light snow began to fall.

"You ever think about leaving New Orleans?" she asked. "Taking a job somewhere else? Go back to Mississippi?"

"Thought about coming up here. Kick around Chicago for a while. Plenty of stories. Plenty of blues players. . . . Depend on what else is up here."

"Bad weather," Kate said.

"Everything thaws."

"Depends on how bad the winter was."

Nick looked into her eyes and reached for her hand in her coat pocket. He traced her warm fingers.

She didn't pull away for a few seconds. The warm coffee in her hand separating them.

"Goddamn, I hate you," she said in her raspy voice.

"I hate you too."

"You need help finding Florida? Don't you?"

"Saddle up, Tonto," Nick said.

41

THE SNOW FELL harder, and the lethargic wipers on Kate's ragged black Karmaan Ghia weren't helping much. One good patch of ice and they'd probably career into oncoming traffic, she thought. She kept her hands tight on the leather steering wheel and her eyes focused on the few feet of visibility. The snow was beautiful among the neon storefront signs and tacky Christmas displays. Mechanical Santas. Plastic Nativity scenes. One had Rudolph grazing by the manger. The things you learn about the Bible.

She'd missed the change of seasons when she lived in New Orleans. After she'd taken the job with the *Picayune*—right out of Northwestern—she'd met people, characters really, she'd never imagined in her middle-class suburban world: voodoo priests who told futures with brittle chicken bones, Mardi Gras Indians with their headdresses full of jewels and feathers, and street kids who thought they were vampires with sharpened eye teeth. *Broken-down bluesmen*. Great writing material.

It was tough to load up her car with Bud, her Jack Russell terrier, and say good-bye to her apartment on St. Charles. But she also missed her family in Winnetka. Her loudmouth Irish cop father, her fast-talking Italian mother, and her five brothers and sisters. Nice to have roots again.

That afternoon, most of the South Side looked sand-blasted

and worn as the wind shot though the holes in her softtop. Nick warmed his hands on the vents and calmly looked into the darkness. The heated air smelled like an old sock.

One day off—day before Christmas Eve no less—and she was going to spend it doing interviews on the South Side. She looked over at Nick's scruffy profile and smiled. *Been too long.*

"Got big plans for all this research?" Kate asked as the wipers squeaked and moaned.

"Not really, just publish my findings," Nick said, leaning over to wipe the condensation forming on the windshield with his glove. "Depends on what I find out. If it looks like she's innocent, I'd like to see the State's Attorney's Office reopen the case. If not, it's still a good story."

"It's exciting, isn't it?" Kate asked.

"What?"

"Knowing the system has failed someone. That they don't have a prayer in the world without you. You have it all there, Travers. It's all there."

She drove into the hazed snow past a commercial strip of used car lots, tire wholesalers, and fast-food franchises. Looked like Airline Highway in New Orleans. Every city has one, a collection of shitty chain businesses and anonymous apartments. A place devoid of personality or feeling. Somewhere to exist.

"How depressing," Kate said.

"You know this ain't about spotlighting on my work. You want to write about Ruby, go ahead."

"No shit?" she asked, as the car thudded over a pothole.

"No shit," Nick said, looking like he might barf onto his boots.

Nick getting sick wouldn't make her feel any better about their past. She'd decided to play it cool and pretend like this fling didn't mean anything. Like she was a big girl with a weak memory. But it still pissed her off. She remembered every detail. That bimbo's blonde—almost white—hair, the woman's damned boobs hanging out of her robe. It would have made more sense or it would have hurt less if it had been someone he worked with at Tulane. But just to pick up some piece of Quarter trash to take back to the warehouse—a place she helped restore—was too much.

Every inch of the red maple floor she stained. All that paint splattered in her hair.

Just the thought made her grind her teeth.

"May take you up on that offer, Travers," she said, trying to take the edge off her voice. "Wouldn't be a bad story for Christmas. Got a lot of great elements working for it. . . . Think she'll talk to me?"

"Don't see why not."

"There's something else about this woman, right? Don't bullshit me. Why are you working so hard on this? You should be sipping on Jack Daniel's with JoJo right now. Maybe going out to the levee bonfires."

She zipped around a yellow snowplow, feeling a slight swerve in her back tires. Nick fumbled with the watch cap in his hands, probably trying to keep his mind off the motion. She sped up and cut back into the lane.

"Ruby's pretty special," Nick said. "One of those blues artists that gave people a chance to remember the South after the migration. It's like she's been stuck in a time capsule all these years and forgotten by historians and musicians . . . but if you talk to people who really know, they realize she's the end of an era. When they put Ruby away, they put away the spirit for a lot of people. The South Side. The blues. It's all kind of been shut off for the last forty years."

His voice grew louder over the car's growling engine.

"Blues changed," Nick said. "I mean, the classic stuff was still performed at revivals and as covers but it didn't grow. It evolved into something else. It switched from a remembering song to a song of protest. Buddy Guy and Elmore King sang about the northern oppression and made the guitar speak for them instead of with them. Shit . . . Ruby wouldn't have survived."

"You okay, Travers?" Kate asked.

"What a waste," he said. "She's given up. You should see her face, she's drained of everything. Completely void of emotion. She lives life out of obligation, trudging through it."

Nick looked out the window and got quiet. She recalled late-night conversations in the old warehouse. Kate couldn't think of anything to say as they rolled through the snow into another section of Chicago with an architecture of nowhere.

She knew all about Nick's series of disappointments. The premature deaths of his parents, some woman who used him to further her social status, and his failed career in the NFL. He rarely spoke of any of those memories. Especially his mother.

Kate drove on in silence.

■

The address for Florida was in a tired apartment complex not far from O'Hare Airport. The cheap apartments were styled to look like English Tudor houses. Brown slats of wood crossed the white concrete siding. The design didn't hide much. Most of the wood hung off the building like broken limbs over molting white paint. Plywood covered most windows with padlocks on several condemned apartments. A group of black teens sat on a Japanese import shaking with rap music as long-dead trees seemed to dance behind them. They eyed her car as she wheeled by them and deeper into the apartment complex.

Kate waved. This neighborhood was like Disney World compared to most places she visited. She pulled into a slot by a ragged Oldsmobile parked among vacant spaces. Nick got out and steadied this feet. He lit a cigarette and adjusted his worn leather belt as she walked to a stoop of an apartment with a plastic wreath on the door. Little lights blinked as fake pinecones buzzed an electronic "Jingle Bells."

She knocked and scanned the almost empty parking lot. Snow had gathered a couple inches on the car hoods. The kid's car boomed in the distant cold. The sky was nothing but a flat expanse of clouds. Deep depression winter, Kate thought as the biting wind ripped through her peacoat.

She knocked again.

Nothing.

Kate checked the mail slot and pulled out a few letters. Old trick she'd learned from a former editor. Not quite ethical. She flipped through them and slipped them back in the box.

"Not Whitaker," she said. "Somebody named Lopez."

Nick walked next door and knocked. She followed and heard a television inside. Canned sitcom laughter. A face soon emerged in the window and looked around. Someone had taped an eviction notice on the door scheduled for Christmas day. A black woman with green eyes and wrinkled skin opened the door a crack, her hair filled with tiny, pink curlers.

"Looking for Florida," Nick said.

"What?" the old woman asked. "You a long way from the beach."

She laughed at that for a good twenty seconds. Kate laughed too, waiting for the comedy to wear off. Nick rolled his eyes.

"A *woman* named Florida," Kate said. "She still live next door?"

Kate could just see the woman's roving eyes above the door's brass chain. She had a mole on her chin that resembled the tip of an eraser.

"Don't know," the woman said. "Only been here since the fall. Sorry."

"Older black woman ever live next door?" Nick asked, pointing to the apartment to his right.

"Naw. Only people I knowed live there is a couple of Puerto Ricans."

They thanked the woman and trudged back to the car. The snow gathered in Kate's eyelashes as she watched Nick fire a rapid drumbeat on her tattered convertible top. A cigarette hung loose in his mouth.

"Maybe she gets the wrong mail, Marlboro man," Kate said.

"And turned into a young Puerto Rican," Nick said, rolling the cigarette to the other corner of his smile. "You mind knockin' on a few doors with me?"

"Oh yeah, I'm so shy I might curl into a ball. Like I said, Travers, welcome to my life. You take the east row and I'll take the west. We'll meet in the middle."

"Let's stick together. I've had a few bad experiences since I've been in Chicago."

"So sorry to hear that," Kate said. "Now go on. This is what I do every fucking day. Somebody messes with me, I'll kick 'em in the nuts. Now go on."

"Hey, Kate?"

"Yeah?" she asked, walking toward the commercial strip.

"Remind me not to mess with you. I kind of like my nuts."

"This much I know, Travers," she said, waving over her shoulder. "This much I know."

■

Nick started at the end of the complex and worked his way down ten apartments before he got someone to open the door. Maybe they were at home and they thought he was an Avon salesmen or a Jehovah's Witness. On the eleventh one, an incredibly short black man wearing a spaghetti-stained T-shirt made to look like a tuxedo stood in front of him.

"Hey, man," Nick said. "I'm looking for one of your neighbors. Woman named Florida. You know if she still lives around here?"

"Well, 'hey man' yourself," he said with a shit-eating grin that dropped into a frown. "I don't know Florida and I ain't got time for this shit."

He slammed the door in Nick's face.

Another five apartments down, an elderly woman carrying a four-pronged cane opened the door. Nick felt like he was trick or treating or Christmas caroling. That was it. He could sing a short song every time someone opened the door. They'd love him.

"Got me a pain in ma gogo," she said. Her face a withered prune topped by a white wig. *Norman Bates, please come get your mother.*

"Where?" he said.

"In ma gogo."

"Gotcha."

Nick walked on and could see Kate working a row of apartments about a hundred yards away. Felt good working with her again. Didn't matter if they were knocking on doors in some shitty apartments. He knew being with her was fleeting, that they'd break away in a few days and return to their own private worlds. Kate wasn't impulsive. She wouldn't let him get beneath her tough exterior. She'd work with him, joke around, but she wouldn't let him know her anymore. He'd ruined all of that and now he was having to pay.

What he wouldn't give for just one more meal at Antoine's when the wine flowed and the conversation rolled and nothing mattered outside their small table.

Years ago, he'd shared a great meal and a couple bottles of wine with her in the old restaurant's Mystery Room. At Antoine's, the menu is more than one hundred years old and each of the fourteen dining rooms are lined with a barrage of images from daguerreotype photos to pictures of long-dead Krewe queens.

That night, the crowd had thinned to a patter of conversation as they walked to a dimly lit back staircase to the second floor. Kate laughed and stumbled as Nick led her into an empty upstairs dining room and closed a squeaky door. The light was so dim, the furniture appeared as shadows in the orange glow. The old floors creaked beneath them as they wandered by the tables smelling of clean linen and the walls of hot wood.

The room had felt enormous. So silent, it buzzed.

Kate led him to an empty chair behind a partition. She was wearing a black summer dress with spaghetti straps and sat on his lap. Nick had felt the blood working through his veins as a door opened and someone switched off the lights. He touched her cheek in the darkness and slid down one of her straps. She wasn't wearing a bra and he kissed her chest. She unbuttoned his pants and she stood as he worked her panties down her legs. *It was all by touch.* In the darkness, he couldn't tell where he started and she ended. It was exciting knowing they could be caught as she breathed louder and began to make soft noises. They both melted into each other that June night in the desolate floor of the New Orleans institution. It ended with the longest, most twisted kiss he'd ever known.

Twenty minutes later, Nick saw Kate about a dozen apartments away chatting with a skinny, black woman in a Bart Simpson nightshirt who smoked a cigarette and held a baby.

She smiled and waved him over.

He lit a cigarette and jogged down the apartment row, his feet beginning to feel like bricks and his face turned to stone. He smiled at the woman.

"This is Ellen," Kate said.

The baby cried as Ellen soothed its curly head. The young mother stuck a bottle back in the child's mouth and wiped her dirty hands on her nightshirt.

"Wish I could help you folks," Ellen said. "But people 'round here ain't too comfortable knowin' their neighbors. Don't know nobody named Florida."

"What about an apartment manager or landlord?" Kate asked.

"If you can get him to return your calls, then you must be a magician. I'll give you his number but he don't know who's livin' here now, let alone few years back."

"What about any old tenants?" Nick asked. "Someone who may recognize the name."

"Take your pick . . . maybe some of the church folks."

"What church?" Kate asked.

"*The church,*" she said, torching a skinny cigarette with a flame as long as her finger. "The First Church of Prayer on Halsted. Everybody 'round here goes to the show on Sunday. Wearin' expensive clothes and talkin' bad things 'bout their neighbors. Best thing goin' if you into that mess."

"Praise the Lord," Nick said.

42

THE FIRST CHURCH of Prayer shook with a hard-hitting spiritual presence that Saturday afternoon. About thirty men and women in street clothes rocked with the music in the back of the huge brick church. Down the length of the building, stained glass windows of apostles glowed like sugar candy as Nick and Kate walked down a side aisle. Midway, they sat in hard wooden seats stamped with the sign of the cross. Kate smiled as she watched the rehearsal heat up. Nick leaned back into his seat and felt the pleasant hum of the music take over the building and the souls of listeners. The pews were almost empty as the choir prepared for tomorrow's Christmas Eve service.

Nick could feel the music deep in his tired limbs. The old church seemingly pulsed with God's energy. Lights, paned in gold and glass, swung from the ceiling, scattering light through the church. A tall Christmas tree sat to the right of the pulpit. The church smelled of dry-cleaned clothes and burning candles. Felt good to be inside as the snow chilled the outside streets. Nick could feel the hot blood moving again through his face and ears.

At the altar, dozens of red candles flickered as the minister took the microphone and looped the cord in his hands, like a Stax soul singer. He was a young man with light skin, a mustache, and a soul patch below his lip. He wore a thick, gold chain around his neck that swung like a clock's pendulum.

"I come a long way . . ." he belted out to the mostly empty

pews. "Come through the sun and the rain, people holding my hand by the grace of God . . . *I come a long way.*"

An organist, bass player, electric guitarist, and drummer jammed at the foot of the pulpit. A lanky, balding man in a gray suit played the organ. Looked like a funeral director as he moved with a quiet enthusiasm.

The beat of the music was not unlike the trademark sound of Muddy's "Mannish Boy." The gospel edge such an important part of the blues. The preacher's growl and elevated vocals emphasized the roots. Something that resonated in Ruby's music.

JoJo always said all you had to do was replace "oh Lord" with "oh baby" and you had a great rhythm and blues song. A lot was the same. The hand clapping, the call and response, and the moaning voices.

All the Delta players had a church background. And almost every great blues singer Nick knew spent some time with a gospel choir. That edge is what gave blues its soul. If you don't have the soul, you're just faking it. It's why most white guys look like mannequins trying to be bluesmen.

Blues is religion.

In the South, the black church was the social center of the community, an outlet during segregation to express feelings. Before television or radio, Sunday services would last way into the afternoon. Picnic tables buckled from good food surrounded by a buzz of conversation.

During the migration, northern cities were overrun with storefront churches to feed the masses. It was a survival of the fittest, storefronts with the strongest base evolved into larger buildings. This was the ultimate. The great whale that devoured nearby competitors. Took a lot of money to run this holy place.

"I want to thank you, Jesus," the preacher sang as he rattled his tambourine. "I want to thank you. I could have been dead! But by the grace of God, *I've come a long way.*"

An old woman in lime green with silver hair sang, "Amen! Amen!" from a front pew.

She was "getting happy," like what Alan Lomax witnessed in

the Cohoma County project so many years ago in the old churches of Mississippi. The women feeling the holy spirit take over their bodies. An African spiritualism. It was hard not to "get happy." Nick remembered going to church in Alabama with his mother and the droning sound of white hymnals. It seemed to stamp out any flicker of human emotion. But in this church, deep soul brought out the deepest part of humanity.

Kate clapped her hands in time with the music as the choir shuffled their shoulders and let it all out. Nick started clapping too, watching the service. The preacher danced on the tips of his toes as a hefty woman reached a high note with the choir keeping the melody.

The band changed into a mellow breakdown of "Silent Night" that raised the hair on the back of his neck. The woman pierced any jaded conceptions about organized religion that he sometimes had. She sang deep and bellowed a wonderful testimonial to her faith:

> *"It was a siiilent night,*
> *Oh Lord, it was hoooly night,*
> *Lord, don't you know all was caaalm,*
> *Lord, don't you know all was briiight."*

The singer was a stout woman with red-tinted hair and oversize glasses. During the last verse, Kate dug her nails into Nick's palm as she listened. Her eyes closed, rocking with the music. The chorus finally broke up after some words from the minister about the Christmas Eve service. Nick walked back to the pulpit. As he followed the center aisle, he felt like he was about to take Communion.

He hadn't been to church in years.

The minister looked down and smiled. Nick introduced himself and complimented the minister's choir. The man thanked him.

"Dr. Anthony Dowdell," he said.

Nick asked him about Florida. The minister shook his head sadly and said he didn't believe he had any parishioners by that name. His face showed a grave concern with a passing light of regret. His tone was even and his handshake warm. *Thank you so much for stopping by.*

Nick thanked him and motioned for Kate to follow him through a back hallway that led to a metal exit door. Outside, several members of the chorus had gathered to talk, scarves around their necks, stomping their feet in the cold. They asked the choir members the same question and they all shook their head, not speaking a word, and returned to talking.

"Let's go get drunk," Kate said.

"Now you're talking." Nick crawled into the Karmaan Ghia's passenger door and sank into the seat. He rolled down the window and lit a cigarette. Kate sat beside him, pulled the cigarette from his mouth, and tossed it out the window.

"No smoking?"

"No smoking," she said, watching him pull the watch-cap over his ears. "That has to be the ugliest hat I've ever seen."

"It was on sale."

"Where? The Salvation Army?"

"Woolworth. A dollar ninety-nine."

"Where do you want to go?" she asked, pulling her hair into a ponytail and wrapping it with a rubber band.

"The nearest bar."

Nick scratched his unshaven face and stared across the parking lot at the great brick church. The minister walked out the front door, still in a robe, and disappeared. Dead leaves scattered on the stone steps covered in a light snow.

The whole neighborhood had the feeling of decaying dark wood. The old Victorians surrounding the church leaned like a James Michalopoulos painting.

Kate started her car and wheeled out of the parking lot. But something caught Nick's eye and he asked her to loop back off Halsted and into the church lot.

"Stop right here," he said as she passed an old Chevrolet. Rust-splotched green.

"Novas sure are ugly," he said.

Kate smiled. She had a beautiful smile.

"Plate match?" he asked.

"Never trust a preacher man," she said.

■

Later that afternoon, Annie and Fannie rode the El downtown with Peetie. The wheels screeched like a scalded cat as the train rattled and rocked. Just as she was getting into a really good *Archie's Digest*, some sex weirdo walked over and kept trying to make eye contact.

"Where you guys going?" the fuckup asked. He was about thirty-five. Suit. And the biggest damned head she'd ever seen. Like a walking potato.

Peetie had his hat slanted over his eyes but she could tell he was listening.

"Hawaii," Fannie said popping her gum and not giving him a look.

He gave an old *har-har* laugh. Guess they did look pretty tough today in complete black leather head to toe. Both of them. Fannie had on this cool silver lipstick and bright blue eye shadow. Annie wore a little black hat like you'd buy in France or something.

Annie put her feet up on the seat before her and played with the zipper on her chest. She looked down at the black lace on her bra.

"I guess you guys hear that all the time," he said, "but you're about the hottest things I've ever seen."

"We know," Fannie said and waved him away. "Now you may go."

"Yeah, go piss up a tree," Annie added.

Fannie whipped out a nail file and began to work on a hangnail. She'd been talking about some new process she'd read about in *Cosmo* all day. Something about soaking your hands in olive oil. Something real crazy.

"I like nasty girls," the man said. "I like it when they're mean to me. You two want to get mean?"

He looked down at his crotch.

Fannie waved the nail file a few inches from his rod. "Mister, you want to keep that little worm? Then you best move on. If you don't think I'll cut your dick off and throw it out the widow . . ." She bobbed her head from side to side. "You are sor-row-ly mistaken."

The man moved on.

Peetie crossed his arms before him and gave a little laugh.

"What did Stagger Lee say?" he asked. First time he'd spoken since she called from the old wooden platform.

"Said it was cool," Annie said. "But he wanted to take care of the exchange tonight. Didn't like the idea of getting out of Robert Taylor for the cash."

"Did you tell him that was the only way?"

"What do you think, dipshit?"

"Just askin', woman, don't be gettin' all testy on me."

Fannie finished with her nails and dropped the file in her purse. "What about that Travers man? We get a second shot?"

"No," Annie said. "As much as I'd like to take his ass out for what he did to Willie . . . Stagger Lee said he'd take care of it. That man won't live to see Christmas."

The brakes of the El screeched in her ears as they stopped downtown.

43

NICK SIPPED ON gas station coffee while he watched Florida's apartment and thought about what Ruby had said about blues fading. He never liked to think the music would die but he knew today's blues lacked an emotional intensity it had with the golden-era folks. A friend of his once wrote that blues was a remembering song just like the African slaves played in Congo Square in New Orleans. Tribal rhythms played on jawbones and wooden horns to evoke the homeland.

There was no doubt the great bluesmen and women of Chicago were recalling their southern home. But, like Ruby said, these days amplification had taken over soul. Life experience didn't mean as much. It was more about learning another's style played louder and fancier.

Where were the spirits of Robert Johnson, Son House, and Charley Patton?

Nick remembered that great line from *Deep Blues*. Something about the Zen-like attitudes of rural musicians: "The intimate link between worlds outside and inside our bodies that city dwellers aren't attuned to but country people simply know."

Maybe that was the key.

Nick took another sip of the foul coffee and kept watching the apartment. They'd followed Florida from church to a grocery store—where they waited for thirty minutes in a parking lot—and then to her new place. It was a brownstone quartered into apartments with heavy concrete steps leading to a glass door.

She'd disappeared into the building ten minutes ago.

Kate had the driver's seat reclined with her arms folded over her chest and a gray wool hat pulled over her ears. She'd buttoned her pea-coat to the very top with the collar high around her neck. Nick looked back through windows coated with frost and took another sip of coffee.

"This stuff tastes like it was made during the bicentennial," Nick said, grimacing.

"What did you expect, Café Du Monde?" she said. "God, it smells awful too. Smells like burnt dog shit."

"Want a sip?"

Kate scrunched up her face and looked up the landing to the door.

Nick sipped on the sludgelike coffee. He watched the door. A group of roughnecks paused by the car but kept walking. Looked harmless. You could tell the mean ones by their eyes. Eyes radiate anger.

Minutes later, Florida appeared at the top of the landing and trotted down the icy steps to the Nova. Even though Nick had seen the forty-year-old picture, he couldn't pick her out of the choir. She'd grown thicker and heavier. Her face was flat as a skillet with wide-set eyes, smallish ears, and an ass the size of Texas. Even larger than JoJo's niece's.

Florida opened her trunk and pulled out a couple sacks of groceries. Her clothes looked about twenty years out of style. A light blue trench coat and leopard-print scarf around her neck.

Nick got out and strolled over to the Nova. His hands hung loose by his sides and he tried an easygoing grin.

"Need some help?"

Florida ignored him, pulling the paper sacks marked FRANK'S FOODS into her arms.

"My name's Travers," he said. "I'm a friend of Ruby Walker's."

"Ruby's in jail." Her mouth downturned.

"I know."

"Then you ain't her friend," she said, slamming her trunk closed and tossing the rattling keys into her bag. Florida looked away, her eyes hot. She had a thin trail of scars on both cheeks that had lightened her flesh. Almost looked like tears.

"Listen, I'm trying to help her out. I know you're her best friend. All I want to know is what happened."

"Thought you said she was *your* friend. Why don't you ask *her*?"

"I need to know where she was the night Billy Lyons was killed."

"That was a long time ago, mister," Florida said. "I have the Lord in my life and don't have time for much else."

Nick put his hand on her shoulder. The material of her jacket felt like a museum piece. "I just want the truth."

"The Lord is the truth," she said, shaking his hand away. "Don't make me call the police."

"Why weren't you at the trial?"

"*Oh please*. Get out of my way." She walked by Nick and moved up the steps, balancing the groceries. She missed a middle step and fell to her knees. One of the bags tumbled down to the sidewalk, its contents scattering across the concrete.

Nick picked up the bag, gathered a bunch of cans and a shaken bottle of generic cola, and brought it back to her. She sat down on the icy steps looking at a gash on her shin under bloodied panty hose.

Her eyes were rimmed with tears.

"I'm really sorry, ma'am."

"Go on! Get out of here!" she screamed.

"I need to know for Ruby."

Florida grabbed a handrail and looked down at the base of the stairs where Kate stood. She looked back up at Nick and quickly turned away. He was on his own.

"Ain't no reason to tell you nothin'. Ruby's in jail and she's been there a long time." Florida pulled herself to her feet and grabbed her bags. She limped to the door. Nick could hear the ice and salt cracking under her feet.

"I know she's innocent," Nick said. "I know she didn't kill Billy Lyons. Who would want him dead?"

"I don't have to listen to this . . . this shit!" she said, cupping a hand to her mouth and then punching a security code on the door. "Get out of my way."

She pushed by him and slammed the door behind her.

"I know you helped her move his body," Nick said through the glass door as she waddled down the hall, her Texas-size ass swaying in her dress. "Why weren't you questioned about the murder?"

She slowed her brusque walk and stopped. Nick's breath froze on the glass pane as he watched Florida put down her groceries, turn, and stare up at him with supreme aggravation.

She stood there for a moment as Nick felt the blood rush in his ears. Then she walked back to the stoop and cracked the door.

The warmth of the hall flooded into his face. He could smell her breath and feel her thoughts. "Well, come on then . . . grab them groceries and make yourself useful. Ain't got all day."

■

Stagger Lee could see Travers from the abandoned lot where he stood among the pieces of wet trash, concrete blocks, and broken bottles. So, this was the man who slipped away from Annie and Fannie. Never knew those two to fuck up. Ever. When they were teenagers, he used to send them into Cabrini-Green to shake down some hustlers. Places that a man would've gotten cut in two seconds. And shit, Annie would come back, a big smile on her face, with that hustler's balls in her hand.

A man couldn't say no to Fannie. And a man couldn't stop Annie.

Man, he'd trained those women right.

Stagger Lee watched the big woman lead Travers and some white chick into her place. He sat there in the cold lot watching and breathing. Hot blood racing through him.

A white light clicked on the second floor.

He breathed and gritted his teeth.

Shame he'd have to take down the man so fast. Without Travers, he'd still be sitting in The Hole, rotting among the backed-up sewers and frozen shit.

Tonight, he'd be reborn.

44

FLORIDA'S APARTMENT SMELLED of baking bread and sweet fudge. Her furniture was fake Victorian, stiff and tiny, with framed posters of Bible verses hanging on the walls. Sunsets, wispy clouds, and inspirational words. Baby dolls dressed in international clothes filled a glass case toward the kitchen. Dutch girls to Geishas. A plastic Virgin Mary and a foot-high Marilyn Monroe.

Nick stood by the kitchen doorway with his arms crossed over his chest, his head almost touching the top door frame, as Kate sat on a bar stool trying to seem like she wasn't listening. Her eyes wandered about the old-fashioned kitchen. A 1950s refrigerator and a gas stove. Even a stainless-steel toaster that looked like it was out of *I Love Lucy.*

"I don't mean to be rude," Florida said, putting away the last of the groceries, "but them days are long gone. I wasn't more than a teenager when me and Ruby come to Chicago."

"You two grew up together?" Nick asked.

"*Mmm hmm,*" she said, playing with the rings on her hands. "In Clarksdale. We drank and partied. Guess you could say we ran a little wild. I'm not too proud of them days. Don't know what else to tell you."

Florida slowly shook her head. She untucked the scarf from around her neck and took a deep breath. The sweet air in the kitchen was beginning to make him feel dizzy. Several plastic trays of red and green cookies and cakes were stacked on the counter. A sack of sugar by the stove with a fat stainless-steel scoop inside.

"Why haven't you been to see her?" Nick asked.

"You have to understand, Billy was my friend too. I loved that man about as much as Ruby. When he would send for Ruby, he would send for me. Bought me drinks. Made sure no one messed with me. That kind of thing. Sharp man in his white suits and white Stetson hat. Real sharp man. He had a bad reputation. People said he was tough, but I knew a lot of that was just an act."

"But he was a gangster," Nick said.

"He did some illegal things, so I guess you could say that." She opened her freezer and pulled out some ice. "But I knew other things about Billy. I knew the other side. The one who left roses for Ruby when she would wake up. The man who tried to get her to stop drinking. He . . ." she trailed off.

"He what?" Nick asked.

"He was so afraid she would be like his mama." Florida dumped the ice into a plastic Baggie and broke it apart with the end of a screwdriver. "He told me one time, his mama ran a house for prostitutes. Back then, it wasn't that uncommon in Mississippi. Billy said she drank herself to sleep every night.

"He said he used to hang out with all the girls and the musicians who played downstairs. Lord, he was always talking about this one man. What was his name? Something like Abadabba. I think that's why he loved the blues. Always talked about Abadabba, the blues piano man. One night, Billy's mother fell asleep, passed out in her bed. Billy said they had these old oil lamps. I guess she knocked one over and caught the place on fire. He grew up on the streets after that. . . . Guess that's why I never blamed him for bein' a hustler."

Nick took a deep breath.

"You ever have a relationship with Billy?" Kate asked, chiming in at the right moment to ease a little pressure. *His Girl Friday*.

"No, ma'am. Billy was like my brother."

"Understand you were close to his child," Nick said. "And that one time you ran off with her."

"Where did you hear that?" she asked. She looked like she wanted to laugh.

Kate looked at Nick. He said, "Ruby."

"You heard wrong. I didn't steal that child. Billy tole me to take her away. When things got rough around Chicago and people made threats against Billy, we'd disappear for a while."

Nick nodded. "Maybe those people killed him."

Florida's face softened. She clasped her hands in front of her face and closed her eyes. The scars below her eyes looked like canyons.

"What was Ruby like the days before the murder?" he asked.

"Ruby could be difficult," Florida said, her eyes still closed. She opened them, picked up the crushed ice, and found a kitchen chair. "Even when we were kids, she could get in the blackest mood you ever saw. Get that lip poked out and that girl wouldn't do nothin'. I don't know . . . before Billy was killed, I guess she was mad. I know she was drinkin' real heavy and cussin' him. But that is just the way it was since she met him. To say she was any different would be a lie.

"Ruby was a jealous soul," she said. "At the end, she followed Billy around. She would kick any woman's behind go near him. That night she told me how much she hated him."

"What time was that?" Nick asked.

"I don't remember, late. We were drinking at the Palm Tavern with Jimmy Scott and Elmore King. About midnight, I left her there. I was mad. Ruby was drunker than I ever seen her."

"Too drunk to kill a man?" Kate asked.

"Apparently not," Florida said.

"What makes you so sure?" Kate asked.

"I helped Ruby dump Billy's body in the lake." Florida pressed the ice pack to her shin. "I helped her get it out of her bed, I drove her crying, and I helped her clean up. Billy was a bloody heap in those sheets and Ruby was a drunk mess."

"Did she tell you she killed him?" Nick asked.

"You said Ruby told you I helped."

"Yes."

"Then why are you here?"

"We want to know why you weren't at the trial or didn't talk to the police," Kate said.

Florida bit her lip and shook her head.

"How did she get home?" Nick asked.

"I don't know."

"I appreciate you inviting us in but I want to know why you took off before the trial." Nick asked. "What happened? Why were you running?"

She kept shaking her head, got up, and limped back into her family room. Nick looked at Kate and she shrugged. In a minute, Florida walked back in with a dusty picture frame. The picture was of a black family in their Sunday best in front of stock-photography bookshelves. Mother, father, two kids. Looked like the all-American family.

Nick smiled, "Who's that?"

"That's Billy's little girl, Nat," Florida said. "I raised her up after Billy died. Billy's wife had died back in Mississippi and she didn't have no other family. His daughter was an honor student, went on to Spelman. I couldn't be more proud of her."

"Was she around the night he died?" Kate asked.

"No," Florida said. "She was with a young friend of hers. I picked her up there the next day and told her about her daddy. She was outside skippin' rope with her little pigtails and bright smile." Florida put a hand to her mouth. "Little girl didn't speak for almost a year."

The refrigerator buzzed to life. A cat wandered into the room, swished its tail, and left.

"Listen, I know people still talk about Ruby," Florida said. "We all want to believe she's innocent. Poor old black woman. Such a sweet, sweet voice. I wish I was half the singer she was. But they have all forgotten about Billy. Billy was a two-time pimp to some people. And that's just a lie. He was a wonderful man and a wonderful father."

"I want to help them both," Nick said.

"I've told you all I know," Florida said. "I got to get started cooking. . . . Y'all excuse me."

"Ruby's made some statements to me," Nick said not breaking eye contact, wanting her to hear every word. "Still says she's innocent. You know this will be her fortieth Christmas without seeing the world? You have your choir and your baked goods and Billy's daughter and Ruby—excuse me for saying this—doesn't have shit. For four decades, she's lived in a concrete cage no bigger than your bathroom. It's easy, Florida, to put your memories on hold, to coat yourself in religion, and say that time has passed. But Ruby cared for you when you came up here. Probably made you more than you ever could be alone. So, let's not play games anymore. This is it."

Florida sat for a moment at the kitchen table. Her head fell into her hands and her body shook for what seemed like several minutes. Kate looked away. Nick watched her sob as he felt the weight of a woman's cries in the silent room. He walked over and looked out the leaded glass window to the street below. He saw Kate's car on the cold, wet streets and the blackened edge of a vacant lot covered in snow.

A hulking man disappeared into the shadows. Nick peered into the night, saw nothing, and walked back in the room.

Florida was crying. The old scars on her cheeks filled with water.

"She's had it, Florida," he said. "I think she's ready to die. So if you don't want any more regrets than you already have, I say let's talk."

"I don't want this conversation going any further than this here room," Florida said, wiping away brief tears. "You hear me? I don't want to be in no paper."

Florida's head bent down to her hands. She sat there for a few minutes with her eyes closed. She looked like she was praying. Nick didn't move. No one spoke.

She began to play with the gold cross around her neck. She

tossed the bag of ice into the sink. It made a harsh cracking noise as it hit.

Florida finally spoke, her voice shaky.

"So long ago," she whispered. "So long ago."

She exhaled a long, deep breath.

"The only thing I never figured out was how she did it," Florida said as she looked down at her linoleum floor and then back at Kate. "We found that man in her bed but the next day I went to the studio to get some things of Billy's for Nat and I seen it."

Nick watched her face, unable to breathe, like she would suddenly stop and change her mind.

"There was blood all over the wall in the recording booth. Big pieces of the wall were chipped away with blood running down its sides like it was crying. Now, why did she move him after killin' him there?"

Nick gritted his teeth. "You could have told somebody, Florida."

"I did. I tole that detective man. But he tole me to keep my mouth shut or else he'd get Nat sent down to an orphanage and stick my ass in prison. . . . Me and Nat left the next day for Memphis and didn't come back to Chicago for ten years."

Nick looked at Kate: "I got to find Jimmy."

45

ANNIE GLIDED AROUND the ice rink at Navy Pier and thought this was going to be the best Christmas ever. She darted in and out of a bunch of wobbly kids and sprayed some old coot in a wool hat with ice shavings. Fannie waved to her from the opposite side of the rink where she was doing her Dorothy Hamill twirl and talking to some yuppie dude and his two kids. That girl was always working it. But Peetie was no fun. That dumb-ass was sitting on a park bench blowing on his hands. She wasn't sure about trusting him, but it could work. Stagger Lee would never suspect a thing. The man was just looking for King to bring the cash and then haul ass to Robert Taylor.

What a gift.

The last Christmas gift she'd gotten was from her mother when she was a kid. Her mother had worked a couple of extra hours bagging groceries so she could buy her three plastic figures: Jiminy Cricket, Pinocchio, and that evil Fox guy. Her mother had wrapped them all up in newspaper and tucked them under a bare tree branch. Annie loved those hard, plastic toys. Slept and played with them until their heads fell off.

She wanted something like that again. Something she could love until its head broke. Something like poor old Willie, God rest his soul. She wondered where he was tonight, was he thinking about her? She tried not to cry as she gave a good run on the blades and then flew around a curve by the Crystal Gardens. She shot a bird to Peetie and kept going around.

Maybe since they were coming into all this cash, she should get Fannie something like thongs and a box of jawbreakers. Or a pack of Bubblicious and a tiara. She remembered Fannie pointing one out in a magazine and saying that thing would make her feel like a princess.

On the next loop, she passed Fannie and told her she was going to take a break. Fannie gave a lazy grin and kept giggling at something the rich white dude said. Annie skated up onto a blade-scarred piece of plywood and walked on quivering heels to a bench. Peetie strolled over with another one of those stinky cigars in his mouth. She stared up at the huge Ferris wheel looming over his head.

"Glad you got wise," Peetie said as the park lights glowed around them in the deep blackness. The snow had piddled down to some grainy microflakes. "Seem like the only thang you two got. Right? Stagger Lee's old. He ain't gonna get no sweeter deal than the one he got in Robert Taylor. Ain't the ole days no more. He don't have the sense to start over. It's like this old goat—"

Annie held up her hand. "Cool it. I got it."

"Girl, you ain't got nothin'. You even look at that man wrong—"

"Listen, you're not even going to be there. Let me and Fannie handle Stagger Lee."

"He ain't going for that circus sex thang. He's the one who taught you that trick."

"That's not what I have in mind."

"Then you mind tellin' me what y'all gonna do?"

"We wait till King gives him the money, then we shoot him."

"Here?" Peetie asked as they sat sandwiched between blasting lights of Chicago and the cold black lake stretching for an eternity beyond them. The wind was a son of a bitch on that little piece of land sticking out into the water.

"Why not? Annie asked, slipping off her skates. "We get the

cash and get gone. Nobody will shed a tear for him, 'specially the cops."

Peetie rubbed his mustache like he was thinking. "And why didn't you do that before, Miss Annie?"

" 'Cause we just got a king-size reason," she said.

"*Ooh, well, well,*" Peetie said. "Work with me, Annie. Work with me, Annie."

Annie rubbed Peetie's face like he was an old cat. If there came time, she'd kill him too, especially if he got too close to the money. Without Butcher Knife-Totin' Annie and Fast-Fuckin' Fannie, he was nothin' but an old cockroach.

Fannie sat down beside her, all out of breath. She slipped off her skates and grabbed Annie's. She reached into her purse, pulled out a compact mirror, and checked her lips.

"That man said he'd give me two hundred to go in the bathroom with him."

"What about his kids?" Annie asked.

"What you think they got a playground for?"

Fannie walked back to return the skates and Peetie took a seat. He puffed the cigar into the snowy wind as a man on a loud-speaker called out that the rink was about to close.

In a few minutes, Fannie walked back and sat down. She had on the cutest cheetah-print hat she'd ever seen. They bought it over at Urban Outfitters after they rode the El back from the South Side.

"I'm with you, Peetie, but Fannie . . . See, Fannie ain't so sure. She kind of believes Stagger Lee can't die. Kind of like a ghost or that thing if you cut off its head, it grows three new ones."

Fannie tossed her hair behind her shoulder: "I'm serious. I don't want that motherfucker coming after me. I love myself too much for that."

Annie looked over at Peetie and shrugged.

"You know how much money King gonna have tonight?" Peetie asked.

"Yeah, we know," Annie said.

"Little man, you think we ain't thought about this already,"

Fannie said. "You know Stagger Lee once beat me with a tire iron 'cause I kept ten dollars from him. This ain't no revelation."

"What about the money?" Annie asked. "This could be the way. This could be it, Fannie."

Fannie watched the yuppie guy disappear with his kids and then reached deep into her shopping bag. She pulled out a long, flat box covered in reindeer wrapping paper. Annie felt her fingers tremble as she took the gift and tore into the box. Inside lay the most beautiful butcher knife she had ever seen. *Chicago Cutlery*. High carbon stainless steel.

Annie squealed and gave Fannie a big hug. "So, we'll do it?" she asked.

Fannie nodded and smacked her gum.

"Willie Two," Annie said, examining the blade.

"But what if King brings his own help?" Fannie asked.

"Like who?" Peetie said, twisting up his face. "That old man ain't got the guts to get mean. Besides, he bring someone and then they know his business, and King don't want no part of that. That's like pissin' in the punch bowl and tellin' your guests."

46

DIRTY JIMMY LOOKED stone-cold tired in the lobby of the ragged brick motel near Forty-seventh Street where he lived. He'd sunk his old frame into a ratty plaid sofa smoking filterless Lucky Strikes and calling out the answers to *Jeopardy*. The coathanger antenna on the fuzzy Zenith caught and sputtered a signal making Alex Trebek's face look green. Didn't seem to matter to Jimmy, he was on a roll with Potent Potables. He kept bragging all that time in bars was finally paying off.

"No, no, no," he shouted, smiling a scruffy toothless grin. "That's a goddamned mint julip. Man said it had mint in it. What is a mint julip? Shit! That woman ain't never touched alcohol. Must be a Baptist."

"Hey, man," Nick said, taking a seat beside him on the couch with yellowed foam sprouting from the holes. The room was as cold as a mausoleum and smelled like Lysol and old lettuce. "We need to talk."

"Yeah, all right," Jimmy said, still staring at the television set. "Ain't no use in trying to talk to these folks. They don't listen. You want to tell me how you make an old-fashioned without Bourbon?"

"Can't do it."

"I know you can't do it," Jimmy said. "See, Trebek likes to drink. That's why I believe him when he acts like he knows the answers. The only thing I don't like is that you never see black people on here. Why's that? I could be on *Jeopardy*. But I don't have the look. You got to be white and have the personality of a dildo."

Nick tapped Jimmy on the shoulder. "I brought a friend with me. We wanted to talk to you a little more about the night Billy Lyons died."

Kate sat down in a chair beside them. She had a notebook in her hand and leaned forward listening, her hair dropping across her face like a veil. Jimmy smiled when he noticed her in the warm glow of the television.

"Say, man, this yore woman?" Jimmy asked.

"Friend," Kate said, looking over at Nick. She arched her eyebrow and patted Nick's leg. "He wishes, Jimmy. No . . . he's still dating his right hand."

Jimmy rolled with laughter in the old lobby. The sound of his cackling warming the dark, cracked edges of the old brick building and down through the caged reception desk. There was a half-eaten can of pork and beans on the table. A thin layer of gelatin on the top like this wasn't the first time he had opened the can.

"Say, man," Jimmy said, his face clouded with cigarette smoke, "I got a friend like that and I'd never leave the house."

"That's a nice shirt," Kate said. "Where did you get it?"

"Maxwell Street," Jimmy said, absently looking at the image of Olive Oyl giving Popeye a blow job. It read WELL, BLOW ME DOWN, OLIVE. "It's just funnin', ma'am. I can change it."

"Then you wouldn't be Dirty Jimmy."

"Well, no, ma'am," he said, looking down at the dusty floor. "Guess I wouldn't."

Jimmy smiled, stubbed out the cigarette in a tin ashtray, and looked over at Nick. "You bring any more whiskey? Love that black Jack."

"So do I . . . Man, I need some direction," Nick said. He put his elbows on his knees, the material of his 501s frayed at the edges. "Okay? You were there the night Lyons died; you were recording with King. Did you give Ruby a ride home from the Palm Tavern later that night?"

"On what, my bicycle?" Jimmy asked. "Or in my Rolls-Royce?"

"How'd she get home?"

"She was to' up. I think King helped her home. Probably tryin' to get a little sweet on the side. Man, he had a thang for that woman. Man, his Alabama ass had just dreamed about a woman like that in the glow of a jukebox. Ruby could do that to you. Her voice was like sweet, sweet, cherry wine."

"Let's go back," Nick said. "The day of September twenty-second, 1959. What were you doing?"

He placed the tape recorder in front of him, but Jimmy continued to be hypnotized by the television. "Aw, man, medieval history. I don't know jack shit 'bout no knights."

Nick looked at Kate and could tell she was trying not to crack a smile. She turned down the volume on the television.

Just as they had Jimmy's attention, it sounded like someone was dancing upstairs. Jimmy reached for a broom handle, stood, and poked the ceiling.

"Shut up, shut up," Jimmy said. "Goddamn Indians. Cookin' some cats up there. Cookin' curry that make your eyes water."

Jimmy ran his hands over his T-shirt like he had pockets and Nick reached into his jacket for a pack of Marlboros. He lit another cigarette with his stainless-steel lighter and handed it to Jimmy. The old man settled back into the musty couch.

"I thought I told you this shit the other night?" he asked.

"You passed out," Nick said.

"Oh yeah," he said, laughing. "Well, all right. Let's see, I told you about Ruby waving a gun around and all that mess. Let's see. You know, Billy stayed upstairs in the studio. He used to walk back and forth. Go up and down to get somethin' to eat or make a call. We was recordin' Elmore. Last song for King Snake."

"What was it?"

"Don't remember."

"What time did you leave?"

"Man, I don't remember what I had for breakfast."

"Pork and beans?" Kate asked.

"That's right. Yeah, man, pork and beans."

"Stay with me, Jimmy," Nick said. He leaned close to the old harp player. He could feel the vibe of apprehension surrounding him. "I need to know it step by step. Billy Lyons was murdered at the studio."

"C'mon, man, she killed that man in her bed."

"Jimmy?" Nick said.

"Man, what you want?"

"Jimmy, tell me what happened at the studio."

"I told you all I know. I ain't holdin' back. C'mon, man, I don't know who killed Billy. And fuckin' up my favorite show ain't gonna make me change my mind."

"But you're sure Jordan was there that night?" Nick asked.

"Sure, man."

"Jordan said he wasn't here," Nick said. "There was no mention of him in the court records."

"Jordan couldn't find his ass with both hands and a flashlight," Jimmy said.

Suddenly, Trebek's voice disappeared. The lights overhead shut off and the buzzing sound of space heaters stopped. Their glowing red rods dissolving into blackness. Nick could hear his own breath and feel Kate's hand on his arm.

■

"Where's a flashlight when you need one," Jimmy said in the darkness.

Nick flicked open his lighter and followed Jimmy to the front desk. A few of the tenants had wandered from the rooms like zombies to gripe and complain. A fat black man opened his door, scratched his balls, yawned, and walked back into his room. An elderly woman screamed and then yelled several times for the woman at the front desk. But the Chee·tos woman was nowhere to be found.

"Goddamned bitch forgot to the pay the bill," Jimmy said,

pulling out a flashlight from a desk drawer filled with loose change, bottle caps, and stray pieces of papers. "Least she got the sense to tell me where this at."

Nick handed Kate the flashlight as they followed Jimmy up a creaking back staircase to his room. Mildewed Sheetrock rotted off the walls. Part of the green carpet had been torn away, exposing buckled plywood thick with twisted nails. The whole damned building groaned as residents shuffled in their discomfort.

Kate cut the beam through the filth all the way to the third floor.

The whole slow trip, Jimmy bitched about the service he got in the place that charged him fifty dollars a week. He said it stank, was nasty, and that even the rats were threatening to leave.

"You want to stay with me over Christmas?" Kate asked.

"Oh missy, that's real cool. But I'm just fine."

Jimmy unlocked his door and hobbled into his darkened room. The wind whistled through the cracks in his windows as another El train passed, rocking the room like an amusement park earthquake ride. Jimmy opened a sixties-style tan suitcase and pulled out a ski jacket and hat with a balled top. The hat made him look like an elderly rapper.

"Y'all sit down," Jimmy said. "Come back on in a second."

Nick took a seat on his unmade bed. Kate found a folding chair and shined the light between them. He felt like they were at camp.

"Guess you couldn't find Williams?" Jimmy asked, his face bright in the flashlight's glow.

"Why's that?"

"Somebody kilt him and his dawg last night," Jimmy said. "Some kind of Satan worship thang, I think. Why else you kill a dawg?"

"Jesus," Nick said.

Jimmy kept shaking his head and his grin closed into a pucker. He stared into a dark corner and looked down at his ratty brogan shoes. The dark room fell silent. The wind howled outside and the floors above creaked with old age and pressure. Somewhere on the ledge outside, they could hear the thumps of heavy footsteps.

"What the fuck was that?" Kate asked, washing the flashlight over the windows.

"Pigeons," Jimmy said, absently. "Hey, man, how 'bout another smoke?"

"That's one big-ass pigeon," Kate said.

The old wooden floor creaked as Nick stood from the bed and grabbed the flashlight. He walked to the window and shined the light on about ten pigeons huddled together in the snow. On the ledge connecting to the El tracks, half of the birds had frozen to death staring into nothing with glazed pinpoint eyes.

Nick flashed the light back in the room at the same metal bed, folding table, and a hot plate. Jimmy's suitcase sat open on the bed with clothes strewn on the floor. Nick patted his jacket for the cigarettes and pulled out another one for Jimmy. He sighed looking at his empty pack.

Suddenly, the window exploded behind him.

Kate yelled.

A force of twenty anvils broke behind his ear and he was knocked to the ground. In his dimming vision, he reached into his jacket for his Browning and tried to stand.

He closed and opened his eyes as if adjusting to darkness. His hand wavered before him as he watched the shadowed image of the largest black man he'd ever seen raise from the broken glass.

The man had a slick bald head with a long black leather trench coat flowing behind him. The man grinned as he looked down at Nick. The brightness of his teeth lit like a jack-o'-lantern in the dim light from a streetlamp outside.

Kate screamed again as the man pulled Nick from the floor by his jacket and slammed him against a far wall.

Nick headbutted the man a half a dozen times and hot wet blood spread across his face.

The man's grip tightened and he tossed Nick across the room.

Kate ran over to the man and attempted a deep punt in his groin, but he backhanded her across the jaw and wrapped his huge hand across her face.

Nick rushed him as the man sank a flash of metal into her side.

Nick yelled and reached again for his Browning before connecting his shoulder with the man's chest. The man grabbed Nick by his hand and bent back his wrist.

The pain brought him to his knees.

Jimmy jumped on the man's back, pummeling the man's head with his fists.

Nick rammed his free hand like a rocket into the black man's nuts.

The man let Nick's hand go and he rolled to the floor, pulling out the Browning and aiming it at the man's mammoth forehead. He could hear their breaths working in the cold room and feel the blood on his face. Nick kept both hands on the gun.

The huge man smiled at him.

Nick thumbed back the hammer.

"Don't even fuckin' blink," Nick said. He couldn't hear or feel anything. The image of the man's face burned in his mind. Something stopped him from pulling the trigger, something stopped him from taking the man's life. His mind flashed to a run-down train station, midnight in Greenwood. Blood. Explosion. Half a man's head gone.

The huge man grunted and dove back through the broken window pane. Nick looked back at Kate and saw her holding her side in the darkness.

Jimmy held her hand.

Nick jumped through the ragged windowsill into the brittle cold and out onto the El tracks twisting into the South Side night.

He took a deep breath and followed the figure—the man's black coat flapping behind him like a cape. Nick's boots drummed on the wooden slats, his labored breath looping a ragged rhythm in his ears as he watched the huge man run toward a bend in the tracks.

The man suddenly stopped, turned, and stood watching Nick in the cold.

Nick could feel the man's hate in the twenty yards and two tracks that separated them. A piercing wind whistled into his ears as he waited to make a move. He aimed the gun at the figure and thought he made out a smile. Nick spit away the blood caking over his teeth.

The man reached in his coat as Nick dropped to a knee, the Browning held tight in his hand. His hand quivered, his heart a rapid booming beat. As he was about to squeeze the trigger, an El blasted across the tracks between them, scattering snow and dirt into his eyes.

After the train passed, the huge man was gone.

47

BY 10:00 P.M., the snow poured down onto the city like a dense fog, covering fire escapes, rooftops, and leaving a blanket on city streets. About an hour ago, they'd gotten back to Kate's place after a Chinese doctor with a lisp had sewn up her wound in black thread and dished out a bottle of painkillers. Whatever the big man used to slash Kate didn't gouge too deep, the doctor said. Only took him just a few minutes to close up the wound while Jimmy and Nick had waited in the lobby talking about Stagger Lee. Then they headed to her place.

Kate lived in an apartment off Dearborn in the Rush Street District. She had a one-bedroom with hardwood floors, a cast-iron tub with clawed feet, cabinets with glass panes, and an old rounded refrigerator. A framed movie poster of Paul Newman's *Harper* hung above her couch. HARPER LOOKS FOR TROUBLE. SEE HARPER LOOK. SEE HARPER.

Nick had ordered a pepperoni with mushrooms from Gino's East and grabbed a six-pack of Budweiser from a White Hen across the street. He propped his snow-soaked boots up on her coffee table, a warm slice in his hand, as he fed Bud a few morsels. The scroungy Jack Russell's tail buzzed like a humming-bird's wings as he yelped for another piece.

"If he shits on the floor," Kate said, grimacing and feeling her side as she twisted in her seat, "you're cleaning it up."

"Hey, I found this guy digging through trash cans on

Napoleon. I've seen him eat molded bread, dirty socks, and cat shit. Deep dish isn't hurting 'ole iron stomach.'"

Kate rolled her eyes and let out a long sigh before twisting the cap off her beer. "Screw those painkillers," she said and stared out at the early snow falling by her eighth-story window. She acted like the whole encounter hadn't fazed her a bit. But he'd noticed her silence on the car ride home and the way her hands trembled on the wheel. But Kate would never admit fear. She would just bitch later that she should have kicked the man harder.

Behind him, Jimmy rattled around in her bathroom, taking a shower and singing a song Nick had never heard.

"Greasy slice?" Nick asked.

"Yep."

Nick handed her a piece and scratched Bud on the ears. The dog licked him on the face and gave another loud bark. He tossed a pepperoni in the air and Bud made a flying leap for the catch.

"What about Elmore King?" Kate asked.

"Doyle said he's set to play at his club tonight. Doesn't advertise, just comes in and does his thing. Either that or stalk him down at the Checkerboard Lounge on Forty-third Street. Heard he likes to cool down there after a show."

"What do you think?"

"His club might be worth a shot," Nick said. "King could put this whole thing together. The murder happening in the studio and any threats from that idiot detective."

Kate had a smallish, twisted Christmas tree the size of a branch on her kitchen table. A single strand of blue lights blinked with ornaments shaped like bones. Completely Charlie Brown.

"Never made any sense," Kate said, still watching the snow flickering by the window, her eyes rimmed with fatigue. "Ruby kills Lyons at the studio, then takes him back to her bed? No one in the world could believe a skinny woman, who's drunk, would take a dead man back to her bed. *And then move him again*. Florida's statement alone about the cop's threats would be enough to reopen the case . . . let alone finding that big-ass shit-head who cut me."

"And killed Williams."

"You think?" her voice slightly trembling.

"I know."

Jimmy walked in the room with a towel around his waist and a turban on his head. He had a toothbrush stuck halfway out of his mouth and a wide toothless smile spread on his face. His chest looked as light and brittle as a bird's.

"Hey, man, you got some cologne?"

Kate said he could use her perfume. He disappeared back into the bathroom and reemerged wearing Kate's flannel robe. He smelled like a French whore. Must've used the whole damned bottle.

"*Wooh*, that pizza smells good," Jimmy said, rubbing his weathered hands together. "I got beans comin' out my nose."

Nick handed him a plate and a cold beer.

"Your clothes should be out of the dryer in about thirty minutes," Kate said.

"I appreciate it, ma'am."

"Jimmy, don't call me ma'am. Make yourself at home, I have plenty of food, beer, gin, and whiskey."

"Travers, don't be a fool. Hold on to this woman. Marry her. Tie her up. Shit, man, do somethin'."

"I'm tryin', Jimmy, I'm tryin."

Kate gave a sly, easy grin and scratched Bud's back. He watched her feet rubbing together. The bright red toenail polish and the one freckle on her right foot. She caught him staring and shot him a glance. She tucked her feet beneath her.

Nick stood, sipped on a beer, and watched the snowplows and city workers from her apartment window. Jimmy devoured the rest of his pizza and swallowed half of the beer in one gulp.

"Why's he after you, Jimmy? Did he kill Billy? Dawkins and Williams?"

Jimmy looked up into Nick's eyes with the sweet sadness of a man who had lost his last hand. He shook his head and said, "You can't beat Stagger Lee. Nobody can beat Stagger Lee. Used to be a wrestler, I heard, come up from Memphis and took over all Billy's territory. I seen him bend steel bars with his teeth. Probably can shit fire."

"I'll take care of Stagger Lee," Nick said.

"You don't know Stagger Lee," Jimmy said. He threw his hands in the air and began to pace the room. "Don't matter now. Stagger Lee gets something set in his mind and that's it."

Nick shook his head.

"Stagger Lee snuffed them men out like a candle, man. What, you think Leroy Williams like to go swimming in the winter?"

"Why would he target those men?"

Jimmy began to walk the room with a slight limp, like one leg was shorter than the other. He had a kind of a skip-hop motion as he looked out the high windows. "Man, I wish I knew."

"Do you remember something Billy said or something he did that was strange or out of character that night?" Kate asked.

"Not really," Jimmy said, sniffing his nose along the arm of her robe. "We finished up 'round ten. Right? Billy was drunk. King was drunk. We was all drunk, man. Billy paid me cash for the session and like I said, I went down to the Palm for a drink. Ruby was there all pissed off. King too. He took her home and she killed Billy."

"What else, Jimmy?" Nick asked.

"That's it."

Jimmy stared out into the black night fuzzed with falling snow, his face lit in Kate's blue Christmas lights. He hobbled back to her sofa and sat down. Bud grunted and jumped into his lap. Jimmy laughed and scratched the dog on his back. The dog's legs wiggled with pleasure.

"That's the itch spot, man," Jimmy said. "You hit that on the dawg and man, he goes crazy."

"So what now?" Kate asked.

"King's her alibi. He drove her home. He knows her condition that night . . . You guys up for some blues?" Nick asked.

"King's place?" Kate asked.

"Yep."

"Y'all go on," Jimmy said. "I can get back to my place. I'm wore out like a catfish who just jumped off a hook."

Jimmy started to stand.

"Sit down, Jimmy, you're not going anywhere."

"Yes, ma'am."

"Jimmy, I don't know if I want to leave you alone," Nick said.

"Why not?" Kate asked. "You have to be buzzed through two doors by a security guard. Anything happens and that guard hits a panic switch. Nobody knows where I live. Besides, even if they did, there are dozens of apartments in this building."

"Jimmy?"

"Man, I just want to lay out. You got cable?"

"Of course," Kate said.

"Y'all go ahead, I'm goin' to have a time. We only get one station back at my place. It's either soap operas or game shows."

Nick looked at Kate. "How about you, can you handle the second half of the night?"

"Only for Ruby," she said.

"For Ruby," Nick said, giving a mock toast with his second Budweiser. "Forty years. *Forty years for nothing.*"

"Y'all be careful," Jimmy said.

Nick watched him.

Jimmy dropped his face in his hands. The old man rubbed his temples, sighed, and then after a long pause said:

"Always mad at King for not lettin' me get my harps that night." He rubbed the gray hairs on his head. "Used to have a whole string of 'em in a leather holder like them Mexican gunfighters wear. But when I asked him if he take me back to the studio when we was at the Palm, he gave me a look like I just fucked his cat. Man reached deep into his pocket, gave me fifty dollars . . . fifty dollars, man, and told me to stay away from the studio and forget about harps I'd had almost my whole life. Why you suppose he did that?"

Jimmy polished off another piece and then disappeared back into the bathroom. Nick could hear his singing reverberating off the tiles. Nick picked up the old harmonica he left on the coffee table and ran his thumb over the rough edges.

"You all right?" Kate asked.

"I want to finish this thing," Nick said. "For once, I want to finish something. Follow through until this thing is over. It's something I've never been able to do. Football. My book on Slim . . . some shit that happened last year in the Delta."

"What happened in the Delta?"

Bud jumped up and crawled into her lap. He had his ears down and his face toward the slice in her hands. Some sympathy begging. She threw a bite onto the floor and Bud scrambled for it like he hadn't eaten in a year.

"If I told you, you'd never believe me."

A row of icicles dropped like daggers above the window. The blue Christmas lights continued to blink as Bud turned three times on the couch before closing his eyes. Nick could still feel the Delta heat in a rundown motel and a battered train station as pure evil enveloped his life. The greed that took out Willie and Henry. Nick's inability to change the past, control time, or fate tore at his mind.

48

ELMORE KING OWNED a blues bar just outside the Loop for blues-starved tourists and conventioneers called The Crown Room. The bar was housed in a renovated movie theater that still had the old marquee above the front doors, surrounded by white lights and green neon listing upcoming acts. You couldn't argue with The Crown Room's taste in blues; they had the cash to book top national talent. The bar was also an unofficial museum of Chicago blues history: Muddy Waters's guitar, Sonny Boy's harp, and most of King's Grammies.

Every cabbie in the city knew to take tourists to the club. The place was clean, safe, and always promised a good time. Nick paid thirty bucks for their cover at the ticket booth and walked inside over a dizzying blue-and-white checked floor, like an opium-inspired illustration from *Alice in Wonderland*. Just inside the door was a glass case filled with King's Grammy Awards and T-shirts and hats with his cartoon likeness. Nearby, a group of German tourists huddled against a glass bar striped with neon.

Nick ambled over and ordered a couple of drinks.

Budweiser for him, a double shot of gin for Kate.

Never hurt to try and get her drunk. Of course it was a fifty-fifty bet. She would either love him or want to fight with him by the end of the night.

One of King's guitars was framed in purple neon behind the bar along with photographs of King with various rock stars. Clapton to Keith Richards. One of the Germans pointed to the guitar and took a picture with a flash, straining Nick's eyes.

The Crown Room was a fine monument to what a broke kid from Alabama could do with a guitar and a little ambition. Nick had met King a few times when he used to play at JoJo's. But JoJo couldn't afford him anymore. Like Doyle said, King had signed a contract with a large Los Angeles record label and was now playing duets with rap artists and fifteen-year-old white blues protégés. All in the name of keeping music alive. He hadn't cut a decent song since his days at Diamond Records with Moses Jordan. King was a part of the West Side school of guitarists, a group of four men born in the South but who only knew a declining Chicago. Otis Rush, Magic Sam, Buddy Guy, and Elmore King. Their music spoke of tattered tenement buildings, unemployment, and of the Chicago dream beginning to disintegrate. Their white neighbors refusing to let anyone past the Black Belt.

The West Siders introduced heavier gospel-style singing coupled with the first use of an electric bass. The sound had more in common with B. B. King or T-Bone Walker than with Muddy or Ruby.

They put emphasis on the guitar as the lead instrument with their urgent, fiery style. String bending. Biting notes.

It was when the blues sound grew closer to rock. The men were a wind of change in the late fifties—as biting and angry as the Hawk—in a style that has remained as the Chicago sound until today.

Kate waited by the edge of a dance floor where dozens of tables sat near the stage. She motioned Nick forward as he carried the drinks.

He watched her butt move in her tight Levi's and heard Junior Wells sing, *"I can tell her daddy's a millionaire just by the way she walks."*

Nick flipped a cafe chair backward and slid the drink over to Kate. She took off her gloves and tucked them in the side of her peacoat before sipping the gin and making a tight face.

"How in the hell do you drink that shit?"

"Same way you drink beer."

"Beer is like water compared to that," he said. "That's like drinking gasoline."

"I like it."

"Glad you don't smoke," he said.

"You want to try to catch him before he starts his first set?"

"No, let's wait. Watch the show and then, when he's had a few, I'll get him."

"Same strategy for me?" she asked.

"What?"

"Thanks for the double, Travers, but you don't have to get me drunk."

A smile pursed into the corner of his mouth and she arched an eyebrow. Nick leaned forward and played with the label on his Bud. First time he'd gotten a good look into her eyes. She just watched him. And he watched her. She gave him a little kick under the table.

"Careful what you wish for," she said.

"I'm always careful."

"You're someone my mother warned me about."

"Me?" he said, still watching her deep brown eyes.

"She warned me."

"I'm a nice man."

"You're the man who ruins a girl's reputation."

"And you're a girl I'd like to ruin."

Nick smiled. Kate looked away and shook her head. "Not this time, Travers. Not this time."

The hot lights suddenly blasted the stage and a little white man in glasses gave an intro to the blessing of Elmore King's presence. *The man. The myth. The legend.* That kind of crap.

But King was a great guitarist, no matter how big his ego had become.

He strutted onto the stage in a black getup that reminded Nick of a silent movie cowboy. Silk shirt with red roses on the shoulders. He looked deadpan into the crowd and everyone stopped talking. He took a step back in the silence as the drummer hit his sticks and counted down.

A long note hissed like a cobra let loose from a shaken box. The sound bit into the air as the crowd erupted in a jolt of whistles and screams. King smiled beating his guitar with his pick and making the Telecaster talk, wail, and cry. He stepped to the microphone and tore into an Elmore James classic with his own, wicked spin:

> "You said you were hurtin,'
> you almost lost your mind.
> 'Cause the man you love,
> he hurts you all the time.
> When things go wrong,
> go wrong with you,
> it hurts me too."

King let his guitar sing the verse with pain and deep-cut emotion, his instrument rolling over the vocals, his one-string bends underscoring the words:

> "You love him more,
> when you should love him less.
> Why do you pick up behind him,
> and I know, pick up all his mess?
> When things go wrong,
> go wrong with you,
> it hurts me too."

By the end of the set, King prowled the club with his cordless guitar in the same style as Guitar Slim. He played and gyrated his hips to blushing women, letting a single note hang followed by an explosive cluster. He licked the frets with his tongue and played the guitar behind his back. He ripped into the final, boiling song with his teeth sunk into the strings and the crowd went crazy.

The drumbeat kicked and the stage lights dimmed.

A man tossed King a towel and he wiped it over his face as he walked down the steps. Nick put down his beer and waited by a back door where a bunch of tourists stood with napkins and pens. King signed a few autographs, took a few pictures, and then motioned for a bodyguard to open the door.

"Hey, Elmore!" Nick yelled over some women with sharp elbows. "Elmore!"

King turned around and looked right at Nick. He stopped for a moment and then walked into a back room. A guard locked the door and folded his arms in front of his chest.

49

THE VIP SECTION of The Crown Room rivaled the classiness of Sammy Davis Jr.'s bedroom combined with Elvis's Jungle Room at Graceland. Really brought "taste" to a new low. The red and blue lighting cast a wild glow on the faces of women wearing pounds of makeup and knife-edged heels. There were low sixties-style chairs, a couple of lava lamps, and a lot of beads separating the corridors to other hallways. It smelled of reefer and incense. Perfume and pig's feet.

Amazing where fifty bucks slipped to the bartender could get you.

Nick scanned faces in the back maze of small rooms. He heard someone moaning as he passed a room and saw a woman's head between a fat black man's legs. The man gave Nick the thumbs-up as he groaned again. In another room, there were four tall, twenty-something women sitting on the floor. A mirror of cocaine sat between them. A gaunt blonde with abnormally large breasts waved him in, her legs spread around the coke.

"Looking for Elmore," Nick said.

"C'mon over," the woman slurred, as her shoulder strap dropped. Her chest was covered in freckles. Nick walked over and looked down at the women. "You want to play?"

"Trying to quit," Nick said.

Two of the women giggled. One leered.

"Don't look at me like that," Nick said to the leering one. "Your eyes will stay that way."

The blonde grabbed his leg and moved her hands toward his crotch. "Stay."

"Tell you what," Nick said, moving her hand off his leg. "Tell me where Elmore is and I'll bring you guys some donuts to go with the sugar."

The blonde rubbed up and down on the shaft of Nick's boot. "Last room down the hall. You can hear him from here, won't shut up."

Nick broke her grasp and followed the hall, covered with recent gold albums, and more pictures with white rockers. King shaking his curls with sweat as he extended his guitar to the crowd.

He heard someone playing a few blues chords through a fuzzy amplifier. Basic stuff being played over and over again. He could hear a black man's hoarse voice say, "That's it. Uh huh. One more time. That's right. C'mon."

Nick turned into the room and saw King with a young white boy and two white women drinking whiskey. The girls looked cut from the same mold as the coke sniffers. Fake boobs, dyed hair, and capped teeth.

Nick knew the kid. Cadillac Mack Miller. Teenage blues protégé who had more money than most veteran bluesmen combined. He played a predictable mix of blues standards with an edgy teen angst. He growled and howled out his fifteen-year-old pain like a minstrel act. Somehow it sold. Teenyboppers and white blues fans ate it up. After hearing one of his songs, JoJo had commented, "How's a kid know about the blues? He ain't had a job, lost a job. Had a woman or lost a woman. Kid don't know pain from ice cream."

Nick tended to think that was true. Blues wasn't necessarily about race, but it was about experience. Besides, Miller looked like a frail woman. Long stringy blond hair, pale delicate skin, and glossy lips.

"Hit it, hit it, hit it," King droned with the ice clinking in his whiskey glass. The girls swaggered to the music. One played with her hair as she arched her back. The other tapped her foot and played with a long strand of gum. "Play them blues, kid, play them blues."

King spoke with all the enthusiasm of a whore asking a man to finish it up. He took another chug of whiskey and looked at the doorway. His eyes narrowed.

"Nick Travers," Nick said. "Remember JoJo's?"

Elmore King rolled his head over to Nick and grinned. Miller played one of King's songs as Nick shook the legend's hand. King nodded and smiled. He drank from a crystal glass with a joint dangling from his other hand.

King leaned his back into the plush, blue chair like he'd just finished a marathon, his eyes red.

"You want a picture or somethin'?" King asked, smiling. The veins in his eyes were angry and thick. His hair was styled with Jheri curl lotion.

"No," Nick said. "Been trying to get in touch with you. See if you remembered playing in New Orleans, ask you about some things."

"Oh, you know I play so many places it's hard to remember," he said, slurring. "Think I played at the Superdome the last time. 'Star Spangled Banner.'"

Nick nodded. *What an asshole. This guy knew who he was.*

King looked over at one of the girls and licked his lips at the big-chested gum chewer. Miller never glanced up from his shiny blue Stratocaster.

The girls couldn't have been less interested in the conversation.

"Listen, I've been in town doing some research," Nick said.

King put his hand on the knee of the woman.

"Been interviewing folks from King Snake," Nick said. "Talking to people about your old boss, Billy Lyons."

King's head rolled back around and he squinted his eyes at Nick. He looked at the ground littered with cigarette butts and beer caps and shook his head. Disappointment, like Nick had just failed a big test.

"You want to interview me, talk to my agent," he said. "I'm just hanging out tonight. Want to enjoy the show."

"Did you get my messages?" Nick said. He tried to keep the force from his voice. Easy roll. Just a polite conversation.

"No. People handle those things for me."

Miller looked up from the guitar. He stopped playing and watched. Outside, the band was jamming and the muffled music sounded like it was trying to break down the barriers.

"Over a bottle of Crown Royal, you once told me Ruby Walker got a raw deal," Nick said. "I paid for the Royal. So don't try to tell me you don't remember."

"Shiiit."

"Listen, man, I'm trying to help Ruby. She says you were with her the night Billy was killed. Dirty Jimmy Scott said you drove her home."

King's eyes bore into Nick's. He had a sleepy-eyed stare. Almost looked like a crazy gunfighter trying to psych out his rival.

Nick was so scared he thought he might yawn.

"Forty years is a long time for silence."

"Get the fuck out of my club," King said.

"What?"

"I said get the fuck out of here," King said. "You people don't know when something ain't your business. My life ain't some kind of goddamned Trivial Pursuit. I'm not some nigger needs to be studied. I'm just a musician. Now get the fuck out of my club."

"Why'd you tell Dirty Jimmy he couldn't go back to the studio that night?" Nick asked. "You scared he'd see Billy Lyons' blood? The holes that forty-four left?"

King stood tall and pushed Nick in the chest. One of the girls disappeared and Miller started playing again. It was the stop time of Muddy Waters's "Mannish Boy." He flipped back his hair like a woman and sneered at Nick.

"Were you with Ruby the night Billy was killed?" Nick asked. "Were you at the Palm Tavern with her? Was she with you? Did you drive her home?"

King sucked in some more reefer and blew it from his nose.

"Kid," King said to Miller. "Get lost for a minute."

Miller shook his head, put down the Strat, and grabbed the other woman by the arm. They disappeared.

"Record company said it'd be good to spend some quality time," King said, blowing reefer smoke and staggering his stance. "As much money as they pay me, I'd waltz with the grand wizard of the KKK."

Nick nodded. The electrifying guitar on stage felt like it was about to rip through the walls and zap King in the chest. Give him a million volts of reality.

"You must think I'm the biggest motherfucker in Chicago," King said, slumping down into the seat. "Right?"

Nick was silent.

King extinguished the orange end of the joint on the bottom of his boot.

"You been talking to folks?"

Nick nodded.

"You think you're smart," King said. "Think you know the whole deal just because of some words of some old man."

"Why wouldn't you let him get his harps?"

"No, sir. I kept my mouth shut and it's gonna stay shut."

"What are you talking about?" Nick said. "Ruby's suffered enough. She's spent most of her life in something you'd use for a closet. She's surrounded by killers and bull dykes. Is that what you want?"

"I just want to live," King said. "Go on."

"If you want to talk I'll be at the Palmer House. . . . It's your move," Nick said. "You can't hide from Stagger Lee forever."

King threw his old-fashioned glass against the wall. He walked away as the whiskey and glass dripped to the floor. As Nick opened his mouth, three guys in Crown Room T-shirts grabbed him by the arms. Nick tried to shake them off, but they dragged him through the VIP halls and back into the bar. People pointed at Nick, screaming for him to leave.

"Let him go, you fucking morons," Kate yelled as they dragged him to the door. She kicked one of the bouncers in the nuts and the man fell away.

Another guy grabbed Kate. Nick freed his arm and knocked the guy to the ground as the other guard twisted Nick's arms behind his back.

He tossed Nick outside. Kate called the bouncer a motherfucker as they pushed her onto the cold sidewalk.

The bouncer slammed the door shut.

On the street, there was hushed snow and the sound of muffled music playing inside the club. The green neon glowed onto Kate's angry face.

"That arrogant fuck," she said, pulling herself to her feet. She touched her sore stomach and marched back to the door.

"Kate," Nick said, looking at the torn elbow on his coat. "You want to go to jail tonight? Let's just go. We'll go at it another way."

"What did you say to him?" she asked, pulling her gloves onto her hands and helping Nick to his feet.

"I asked him about not letting Jimmy get his harps," Nick said. "King said he wasn't going to say shit about what happened and then he told me to get out of his club. Told me he didn't want to be studied. He was pissed."

Kate muttered under her breath as they walked under the rusting El tracks back toward the city. "Motherfucker."

"You want me to wash your mouth out?" Nick asked.

"Fuck you," she said.

Nick grabbed her hand and pulled her close. Her eyes were still heated and he could smell the gin on her rapid breath. A taxicab passed. The El rolled by. Nick smoothed his hand across her cheek and tucked her brown hair behind her ear. Her eyes were huge brown discs.

"How's your stomach?"

"Sore."

"Too sore?"

"Leave me alone, Travers."

Her mouth parted and her head tilted.

And he kissed her.

50

NICK KEPT KISSING Kate all the way up the Palmer House elevator as his hand ran underneath her coat and over her warm back. He could feel her lips on his ear and her fingers messing his shaggy hair. They lost their balance when the elevator stopped at the fourteenth floor, and her mouth pursed into a slow grin. Nick's stomach burned, smelling her hair and tasting her lips. He knew he'd waited so long to be with her again. When he was with Kate, he was at home. Nothing existed outside their loop.

He led her by the hand down the corridor to his room, sliding the card into the lock and kicking in the door. The bedside lamp was on and soft snow fell outside. Completely weightless, shifting in the Arctic wind.

She walked ahead, grabbed his hand, and pulled him onto the bed. He held her back and set her down onto the cool sheets smelling of bleach. He kissed her neck and she arched her back. She wriggled free of her peacoat, and Nick threw it onto the floor as she kicked out of her shoes and kissed him with an open mouth.

Their tongues worked together, tasting her sweetness and the gin on her beautiful breath.

"Are you sure you're okay with this?" Nick asked.

She nodded.

"What about your stomach?"

Kate grabbed his hand and pushed it on the warm skin surrounding a bandage. He moved his hands under her black sweater and cotton underwear. She was braless and Nick brushed his hands over her breasts and down again to her stomach. He could feel the taut muscles and the curve of her hips. She pulled him on top and opened her mouth more. He tasted her rich saliva and felt her hips grinding into his. He pulled up her sweater and kissed her stomach and chest. She arched her back again, and he kissed the spot between her breasts. She sighed and made soft sounds. He felt weightless as the falling snow, like they were drifting downwards as she fumbled for his zipper.

He kissed the narrow part of her waist and stomach trailing up to her breasts again. She straightened her hands above her head and he lifted the sweater away. Her hair was still damp from the snow and he smoothed it behind her ears. He kissed her thick eyebrows, nose, and dimpled chin. He kissed her glorious neck and thick, rubbery lips and unbuttoned her faded blue jeans. She gripped the edge of her jeans and pulled them down past her white Calvin Kleins as Nick stood back from the bed and stripped down to his Scooby Doo boxers.

He dove back into bed and brought her with him under the warm blankets. She laughed as he pulled away their last pieces of clothing. Finally, they were back together, cold feet feeling each other, knowing he was right where he needed to be.

On the second go around, their bodies worked, coated with sweat. She rolled on top of him and landed her hands on his chest. Her eyes closed as if in meditation, her brown hair swaying down onto his face. They stayed that way for a long time, a drop of sweat rolling off her nose and into his eyes, until he wrapped his arm around her back and spun her back to the bed.

He kissed her forehead and cupped his hand to her face.

As he stared into her brown eyes, he felt the days, weeks, and years break away from them. Her mouth on his, her sweet smell all over his body, was a homecoming.

■

For the last few months, Nick had been having strange dreams about the blues. Maybe he should've seen a psychologist, stop mixing Jack and Dixies, or stop trying to enter dead people's lives. But ever since he spent a late summer in the Delta last year, Robert Johnson had entered his mind and spoken to him in the deepest layer of his subconscious. Or maybe Robert Johnson had become his subconscious. Either way, the master blues guitarist who died in 1938 broke free early that Christmas Eve morning. Nick could see him standing at the foot of his hotel bed, in his creased pin-striped suit, a beaten black guitar case in his hand, smiling a wide grin on his deep black face.

What is it, R. L.? Nick heard himself say.

You brought yourself into a world of pain, Johnson said, *pulling a fedora lower over his bad eye.*

Had to.

Why do you believe in a world that doesn't believe in you?

Stubborn.

That Elmore King's a joker ain't he?

He is.

You know he holds that old, rusted key.

To what?

Freeing the blues.

Nick broke out of the dream, hearing a scratchy song spinning in a jukebox that glowed like rock candy before dissolving in his waking eyes. He could feel his ragged breath catch somewhere down deep in his chest soaked in sweat, as snowflakes the size of sand bits scattered on the ledge.

The red lights on the alarm clock read 2:00 A.M. *There was still time to catch him.* Without a word, Nick brought his feet to the floor and looked back at Kate sleeping. He leaned over and kissed her on the ear. She smiled, moaned, and pulled the blankets close as he grabbed his watch from the nightstand and hunted for his clothes.

"Where are you going?" she asked, half-awake.

"Downstairs for a drink." He pulled on his socks and jeans and sat down for his boots. "Can't sleep."

"Now?" Kate stirred in bed. "Hold on, let me get up."

Nick leaned to her on the bed and kissed her on the mouth.

"I'll be right back." He stood and watched Kate close her eyes again. He searched in his army duffel bag for his stainless-steel Browning and his Tom Mix boot knife. He grabbed an extra clip and quietly slid the gun into his coat pocket.

> *"Oh, baby don't you want to go*
> *Back to that land of California,*
> *to my sweet home Chicago."*

51

IF THERE WERE a heart of the blues, it would surely beat like the tattered drum in the Checkerboard Lounge. The blues joint was housed in a rugged, brick building down on Muddy Waters Avenue where guys on the street drank cheap booze from paper bags and warmed their hands over oil drum fires. But the neighborhood didn't keep the blues pilgrims away—everyone from James Cotton to the Rolling Stones jammed there. In the capital of the blues, with so many false temples, the Checkerboard pounded like truth itself.

Early that morning, a ragtag band played the drivin' chords of a Jimmy Reed song as a big woman in white pants and an orange fur coat shook her ass near the stage. In a corner booth, an old timer sat grim-faced under a cheap baseball hat, a Budweiser sign burning above him. Swivel school chairs with hard wooden backs surrounded long thin counters the width of ironing boards on a linoleum floor buckled with water damage.

Nick ordered a Bud from the bartender and took a seat.

Garland, white Christmas lights, and fake snow sprayed from a can framed the mirror in front of him where he studied his haggard face. He looked like he belonged here. A street guy. Unshaven. Drawn eyes. A watch cap on his head. Nick took a sip of the Bud to hopefully soothe his lack of sleep and still-pulsing hangover from the night before.

He'd give King another twenty minutes, then he was out of there. The Christmas lights, the blues coming from the stage, and the softly falling snow on the decaying brick outside had him thinking about R. L. again.

He wondered what Johnson could have accomplished if he hadn't been murdered in Greenwood. Would Johnson have preceded Muddy to form the first modern blues band? How would his music have evolved from his country roots singing of bare crossroads and midnight meetings with Satan? Johnson had been dead almost a quarter century by the time Nick was born. His legacy had manifested in the lives of Chicago masters like Johnny Shines, Muddy, Wolf, and Sonny Boy.

But Ruby was still here. Ruby had a completely different legacy still left.

Nick heard some commotion by the door and watched Elmore King strut in, shaking hands with several people. King was a hero to the South Side and his people wanted to be near him. He patted their backs, talked about his latest album, and finally took a seat at the bar next to Nick. His smile dropped and his eyes stared at the jug-size whiskey bottles. The bartender poured a tall glass of Crown Royal on the rocks and sat it before him.

"We come a long way from New Orleans," Nick said. "We could have talked about this at JoJo's."

"Figured you be here." King took off his cowboy hat and laid it on the bar before turning to the stage and sipping on the Royal.

The band changed into an instrumental of Ike and Tina's "Everythin's Going to Turn Out Alright." The guys on stage couldn't be making much, just enough to cover their drinks at best. In old T-shirts and jeans they tore into some blues covers. But there was a difference in their playing. These guys were saying something with the music. You could tell they were feeling it, not like King going through the motions earlier that night.

"Funny, I couldn't get these guys a record deal," King said. "White people run the blues now. I never thought our own people would stop caring for us. But I look out at the crowds at festivals across the country and all I see is white faces. No offense, man. Just makes me think."

Nick finished his beer. He watched King staring at the stage.

"Where's your protégé?" Nick asked.

"Fuckin'," King said, sipping the Royal.

Nick kept watching his face until King finally turned to him. His face parched and worn as old leather.

"You a professor?" he asked.

Nick nodded.

"I'd like someone to write a book about my life," King said. "I'll put my name on it as the only official history of the Elmore King experience. How'd you like them apples, man? Cash be shootin' out the ass."

"I don't take bribes."

King flared his nose and squinted his eyes. He turned back to the bar and put down the drink. His shoulders slumped as he stared at the flickering TV set. A man walked over and said he just wanted to shake a legend's hand. King forced a smile and signed an autograph.

Nick placed his elbows on the bar and remained quiet. There was nothing to say, this was King's move.

"You understand what you're doin'?" King asked.

"You want to explain it to me?"

King's mouth curved into a grin as he looked to the door. He looked back at Nick as a brittle wind shot through the room. A slump-shouldered black man took a couple's cover, nodding them into the door. The man leaned back against the wall and worked on a Polish sausage.

"You waiting on someone?"

"Yeah," King said. "He said he'd be here."

King stared at an old clock hanging on the wood-paneled wall. On stage, there was a poster of Robert Johnson, covered in torn, plastic sheeting. It was the shot of Johnson grinning with the guitar in his lap and the world seemingly by the balls. R. L. before the darkness set in. Above the poster, a curtain shook with a cold wind as the front door opened again.

King looked at the patron then back at the top of his drink.

"Man, you're ripping away something," he said. "And there's something mighty ugly beneath it."

Nick watched his eyes.

"You want to tell me why you did it?"

King laughed through his nose. "Goddamn, dude, don't you let up?"

"I have a pretty good idea what happened," Nick said. "Billy had you locked in. He tied you with that contract and King Snake was going nowhere. A man like you doesn't sit idle. You could almost taste that fame, couldn't you? . . . I know you hired Stagger Lee."

King laughed again and watched Nick. A smile smeared on his face. "You have no idea."

He looked at the old wall clock again and then at the door.

"What dragged you away from your ranch and your groupies?" Nick asked, finishing the last of his Budweiser, still reeling with the thought of Kate in his arms.

King played with the napkin around his Royal. He lovingly wiped away the condensation from the glass before watching his reflection in the warped mirror in front of him.

"I guess I'm tired of being jerked around," King said, almost to himself.

Nick watched him. The man's beaten face almost falling from the bone.

"Guess my friend is tired of this shit too," King said, leaving his drink on the bar and laying down a few bucks. "Goodnight."

"What is it? Who are you talking about?"

But it was too late. King walked out of the front door and onto the desolate street shining in the intermittent glow of a few lights. Nick followed into the early morning chill and saw King about ten yards away walking down Forty-third Street.

"King!" Nick yelled jogging over to the man.

King stopped, looked down at Nick's coat, and then stared up into his eyes. Nick self-consciously felt his pocket and touched the butt of the Browning. King put his hand on Nick's shoulder as the muffled blues wailed across the bleak landscape.

"I need some help," King said.

"Yeah, right."

"Listen, what I tole you with JoJo that night was right on," King said. "You come with me tonight and I'll tell you the whole deal."

Nick looked down at the cracked sidewalk under his boots and back into King's ancient eyes. The man slipped the black cowboy hat back on his head. "You want to help that ole woman or not?"

52

NAVY PIER RAMBLED a half mile into the freezing black water of Lake Michigan in a testament to a Chicago that no longer existed. The place had been used for shipping warehouses, World War II troop training, and even a college campus. To Nick, all the red-brick buildings looked like a collection of small football arenas connected on a long, rectangular floating sheet. In its present life, the pier had added an indoor garden, a movie theater, and even a small amusement park complete with a huge Ferris wheel. He was sure the wheel was supposed to add a whimsical edge to the hulking structures with domed tops. But at 3:00 A.M. on Christmas Eve, it reminded him of the one in *The Third Man*. Dark and ominous.

Something about silent amusement parks, cold black water, and early morning exchanges turned his stomach. His head still whirred with beer and lovemaking as a vicious wind tore deep off the lake. He wrapped his arms around himself.

On the ride from the Checkerboard in his two-ton Mercedes, King had told Nick about the threats from Stagger Lee. King, his cowboy hat pulled low over his eyes, said he was innocent. He said Stagger Lee was blackmailing him and he had an old doctor's bag stuffed with cash in his trunk. Nick had asked why an innocent man pays someone off, but King had just cranked a Bobby "Blue" Bland song louder as he wheeled toward the pier.

The answers will come, King promised.

Dock Street sat empty. At the top of a wide staircase, the skating rink was closed and the carousel sat covered. A red light from another pier blinked in the muddled air. A thick fog rolled off the lake mixing with the intermittently falling snow. Water slammed against pilings like a fist.

The falling snow looked like pieces of cut lace.

Nick could hear his boots crunch below him in the electric silence as he reached in his coat pocket and switched off the slide release on his Browning. King kept pace beside him, scanning the never-ending fog, his black boots clicking on the concrete edge of the pier.

"After this, let's find Peetie," King said.

Tall green streetlamps lined the pier's edge like matchsticks. Nick took off his right glove and felt his hand sweat around the walnut handle of the gun.

"Why?"

"He's been playing you, man. Me too. He knows everything."

"Is that why Stagger Lee is after you?"

King looked confident, his shoulders reared back, as he walked through the fog. Nick felt his heart pound as he searched through the swirling wind. King seemed like he wanted to kick somebody's ass as he kept walking and spit on the frozen ground.

"If something happens to me," he said, looking over at Nick, "I want you to hear a song."

"How 'bout you be straight with me for once?" Nick said. This was getting ridiculous. Kate's warm body was waiting for him back at the hotel as King played the same mind games he'd started in New Orleans.

"Close your mouth and listen, man," King said. "I kept all my masters from King Snake and Diamond at my ranch. Bet you didn't know that. Did you?"

Nick shook his head.

"I want you to listen to the Sweet Black Angel."

"C'mon, I've heard all those songs."

"No, listen to me." King said. He'd stopped walking, his face tight with concentration. "I want you to hear that song. *Everybody needs to hear that song.* I'm tired of cleaning up everybody's shit. Man, I paid my dues. Too many times."

King looked over at Nick and gave a confident nod as the fog enshrouded his tired face.

■

Annie and Fannie skipped though the snow out toward the docks where they used to catch tour boats in the summer. Kind of fitting they had to come here tonight; Navy Pier was the place to clean up. When it was warm, all they had to do was wear some really flimsy satin dresses and they'd come home with more than five hundred apiece. Fannie would distract the men while Annie went through their pockets. If the guy noticed, she'd just feel around like she was looking for his rod. Or pinch him in the ass.

Nothing to it, Annie thought, looking for security guards. Tonight, she just had to make sure Stagger Lee was looking for his own rod when she got him.

Willie II felt grand in her pants as she hopped and skipped. A slight metallic jingle on her leg. She smoothed him like an erection. *Willie, Willie, Willie.* That blade seemed to give her strength.

"Walkin' in a winter wonderland."

"Where's Stagger Lee at?" Fannie asked, blowing a bubble as big as a softball and tearing it down with her fingers. Hot air erupted from its torn edge.

"At the end," she said, slowing down and laughing. "He said sweep back to the end."

"That where this King cat at?"

"Yeah, the King got to give up his booty."

"You ready?" Fannie asked. "Cause we don't have to do this. We can wait till later."

"Where?" Annie asked, shaking her head with disappointment. "At Robert Taylor with Twon around? This is it. We have the car, the money in hand, and Stagger Lee's mind on other things. As soon as I get the cash, Stagger Lee is going to meet Willie Two."

"Why can't you just call him Willie?"

"You are so silly sometimes, Fannie. It's not Willie. It's his sequel."

Fannie kept smacking on her gum as Annie looked down toward the end of the pier and saw two men approaching Stagger Lee.

∎

Stagger Lee stared into nothing. He could feel the fog roll through him as the snow floated down from above. He wanted to spread his arms wide, stare at the sky, and bark at the moon. He could feel the perspiration beneath his heavy, black leather coat; his own odor sickened him. Behind him, Stagger Lee heard steps cracking and felt for the blue steel. 44. *How sweet this was going to be.*

He turned and searched through the fog, watching King and the white man called Travers come toward him. *It couldn't get any sweeter.* He stood his ground. They would come to him and his girls would clean up.

"You can't bleed me forever," King said, a fat leather bag in his hands. The wind ripped between them. "This is it. You hear me? I don't care anymore. Nothing is worth this kind of shit."

King stared back red-eyed, breathing quick smoke from his nose. The white man stood by his side. *Fool.* Stagger Lee could tell his blood raced through Travers's heart in fear. That sweet fear zipped along those veins. *Keep that fear, boy. Keep that fear.* Stagger Lee crossed his arms and listened to the cold wind howl.

"You or any of your gang come 'round my home again and I'll kill you," King said.

Stagger Lee smiled at him and watched the white man keep his hand in his right pocket. He knew the girls were right behind them. When the shit went down, they would take care of his ass like they should've the other night and the way he should have at Jimmy's.

"We're done!" King yelled and threw the bag at Stagger Lee's head like a medicine ball.

Stagger Lee caught it as the wind howled some more. The snow fell and melted on the crown of King's cowboy hat.

"I don't sweat you no more," King said as he was about to turn away. "We're done, motherfucker."

"No," Stagger Lee grunted. "You're done." He whipped out his blue steel .44 and shot Elmore King in his neck and through the heart.

■

As the gun shot thudded off the Navy Pier's walls, Nick pulled out the Browning from his coat and leveled the gun at Stagger Lee's head. Stagger Lee disappeared for a moment in the fog and snow. Nick heard a cable snap against a buoy and the cold waves pound against the pier. His hands shook around the stinging metal as he stared down everything he'd searched for since being in Chicago. *Stagger Lee.*

Back out of the fog, Stagger Lee was a tight cord ready to spring with his gun aiming right at him. Nick squinted his eyes into the wind and snow, waiting for one of them to fire. He was about to squeeze the trigger until he felt a sharp blade at his throat.

A pair of wet lips kissed his ears and then a tongue licked his cheek. Stagger Lee's arm lowered. A nausea ate at Nick's stomach as he let out a breath and dropped his gun. A flurry of snow and fog covered Stagger Lee as the white girl from the other night slapped him hard across the face.

"You stupid fuck! What'd you do with my knife?"

Fannie grabbed her by the arm and pulled her away. Nick moved slowly, keeping his hands in view, as Fannie walked back. She rubbed his ears then planted a huge wet kiss on his mouth, sticking her tongue almost down his throat.

He pushed her away and spat.

Fannie cackled with laughter as Stagger Lee reemerged and walked toward him, his .44 dangling in his hand.

"Just thought you needed a little goodnight peck," Fannie said, blowing him a kiss. The white girl slapped Nick again, a long butcher knife in her other hand. Nick was looking over her shoulder at Stagger Lee when she kicked him square in the nuts.

Nick fell to his knees. An immense pain blossomed through his entire body. He saw flashes of red and broken membranes through the back of his eyelids.

On the ground through flickering eyes, he saw Stagger Lee walk over to King and roll his body with a massive black cowboy boot. He planted his foot on King's stomach, like a safari hunter, then from several feet away aimed his .44 at Nick's head, and said, "Get your business done, Annie."

Annie rammed her platform shoe into Nick's side about a dozen times. He felt every inch of breath escape from his body. It was as if a giant hand had crushed his ribs and taken every bit of life from him. His bare hands groped for the concrete walk. Finally, she finished kicking and Fannie straddled him on the cold ground, gripped his hands over his head, and then began to rub her hips into his. She licked his face again and Nick spit into her eye.

She got off him and wiped the spit with her cheetah-print hat. Nick felt his jaw clench and his anger beating inside.

Stagger Lee ambled over and looked down on Nick like he was atop a football pileup. Nick could only see his black cannonball head and the white of his eyes framed by the fuzzy snow. He held his breath and closed his eyes waiting for Stagger Lee to fire. A blue steel .44. *Lyons, Dawkins, Williams.* Stagger Lee gripped Nick by the front of his coat and pulled him to his feet. The whole pier felt like it was rocking and Nick's head still thudded with the explosion of the pistol. His legs tingled and his nerves buzzed.

Stagger Lee's breath smelled cancerous and rotted.

"Fuck you," Nick said.

The white girl stood by Stagger Lee's side as he put away the .44 and reached against his belt. Nick could feel a thin rod of metal against his ear. Nick had his hand around Stagger Lee's wrist and could feel the taunt tendons. He knew any movement would cause him to sink the tip into his brain. Nick kept holding his breath, the cold metal playing around his ear canal. The snow caught and burned on Stagger Lee's fevered head.

"The woman you set up. Her name is Ruby Walker. Remember it."

Stagger Lee pulled back his fist, holding an ice pick, and punched Nick in the nose. Nick's mind flowered into colors and jagged black-and-white dimensions as Stagger Lee dropped him. He rolled to his hands and knees on the icy sidewalk as Stagger Lee let a kick fly into his side.

■

The worn leather bag lay by Stagger Lee's feet. *This was it*, Annie thought. Everything they'd been waiting for. She thought about the sickeningly sweet smell of the jerk shacks, Stagger Lee beating Fannie with ice cubes rolled into a sock, and the way he'd choked her at the Sears Tower. Annie nodded to Fannie, drew her lips together, and got a good grip around Willie II. She pointed the end into Stagger's Lee's side and tore into him with the blade.

The huge man howled.

He clawed at his ribs and yanked the knife from his body before flinging the blade deep into the black water and grabbing Annie by the throat. Her eyes felt like they were about to pop from her head as he yanked her from her feet and held on with both hands. She heard a cracking and popping in her voice box as her vision blurred. She made a gurgled scream as Stagger Lee rammed her head into the sidewalk.

Someone fired two shots and she saw Stagger Lee's arm explode into a bloody mist. But it was as if he didn't feel a thing. He reached into his coat for the ice pick and tore into her body. She could feel the steel jabbing through her flesh and into her bone.

As she gagged on the blood in her throat, she imagined a little brick town where sunsets were yellow circles, teenagers met at malt shops, and the world was yours with an ice-cream truck.

■

Fannie stood there paralyzed as the two shots went through Stagger Lee's body. She had Nick's Browning loose in her hand as she watched Stagger Lee bend over her friend with a bloody ice pick. Nick rolled to his feet and walked slowly behind her. Startled, she turned the gun on him with shaking hands. Nick looked into Fannie's almond-shaped eyes and opened his right hand. Her head and body shook as she let the gun drop upside down onto her index finger.

As Nick grabbed the Browning, Stagger Lee aimed his .44 at him and motioned to Fannie with his gun. Nick kept the muzzle in line with the center of Stagger Lee's bald head. He held Fannie's arm but she slipped through his fingers and joined Stagger Lee at his side.

The shifting wind blew the snow in drifts like loose sand along the sidewalks.

Stagger Lee was covered in blood, his left arm hanging loose and bloody by his side. His flank coated in a sticky red mess. Nick watched Stagger Lee grab Fannie by the hair and pull her into him, locking her head into the crook of his bloody elbow.

Stagger Lee's teeth were bare as he grunted, grabbed the leather bag, and walked back into the snow and fog until he disappeared.

53

NICK CALLED THE Palmer House from a downtown pay phone, blocks away from the pier. The phone booth sat near a highway overpass painted with graffiti and next to an abandoned gas station. Place was empty and bare, its gas pumps ripped away long before. Nick coughed in the frozen landscape listening to the phone ring. His nose had finally stopped bleeding but his sides screamed with every breath. As his lungs constricted with pain, he knew Annie and Stagger Lee's kicks had cracked a few ribs.

But wheezing in the cold air, he thought of Elmore King and felt lucky. The image of King's slumped body on the cold ground with his eyes staring up into the sky burned in Nick's mind. The operator patched him through to his room and Kate answered.

"Jesus, Nick, where are you? I was about to call the police."

"I think they're already on their way," Nick said, slumping into the booth and closing his eyes.

"Where are you?"

Nick told her as he lightly felt his broken nose.

"King's dead."

"Holy shit, what happened?"

"I'll tell you when you get here . . . we ran into Stagger Lee again."

"Why'd you lie to me?"

"No really, I'm fine," Nick said.

He could hear Kate's breathing.

"Just hurry."

Nick's mind buzzed with King's last words as he walked onto the buckled asphalt of the dead lot, leaned over, and threw up. He coughed and almost choked, then stood and paced the lot. When his head stopped reeling, he reached into his wallet for a business card and walked back to the pay phone.

He dropped another quarter into the slot. On the third ring, Doyle's answering machine picked up.

"It's Nick. Listen, man, some serious shit has just gone down and I need some help. If you get this, meet me and Kate over at—"

Someone picked up the phone. Dropped it. And picked it up again.

"This better be some *seriously* serious shit to wake me on my only day off in the world. What time is it, man? Six?"

"Four," Nick said. "Where does Elmore King live?"

"Place called Woodstock. Why? Beating on doors early Christmas Eve ain't a good way to make friends."

"King's dead."

Doyle didn't say anything.

"I need your help . . . I need you to give me directions and meet me at his place."

Doyle didn't speak for a few seconds and then rattled off where Nick needed to go. The old tracker's voice brittle on the buzzed connection. But Nick didn't have time for consolations or eulogies, he only thought about Ruby and a promise made days before. He could almost feel her small hand in his. *Fading blues.*

Nick hung up and walked over to the white glow of the streetlight. *Elmore King was dead.* A blues legend had gotten blown away right in front of him over something he'd started. Nick walked to a pile of concrete blocks and sat down. He held his head in his hands as he listened to the traffic race above him. He closed his eyes, trying to keep his mind off King.

He rubbed his temples and rocked back and forth. It was so

cold, he felt his clothes were nothing, the inch layer of wool and cotton around him just paper. His teeth chattered and he fought the urge to vomit again. *What have I done? What have I done?*

He looked down at the blood covering his boots and jeans. His own? King's?

Nick felt like he'd sat on those concrete bricks for a century when Kate pulled into the parking lot and jumped out of the car. He slowly stood as she helped him ease into the black convertible. Thank God, the heater was fully in effect.

He gave her directions to King's country ranch.

As they pulled back onto the street, a patrol car roared past with its lights spinning and sirens blaring. Kate shook her head and bit her lip.

"This is not right," she said. "This is not right. You can't leave something like this. You left the scene of a crime."

"If we don't get there," Nick said, "someone else will."

"What the hell are you talking about?" she asked. "This is fucking nuts."

Nick told her to pull over. As the car continued to roll, he opened his door and threw up into the passing slush. He closed the door and wiped his lips with his jacket. She stopped the car and pulled up the emergency brake.

Kate moved close and Nick wrapped his arms around her. He held her tight and kissed her forehead as the car idled on the city streets. He could feel her chest rise and fall.

"You son of a bitch," she said. "You scared the shit out of me."

"I scared the shit out of myself."

For the next hour, they drove in silence along an anonymous interstate to a rural Illinois county an arm's length from Chicago. They passed franchise upon franchise, dozens of super-size gas stations, and rows of houses that looked like they were constructed by insects. Nick had never felt so unimportant in his life.

54

ABOUT 7:00 A.M. they waited for Doyle at the entrance to Elmore King's ranch. Kate had fallen asleep in Nick's arms as he scanned the gray dawn for a battered Volkswagen. The morning sky was a mixture of black and red like something out of a Dali painting as gray light leaked through dead cornstalks and winter weeds partially hidden in snow.

Nick flicked on the Karmaan Ghia's windshield wipers again to clear the frost. The red and black turning a bluish gray in a flat and hard morning. He looked at his bloodied reflection in the mirror and shook his head as he listened to Kate's sweet breath in his ear.

He brushed his hand over her cheek. A semi passed, rattling her little car and she yawned, her eyes still closed.

Nick kissed her cheek with his broken lips as he heard a horn in the distance play "Dixie."

Doyle pushed his horn again and Kate opened her eyes as the van chugged and spurted beside them. Doyle's gray-bearded mug, craning from his open window. Nick had never been so glad to see anyone.

"You look like you've been dating Mike Tyson," Doyle said.

"Yeah, I've ruined my good looks," Nick said through his open window.

"Follow me," Doyle said, running the van down a crooked dirt road to a huge white house a dead blues singer called Crossroads.

■

Doyle had on a tattered blue robe and black Chuck Taylor high-tops as he walked to the grand porch of the faux antebellum home and knocked. The door opened and Doyle disappeared for about twenty minutes. He reemerged grim-faced and hugging an older black woman in the frame of the front door.

Soon, Cadillac Mack Miller walked out by the woman, and he and Doyle trotted off the porch, walking around the back of the home.

Nick could hear the Karmaan Ghia's engine tick in his ears after Kate cut the engine. Doyle motioned for them to follow the teen protégé to a slat fence behind the house.

"Servants' entrance?" Kate asked.

"Who knows."

On the other side of a gate sat an Olympic-size swimming pool. Empty. Only a blue and white cord and an old life preserver sat stiff in a foot of frozen brown water.

The kid, in a black Levi's jacket and jeans, rounded the edge of the pool and walked over to the diving board. Across the pool, and separate from the house, stood an elongated brick building. Looked like a sun room or an old greenhouse with dozens of broken panes curved over half the roof.

Miller tossed back his stringy blond hair, yet to say a word or show a drop of emotion, and handed Doyle the key. Doyle scratched his beard, walked inside, and flipped a switch. Dozens of fluorescent lights sputtered to life above them.

The room was haphazardly stacked with old jukeboxes, pinball machines, and pool tables. Someone had grouped a few plastic chairs in a circle for a jam session. A couple of amps lay toppled on the floor.

Place made Nick think of Chuck Berry's pad in *Hail, Hail, Rock and Roll*. He thought of that scene at the end when Berry sat in that room of red carpet and played some of the loneliest lap steel Nick had ever heard.

Doyle followed Miller to a back corner of the building packed with a mountain of bent cardboard boxes marked with scrawled black pen. The boxes smelled like the inside of a fading photo album—full of old heat from disintegrating moments.

"I don't think we can truck all of this," Doyle said.

Nick crossed his arms over his chest and nodded. He looked at a huge pile of amplifiers and broken instruments that sat discarded among the mess. Loose papers littered the floor and piles of old concert bills were stacked in old milk crates.

"Sweet Black Angel," Nick said. "He said we had to hear her song."

Doyle sighed. "Let's start box by box. Hey kid, move those amps and all that crap in the corner, okay?"

Miller began hoisting the crates in his arms. Nick pulled the top box teetering a few feet over his head and checked its contents. Six-millimeter master tapes in skinny cardboard boxes. Each marked. Most of these came from a 1966 session for Diamond.

Nick set them aside. Kate and Doyle were doing the same thing, taking a few boxes they needed outside and to the van. Nick's labored breath came out in cloudy spurts as he searched through countless boxes, setting aside a few that contained sessions that would have included Ruby. *Unbelievable he'd kept all these.* For a blues tracker, this was like breaking into King Tut's grave. Old photos, cardboard ads, outtakes, and numerous studio sessions. When he found what he needed, he had to come back and shuffle through King's life. If he was ever allowed back in it.

Nick took a deep breath as he saw six twisted cowboy hats on top of an old amplifier. He shook off the black feeling and hoisted off two more boxes filled with more master tapes and a hundred feet of guitar cord.

An hour later, Doyle had loaded his van with what they needed and headed back to Chicago. Nick carefully put every mike stand, amplifier, and box back in its place. Outside the fence, Kate was waiting in her car, her exhaust beating hot air in the chilled Christmas Eve morning.

As he walked out of the sun room, shards of light shot through broken panes of glass crisscrossing the face of Cadillac Mack Miller. Miller sat on an overturned milk crate in the cold and worked on three strings of one of King's broken guitars. He stopped, returned a loose string, and worked off a hollow version of one of King's classic tunes. Without an amp, the electric sounded small, lonely, and almost dying.

The teen's face was obscured by his blond hair as he labored for a sound that was not his own.

55

Hours later, Doyle walked next door to his record shop near the Miracle Mile and bought a dozen donuts and three large coffees. But Nick didn't need caffeine, the adrenaline pump was working just fine as he listened to another reel of tape. *King Snake's Greatest Hits*. The complete recordings. Every take, every cough, and every sigh of when Billy Lyons started the machine. He felt he'd been connected back to the late fifties and to a world that only existed in a tattered memory. The sound of Lyons calling the countdown to the songs raised the hair on his arms.

King had told him to look for the Sweet Black Angel, so they'd grabbed every disintegrating cardboard box filled with Ruby's old music. But Doyle, God bless him, grabbed other singers too. He grabbed thirty reels from 1959. Some of the last music Ruby sang and some classic stuff from King.

Kate was asleep in an office chair with Chicago working in an electric pulse around the shop when Nick saw the faded writing on the boxed reel, *Black Angel Blues*.

But it wasn't Ruby.

It was Elmore King. A reel from September 22, 1959. He tipped the marked end toward Doyle.

Doyle just shook his head and crashed his big frame into his office chair, a trace of chocolate icing on his lips. "Unbelievable, man. Unbelievable."

"You think?"

"Only one way to find out," Doyle said.

Nick handed him the brittle tape and let Doyle loop it through the reel-to-reel. Nick's hands shook too much to handle the music.

This was another version of "Black Angel Blues." A song first recorded by Lucille Bogan in 1930 but most recognized by Robert Nighthawk's cover in 1948. Nighthawk, a master slide guitarist from Helena, cut a mean version of the song for Aristocrat.

Elmore King's recording started out with Billy Lyons saying, "Okay, this will be take one. 'Black Angel Blues,'" in the metallic burn of a studio mike. The band tore into an uptempo, electric variation of the refrain and then he could hear Lyons's voice saying, "Again. No, again."

"Who's that?" Kate asked.

"Billy Lyons," Doyle said, with sleepy eyes.

The band started back into the song and the same thing happened several times again. Finally, King broke into the classic chorus of the song.

"*I got a sweet black angel,*" he sang roughly. "*I love the way she spreads her wings.*"

"Was this version ever released?" Nick asked.

Doyle shook his head and tossed Nick a cigarette. Kate stirred in her seat and wiped the sleep from her eyes. Nick lit the cigarette and strained to listen to the recording. He grabbed a pen and paper from Doyle's desk and began transcribing.

KING: "*I ask my black angel for a nickel, you know she gives me a twenty-dollar bill.*"

Doyle drummed his fingers on his desk, took a bite of a powdered donut and a puff off his cigarette.

KING: "*I ask her for a small drink of liquor, she gives me the whole whiskey still.*"

The band played through the entire song. After the final turnaround, they quit but the recording kept playing through. Doyle started to press stop but Nick reached over and cued forward. He stopped when the squawking began.

Through the brilliant, crackling hiss, Nick heard the voices of the band members keep talking. He could hear the gathering of instruments and loose good-byes.

A door slammed a few times and Nick could imagine the old studio back in the day. The gray recording machines that resembled NASA supercomputers looped with tape. Microphones that looked like honeycombs. He could imagine King placing his guitar back in its worn black case and Billy Lyons smoking a cigarette as he logged the session, a white Stetson slipped back on his head.

LYONS: *"Got to be rougher, man."*

KING: *"Huh?"*

LYONS: *"You playin' like a woman."*

NEW VOICE: *"Cool it, Billy."*

Doyle turned off the reel-to-reel and leaned back into his seat.

"Who's that?" Nick asked.

"Can't you tell?" Doyle asked.

Nick shook his head.

"Moses Jordan, man. He didn't tell you he was there?"

Nick shook his head again and Doyle flipped the switch on the reel-to-reel; 1959 began again and Nick's heart slammed in his chest.

LYONS: *"Man, I pay him. He can take it."*

KING: *"If I don't get my cut this time, I'm walkin'. This whole thing fallin' apart."*

LYONS: *"This is Chicago, boy. We do things different in the city."*

Inaudible discussion and yelling.

JORDAN: *"Y'all cool out. C'mon. Cool out."*

Footsteps thud across the floor and a door slams, the sound of labored breathing.

KING: *"That motherfucker has all of us by the nuts."*

JORDAN: *"Remember what I tole you."*

KING: *"Man, takin' all my work and gamblin' it away. Tell me, Moses, what's the difference between Chicago and Alabama? You tole me when you brought me up here it'd be different."*

JORDAN: *"It will. You're the finest guitarist I've ever known."*

KING: *"Why'd you make me sign with that man? You lied, man. You lied."*

JORDAN: *"Be cool, I got the whole thing. We got the whole thing. Go on."*

KING: *"You're talkin' a mess but you don't play."*

JORDAN: *"I want you to get Ruby out tonight."*

KING: *"Why?"*

JORDAN: *"Keep her away. Take her out. Here, take this."*

KING: *"Aw, man."*

The door opens again and the room remains silent.

KING: *"Who the hell are you?"*

JORDAN: *"Get gone."*

KING: *"Goddamn, you a hoss."*

JORDAN: *"Go."*

The door creaks open and bangs shut. Some loose jazz-style drumming starts for about thirty seconds. Someone coughs and the door to the studio opens again.

LYONS: *"Jordan, it's ten o'clock. Get out here. Hey, you—"*

The studio fills with thuds and crashes.

LYONS: *"You motherfuckers, you motherfuckers . . ."*

Piano keys clank.

Cymbals turn over.

The microphone topples over and buzzes with feedback.

The sound of what seems like bloody flesh being torn apart. *Over and over.*

Then in the vibrating, electric silence caught on skinny brown tape over forty years ago came the final violent sound. A sharp gunshot and a high-pitched scream. Sounded almost like a child in the magnetic hiss.

The tormented moans match a desperate writhing somewhere near the microphone. Heavy footsteps thud across the floor, a door slams, and one man's breath soaks the final few moments of the tape.

The door opens again.

KING: *"Sweet Jesus, what have you—"*

The tape reached its end, flipping its tail over and over on the reel. Doyle's face had turned white and the cigarette had burned to a nub in his fingers. Kate watched Nick.

"We need more?" Nick asked.

Kate shook her head.

"Kind of makes Sonny Boy's *Little Village* session seem like a PTA meeting," Doyle said. "Always thought that fifty-fifty was a hell of a split."

"Doyle, can you drive Kate to the State's Attorney's Office?" Nick asked. "It's down on Randolph."

"I know," Doyle said, still in shock. "Be glad to."

"What about you?" Kate asked.

"I'm going to grab Jimmy," Nick said. "Make sure he's all right. We also need Peetie, I bet he can put the rest together with Dawkins and Williams."

"South Side?"

"No, I heard he's down at Maxwell Street."

■

A pinkish blue light leaked from the end of the State Street corridor that morning, as Moses Jordan's Mercedes rolled through the Robert Taylor Homes. He passed dead trees, rusting playgrounds, and huge trash bins filled with burning rubble. Made him sick to see all the filth and the cancer that plagued the dream. He couldn't wait to see it all cut from the South Side, so the healthy areas could thrive and grow once again.

He remembered when they built the towers and demolished neighborhoods, failed self-respect, and lies that followed. For a few years the plan worked, until unemployment and drugs began to twist at the people. The children who were born here never knew anything else but poverty and pain.

Just one more thing he needed and he'd be done with Robert Taylor. Forever.

Jordan's Mercedes slowed at the end of the corridor. 5326

South State Street. *The Hole*. Jordan took a deep breath and walked into the dead city towering above him. He'd be fine with Stagger Lee, Jordan thought, smelling the piss-soaked hallways. The man knew where the money came from.

He should have never sent Elmore to do his work last night. But Elmore understood Jordan could never be seen with Stagger Lee. He knew the hope of the South Side meant the world and made the effort to take the cash.

But Stagger Lee said Elmore had never shown.

Jordan would go in, find out what Stagger Lee wanted now, and leave this mess.

An old woman cried in a corner, talking to a mangy cat. Jordan walked around her and put his hand over his nose to filter out the smell. Damn. He pushed the elevator button. Nothing. No electricity.

Jordan opened the door with his foot, walked around the crap on the bottom step and up the emergency steps over piles of garbage in the halls. Garbage bags of old food had frozen into bricks. Icicles hung from ceiling tiles and entire doors were coated in clear ice. Down the hall, a fluorescent bulb buzzed on and off and he could hear the motor on a gas generator.

Felt colder in here than on the street. Stagger Lee must've tapped into some power upstairs or something. No way you could live in this shit unless you were a polar bear. Surprised he'd stayed on. Guess he was still working a few more of them nickel-and-dime crack deals to make sure he gets rid of the product. *Crack, Stagger Lee's legacy*.

For years, Jordan had combed the South looking for talent. He'd gone all over the southern states with promises of records and Chicago. He'd brought hundreds to the big city from little old country towns. But if he could just go back and change that meeting in Memphis in '59, he'd do it in a second.

A white record promoter he knew had used Stagger Lee before and told Jordan he was the man to take care of any troubles. So on a hot August afternoon, Jordan sat in Handy Park and watched a slide player work out on a Son House song. The biggest man he'd ever seen took a seat on the green park bench by him.

Jordan remembered feeling the man's heavy breath. Stagger Lee, just a young man then, didn't talk. He just listened to what was to be done, took the money, and left. Never saw him again until after Billy was killed.

But Stagger Lee never left Chicago. That piece of shit stayed and picked off each part of Billy's old territory. He became the new leader of the South Side and when Robert Taylor was built, the man really went for the throat of the people.

If he'd just never gone to Handy Park that day. Maybe. Maybe. But you can't change the past. Dwelling on mistakes wouldn't make change come any faster. Today was all that mattered. Today would make the difference.

When he reached Stagger Lee's floor, a fat little black boy with a shotgun waved at the end of the hall. The fat boy opened the door and Jordan saw Stagger Lee standing by an open window in a bare room. He had on a long, black leather jacket, black jeans, and cowboy boots. No shirt and a dog collar. He held a bloody towel to his side.

The door slammed behind them. A whole mess of locks clamping shut. Jordan took off his checkered hat, listening to generators whirl.

"Stagger Lee," Jordan said. "How you doin', man?"

Stagger Lee whipped out a .44 from his jacket and stuck it right in the middle of Jordan's forehead. Jordan's legs felt like a broken guitar string and he dropped to his knees.

Jordan swallowed.

"Tell me what you need," Jordan pleaded. "What do you need?"

"What do you have?"

"Money, man. I'll get you all the money you want."

"Money didn't help your friend Elmore King," Stagger Lee said. "It's gonna be a cold, cold Christmas for that dead mother-fucker."

Jordan ground his teeth, staring down the long barrel of the gun. He swallowed again. Slowly.

"You talk to a man name Travers?" Stagger Lee asked.

"He came to see me but I didn't say anything," he said, hearing the slow twirl of the gun's cylinder. "I'm not stupid."

Stagger Lee breathed in his ear as his hands shook and throat constricted. He couldn't breathe, everything was so tight. His eyes watered and tears splatted against his cheeks.

"Please, please."

Stagger Lee pulled the trigger and the hammer fell on an empty cylinder. He pulled the gun back and stuck it into his coat. Jordan looked up into Stagger Lee's eyes covered in bug-shaped sunglasses. There was a smear of blood on his stomach and bloody holes on the arm of his jacket.

"What's it worth to you to make all your problems go away?" Stagger Lee asked in the empty room. "What's it worth to you to make all the questions about Billy Lyons and Ruby Walker fade out?"

"Everything," Jordan quivered and felt the warm piss spread down his thigh.

THE MAXWELL STREET Market buzzed with a nervous energy that Christmas Eve. Vendors in worn tents and dented vans hawked used tires, flannel shirts, cheap jewelry, and tools splotched with rust. Mexicans huddled by heaters with their dried peppers, cactus paddies, and cockfighting videos. The whole street smelled of corn tortillas and cheap leather as a few hardcore musicians played raunchy blues. Their weathered fingers worked over frets through cut gloves as their music fuzzed from torn speakers.

The market was the old gateway to the blues. The place where Little Walter first blew his harp in Chicago. The spot where Robert Johnson's old traveling partner, Honeyboy Edwards, came to establish himself after the legend's death. This was the proving ground for Hound Dog Taylor, Snooky Pryor, and Jimmy Rogers. The tales of a day's rewards were legendary. Bathtubs overflowing with dollar bills for country musicians fresh from the Mississippi Delta. One of Nick's favorite stories was about a guy who made money with a performing chicken. The guy could command the chicken to sit, speak, and roll over like a dog. *Only on Maxwell Street.*

Even though the century-old market had moved near the railroad yard off Canal, there was still a lot of character left. Some complained it was a little too clean but there was plenty of chaos and mounds of junk to buy.

Dirty Jimmy stood talking to an older black couple who sold velvet paintings of flowers. He asked them a couple of questions, they shook their heads, and then wandered back to Nick.

"They ain't seen him," Jimmy said, his ski hat pulled so low on his old head Nick could barely see his eyes. "Man, that jive-ass huckster is gone."

When Nick had stopped by Kate's place to check on him, the old man said he wanted to go with him. Nick tried to talk him out of it, but Jimmy said he knew the market like the back of his own ass. How do you argue with that?

So after Nick took a long, hot shower to clean off the blood, he finally agreed. He was in no condition to fight it. His head and ribs throbbed. His hands shook. He hadn't slept in twenty-four hours and was afraid he would be out if he blinked.

Jimmy looked down the endless rows of vendors, tents thudding in the brittle wind, and took a deep whiff of the pungent smells as if he were a bird dog. The sky was hard and flat. A blackening gray. Somewhere, a cheap cassette player played Burl Ives's "Holly Jolly Christmas." What Nick wouldn't give for just one of those humid summer nights back home where your T-shirt sticks to your skin.

It was late in the afternoon and most of the vendors were starting to pack up. Nick and Jimmy walked the market for a final time. They crossed over Roosevelt Road past an old diner. He was sure Peetie was gone.

They walked past an old man selling pirated movies on video, a man that specialized in risqué belt buckles and another that sold nothing but singing Christmas trees. Nick was about to pack up the expedition and head back to Kate's for a warm drink when he happened to glance in the weathered diner facing Roosevelt and saw Peetie's face halfway into a cheeseburger.

"What's up, man?" Jimmy asked, his face looking hard and frozen in the streetlights.

Nick nodded to the diner and smiled.

"That dipshit better bend over," Jimmy said.

"Why's that?"

"He 'bout to get the ass kickin' of his life."

◼

The White Palace Grill was a twenty-four-hour diner with orange vinyl booths that smelled of decades of hamburger grease. Nick stared at a hand-painted menu above as two workers hunkered over donuts and meatloaf at the counter. He watched a tired waitress with hair the color of copper wiring walk over a faded red and white floor chomping on gum. Bacon and eggs sizzled on the open grill.

"Hey, man, how you doin'?" Peetie said, offering his hand and putting down his cheeseburger. "Listen, just about to call you and see how thangs went. Hey Jimmy, what's up, brother? Good to see you, dawg."

Jimmy and Nick stood back from the booth and Peetie pulled back his hand. He had on a green suit and green hat. Reminded Nick of a leprechaun.

"What's up, man?" Peetie asked. "Look like somebody just pissed on your Christmas tree. Let me buy y'all a burger with extra cheese. Jimmy, I know you're a cheese man."

Jimmy looked at Peetie like he was something he had found on the bottom of his shoe.

"How 'bout you tell me about Moses Jordan and Stagger Lee," Nick said. "And I won't kick your narrow little ass."

Jimmy laughed and looked down at Nick's feet.

"What size you wear?"

"Eleven," Nick said.

"Eleven lots bigger than yore rectum, Wheatstraw."

"What? Stagger Lee?" Peetie pulled out an unlit cigar from his green suit jacket and twisted it into his puckered mouth. "Y'all drunk?"

"King's dead," Nick said.

"Yeah, man, I heard that on the news. Shit, everybody 'round here been talkin' about it. Takin' it real hard. Killed out on Navy

Pier or somethin'. Who would want to kill such a sweet, sweet man?"

Peetie took off his green hat and held it over his heart.

"King told me you set him up," Nick said. Jimmy stood beside him nodding. "Thought we were friends, Peetie. You been playin' me?"

"No, man, we're cool. We're cool." Peetie held out the palms of his hands and bobbed his head. "You know I'm a peace-lovin' man. Don't want no trouble."

Nick stood with his arms crossed, watching him.

■

Nick finished his second cup of coffee and could feel the caffeine pumping its magic into his tired limbs. Sleep deprivation wasn't so bad after the first twenty-four hours, he thought. It was actually like running a marathon, as if your body went back to the caveman instincts.

"This won't take long?" Peetie asked. "Right?"

A nub of a cigarette burned in a flat metal ashtray before him.

"Depends on what you have to say," Nick said.

Peetie tipped his bowler back on his head. "My auntie said she wanted me to take her to service tonight. Real important to the old woman. Candlelight and all that. Me? I just want to get drunk and watch that *Ain't It a Wonderful Life*. Man, that George Bailey a trip, runnin' through his hometown when it's filled with cathouses and honkytonks. But shit, man, to me Pottersville looked better than that other world where he livin'."

Peetie laughed and laughed as Nick stared out the window into the blackness. On Canal, a few vendors were still packing up and heading out for Christmas. A wino in a Santa's hat walked in the diner and asked if anyone wanted to hump for a quarter.

No one responded and the old man left rejected.

"Tell me about Stagger Lee," Nick said.

"I don't know no Stagger Lee. What y'all talkin' about?"

"Peetie, you gots the intelligence of fly shit," Jimmy said. "The man knows. So get your head out yo' ass and tell this man the truth. Quit wastin' his time."

Peetie straightened his coat and dropped the green bowler back in his lap. A sprig of holly in its brim. He clicked his tongue and sighed before looking Nick in the eye. His cockiness fell as he laced his hand before him.

"*Ooh, well well.*"

"You work with Stagger Lee?"

"Aw, man," Peetie started to move out of his seat. "Y'all talk about your dreams together."

"Listen, you little bastard. I almost got killed this morning. You want to hold out? That's cool. I'll call the cops right now and you can tell them all about the con job you worked on Elmore King. I don't have time to fuck with you anymore."

Peetie's face froze and his eyes shifted.

"He tole me he'd kill me, man," Peetie said. "He just asked me to take a message to King. That's it. I didn't have a choice. That was Stagger Lee's deal, I didn't want no part of it."

"Where is he now?" Nick asked.

"Dead," Peetie said. "Word has it, he got killed by one of his own folks."

"Man," Jimmy said, "that dude don't die."

Nick lit another cigarette and took a sip of the coffee. He wanted to reach over and choke Peetie's skinny neck. The old man's Adam's apple bobbed up and down as he spun more webs of shit.

"I know a man who seen his body," Peetie said. "Guess he crawled back to Robert Taylor like an old dawg and just fell out. I say hallelujah. I hated that motherfucker."

"What about Moses Jordan?" Nick asked.

"What?"

"Why did he hire Stagger Lee to kill Billy?"

"*Shiiit.* You got to be kiddin' me, man. Jordan killed Billy Lyons? That man act like his shit made out of gold."

Jimmy glared at Peetie but Peetie just ignored the hard glances.

"I wasn't there, Jimmy," Peetie said, pointing his finger at Jimmy. "You the one at that session, so don't look at me like you a saint."

"Peetie, you so greasy they could use your sweat to cook chicken."

Peetie leaned back in his seat and tried to relight the wet cigar. He ordered a donut from the waitress and kept trying with the match. The wet, burning smell of cherries and vanilla made Nick want to puke.

"Dawkins and Williams?" Nick asked.

"Hey, man, King can say what he wanted about me, but I didn't have nothin' to do with any of that killin'. But if Jordan had Billy killed . . . man, I don't know."

"You fuckin' with me, Peet?" Nick asked. "Please don't be."

"No, man, I ain't fuckin' with ya," Peetie said. "That piece of news about Jordan just jumped up and bit me in my ass. C'mon, let me go, quit tryin' to stick my head in the toilet. It's Christmas. Got to be with my family."

"Elmore ain't having Christmas," Nick said.

"Sounds like he the one who started all this shit. If he let Jordan swim in his own shit we wouldn't be here right now. But I guess King figured he got to take care of the man who made him *the deal*. Right? Can I please call my auntie, man? She got to be twistin' in her panty hose right now. I suppose to be back 'bout now."

"You're not going anywhere, man," Nick said slowly. He leaned against the cold glass and was hypnotized by the loops his cigarette made in the ashtray. He yawned and felt in his coat for his leather gloves.

Just as he was about to ask Jimmy to let him out of the booth, Peetie shot out of his seat, sprinting to the front door.

Nick bolted over Jimmy's lap and ran after Peetie as the cook yelled for him to pay the tab.

Out on Roosevelt, a cab swerved and skidded to avoid hitting Peetie as he darted across the street toward a bridge in the darkness. Nick waited in the center yellow line for a semi with a blaring horn to pass before following the old man down a grass embankment and into a gravel valley filled with rusting railroad cars.

57

STAGGER LEE KILLED Fannie as soon as they had gotten back to Robert Taylor. The woman had no pride. She'd tried to put the move on him, tried to make his dick hard. So he took her to the top floor of The Hole and let her get through her act. They sat up there in the black cold as the wind ripped through broken windows. She cried with her teeth chattering as she stripped for him. She was naked in below zero air trying to get his pants down when she died. She kept on saying it was going to be all right. And so he let her put her head between his legs and stuck the ice pick through her brain. Guess she was upset about the white girl. Kept repeating Annie's name as her eyes crossed.

He didn't play.

That was his only rule.

He didn't play.

That man Travers had brought this world of pain on himself. He was the one who really killed Elmore King. He was the one who killed Annie. And even Fannie. This was Travers' final moment, Stagger Lee thought, watching through the slit in the railcar door. He looked to the gravel littered with snow and listened. He moved the bag of cash to a far corner and pulled the bloody ice pick from the dead man in the Santa hat.

He watched his breath in the cold, the flesh around his knuckles turning gray as the heat came again to the bloody wound at his side. Stagger Lee kept a knee on the rusted floor as he pulled out his .44 and waited to finish his business.

The South Side way.

Nick loosely held a cigarette in his mouth as he kicked the stones in front of him. He'd found Jimmy wandering down the lonely tracks five minutes ago and Peetie had to be long gone. But he kept searching as Jimmy rattled on about the old days. He could name all the lines: Frisco, Illinois Central, L&N, Sante Fe, and Union Pacific. Jimmy knew them all. Each of them part of the old highway. A unique world of freedom without bounds.

"Used to live in places like this," Jimmy said, a slight shuffle in his step as he walked through the railroad yard. "Just ole hobo camps. In Mississippi, we had little villages of 'em. Have about five men to an ole railcar. Man, we went all over the place from Helena to St. Louis over to Chicago then back to the Delta. We'd play cards, play a little harp. Traveled a little bit with Honeyboy, some with Little Walter."

"You never told me that."

"I ain't one of those people who makes themselves known by sayin' I knew so-and-so. You know? If you played the blues one time or another you ran into some other player. You a professor, right? Don't you hang out with other professors?"

"I try to avoid it," Nick said, walking through the forgotten monoliths. Be a good way to start his story about Ruby Walker and King Snake. *Dirty Jimmy Scott, forgotten bluesman/hobo walking through an old railroad yard on Christmas Eve.* Where the hell was Peetie?

"Yeah, but you know what I'm sayin'," Jimmy said. "We had a time. Never felt so free in my life. I got married and got respectable and that kind of ended thangs. A wife with child won't put up with all that mess."

"When did you stop ramblin'?" Nick asked.

"I guess the word *home* just started meanin' somethin' to me. I like the way it sounded. Meanin' a warm place to sleep, some stew ready fer you when you get home. Sometimes even tomcats want to be loved."

Nick tossed away his cigarette and reached in his coat for a couple more smokes.

He lit both and handed one to Jimmy. The men stopped in the middle of the dozens of rusted-out railcars. It was like being in a museum, watching the decay on an important part of history. All the railcars full of the sweat of Chicago now left to rust.

The moon was an unreachable gold coin above them.

"You ever regret it?" Nick asked.

"What?" Jimmy asked.

"Way you spent your life?"

"Not a minute, man," Jimmy said. "Not a minute."

"Don't blame you. C'mon. I'll buy you a steak dinner and a few beers. Peetie's gone."

"How 'bout some Irish whiskey?" Jimmy asked.

"Whatever you want, man," Nick said, trudging toward the narrow road behind the Maxwell Street Market. The cold air buzzed his fatigued mind, each step crunching in his ears.

A blur of green flashed across his eyes.

"Goddamn!" Jimmy yelled. "Catch his ass."

■

Stagger Lee could hear steps. Some men talking. His finger wrapped the cold steel of the .44. Every nerve was ready to leap from the old car and take out Travers. Then he'd take care of Peetie. Little shit all scared, trying to pretend like he didn't know what Annie was up to. Peetie thought he was clear of this mess. Thought he could go back to his jive-ass shop but he'd be dead before Christmas morning too. It was time to bury *all the past*.

He coughed out some blood and spit onto the ground, the red twirl of blood and saliva dripping to the gravel below.

Stagger Lee had all he needed with him. The money from Jordan and King by his side in the old leather bag. All of it. Maybe he'd come back to Chicago. Maybe he'd disappear. Not much left. He'd sucked everything he could from the projects. Besides, the city wanted to shift the poor people all around Chicago now. His world would be gone by the end of the year. The State Street city nothing but a memory.

He watched Travers share a smoke with Jimmy Scott who was just hobbling along. The smiles on their faces made Stagger Lee want to howl. Then they started to run.

One hand felt for the huge sliding door while the other held the heavy gun.

■

Peetie dipped through another long row of boxcars and then disappeared again. Nick slowed his run to a fast walk, his Browning out in his hand. Somewhere in the distance a train whistle blew. Nick stopped and listened. The whistle blew again and the tracks and old trains shook with its approach.

"Peetie?" Nick yelled.

Nothing. Industrial powerlines stretched overhead like a web.

"I'm not going to hurt you. C'mon, man. Let's talk."

The ground shook more and all the loose rusted parts of the train rattled. He yelled again.

About ten yards away, Peetie emerged from the shadows with his hands raised above his head. His shoulders were hunched and his teeth clamped tight. One eye was shut.

"Man, I'm not going to hurt you."

Peetie shook his head and looked away.

Just as Nick turned, Stagger Lee flew from the doors of the railcar, his black overcoat whipping around him like wings. He looked like a huge raven descending to the earth as he slammed Nick to the ground. His gun skittered across the gravel.

Nick felt the air force from his lungs and his vision dim as he reached for his lost gun but Stagger Lee found it first. Stagger Lee threw the Browning over his shoulder and struck Nick in the face with the butt of his .44.

"Hold on," Peetie yelled.

Stagger Lee quickly aimed the long barrel at Peetie and fired off two quick shots, nailing the old man in the chest. Peetie toppled over.

Nick tried to roll free but the weight above him flattened him to the ground. Stagger Lee twisted the gun into Nick's side.

He connected his fist into Stagger Lee's throat.

The hammer edged back and Nick closed his eyes.

Stagger Lee grunted as Jimmy slammed a red brick into the big man's head.

Nick heard a booming gun shot and pain exploded through his thigh.

Stagger Lee knocked Jimmy away with one hand as Nick drew up his leg and reached into his boot for his knife. The pain, a throbbing pulse of his heart. He grabbed his Tom Mix special, flipped open the blade, and stabbed Stagger Lee in the gut. He felt the weight roll off of him as Stagger Lee made an animal groan that echoed off the railcars.

His hands tore for Nick's face.

Nick broke free from his grasp and kicked Stagger Lee in the head with his good leg. Stagger Lee lunged for Nick and gripped his neck, locking with all his strength. Nick felt the blood rush to his face as he slashed with the knife into Stagger Lee's arm.

He made a deep stab to Stagger Lee's shoulder. Another giant howl and Nick was free. He rolled off the gravel to his feet.

Nick pushed Stagger Lee as if he were a quarterback, ramming his head up into the huge black man's chest and knocking him to the ground. Nick reached down and yanked his knife free and kicked Stagger Lee in the head.

A long stretch of railcars passed. Somehow Jimmy had crawled onto the one where Stagger Lee had hidden. The train whistle blew. The old diesel engines hummed as Jimmy stretched out a hand to Nick. "C'mon!," Jimmy yelled, the rusted boxcar moving along.

He soon disappeared as the train rolled. Nick hobbled for Jimmy, tripping hard and cutting his hands on the sharp rocks. He tripped again, trying to run for the open car and Jimmy's hand.

His heart thudded in his ears. His leg screamed with pain as he found a foothold and pulled his body into the car.

Nick rolled onto the rusted floor, his vision blurred, trying to catch a decent breath. Jimmy lay next to him, holding his chest.

Nick closed the bloody knife and stuffed it back into his boot. The train creaked and moaned underneath him. He was about to help Jimmy when he saw a thick hand covered in blood wrap around the door.

Stagger Lee's bald head appeared.

His eyes bloodshot and teeth clenched as he groaned. It was as if he was trying to lift up the car. He groaned again, hooking a foot on the floor. Nick punched him in the face as Stagger Lee tried to bite his hand. Nick kicked at his head and Stagger Lee lifted his mammoth weight into the rolling car. A perfect moon shone above him before the shadow of the Roosevelt Bridge closed over them. When they passed through, Stagger Lee raised to his full height and smiled.

And then Nick heard the shots.

Three. Rapid. The sound blasting through metal walls as if they were in a steel drum. As the shots cracked off the metal of the freight car, Nick opened his eyes to see Stagger Lee waver and lose his balance. His eyes wide in disbelief as he fell backward and disappeared into a black gaping hole.

Jimmy sat against the far wall with Nick's 9 mm in his hands. The train picked up speed, a whistle blew, and Nick felt the blackness sweep over his mind as he drifted far away.

58

LATE CHRISTMAS EVE, the snow felt like feathers on Kate's eyelashes as she walked the Maxwell Street Market. Banners flapped on streetlights illuminating the scattering snow. The vendors were gone. Some had left broken crates and trampled boxes. Newspapers rolled down the vacant street and a few junk cars rambled by as she walked across Roosevelt Street.

A cab chugged heat from its tailpipe waiting for her return.

She'd spent the morning at the State's Attorney's Office and the rest of the day at the *Tribune* writing her story. She had to handle the studio tape part carefully so she wouldn't get sued but still, the story fleshed out into something great with earlier notes from Florida and Dirty Jimmy. Should be plastered on 1-A across the city tomorrow.

She felt good until she returned back to her apartment, picked up Bud from her neighbor, and checked her messages. Two from Richard, who said something about wanting to fly up and talk through things. But none from Nick.

She called the Palmer House and Doyle, but nothing.

Kate told the taxi driver to go ahead as she walked to the White Palace Grill. The tri-corner diner's wrap-around sign advertised BREAKFAST, LUNCH, AND DINNER 24 HOURS, and a Polish sausage dinner for $2.50. A Middle Eastern man in a hooded sweatshirt had his arms wrapped around a bloody steak. An old red-headed waitress refilled his coffee cup. A plastic Christmas tree blinked its lights by a green metal register with thick push buttons.

"Merry Christmas," the redhead called out.

"Hey," Kate said, pulling off her gloves and ordering a cup of coffee. She sank her head into her hands and listened to Elvis singing "Blue Christmas." There were few places lonelier than a diner on Christmas Eve. There was a deep melancholy for those who worked that night or who had no family. For some, this was as good as it gets.

Kate felt her shoulders shake and watched her tears drop onto the paper placemat. She covered her mouth with a napkin. She remembered a few years ago spending Christmas with Nick, Loretta, and JoJo at the Jacksons' townhouse on Royal. The smell of Loretta's spicy jambalaya filled with red and green pepper and WWOZ on their old console stereo. Nick and JoJo had sat on that crooked balcony smoking and talking about music.

After dinner, she'd walked hand and hand with him back through the French Quarter. Christmas lights blinking from the old rusted balconies with the sound of soft music playing high above the dead streets. They walked over a barren Canal Street and back to the warehouse on Julia and made love in a pile of blankets and pillows beneath his industrial windows. Their bodies were coated with sweat and their chests heaved with breath as the sound of Mississippi tugboats and stray horns floated through the Warehouse District.

Kate rubbed her fingers over her face and took in a deep breath. The Middle Eastern man put his hand on her shoulder and asked if she was all right. She said she was and ran the napkin over her cheeks. Through the glass sheets that wrapped the diner, she watched the snow softly fall in the streetlamp's glow. She took a sip of the burnt coffee.

"Been a hell of a night," the waitress said.

"Yeah."

"I never seen the market so busy, then all those cops came and it's just been a mess."

"Cops?" Kate asked. "What happened?"

"Oh, you know. Chicago. Somebody was shooting down by the railroad yard or something like that. Well, you know how it is."

At the paper she'd been so into her story, she hadn't heard a word.

Kate stood and tossed a couple dollars on the table.

"When did the police leave?"

"A few hours ago," the waitress said. "After they found that dead guy . . . real Merry Christmas, ain't it."

59

THE ROLLING AND tumbling of the train threw Nick in and out of dreams. He dreamed of riding the cold waves, his view half above the blackness of Lake Michigan. He struggled to reach a green luminescent glow in the center of the lake. When he reached the glow, he saw it surrounded a bloated man in a pin-striped suit. Suddenly, a wave rocked and broke over the body and he saw another face appear. It was Ruby. But as he struggled to catch her, black water circled her face and she disappeared. As she slipped under, a million battered suitcases shot from the water like torpedoes.

Nick struggled with the hand on his shoulder. He pushed it away and scrunched up his body on the cold ground. They pulled at him and he felt the hand try for him again.

"Nick?" the voice called.

Nick scrunched his eyes tight.

"Nick?"

As he rolled, a pain ripped through his thigh and his eyes opened. Jimmy Scott looked down at him in the darkness and shook him again.

"Fever got you, man," he said. "Got to keep awake, man. C'mon. Wake up."

Jimmy pushed a plastic flask to his lips and Nick took a drink of whiskey. Nick coughed and some poured off his chin. He closed his eyes and opened them again. His leg felt heavy and hot. A red bandanna twisted tight over the wound.

"Thanks, man," Nick said. "Where are we?"

"Don't know," Jimmy said, smiling. His face looked gray and parched like a road map as the moonlight shone though the sliding door. They weren't moving.

Nick had never been colder in his life.

"Chicago?"

"I know we ain't in Chicago."

Nick unwrapped the bandanna and ripped open the hole in his jeans and thermal underwear. The wound had clotted with a purple halo surrounding it. Didn't feel too nasty. Nick could move his lower leg, which was a good sign.

Nick borrowed the whiskey from Jimmy, poured some on the bandanna, and cleaned the wound. He took his Tom Mix knife and cut the tail from his flannel shirt and wrapped his leg.

"Help me up," Nick said, holding out his hand.

"Don't know if I can," Jimmy said.

Nick looked at him and Jimmy pulled open his jacket to show a bright splash of blood in his stomach. He coughed a horrendous, guttural sound. "Got me deep, man. Got me deep."

Nick used the edge of the door to pull himself to his feet. His leg screamed as he clenched his teeth and pulled the door wider. A field of yellowed weeds stretched for miles around him. Snow lightly covered the brown earth.

"I'll be right back," Nick said.

"Don't be gone too long," Jimmy said. "This guy ain't gonna be no good company."

Nick hobbled over and looked down at a twisted heap in a red-and-white suit. It smelled of human waste and alcohol. Dried blood covered the fake fur of a Santa's suit.

"You know you goin' to hell when you kill Santy Claus."

"I think Stagger Lee was already in line," Nick said.

Nick kicked the body farther into the corner and exposed a brown leather doctor's bag. He picked up the heavy bag and dragged it back into the light. In the thick moonlight, he pried open the flap and looked inside.

Packs and packs of crisp green paper bundles.

"What is it?" Jimmy asked.

"Stagger Lee left us a present."

■

Nick walked the barren tracks searching for someone to help. Where the engine had left ten cars, still coupled but alone, there was a small wooden shed and a long dirt road leading through snow-covered trees. Their leafless branches looked like the bony fingers of a skeleton.

Nick tried the shed door but it was locked.

He tossed a rock into the window and the glass shattered.

Nick used his arms to lift his bad leg into the room, sat on a low file cabinet, and dragged his good leg though the window.

He rested for a moment.

A metal desk filled most of the room with bulletin boards hanging on the plywood walls. A water cooler sat frozen in the corner, a big bubble spread wide in the center of the ice. Nick sat in the chair by the desk and tried the phone. No dial tone. He checked the plug and hit the hang-up switch several times. Still dead.

He rummaged through the drawers for anything they could use for warmth. He found some musty moving blankets and a pack of kitchen matches. He opened the door and walked by the shed, pulling off pieces of dry, brittle wood. He wrapped the wood and matches in the blankets and limped back to the railcar.

Jimmy sagged against the far wall, his breaths coming in quick smoky gasps. His face looked gray as he coughed into his glove. Nick plunked down the blanket and wood and pulled himself into the car. He unwrapped the blanket, spread it around Jimmy's lower legs, and struck a match.

The wood caught in a sudden burst of flame.

The corner smelled of the dead man and Nick grabbed the

body and tossed the limp weight outside. A trail of blood followed.

"Glad you got rid of him," Jimmy said. "Ain't no good for talkin'."

He hacked again into his hand.

The smoke drifted up into the ceiling as Jimmy and Nick huddled by the fire on the floor. Nick wrapped himself in the other packing blanket and poked at the small fire with his boot.

"Wish we had somethin' to eat," Jimmy said weakly.

"Hey now, ain't no room service in the woods."

Jimmy laughed.

"I remember sometimes we wouldn't eat fer days then end up in a little place like this," Jimmy said. "We'd find some farmhouse and get some hog parts from a farmer. Maybe a foot or a snout. Some ole guy always had a pot. We'd get that pot goin', put that pig foot in there, and man, would it smell good."

"One foot?"

"All we needed," Jimmy said, his mind decades back. "Some ole guy have a potato, another a carrot. You get some salt, maybe dig up some roots and grass. That way that stew would grow. You'd keep watchin' the stew and say you got to add somethin' if you want some. So them hobos would find all sorts of things in their bags. One time this guy gave me an onion like he found a chunka gold."

"I'll get you a whole pig when we get back to Chicago."

"I ain't goin' back," Jimmy said.

"C'mon now, we'll be back. Just need to warm ourselves a little bit, then I'll go for some help."

"You go on," Jimmy said as the fire crackled and popped by his foot.

"No way."

"You do me a last favor?"

"Anything."

Jimmy reached with a shaky hand into his coat for his harp. He pulled out a worn Hohner Marine Band. A thumb-size dent in the tarnished silver metal with the paint on the reed starting to flake. Jimmy pressed it into Nick's hand and closed his fingers around it.

Nick shook his head.

"Tell me more about that pig foot soup," Nick said. "What can I bring?"

"Thank you," Jimmy said and closed his eyes.

"What can I bring?" he asked again.

Hours later, as the night closed around the old railcar and the fire smoldered, Jimmy stopped breathing. Nick tucked the old blanket around his friend, jumped out of the railcar, and followed the dirt road coated in ice.

60

THE DAY'S WALK melted into two days of frustration in Chicago when Nick found out Jordan had disappeared. He'd stalked him at his home off Drexel and waited for hours outside the old Diamond studios with no luck. After his bill came due at the Palmer House and Richard had arrived at Kate's apartment unannounced, he decided it was time to complete his journey. He packed his tattered, green duffel bag, drove to Dwight Correctional one last time, and then boarded the *City of New Orleans* home as the worst snowstorm since 1967 pelted the city.

Ruby was on her way. That's all he could ask, he told himself on the trip south.

■

Four months passed before Moses Jordan had to answer questions about the murder of Billy Lyons. He'd tried to fight it with lawyers, an extended vacation from Chicago, and mostly feigned cries of innocence. But the Cook County State's Attorney's Office finally brought in Jordan that April. Nick was sitting on the roof of his warehouse grading papers on postwar blues when he got the call from Kate that Ruby was about to be released.

As the sun faded over the Mississippi River with a light breeze scattering papers across his beaten deck, he decided to see it through. Jordan was back, she said. He'd been trying to regain his place as a South Side leader after Kate's articles and the investigation.

The next afternoon, Nick was in Chicago driving toward Diamond Studios. He hadn't seen Jordan since the breakfast they'd shared at Lou Mitchell's in December. On that day Jordan had said Jimmy Scott was senile and Stagger Lee was a phantom.

A crisp city rain beat the gray and brown buildings of the South Side as Nick headed north from O'Hare. He knew the man had denied that was his voice on the tape and having anything to do with calling the hit on Billy Lyons, Franky Dawkins, and Leroy Williams. He told newspaper reporters in a prepared statement that Williams's son and Jimmy Scott were unfortunate casualties of a decaying world.

Shit, the old man would never see the inside of a jail unless he was connected to the recent murders. Kate said the statute of limitations on murder for hire was something like five years. Still, Doyle Brennan said the news of his involvement had hurt Jordan in a more personal way. Most of his charities had dissolved. His friends in city hall ignored his functions and all but a small group of his zealots still clung by his side.

As Nick pulled in front of the two-story brick storefront of Diamond Records, he saw a single light clicked on in the darkness. A sudden roll of thunder hammered through the streets setting off car alarms. Nick took a deep breath and ran for the old studio.

The front door was locked.

He knocked several times, rain soaking his face and jean jacket.

Jordan emerged from a back hallway and walked to the glass door. He had his hand on the lock before looking up into Nick's eyes. His gaze broke for a moment and he shook his head. His face looked haggard and beaten. He wore a single gray jumpsuit splattered in paint.

Nick tried the door again. The long metal handle was bent and tarnished.

Jordan shook his head again and walked back into the cavern of the old studio.

As the rain drummed all around him, Nick walked around the building until he found a dented metal door by a loading dock. He hopped up onto the platform and tried the back door. It was open. He followed a darkened hallway and heard the sound of old Diamond blues playing and the sound of rough scraping.

Jordan stood on a creaking ladder in the hall working on caked paint along a door frame. A little cassette player sat at the base of the ladder. He looked down at Nick from his perch, slowly walked down the ladder, and shut off the blues.

He folded his arms over his chest and nodded his head. It was almost as if Nick was the one who had screwed up and Jordan was about to give the lecture. They stood there for a few moments looking at each other—the rain pinging away on the old roof above—until Jordan finally spoke.

"Heard they lettin' Ruby out."

Nick nodded.

"Then I guess you can leave us alone."

Nick didn't say a word. He just watched Jordan's jowled face twitch in the dim light and left him to work his own explanations in the uncomfortable silence.

"You've made me into something I'm not," Jordan said.

The water clicked and beaded off the front pane glass window. The halls smelled of hot vinyl and fresh paint.

"I didn't make you anything," Nick said. "You brought him into everyone's world."

Jordan looked away at the front window where decaying warehouses and vacant lots were being drenched in the afternoon shower. The streets rolled with the downpour.

"You've ruined everything I've tried to do to this neighborhood. Do you know how many failures you're responsible for, son? Do you have any idea of the lives you've ruined?"

Nick let him talk.

"I've been working my whole life to help others. I've made

some bad decisions. But you got to look at the whole picture. A single man's life don't mean that much."

"I'll let Ruby know."

"I didn't have anything to do with any of them being killed . . . You can't control Stagger Lee."

"I thought he was an urban legend."

Jordan looked down at the paint splattered on his old walking shoes.

"I just have one question," Nick said.

Jordan looked up. His droopy face hanging in the hall's glow.

"Why did you want Billy dead? I understand the others were just to cover your ass. They lied for you in the depositions. But what was so damned important about Billy?"

"I don't know what you're talking about."

"I know you got control of all the recordings, King's contract, and were able to make a sweet deal with the Diamond Brothers. But there had to be something else."

Jordan walked to the front window. Trails of water droplets scattered over the clear panes in a million directions. Completely random paths catching in the gray light.

"You need to go now," Jordan said softly.

"I want an answer." Seemed strange sitting there with a legend of Chicago blues and calling him a liar. This man was one of his heroes.

Jordan stabbed his stubby finger into Nick's chest. He looked like he wanted to get his words past his clenched teeth but something was holding him back.

"Let me tell you one goddamned thing," Jordan finally said after the fifth jab. "You think you know me? You study my songs, you write about my life and my travels. Makes you a bluesman, does it? *You understand so much about us. You want to be us.* But you know what? You can never be us. You ain't shit. Now get the fuck off my property before I call the police."

"I don't give a shit, call them," Nick said. "I want to know why you had Billy killed. Power? Did he have too much control?"

Jordan kept looking at the decay in the broad window before him. The Diamond Records logo was painted backward in the middle of the glass pane.

"Get out."

"You know, I used to keep a picture of you in my office. Man, I thought you were brilliant. I can name every song you wrote and the date it hit vinyl. But now . . . I just see a warped old man."

Jordan swung at Nick and popped him hard in the ear. Nick felt his ear tingle with the jab and the blood rush through the cartilage.

He smiled.

"Always knew you had it in you," Nick said. "Knew you could do one thing yourself without having someone handle it. Now you're on your own, you'll have plenty of practice."

Jordan pushed him hard with the flat of his palms. "Leave."

Nick turned to walk away but at the end of the hallway, near the old loading bay where records were shipped, he turned back to Jordan. He could hear the hollow sounds his boots made in the concrete cavern.

"They never found Stagger Lee," Nick said.

Jordan looked away, a tattered red rag in his hand.

"He'll always own you," Nick said. "That's something you'll always have in your life."

Nick was sure the sound of his boots grew smaller and smaller until he closed the door behind him and walked out into a Chicago rain.

61

THE BRIDGES IN Chicago are synchronized in a ballet of screaming steel and clanging gears to allow sailboats and cargo ships to flow from Lake Shore Drive to the Eisenhower Expressway. Something like fifty of them all around the city. Of course, a lot of people probably hated them because they clogged up traffic. But they reminded Nick of something out of Venice or Paris. Something romantic about the serenity of spanning the churning water below. He leaned over the Michigan Avenue bridge, by the *Tribune* Tower, and watched an architecture tour boat cruise underneath the steel grate. A cool spring breeze rustled his hair as he lit a cigarette.

He couldn't stop thinking about the dream with Billy Lyons surrounded by the green glow. His mind flashing to thoughts of Elmore King and Jimmy Scott. King. The twisted knot of lies that clung so tightly for almost forty years. Billy Lyons sealed away in the hardened earth of Illinois, so far away from the Clarksdale sun.

Promised land.

He had spoken to Kate a few times since he left the day after Christmas. He'd figured there wasn't much to talk about with Richard hanging out at her place. But she'd later told Nick he shouldn't have worried. Richard left the day after he arrived. Nick smiled at the thought of that pompous asshole getting the high hat.

Kate walked quickly out of the *Tribune*, her jaw muscles clenched. "She's gone," Kate said. "Ruby got an early release and didn't even tell us."

"When?" Nick asked squinting into the wind and looking toward Lake Michigan.

"Last night," she said sweeping the hair out of her eyes. "Somebody from a prisoner's release program took her to the bus station. That's all they know at Dwight. Or say they know. Didn't even take anything from her cell. Get this, she wore the clothes she had on in nineteen fifty-nine."

Kate crossed her arms across her chest. "Where could she go?"

"Have a good friend already on it." Nick smiled.

"You want to share your information?"

"Let's just say she's not within driving distance."

"I see . . . Still, I can't believe she didn't call to thank us or anything."

"What did you expect, Kate? Flowing tears at her release? Cameras flashing?"

"Shit, my editor's gonna be pissed."

Nick tossed the cigarette on the bridge and ground it under his boot. "There's always the *Picayune*."

"Oh, no. Took me years to get here, Travers. I have my family here, my friends. What more could a girl want?"

He stared out at Lake Michigan and said, "Depends on what you're looking for."

"Would you quit spouting off bullshit and tell me what you mean, Travers. We've been playing this game for ten years."

A group of men in identical blue suits wandered by, pushing Kate closer to Nick on the bridge. She grabbed his arm and looked up into his eyes. She raised her eyebrows in impatience.

"How about when I'm with you, I don't want to be anywhere else in the world. I am completely happy."

"No shit?"

"No shit."

"That's pretty good for a con artist." Kate smiled as Nick

tucked her brown hair behind her ear. "We're still going to dinner? Rosa's. Drinking. A possibility of dancing. Right?"

"I'm serious." Nick pressed his index finger to her thick lips and traced his hand down to her chin. He slowly lifted up her head, leaned over, and kissed her. Steady, closed mouth. Deep. He could feel the spring wind rattling his blue jean jacket. She kept her eyes closed as he kissed her on the forehead.

It was one of those moments when you understand mortality with an unshakable clarity. You seem to understand the moment for its fleeting beauty, its arcane details, and gift of the one you love.

"Come back with me," he said.

She made a motion with her lips like she was trying to say something but he could tell no words would come.

EPILOGUE

THE MISSISSIPPI DELTA blurred across my vision as the tired old Greyhound rolled down Highway 61 and into Clarksdale. I felt like I was floatin' in my high seat as I watched the sun-bleached two-lane, the tilled brown earth of the cotton fields, and abandoned brick buildings crawlin' with kudzu. I just knew anytime a guard would shake me and tell me it had all been a dream. I'd have to dress and wait for the locks to pop down the row of prison cells in an invitation to relive my tired life.

But I could feel the warm spring sun on my brown arm as I leaned close to the glass and watched a landscape I could almost taste. When I closed my eyes I believed Chicago had been an illusion. I didn't know the person who wanted to leave Mississippi. She lived somewhere on the opposite side of the earth.

My soul felt parched for home.

I had no family left. I had no job. Hell, I didn't know what I was going to do once my ride ended and the hundred and eighteen dollars I made in jail disappeared. Didn't matter, I was free.

I would sleep in the streets. I'd work the fields. I just wanted to feel the sun and watch those blessed dark clouds roll over this sweet earth once again.

The bus slowed and rolled off the highway into a downtown I once knew. It was as if a giant flood had washed the town clean of memories. I knew the buildings and the streets but everything else had changed.

When we rolled to a stop, I hung back waitin' for the bus to clear out. I could feel my heart in my throat and shakiness wrap my body. I couldn't move. I couldn't breathe.

"Ma'am?" the bus driver called.

I felt the torn edge of my old dress and rubbed my hands in my lap.

"Ma'am, this is it."

I closed my eyes, gritted my teeth, and walked down the aisle. The door would shut any moment. I couldn't get off. They wouldn't let me go.

I stepped down over the rubber-coated steps and onto the cracked asphalt. I hadn't breathed since I left my seat.

I got my old trunk, coated in travel stickers, from under the bus and walked through the cool day into the station. Glad Travers had helped me slide out of town without no one's notice.

As I crossed through the dark bus station, I heard the hard clicks of shoes behind me. A black gentleman with nice silver hair in a suit and a shiny pair of wingtips walked toward me.

He stuck out his hand and I took it.

"Heard Chicago wasn't for you."

"No, sir," I said and looked at my forty-year-old shoes.

"You hungry? Know a good barbecue place down the road."

"No. I'm fine."

"Nick tole me you didn't want help."

"I know who you are," I said. "He tole me to call you if I need anything. Would you give Mr. Travers somethin' for me?"

And I handed him my notebook, my journal I had kept for so many years. He tucked it under his arm.

"Nick has somethin' for you too," he said. "At a bank down the road, there's an account in your name. I can show you if you like. More money inside than I made my whole life."

I nodded, a bit confused, and he grabbed the rotted leather strap on my trunk and hoisted it to his side. I closed my eyes as I felt the spring breeze pass through me and shake the trees downtown. His heels clicked alongside me.

He looked straight ahead as he walked and said, "You want a job singin'? Me and my wife got a bar down in New Orleans. Could use someone to sing them ole-school blues."

"I don't sing the blues anymore. I left my blues up north."

"You know what they say," he said. "If you can't sing 'em, means you got 'em."

He kept walkin', the trunk in hand, and nodded with a simple understanding.

"Let me know when you want to come back," he said. "Lot of folks lookin' for you."

Then something happened I hadn't felt in a long time. My face tightened into something I once remembered as a smile.